A NOTE ON THE AUTHOR

PARKER BILAL is the pseudonym of Jamal Mahjoub. *The Burning Gates* is his fourth Makana Investigation. Born in London, Mahjoub has passed through Sudan, Egypt, Denmark and Britain, before settling in Barcelona.

THE
BURNING
GATES

PARKER BILAL

BLOOMSBURY
LONDON · OXFORD · NEW YORK · NEW DELHI · SYDNEY

Bloomsbury Paperbacks
An imprint of Bloomsbury Publishing Plc

50 Bedford Square
London
WC1B 3DP
UK

1385 Broadway
New York
NY 10018
USA

www.bloomsbury.com

BLOOMSBURY and the Diana logo are trademarks of Bloomsbury Publishing Plc

First published in Great Britain 2015
This paperback edition first published in 2016

British Library Cataloguing-in-Publication Data
A catalogue record for this book is available from the British Library.

ISBN: TPB: 978-1-4088-4108-2
PB: 978-1-4088-4110-5
ePub: 978-1-4088-4109-9

2 4 6 8 10 9 7 5 3 1

Typeset by Hewer Text UK Ltd, Edinburgh
Printed and bound in Great Britain by CPI Group (UK) Ltd, Croydon CR0 4YY

To find out more about our authors and books visit www.bloomsbury.
com. Here you will find extracts, author interviews, details of forthcoming
events and the option to sign up for our newsletters.

The world grows dark,
The shadows have spread over it,
Now is the glimmer of dusk.

The Epic of Gilgamesh,
Eighteenth century BC

Prologue

They came out of the wall of sand like figures from a nightmare. In single file. Blindfolded. Hands tied behind their backs, a loop of rope binding them together. If one of them fell the others had to stop and haul him up. Five men, leaning forward against the wind, the weight of the dust storm pressing them back. They seemed to have no sense of where they were going.

The blind leading the blind, was Cody's first thought.

Some kind of religious dream maybe, but he was too out of it to care much. The sandstorm was so thick you couldn't see more than five metres in any direction. Black smoke swirled around him. Burning metal and rubber. Sand. Everything was on fire. And death, he could smell death. The smoke choked his throat and lungs. He lay there, gasping helplessly as the ragheads came towards him, stumbling along in single file. Where did they think they were going? It was almost comical. They bumped into one another. One of them nearly fell. They were moving forward in a slow weaving pattern, like a snake dancing.

Cody didn't know how long he'd been out. His head was still ringing, still trying to piece it together. He couldn't hear right.

The smell of burning metal and flesh was seared into his nostrils. A vehicle on fire. The stench of gasoline. The remains of the Humvee they'd been driving in, with a hole punched right through it. Tyres burning. An IED. They were all dead. That much he was sure of.

When he turned his head he saw the legs and lower body of his buddy Jo Jo. The rest of him was gone. What was it for? They risked their lives every time they went out on patrol, but who were they trying to protect? 'If we weren't here, what would the terrorists have to fight?' If he'd asked the question once he'd asked it a thousand times. It made no sense. Sergeant Andrews had said, 'Don't sweat that stuff. Think about the mission. Think about watching your buddy's back and staying alive. You think any other way and you'll never make it.' Fine advice, he thought at the time, except that it didn't help Andrews. That much he remembered. Routine search. How dumb was that? They'd done it a hundred times. They kicked in a metal door and turned the place upside down. SOP. Standard Operating Procedure. The family all wailing out there in the dark. Old lady and her kids. One of the girls was a looker. Ripe. At sixteen with a body on her that set the men drooling. They went over and flashed lights in her eyes. Pushed her around a bit to see her tits move. Then somebody out in the yard yelled they had something. Flares and AK ammunition. The men were lined up along the wall. Where'd you get this stuff? No answers. The hajjis all mumbling and the interpreter doing his best not to look like a dick. There was a door on the far side of the compound. Sergeant Andrews must have been tired to do something that dumb. A couple of men were on sick leave and they'd pulled night patrols three days in a row. Whatever it was, he yanked open the door without thinking. There was a click. Heat. The whole thing went up. He was knocked backwards. The whole corner of the house had gone. Nearby was what was left of Andrews. Just a headless twitching torso, blackened and burned meat. They lost it then. They turned on the hajjis and beat them, just clubbed them and kicked them until they had no strength to go on. Three of them dragged the girl inside. It must have got out of hand because she freaked out and started screaming. The rest of them were standing around. Her father and brothers were kneeling out there in the dust crying, listening to her screams. 'Serves you right, motherfuckers.' Somehow the girl got loose. Hysterical, she climbed out through a window and was running into the darkness. He and a couple of others jumped into the Humvee and went after her. All he could see was the girl's naked ass jogging into the darkness and Jo Jo next to him was saying how this was one monumental fuck-up. Kept repeating it over and over. Monumental fuck-up. Cody turned to tell him to shut it when they hit something. The lights went out and when he opened his eyes he was in the sandstorm and everyone else was dead. Game Over.

The five ragheads had stopped moving. They stood huddled in a circle, unsure of their direction. He must have passed out then. Either way he closed his eyes and when he opened them again Wild Bill Hickok was leaning over him. Well, it looked like Hickok or perhaps he was thinking of General Custer? Blond hair blowing around his weatherbeaten face. Tapered beard and drooping moustache. Wraparound shades. He was saying something. Cody couldn't make out the words. He felt himself being lifted up and he drank eagerly from the bottle of water.

'How bad is it?' he spluttered. There was a ringing but his hearing was coming back.

'Broken ribs, a busted arm. Some shrapnel in your shoulder. You'll live.'

'The others.'

Hickok lowered the bottle. 'What's your name, soldier?'

'Jansen, Cody, sir. Private First Class.'

'Well, Cody, you're one lucky son of a bitch, I can tell you.'

He squinted at the insignia on Hickok's shoulder flashes. Crossbones and some kind of animal like a dog, only it wasn't a dog.

'What are you, Special Forces?'

'Hell, no. We're the goddamn horsemen of the apocalypse.' Hickok threw back his head and laughed. Cody knew then who they were. Contractors. Mercenaries. Soldiers of fortune. The whole team wore uniforms with the same insignia on the shoulder; a red circle with a green jackal over crossbones. Private contractors pretty much did what the hell they cared to, and earned about ten times what any ordinary grunt did into the bargain.

A Latino named Raul bandaged his wounds.

'Who are they?' Cody asked, nodding at the Arabs.

'Insurgents.' Raul chuckled. 'We do it some times, just to fuck with them. Tie them up and let them go. They don't know which way to run. Tires them out, gets them panicked. They're out in the open but they can't get away.' He laughed some more. 'It softens them up for interrogation.'

'Are we going back to Dreamland?'

'I don't know, man. I just follow orders.'

As they were about to lift him up to place him in the back of one of the SUVs, a tall man dressed in black strode up. On his head he wore a bandanna, also black, tied pirate style so that the tail hung down his neck. He had a fancy shoulder holster in which nestled a big chrome-plated automatic, a Desert Eagle by the look of it. A nice piece. There weren't many men who would dare walk around in black. It made you stand out. He looked like some kind of Viking god come down from Valhalla to give them all a hand. He came over and knelt beside Cody, resting a hand on his shoulder.

'You're safe now, son. We'll take you back to your unit.'

'No.' Cody grabbed him by the wrist. 'I'm not going back there.'

The man smiled. 'Don't sweat it, kid, you can stay with us until you're better.'

Cody watched him walk away.

'You'll be all right, kid,' said Wild Bill. 'We have our own palace outside Falluja. You can rest up there.'

'Who is that guy?' Cody asked.

'That, son,' grinned Hickok, 'is God, or the closest you're going to get to him in this life.'

Chapter One

Cairo, September 2004

Makana stood by the ferry station watching the sunset drape its cloak over the city. By the time September came around the summer heat usually began to diminish and the nights to cool down, bringing some relief with them. It hadn't happened yet, but hopefully it would, and soon. For now purple and magenta streaks cut the sky like the flying banners of some old, forgotten army. There was something unfinished about this city, he decided, as if the medieval world refused to let go its grasp. It added to that sense of confusion, as if the present might just be swept away from one day to the next, and all would return to how it was in the days of the Mamluks, or the pharaohs even, when this was nothing but a patch of sand and a river. The more you looked at it the less substantial the present appeared. A thin layer of flood water that had washed over the old world and left behind ugly buildings and flying buttresses like listing shipwrecks scattered about.

Right now it was a city preoccupied with war. Ever since the invasion of Iraq. Over the last eighteen months the protests had died away and most people had resigned themselves to the fact that nobody was going to pay any heed to their demands, but

6

there remained an undercurrent of anger and resentment, a sense of betrayal. The occupation of another Arab country by a Western power, a Christian one at that, put everyone ill at ease. The government did its best to reflect the common sentiment, with the president issuing statements of sympathy for the Iraqi people and calling for the restoration of power as soon as possible. Few really believed this was any more than amateur theatrics to keep the people at bay while not upsetting the Americans.

Inside the ticket office sat a small unshaven man who kept up a steady stream of chatter with anyone and everyone who passed him by. In front of him lay a messy heap of banknotes and coins that he shuffled with the confidence of a croupier in Monte Carlo, passing tickets back through the roughly cut hole in the glass with speed and dexterity.

'*Yallah, ya basha.* Buck up your ideas before the Americans start landing.'

'Why would the Americans come here?' The man behind Makana wore an old check shirt covered with a liberal sprinkling of fishscales.

'You ask why? Aren't those two eyes in your head? Why? To liberate us from the oppression of our leaders, just like they did in Iraq.'

'Don't hold your breath,' offered a woman in black with tired eyes. 'We have nothing they want.'

'You wait,' nodded the croupier confidently, shuffling coins in the direction of the next line, a girl of sixteen cradling a baby she could barely hold up. 'When they finish with the Iraqi oil they will be thirsty for good water and they'll be right over.'

The man in the fishscales lingered, his face a twisted knot of anguish. 'Who do you think put the president in charge? He's in their pocket. They'd never move against him.'

Makana left them to it and wandered down the ramp to the quayside where the other passengers waited. Already in the distance the water taxi was visible. Sitting low in the water, the vessel cut across the river at a good pace. Beyond it Makana could see the bridge that linked this side of the Nile to the island of Gezira. When he had first arrived in this city the river had been spanned by a quaint iron structure whose design harked back to the last century. The Boulac Bridge came with its very own myth attached, namely that it had been built by one Gustave Eiffel, better known for a certain tower in Paris. The legend went further, claiming that on discovering that the swing bridge would not open as intended, M. Eiffel had hurled himself from it in despair. As with so many stories in this city, the facts were seasoned with a good sprinkling of imagination. The bridge was not designed by the same engineer who had built the famous tower, and as for his suicide, this too appeared to have been an embellishment. Romance had eventually bowed its head to reality and the narrow, impractical bridge was replaced by a clumsy concrete structure that hummed day and night to the tune of thousands of vehicles flying back and forth over the river.

The boat ride was a pleasant alternative route, an idyllic interlude, a humble reminder that without this river the city would not, in all its fury and ferocity, exist. Ten minutes later Makana stepped ashore on the far side and walked through the tree-lined streets of Zamalek while the birds overhead sounded their shrill excitement in the last rays of daylight.

The house was a large villa, set back elegantly behind a row of enormous banyan trees. Ali Shibaker was already kicking his heels in the dust outside. Tonight he was dressed in full artist's regalia: a velvet jacket that he kept in a bag full of mothballs and a beret that seemed to have acquired a crown of cat hairs somewhere along the line. Makana remembered the jacket from the early years when they had both been strangers in this city. He had no idea where Ali had got the notion that this was how artists were supposed to dress, but it wasn't a subject that came up easily in conversation. Ali felt he had to look the part, and on the rare occasions when he saw him like that Makana felt obliged not to comment.

Appearing in public as an artist seemed like a nerve-racking business. Shibaker couldn't stand still and insisted on tugging nervously at the silk scarf around his neck, which wouldn't hang right. If Makana hadn't shown up in time he might well have succeeded in strangling himself.

'Where have you been? I've been waiting for ages.' Makana muttered an apology. He knew better than to argue when Ali was in this mood. 'Let's go in. We don't want to be late.'

They were, by Makana's estimate, right on time, but he thought it unhelpful to say so. Instead he followed Ali through the gate, past a couple of men who were checking invitations. They didn't bother with Ali, who no doubt had been in and out a dozen times already while waiting. Instead they gave a sigh of relief, happy to see the back of them.

The garden was a wide, cool expanse of green lawn, edged by shrubs, tall neem trees and palms. Indeed, it was so crowded with vegetation that the outside world seemed to pull up sharply at the gate, ceasing to exist, giving way to another age. A path lit by old-fashioned oil lamps marked the way up to the house. The flickering light lent the scene a timelessness, putting Makana in mind of the Ottoman pashas in the nineteenth century, living inside a silken cocoon, oblivious to the wretched fate of the world outside. Certainly, the handsome villa that stood at the far end of the lawn might have dated from that age. Steps rose up the front to colonnades and a veranda running along the front of the house. Open French louvre doors on the right led to a brightly lit set of interconnecting rooms. The hum of voices and faint music drifted out to mingle in the night air. On both sides of the stairway long tables covered by white cloths had been set out and laden with food and drink. Makana slowed, suddenly acutely aware of his hunger. Ali tugged him along impatiently.

'There's no time for that now.'

A woman in an elegant black dress, wearing a translucent shawl that did a bad job of covering her bare shoulders, exchanged a smile with him.

'Don't talk to that one, she's a snake!' Ali hissed, managing to smile at the same time. But the woman was clearly not going to be passed by. She stepped into their path and extended a hand.

'Ali, you weren't going to go by without even saying hello?'

'Never.' He clutched her hand in both of his and did a convincing job of looking like a devoted admirer. 'How lovely to see you, Dalia.'

'Aren't you going to introduce your friend?'

'Yes, of course. This is Makana, my manager.'

'Your manager, really? Well, we must get together.' She was an attractive woman in her forties. Her eyes had a somewhat faded spark of mischief.

The smile stuck to Ali's face as he dragged Makana onwards. 'Who was that?'

'Dalia Habashi. Another dealer. Hates Kasabian, of course. Doesn't have a fraction of his taste. Look at the way she's dressed, flaunting herself.'

'Do you think it was wise telling her I'm your manager?'

'Of course, why not? It makes them think you're important.'

'But don't you think she might find out?'

'Let me worry about that. I know how this business works.'

Makana fell silent. Ali was as jumpy as a cat in a dogfight. They walked up the stairs to be met by a large man wearing a silvery grey suit. Although he had never met him before, Makana knew at once that this had to be Aram Kasabian.

'Ali, Ali, where have you been? We've been waiting for you.'

For a man in his sixties, Kasabian had the smooth features of somebody twenty years his junior. His wavy grey hair matched his suit in colour, his hand was cool to the touch and he gave off an aroma of expensive cologne. Makana was wearing his best jacket and yet it still seemed as if the waiters were better dressed than him. He felt Kasabian's well-trained eye appraising him.

'And this is the man you've been telling me about.' He stretched out a hand.

'This is Makana,' said Ali perfunctorily. 'We've known each other for years.'

'Welcome, *merhaba*.' Aram Kasabian leaned over as he ushered the two of them in. 'We will talk later, Mr Makana,' he said confidentially.

They stepped through the first set of double doors to find themselves in the midst of Kasabian's well-heeled guests. The lights seemed very bright after the relative gloom of the veranda. The two front rooms had been turned into galleries. The walls were hung with framed canvases of various sizes. Makana watched Kasabian slide through the crowd with practised ease, pausing to shake a hand here or exchange a greeting there before arriving at the far end of the room where a small stage had been set up. He spoke like a man who was not only used to speaking in public but who enjoyed it. His natural charm soon had his guests nodding and chuckling.

'This is always a great honour. The autumn exhibition has now become, I am proud to say, a key event in the cultural calendar of this great city. It gives us the opportunity to discover some of the wonderful talent that surrounds us as we go about the rather dull business of earning a living.' He gestured at the walls around them. 'Artists allow us mere mortals to dream. Their vision enriches our lives. Each year we discover brilliant new talents and this year is no exception.' He mentioned several names that meant nothing to Makana and pointed out certain people in the room. There was some polite clapping. Kasabian went on to thank a few of the private patrons and sponsors without whom, he emphasised, the exhibition would not have been possible. There were more smiles and nods as they enjoyed their moment in the spotlight. Everybody seemed pleased to be there. Makana knew that for Ali this evening meant a lot. The guests who thronged the room, clutching non-alcoholic grape juice in champagne glasses, were the cream of society. Wealthy entrepreneurs, businessmen and investors, bankers and men of industry, along with a good sprinkling of embassy staff and expats. They were the patrons every struggling artist was hoping to captivate with their work and maybe make a few sales.

When Kasabian finished his speech the noise level rose as the guests resumed their conversations. Some moved around and for a time Makana moved with them, grateful for a break from Ali's fretting. He was now busy chatting away with potential buyers. To Makana he resembled a man out of place. Most of the time he was Ali the Mechanic, who ran a car-repair shop just off Sharia Sudan Street.

From the snippets of conversation he picked up Makana concluded that wealth did not qualify a person to understand art. The pictures reflected a range of style and quality. It was a strange business. The fortunate ones would find their way to a wall in a house or private flat, in the lobby of an embassy or the boardroom of an insurance company, proof of the sophistication and taste of their new owners. Makana stared at a picture of a bowl of what might have been artichokes but on the other hand could have been a family of dead frogs.

'Are you really his manager?'

Makana turned to find the woman he had briefly met earlier, Dalia Habashi.

'I'm afraid Ali is a little nervous this evening. I came to lend support.'

That made her laugh. 'Well, at least you're honest about it.' She leaned over to whisper. 'Which is more than most people here are.' Her eyes lit up when Makana produced his cigarettes. 'You're a mind reader, but they won't allow it in here, I'm afraid. Let's go outside.'

The veranda was lit by the soft glow that came from a huge copper lamp with glass sides, hanging from the ceiling above the stairs.

'It used to belong to King Farouk,' whispered Dalia Habashi.

'He left it behind as a parting gift?' queried Makana, lighting both of their cigarettes. Dalia Habashi leaned back and exhaled at the stars.

'Not at all. How it came into Aram's possession is a mystery.' She cocked an eyebrow. 'But then you know all about that.'

'Lamps?'

'Aram's mysteries. I understand you are here to help Mr Kasabian.'

'Then you know more than I do,' said Makana.

'You're discreet. I like that. Sounds like an interesting life, investigating people. Is it?'

'It has its moments.'

Dalia Habashi smiled. Her accent was Lebanese and she had that olive complexion that spoke of being bathed in money for generations.

'What did Ali tell you about me?' A mischievous gleam twinkled in her eyes.

'I'm afraid he isn't making much sense tonight.'

'You're being diplomatic, or evasive.'

'I've never really thought of this city as being a place for art collectors.'

'Oh, you'd be surprised. The Cairenes, the wealthy ones at least, like to think of themselves as closer to Rome or Paris than to, say, Khartoum.'

Mention of his hometown prompted a stab of anguish in Makana. 'I don't need convincing of that.'

'There is a market for artworks, certainly, but it tends to be less about quality than about who you know.'

'Who would have thought?'

Makana saw her eyes pass over his shoulder and turned to see a broad-shouldered man in a blue-striped suit. From newspapers and television appearances Makana recognised him as Deputy Minister Qasim Abdel Qasim. People were falling over themselves to shake his hand. In itself this wasn't all that surprising. Qasim had a lot of influence nowadays. He was part of the inner circle of the ruling National Democratic Party and a close personal friend of the president's son. You couldn't get much better connected.

This was what these events were really about – being seen with the right people. And it seemed that Makana was about to become one of the chosen ones, since Qasim was headed straight towards them. The deputy minister was clearly interested in

14

speaking to Dalia Habashi, who in turn seemed reluctant. There was a slightly awkward moment, which Makana's presence did nothing to alleviate. When introduced, Qasim ran his eyes over Makana and dismissed him as insignificant in the general scheme of things, but then a frown crossed his face.

'Makana? That name rings a bell. What business are you in?'

'Mr Makana is an investigator, so watch what you say.'

'An investigator? Really? I must be mistaken. I thought you were someone else.' Qasim apologised as sincerely as any politician was capable of doing and turned to start chatting to Dalia Habashi about things such as mutual acquaintances, perhaps in the hope that Makana would take himself away, which he might have done, except that he objected to having to move for a man like Qasim. And besides, Dalia Habashi had not asked him to leave. Instead she turned and handed him a card with her name and the address of the Zerzura Gallery.

'You must come and have a look. You never know, you might decide to become a collector.'

'I'm sure an investigator hardly has the time to take an interest in art,' said Qasim. He didn't exactly sneer, but it came close. Makana wondered if the deputy minister had somehow mistaken him as a rival for Dalia Habashi's affections. 'Now I remember where I heard your name,' Qasim said suddenly. 'You were involved in that business last year in Siwa.'

Makana's part in the events in Siwa involving a supposed arms shipment and a wanted terrorist had not been made public. The deputy minister would have read about them in an intelligence report, or been briefed by somebody in the know. Whatever it was, he now regarded Makana with what looked like deep suspicion.

'You have a reputation for getting yourself into trouble.'

'I'm honoured to have any kind of reputation at all,' said Makana before making his excuses.

'I mean it, you must come and see the gallery.' Dalia Habashi said in parting. Makana returned her smile, if only to annoy Qasim.

'I'll certainly try.' He turned to find one of the waiters standing before him, dressed in spotless black and white that made Makana feel like he'd just crawled out of a cave.

'Mr Kasabian will see you now,' he said.

Kasabian's office was on the first floor at the back of the villa. The old house was surprisingly robust, if a little run-down. There were artefacts of historical and artistic value dotted around. Paintings of red-faced pashas in tarbooshes, landscape scenes of camels in the desert along with several views of the pyramids and assorted ruins. Twin ebony statuettes of Nubian slaves bearing spears caught Makana's eye. Modelled on some of his ancestors, no doubt. A reminder of his place in the scheme of things. By the time they had climbed the creaking staircase and walked down the hallway, the sound of voices coming from below had dimmed to a distant murmur. Once he stepped inside the office it was as silent as a sealed tomb beneath the sea.

Aram Kasabian was pouring himself a whisky from a drinks cabinet the size of a small handcart standing beside a large wooden bookcase that ran around two sides of the room.

'We can't serve alcohol at these events. It's bad for our reputation and besides, people go mad at the hint of free alcohol. They behave badly.' He gestured at the array of bottles. 'Can I offer you something?'

'No, thank you, I'm fine.'

'Please.' Kasabian gestured for Makana to take a seat. Two high-backed armchairs facing the desk were upholstered in soft leather held in place by brass studs. It felt like sinking onto the upturned palm of a giant genie. Kasabian held open a silver cigarette box lined with aromatic sandalwood. Makana helped himself as Kasabian sipped his drink and moved behind the desk. The room was lit discreetly by a desk lamp and some kind of lighting that ran along beneath the shelves on the walls. Through the glass of the window behind where Kasabian sat, Makana could see the Nile. Beads of light trickled across the bridge like tracer fire aimed at the distant outlines of hotels and apartment buildings in Dokki. Makana took a moment to study his host a little more closely. In here, under these lights and away from his guests, it was easier to see Aram Kasabian's age. His silvery hair was straight and slightly longer than it perhaps ought to have been. He constantly pushed it back from his face with a practised movement that betrayed a certain vanity. Then he folded his hands together on the desk.

'I'm not sure where to begin, to be honest. I had been wrestling with this problem for some time when by chance I mentioned it in passing to Ali. He told me about the line of work you are in. I immediately realised you would be perfect for this job.'

'That rather depends on what Ali told you.'

Kasabian opened his hands outward. 'He's a loyal friend and I am sure that he was only trying his best to help you. Over the years, however, I have learned to be wary of offers of help. People invariably want something more in return.' He paused to lean back and swirl the ice in his drink. 'Ali tells me you have a reputation for honesty and discretion. Both of these qualities will be needed for the task I would like to propose.' Kasabian took a moment to make himself comfortable, resting his head against the back of the chair.

'Perhaps if you told me what you had in mind.'

'Of course. I apologise if I seem evasive. It's a strange business. Recently I was approached by a wealthy client from America, through an art dealer in New York.' Kasabian chuckled. 'As you can imagine, there are not many occasions when a foreign buyer has reason to call on us. I was surprised and yes, somewhat flattered.'

'How long ago was this?'

'Just over a week.'

'And you'd never had contact with this man before.'

'Never.'

'Did he say how he came across your name?'

Kasabian looked a little nonplussed. 'Well, I assume it was through the dealer, Mr Norton Granger. Since he mentioned him by name.'

'You've had dealings with this Norton Granger before?'

'No. I know him by reputation only. One of the finest houses in America.'

'And you were flattered that your reputation had arrived in New York.'

'In a way, yes.' Kasabian smiled and folded his hands together. He looked uncertain whether to continue.

'Please go on.'

'Very well. This is where it becomes interesting. The buyer claimed to be looking for a number of very rare pieces of modernist work that have been missing for almost a century. You understand, Mr Makana, that the art world is full of such mysteries. Paintings appear and disappear with unfailing regularity. So I was not unduly shocked, although the idea that such a masterpiece might have found its way here, that it could be in Cairo, right under my very nose, so to speak, did surprise me.'

Kasabian spoke with authority. Little happened in the art

world here that did not somehow come to his attention. Nothing of great value would be in circulation without him getting a sniff of it. Makana had made his own enquiries prior to coming here this evening, enough to know not only that Kasabian was respected but that he was a shrewd and wily customer. Beneath the smooth, easygoing manner was a hard-nosed businessman and tough negotiator. He also had political protection. Friends in high places, like Qasim no doubt. You had only to glance at the guest list to know that.

'Might I ask the identity of this buyer?'

'For the moment I'm afraid that must remain my little secret. It's not that I don't trust you, but his approach to me was conditional on maintaining his anonymity. This is understandable under the circumstances. One expects it.' Kasabian gave a philosophical shrug. 'A stranger in our country, and particularly in the business we are in . . .' He left the sentence unfinished. 'One has to be cautious.'

'And is he here in this country at present?'

'Yes, he came here to find me, to find this work.' Kasabian nodded gravely.

'Is that usual, for someone to come all this way for a painting?'

'Yes, but if he is right then we are not talking about one painting but about a collection. A very special collection.' Kasabian gave Makana a stern look.

'What brought your American client to Cairo?'

'According to him, rumours began to surface in New York a few months ago that someone was trying to sell a painting, *The Tower of Blue Horses* by Franz Marc, a German Expressionist.' Kasabian chuckled, which lent him the air of a jovial uncle. 'Cairo is hardly the place one imagines finding such a priceless work.'

'But nevertheless he flew straight here. It must be a valuable painting.'

'*The Tower of Blue Horses* went missing during the Second World War. Nobody has seen it since. Today it would be worth a fortune.' Kasabian resettled himself at his desk, setting the heavy glass carefully on a place mat.

'Forgive my ignorance, but it strikes me as a little odd that such a painting could wind up here.'

'I understand your scepticism.' Kasabian allowed himself a smile. 'The art world is nothing if not full of surprises.' He leaned forward, his face half in shadow. 'It is a curious fact. On the one hand we collectors crave exposure for the works we buy, and on the other, we hide them away, for decades, sometimes for centuries.'

'You said there were more paintings?'

'Absolutely. If the information is correct, we are talking about a unique collection of some of the great masters – Chagall, Matisse, Picasso, Nolde . . .'

'And your client is aware of this?'

'Oh, yes.' Kasabian peered into his glass.

'Can you explain how such a collection of masterpieces might arrive here?'

'Well, for that we have to go back to the Second World War. Just before it, in fact. In 1936 Adolf Hitler ordered a purge of modern art from German museums. Hitler, as you may know, was himself something of an amateur painter, but very traditional. He detested the avant-garde. He saw the development of modernist forms such as Expressionism as degrading to the German spirit.' Kasabian shrugged. 'He was a small man with very conservative views. He didn't like change. He associated this new art with Jewish interference in German life. So he confiscated thousands of pieces and arranged for them to be displayed publicly with the idea of ridiculing them and the artists who produced them, many of them Jews, of course. Degenerate Art, as he called it, threatened to corrupt the minds of all good people; it filled them with images that were impure and unclean.'

'He was ahead of his time,' said Makana. 'I can think of a few people around today who would agree with him.'

'Yes, indeed. There is not that much of a gap between Hitler's views and those of our religious purists.' Kasabian sipped his drink.

'I may be missing something but I still don't see the connection with the here and now.'

'I'm coming to that. When the Nazis realised they were losing the war they started to move artworks out of Germany for safe-keeping. A number of them have never resurfaced.'

'Not even on the black market?'

'Not even there.'

'So how did they wind up here?'

'We can only speculate on that, but if you like I can give you my personal hypothesis.'

'Please.' Makana reached for a cigarette and lit one.

'We all remember the First Gulf War of 1991. Well, when Saddam's forces invaded Kuwait his soldiers behaved like barbarians. They ransacked and they robbed, including a number of private art collections. None of us had any real idea what they might have contained, but we suspected that some great works were hidden there.' In Kasabian's measured tones Kuwait City sounded like a modern-day Aladdin's cave. 'In a few months some curious works began appearing on the world market. Some of these, it was suspected, came from the private vaults of Kuwaitis now in exile. Little information was forthcoming because owners are not always keen to explain how they came by certain works.'

'And you think that's how this collection wound up here?'

'It's the only explanation, in my opinion.'

Makana recalled the time. The year the Americans had expelled Saddam from Kuwait was the year he had fled from Khartoum. The sight of US forces gathering in Saudi Arabia had outraged pious souls in the region who saw sacrilege in the presence of infidels on holy soil, even if they were there to defend it. Makana was struggling against his own version of religious zealotry at the time, so he had little sympathy. Not that he was a supporter of the American-led aggression. He recalled the images of the road to Baghdad littered with blackened vehicles of the retreating Iraqi forces. They seemed to deserve one another, the Americans and their unruly puppet.

'That was more than a decade ago. Why has it taken so long for these paintings to surface?'

'These things are rarely straightforward.' Kasabian got up to refresh his drink. 'It may not be a coincidence that the Americans are once more knocking on Saddam's door, as it were.'

'You said this American came to you out of the blue?'

'I have no reason not to trust him. Especially since he came to me recommended by such a respectable dealer as Norton Granger.'

'Did you check on him?'

'I understand your concern,' Kasabian smiled. 'It is in your nature to see conspiracy everywhere.' Makana was beginning to tire of that smile. Kasabian's manner suggested there was something here he could not be expected to comprehend. 'But the art world is a high-risk business. There are no assurances. Anyone who expects it will grow old and poor very quickly.'

'Where do I come in?'

Kasabian settled back in his chair. 'As I mentioned, there

have long been rumours of what disappeared from Kuwait during the Iraqi invasion thirteen years ago. But that is all, just rumours. Sellers are often reluctant to say how they came into possession of a certain painting or sculpture and many buyers are equally unconcerned with such . . . formalities. If the piece is for a private collection nobody will ever see it without permission.'

'I take it you have no moral problems with selling potentially stolen items.'

'I am a dealer, Mr Makana. I take what comes to me. It is in the nature of the game. I didn't steal the painting, you understand. And if I didn't sell it, my nearest competitor most certainly would.'

'I get the feeling you have an idea where this painting might be.'

'Very astute, Mr Makana.' Kasabian took a sip of his drink. 'My client insists that the rumours he has heard associated this painting with a certain Iraqi colonel of the Republican Guard by the name of Kadhim al-Samari.'

'It sounds as though he came here well informed.'

Kasabian shrugged. 'He's American. With a few friends in Washington he could have access to some of the most powerful intelligence services in the world.'

'But still he came to you.'

'To him this is a foreign country. I assume he came to me because of my knowledge of the region and how things work here.'

'In other words, he knows who has the painting but not how to find him.'

'That is my understanding.'

'And you think that this colonel of yours might be in this country?'

'It's possible. Naturally, before contacting you I made a few enquiries of my own, in the hope of establishing contact. That is the key to my work, Mr Makana: circulating, making my name known.'

'But you came up with nothing.' Kasabian's smooth charm was beginning to grate. The more he strived to convince him of his sincerity, the more Makana began to wonder what it was he was not telling him.

'Correct. No trace whatsoever of a Colonel Kadhim al-Samari. If he is here he keeps a very low profile.'

'What is it you would like from me, Mr Kasabian?'

'I want you to find this man Samari. If our American friend is right, then we have a priceless collection under our very noses. If he is wrong, well, my reputation is at stake. I cannot have this man going back to New York to report that I was anything but completely thorough. It goes without saying that you need to be discreet. We don't want the world to know of our interest in this man.'

'What do I do when I find him?'

'Nothing. Report back to me and nobody but me. Not a word to anyone else. Any approach must be handled very delicately.' Kasabian beamed once more. 'We don't want to scare him off.'

'I understand.'

'I hope so. You can make the arrangements for fees and so forth with my assistant, Jules. You will be handsomely rewarded, but I want you to report only to me. Is that clear?'

'I think so.'

Kasabian leaned forward to rest his hands on the desk. 'Please be aware, Mr Makana, there are many people who might be interested in this information. I don't want you to be in doubt about where your loyalties lie.'

Makana got to his feet. 'This is a big city, Mr Kasabian, but a small town. I wouldn't get very far if my clients couldn't feel they could trust me.'

'Very good, then we understand one another. Discretion is the key.' Kasabian got to his feet and came round the desk. Makana shook his hand and headed for the door. Kasabian's assistant was sitting in a chair just outside the door. He leapt to his feet as it opened.

'This way please.' He indicated a door on the other side of the hallway. A small brass plaque read Jalal Sirhan. 'Jules' as Kasabian had referred to him was a small, concise man, in his forties. He was wearing a grey suit that was immaculate, if a little tight. His office was small and discreetly furnished, without the clutter of Kasabian's. It barely looked lived in. He closed the door gently behind them, went round the desk and produced a card with two telephone numbers on it and a fat brown envelope.

'I hope you do not object to being paid in US dollars? There are two thousand five hundred here and you will get the same amount again when you finish your work. Mr Kasabian wants me to tell you that there will also be a bonus, depending on the degree of success you achieve. Obviously your expenses are apart from this. Keep a record and there should be no problems.'

'I could get used to working in the art business.'

Jules smiled without humour. 'We are always looking for people who can be discreet.'

Downstairs the guests were beginning to disperse. Makana found Ali on the veranda, busily chewing his way through a mound of pastries.

'Where have you been? I'm starving.'

'I was talking to Kasabian.'

'Let's get out of here.' Ali wiped his mouth with a napkin as he followed Makana along the veranda. 'How did it go?'

'I'll tell you later.'

There was a commotion ahead of them as they approached the gate to the street. A young man was arguing with two of the waiters. The man, in his thirties, was dressed in casual Western style with elaborate jeans and a shirt with a lot of studs on it. His hair was thickened with some kind of glistening oil that made it hang down the back of his neck. Dalia Habashi appeared to be trying to intervene on his behalf.

'What seems to be the trouble?' Makana asked.

'Oh, they are just behaving like animals.' Dalia waved a hand and turned away.

'Look,' began Makana, 'I'm sure there's a way of resolving this peacefully.'

The man who was being manhandled towards the gate turned to address Makana. 'Listen to him, he's a genuine statesman.' He smiled. 'Why don't you go and save somebody else's life?'

Dalia was yelling at the waiters again. 'Let him go. He hasn't done anything.'

'Sorry, Madame, we have our orders.'

Taking advantage of the distraction, the young man managed to wriggle free. He shoved Makana in the chest and then swung a clumsy punch at one of the waiters before overbalancing. He scrambled to his feet and ran out into the street where he jumped onto a yellow Yamaha motorcycle. The engine roared into life and he sped away.

'He won't be back,' the waiter sniggered.

'Why is it that at the first whiff of authority men in this country have to behave like brutes?' Dalia Habashi asked nobody in particular before stalking off. Makana wanted to ask her who the man was and what he had done to be ejected like that, but she was already gone.

Ali had finished his snack. 'I'm starving,' he said, brushing the crumbs off his hands. 'Let's get something proper to eat.'

Chapter Two

Sindbad was waiting in the car when they came out of Kasabian's house. On the way into town Ali was in a talkative mood, excited by the evening's events.

'It's not that I enjoy these things.'

'Of course not.'

'But you know how it is, one is expected to socialise.'

Makana let him talk. His mind was on the meeting with Aram Kasabian. An Iraqi colonel and a German Expressionist painting. He was pretty sure he'd never come across such an odd combination before. More than that, he wasn't sure how far he trusted Kasabian. Makana had dealt with a lot of people in his time and most of his clients had something to hide. It was in the nature of the business. That's why they came to him, expecting their problems to be dealt with in a discreet fashion by a man who had nothing to gain by exposing their secrets, and everything to lose.

26th July Street was packed. The usual deadlock. Vehicles of every shape and size jammed like logs in a narrow cleft. Brakes squeaked, horns croaked. Faces stared out from the metal cages

27

around them, praying for freedom. It was a particularly oppressive spot, hemmed in on both sides by tall buildings and crushed beneath the weight of the overpass. It felt like being enclosed in a gloomy concrete tomb. The gaudy flash of bright electric lights running along either pavement provided the only distraction. People going on with their lives, not stuck in limbo. Not so much entertainment as a form of exquisite torture. Even the red prawns being shovelled onto a mound of crushed ice seemed to have a better fate. Intellectuals hunched around a low-lit table in Simonds café. A row of electric mixers whirred sugarcane into an angry white froth. And everywhere there was music and blinking lights. Money changers, plastic shoes, striped shirts and coloured lamps.

Makana wondered about Kasabian's mysterious American client. He seemed to trust him. At least he was willing to seek out a fugitive bearing stolen goods on his behalf, which meant that the painting, if that was what he was truly after, had to be worth a lot of money.

They inched forwards, edging past a bus that was lodged across the road. A crowd stood around offering opinions but the bus wasn't going anywhere. A wheel had fallen off. The axle was ground into the tarmac like a broken tooth. The passengers inside peered out at the cars slipping by and wondered when they would begin moving again. A traffic policeman waved an illuminated baton that looked like a child's toy. Ali was still talking.

'You never know. I mean, they probably won't buy anything today, but six months or a year from now, maybe they'll remember my work.'

It was a nice idea, but seemed like a flimsy premise upon which to base your existence, but then what did Makana know? Was it any different from him waiting for someone to knock at his door with a problem? He was in business because those who were charged with upholding the law were no longer to be trusted, or didn't care enough to do anything about it. Some of his clients had tried the law, been up and down every avenue available before turning to Makana. Some didn't want to risk making their private affairs public, because they were innocent and no one would believe them, and some because they had something to hide.

'He's been good to me,' Ali went on. 'Kasabian, I mean. A great support over the years. Not so much in sales, perhaps, but you know, just being there.' Ali twisted round in the front seat to look back at Makana. 'How did it go, by the way?'

'Well, we'll have to see how it works out, but thanks for the introduction.'

'Don't thank me, he's a good man to know. Lots of contacts. And besides, that's what we're here for isn't it? To help each other. That's all we can do. Speaking of which, when are you going to trade this wreck in?'

Makana noticed a stiffening of Sindbad's thick neck. Generally, when Makana had people in the car with him Sindbad made a point of minding his own business, but the Datsun was a sensitive issue. Sindbad loved the car as dearly as his own offspring.

'Actually, *ya doktor*, this fine car has served me well for many years.'

'It's served a lot of people well by the looks of things,' said Ali, brushing his hand over the scarred dashboard. 'I can see the road through the floor here.'

Sindbad wagged his head philosophically. 'It needs a gentle hand.'

'Please, let me repay you,' Ali implored, turning to Makana.

'You don't owe me anything.'

29

'You know what I mean. I would never have had the courage to go there by myself. I'm serious, come by the workshop. I'll find something that will suit you.'

As they started to move on, Makana said he would think about it, feeling Sindbad's eyes on him in the rearview mirror. There was no written contract between them, but it was understood that Sindbad would be available for Makana as his exclusive driver whenever he needed him. In return he was paid a modest salary. When Makana had no work for him, Sindbad returned to being a regular taxi driver. Day-to-day running costs were Sindbad's problem, but if it came to major repairs or damage then Makana would be obliged to share some of the burden. All of which meant that he had some stake in the vehicle. Sindbad's faith in the Datsun was unshakeable, to the point where he remained blind to its faults. Even suggesting that it needed to be seen by a real mechanic, and not his brother-in-law or some other neighbourhood cowboy who thought he knew something about automobiles, was akin to heresy.

The traffic eased as they hit the downtown area where the evening was in full flow. In a few minutes they arrived at Aswani's to find the oversized chef huffing and puffing over the hot grill. He came across to say hello, snapping the sweat from his brow with a finger and shaking it off on the floor. It was that kind of a place.

'I have fish today, how about that for a change?' He stared at them as if daring them to defy his recommendation. But Makana had learned over the years to rely on the cook's judgement. If Aswani said fish, then fish it was.

'Sounds good,' said Makana.

'Oh, and by the way, could you tell your strange friend to stop pestering my clients? It ruins the digestion to have to keep fending him off.'

Makana didn't need to look far to catch sight of the offending person. Barazil was impossible to miss. He was tall and as thin as a cane, dressed in what could only be described as rags. It wasn't that he had no clothes, just that everything he had was not so much a possession as a potential profit. Makana could not recall where he had met him. He seemed to always be around, moving through the city with smooth confidence. Instead of a home, Barazil had a storeroom, an old garage with a collection of outsize padlocks attached. Inside he kept everything from refrigerators to sacks of rice to toy aeroplanes. Racks of leather jackets that had never seen an animal in their lives. Stoves, electric heaters, acrylic blankets printed with tigers and superheroes, pop stars you'd never heard of. There were stacks of chairs, aluminium buckets, toilet bowls, boxes of rainbow-coloured feather dusters. You had to admire the sheer range. He was the king of the cheap and shoddy product, a modern-day pasha of the provisional. More to the point, as far as Makana was concerned, he was a reliable source of all manner of information. Today, however, he had brought along a bag full of telephones for Makana to try out. With a sense of occasion Barazil sat down, ushering in a characteristic odour of unwashed nylon and mothballs.

'You have to have one nowadays. Otherwise the world will forget you.'

'You say that as if it's a bad thing.'

Barazil laughed and slapped the table, hee-hawing like a donkey. 'I swear, half of the things you say I can't understand, and the other half make me cry tears.'

Like all good salesmen, Barazil was a showman. Makana had been considering the idea of a mobile telephone for longer than he cared to admit. The old landline was sluggish and unreliable and Umm Ali had the inconvenient habit of disconnecting the line when he was late with the rent, although she would swear on the life of her late husband that she had never tampered with it. The idea of being available at all times of the day and night, regardless of where you happened to be, made sense in many ways. On the other hand, who wanted to be available all the time?

'How much are you charging for these things?' Ali asked, prodding the items on the table with a wary finger.

'I swear on my mother I would never ask anything more than a fair price.'

'Don't get him started on his mother,' said Makana, glancing over to see where Aswani was with the food. The grills behind the counter were billowing smoke and flame through which Aswani's helpers rushed back and forth. At times they looked as if they were stoking a steam engine, at others fighting a fire. At the centre of the storm stood the portly figure, issuing orders like a field marshal, inspecting every dish before it went out. The place was crowded. Large groups of traders from the bazaar, wholesale vendors, craftsmen, all gathering at the end of the day. There were the odd visitors, the occasional tourist who looked about them with wonder and a degree of unease, a little unsure if they wanted to do this after all. And then there were the night owls, the nocturnal creatures who flitted from place to place doing the rounds, looking to pick up any opportunities that might be available; newspaper vendors, boys bearing trays of cigarettes and chewing gum, ballpoint pens and lighters. People like Barazil, who was hastily tearing off strips of bread and dipping them into the appetisers with the enthusiasm of a man who has no idea where his next meal will be coming from.

'What happened to your mother?' asked Ali, undeterred.

'My mother sold me to a circus when I was six.'

'That's terrible. How much is this one?'

'That, *ya sidi*, is the best I have,' Barazil gulped between mouthfuls. 'You have good taste.'

'Were you really in the circus?'

'For ten years I was jumping through flaming hoops, climbing ropes, turning cartwheels. I slept in a box of straw with a chimpanzee. Until I was twelve I thought he was my closest relative. Because you are a friend of the *basha* I will give you a fair price. You can take pictures with this one and play music.'

'Music, really?' Ali's eyes widened as he leaned forward eagerly for the demonstration. Makana was all but forgotten. He turned the instrument over in his hands and thought about the envelope of cash in his pocket. The time to buy such a thing was now, rather than wait until money became scarce again.

'Is this the smallest you've got?'

'Small, you want small. All you have to do is say so.' Barazil reached into his pocket and with a flourish produced something that would have fitted into a packet of cigarettes. It folded open. 'This is my very own, but you know what? You can have it. Just say the word. It's brand-new. Less than a week out of the box. Try it.'

It looked like a toy. To his alarm it begin to vibrate in his hand. Makana looked up. Barazil was grinning, displaying a row of yellowed teeth, speckled with scraps of chopped parsley. He was holding up another device.

'I'm calling.'

'What do I do?'

'Just press the green button. You can change the tone if you like. I have hundreds of different ones. Your favourite song. Happy Birthday. Sheikh Imam. Amr Diab. Whatever. You name it.'

You couldn't fault Barazil for lacking enthusiasm. He never tired of explaining things to potential customers, even those who stubbornly refused to grasp even the most basic concepts.

'When you finish you just press the red one and the call is over. There are other features. You can hold one call on the line and answer another, for example. You can store all the telephone numbers you have in it.'

Makana weighed up the device in his hand. 'How much?'

Barazil segued smoothly into his closing routine. 'No, no really. I can't take your money.'

'Just give me a price.'

'I can't. I swear on my mother's grave.'

'I thought she sold you to the circus?' Ali looked up from the device he was studying, from which an alarming range of songs was already emanating.

'That doesn't change the fact that she's my mother.'

'Give me a price for both of them,' said Makana. Ali began to protest, but Makana indicated for him to be quiet. Barazil, sensing victory, named a price. Makana offered half that and eventually they settled somewhere in the middle.

'You drive a hard bargain,' sighed Barazil as he got to his feet. Aswani was approaching bearing heaped platters of grilled fish, but Barazil knew not to overstay his welcome. 'From the mouths of my children,' he said, tucking his money away.

'I thought you were married to a chimpanzee,' said Aswani. 'I didn't know they could have children with men.'

But Barazil was already gone. Makana began to eat. The fish was grilled to perfection. Aswani squeezed lime juice liberally over the smoke-blackened scales and withdrew. Ali was oblivious. He sat poring over his new device, as delighted as any child with a new toy.

34

'You understand this means you have to bring the car in for me to fix.'

'I'll have a word with Sindbad, but he's very attached to that car. Eat before it gets cold, then tell me what you know about Kasabian.'

When Ali Shibaker first arrived in Cairo he had decided he would turn exile into an opportunity to develop his artistic talents. He had taught at the Institute of Fine Arts in Khartoum, restricting his own creative work to spare time and holidays. The dream of transforming himself into a real painter was more romantic idealism than pragmatism. Kasabian had been helpful right from the start.

'I went to see him early on. I showed him my paintings and the man gave me money to tide me over. Never asked for anything in return, always fair on prices, never had a problem with him.'

Cairo had a strong tradition of welcoming refugees from the Arab world and beyond. Men and women had found a safe haven here for centuries, as well as a cultural climate in which to nurture their work; writers, poets, artists. Kasabian worked tirelessly on their behalf, set up exhibitions, often reaching into his own pocket to do so. In those early days, Ali had thought it might be possible. Over time he began to see just how difficult it was. The Egyptians had their own artists. To them, Ali would never be more than an exotic distraction. There were occasional breakthroughs, but not enough. Finding a teaching post met with equal resistance. When he finally came down to earth he opened a car-repair workshop. Cars had been a hobby of his since he was a teenager. In the evenings he retired to his studio above the workshop.

'You didn't have to buy me that telephone, you know?'

'We're celebrating,' Makana reminded him. 'You found me work.'

'Just like in the early days,' Ali nodded. 'Remember that? We always shared what we had.'

'Things haven't changed all that much.'

'You still haven't told me what Kasabian has asked you to do for him.'

'I'm not sure he would appreciate my talking about it.'

'I understand. Just do a good job, will you? He's important to me.'

Aswani appeared with more food. This time a handful of red snappers, along with salad and rice. For a time the two men occupied themselves with eating, then Ali's curiosity got the better of him again.

'Did you ever get to the bottom of that business with your daughter?'

Makana looked up, wondering where the question had come from. He reached for a napkin and wiped his mouth, having suddenly lost his appetite.

'No,' he said. 'Nothing ever came of it. Just rumours I suppose.'

'The worst thing is not knowing.'

'Yes, I suppose it is.'

'Something like that can drive a man mad.'

'I try not to think about it,' said Makana, reaching for his cigarettes.

Nothing more was said on the matter, but the mood had changed. While Ali ate and fiddled with his new possession, Makana smoked and looked around him. When they had finished eating he paid Aswani and walked Ali down to the main road to find a taxi.

'Aren't you coming along?'

'No, I think I'll walk for a bit.'

'Probably ate too much,' laughed Ali.

'Yes, that's probably it.'

'Don't forget to come by with the car, before it's too late!'

Makana waved, then turned back to the city and the empty streets, the shuttered shopfronts, and began to walk.

Chapter Three

Makana never gave up hope that one day he would find his daughter. By now Nasra would no longer be a child, she would be almost eighteen years old. He could only imagine how much she had changed. All his attempts to locate her had failed, and the hardest thing was coming to terms with the fact that there was nothing more he could do about it. For the moment, at least. He would find her one day, he was sure of it. He had to believe that, just as he was convinced that she was still alive.

For ten long years he had thought she was dead, that she had died along with her mother on that night when everything had changed for ever. But if life had taught Makana anything it was that it was never done with surprising you. When he first heard the rumour three years ago that she was still alive he had thought it a trick by his old enemies, a way of getting to him, of forcing him to come home. He had set about trying to find out, pulling as many strings as he could. None of his efforts had produced any substantial leads. If she was alive she was living a discreet existence, possibly under another name. Eighteen years old. Almost grown up. It would mean he had missed her entire childhood. A feeling of dismay came over him, filling him up like the dark water he had seen close over the car in which Nasra and her mother had vanished all those years ago.

A part of him had never managed to shake off the feeling of guilt that somehow he had caused their deaths. Hardly a day went by, even now, all these years later, when he didn't feel that combination of shame and regret. It was impossible to shake off the feeling that he had failed them. He should have been able to find another way out, an alternative. He could have cooperated instead of stubbornly sticking to his principles. What did principles matter when measured against the life of a loved one? He could have yielded. How many times had Muna urged him to compromise? But he hadn't listened. He was a detective, a police inspector, and his job was to uphold the law. 'If we let them define what we believe in, then what do we have left?' All around him everything he had believed in was being broken down. A free press, justice for all, the law, the courts, the judges. Everything was being twisted into new shapes that would give the regime the control it wanted. Makana refused to go along. Not the smartest plan in the world, which was why he ended up in prison, why he was beaten and tortured at the hands of his former adjutant, Mek Nimr. In the end he saw there was no way out. That the only option left to him was to flee, to leave the country and never come back.

Makana walked on, trailing through the deserted streets towards the distant pull of lights and movement. In all these years he had never managed to find any satisfactory answers to these questions, but that didn't mean he would ever stop trying. So absorbed was he in his own thoughts that he almost went right by it.

The bar was set in one of the narrow, uneven alleys behind Nasser Station. A simple walk-in place, open to the street. Light

39

spilled out of two entrance openings with their metal shutters rolled up. The walls alongside were adorned with faded logos advertising Coca-Cola and the familiar white star of Stella Beer. Chairs and tables were spread about on the uneven flanks on both sides of the road. An old, hand-painted sign on the wall read *Bar Kadesh*. The name was accompanied by a few roughly fashioned hieroglyphs and a chariot bearing Ramses II into war. The place had been around for decades, or perhaps even centuries.

Finding Marwan was easier than he had anticipated; before he'd even walked through the door he heard his name being called, and when he looked round he saw the large, clumsy figure fumbling with his trousers as he lumbered out of the shadows at the corner where the rather rudimentary toilet was.

'I thought it was you.'

The light was behind him but Makana instinctively registered the silhouette.

'How long has it been?' There was a touch of irritation in his voice which reminded Makana of the outsized chip Marwan always seemed to carry on his shoulder. 'Come on, have a drink with me, for old times' sake.'

The interior was noisy but the clientele seemed to know Marwan well enough to get out of his way. The Kadesh Bar was known to be frequented by off-duty police and security officers. The lower ranks, non-commissioned officers, along with the kind of thugs they hired from time to time to do their dirty work. In no time they were seated around a table in the corner with two cold green bottles of Stella in front of them.

'Actually, I was hoping to run into you.'

'You're toying with my feelings now.' Marwan wagged a finger and reached for his glass. 'I'm always here. Everyone knows that.' Marwan poured beer down his throat, his Adam's apple bouncing like a runaway rubber ball. The drink unleashed a sentimental streak. 'You remember where we first met?'

Naturally, Makana remembered. It would be hard to forget. It was out on the Red Sea coast. A bomb had exploded in a hotel. Marwan had been part of the State Security team whose job it had been to keep an eye on a Russian named Vronsky who was killed in the explosion. Marwan was part of the surveillance team and was busy tidying up afterwards when Makana turned up. That was about six years ago. Since then they had bumped into one another on a handful of occasions. It wasn't like they were friends, but you didn't get anywhere in this world without contacts. Makana's life depended on that fact in more ways than one.

For a time they talked about the past, cases they had worked on, people they knew. Makana was about to make his excuses and leave – hanging around with drunken policemen was not his idea of fun – but he needed information and Marwan seemed to have something on his mind. He called for another beer, which appeared as if by magic at his elbow. Makana had barely sipped his first. He braced himself and then tried to stave off the deluge by asking a question of his own.

'How's Lieutenant Sharqi?'

'Sharqi?' Marwan didn't so much say the name as spit it. Foam flecked the table, missing Makana's hand by millimetres. 'People like Sharqi always manage to come up smelling of roses. They take care of him. He's presentable. Young. Smart. Knows about computers. The Americans like him. That's important. He'll go a long way. I think Colonel Serraj is grooming him, maybe to take his spot one day.' Marwan shrugged as if this was of no importance to him. Another bitter pill life had cast him. He drowned it with more beer for a time before finally coming up for air. 'You were involved in that business out in the desert, weren't you? Well, there was a lot of finger pointing after that. The operation went bad. Heads had to roll. They put a nice twist on it as usual, some stories in the papers about catching a few terrorists. You know how it goes. But a few of us found ourselves locked in a corner. Someone had to take the blame, right?'

'I'm sorry to hear that.'

'Hey, it's not a problem. Actually, I'm glad. I've gone back to what I always was, a plain, honest policeman.' It had an odd ring to it, the concept of a plain, honest policeman, but Makana said nothing. 'I started out in the force and now I'm back there. Did you know my father was a policeman? Sure. Things were different back then. There was . . .' Marwan's glistening lower lip trembled as he searched for the word he was looking for. 'Dignity. That's it.' He thumped a meaty fist on the table that made the glasses jump. The men at the next table nudged one another and grinned.

'So where are you now?'

'Amn al-Merkazi. They even promoted me.'

'*Mabrouk*,' said Makana. Marwan brushed the compliment off with a shrug, as if it was nothing more than he deserved.

The Amn al-Merkazi, or Central Security Force, CSF, was a paramilitary arm of the police, halfway between riot police and the army. They were armed and violent, the heavy brigade. Generally feared, they were a law unto themselves. Not so much a promotion as a sideways shift, then. Somebody thought Marwan was a liability and so they had farmed him out to a spot where he could do as much damage as he wanted and it wouldn't matter.

42

'Sure, I'm a first lieutenant now. How about that?'

'Not bad. So something good did come out of all that.'

'It certainly did.' Marwan leaned his elbows on the table, almost tipping it over. 'So, tell me, what are you up to?'

'The usual things.' Makana sat back and lit a cigarette. The noise had abated somewhat. 'Actually, you might be able to help me – unofficially, of course.'

'Naturally. You know me, I'm always there for a friend in need.'

He didn't add the words 'for a price', but it was understood that nothing came for free.

'Have you ever heard of a man called Kadhim al-Samari?'

Marwan drew back his big head and his nostrils flared rather like a horse encountering a snake in its path. His eyes were bloodshot and unfocused.

'Why are you interested in him?'

'It's nothing big. The name came up and I was curious. He's Iraqi, isn't he?'

Marwan might have been drinking, but the look he gave Makana was as sharp as a pin. 'You're moving in murky waters, my friend. That much I can tell you.' He raised a hand. This time a bottle of Arak Haddad arrived on the table along with two glasses filled with ice. He poured a glass for both of them. Makana knew there was no point in protesting. He understood that this was a kind of initiation ritual. In a society governed by religious piety, breaking the rules invariably involved being tested on how far you would step over the line of respectability. A kind of pact of mutual culpability. Makana watched the clear arak turn milky in the glass.

'You do know him then?'

'Not personally.' Marwan lowered his voice and his eyes fixed on Makana as he leaned in to him. 'By all accounts a very nasty piece of work.' The big man swallowed and reached for his glass, which he drained in one. 'He was a senior officer in Iraqi military intelligence. If I remember correctly he was based in Falluja – where the fighting is going on right now. He disappeared, of course, right after the American invasion. So what's this all about?'

'Well, I was just curious.'

'No, no.' Marwan refilled both of their glasses to the rim. 'You're not getting away with that. This man is way out of your class. No offence, but he was one of the most high-ranking members of the Baath Party under Saddam.'

'You've seen reports on him?'

The big man gave a clumsy shrug. 'It's what I used to do, read intelligence reports. And I have a good memory for names.' He tapped a finger to his forehead.

'Do you have any idea if he might be in this country?'

'Here?' Marwan laughed out loud before his face grew serious. 'Even if I did know, I wouldn't be telling you.'

'Why not?'

'Because it would be classified.' He pushed his glass aside and leaned his elbows on the table. His eyes were rimmed with red. 'We're supposed to be helping the Americans, our friends, remember? We couldn't possibly be giving shelter to a man who is a fugitive. You never know who might be listening.' He raised his voice. 'Isn't that right, Amm Ahmed?'

'Isn't what right?' A bald man at the next table leaned out.

'That you never know who might be listening? The Americans have ears everywhere.'

'And the Jews. Don't forget the Jews,' cackled the other man. Marwan was enjoying the moment, playing the big man. He raised his glass in salute.

'Here's to the victory of the just and the triumph of the brave.'

'Sounds like you've had your fill for tonight,' said Makana, getting to his feet. 'I have anyway.' He paused. 'What we just talked about . . .'

'You don't have to tell me,' Marwan squinted up with blood-shot eyes. 'It's between us.'

After giving him his new number Makana headed for the street. As he edged through the crowd, he wondered about the wisdom of involving Marwan, but to find Samari he needed someone on the inside of the system. He wasn't exactly the kind of person he liked to put his faith in, but when it came to making a little money on the side Makana knew there was nobody more trustworthy and dependable than Marwan.

Chapter Four

The next morning the sun was bright and Makana felt a slight throbbing between his temples. He had slept badly. The combination of alcohol and the matter of Nasra having resurfaced during his conversation with Ali had left him in a sleepless daze. He had passed half the night in the big chair on the upper deck of the *awama*, to which the overflow of cigarette butts in the ashtray and the soreness in his throat testified. He stepped over to the railings and looked down to see Umm Ali and Aziza tending the little vegetable patch they kept on the riverbank. Aziza was the only one of the children left at home. The boy, still a teenager, was rarely to be seen. He hung around with some disreputable types his own age who lived in the neighbourhood and was busy charting a course for himself towards a life of delinquency.

It was a beautiful morning, despite the grumble of traffic and the raucous discord of car horns. A small family of ducks quacked in reply as they wandered in single file along the river's edge. By the time Makana had washed, shaved and dressed there was still no sign of Sindbad. He reached for his new acquisition and was about to press the button to make his first call when he heard the strangled squeak of the Datsun's horn from up on the road. He waved to Aziza as he walked up the path under the big eucalyptus tree. When he reached the road he found an apologetic Sindbad.

'*Maalish, ya basha*, she was tired this morning.' Sindbad had his own way of explaining the car's mechanical problems.

'Maybe we really should consider Ali's offer of assistance seriously?' It was only a suggestion. Sindbad grunted.

'My brother-in-law knows all about cars.'

'He's the one who usually repairs it, isn't he?'

'Oh, he's a real expert.' Makana fixed him with a look that made Sindbad crunch his eyes tightly shut. 'Really, he can fix anything.'

'Except he never does, not really. Think of it like going to the doctor.'

'The doctor?'

'If you went to a doctor and he gave you some bad news, you would ask for a second opinion, right? I mean, you would perhaps consult another expert before preparing for your funeral.'

Sindbad muttered a soft invocation to Allah under his breath before turning the key. He beamed with delight as it came to life. Happily he struggled with the gearstick which stubbornly refused to go where it was told. At last he accepted the inevitable. 'Yes, a second opinion.' Then, as if by divine intervention, the gearstick slid smoothly into place.

On the way into town, Makana tried out his new telephone. He called two people. First, a contact in a real estate agency in Maadi. He asked him to enquire whether anyone by the name of Kadhim al-Samari had bought or rented any property in the last few months. He didn't think there was much chance of this yielding worthy results, but it was worth a try. Then he called Fathi on the immigration desk at the international airport, who had access to the entry visas processed at the airport.

'How far do you want me to go back?' Fathi asked, his tone already implying futility.

'Start with the American invasion of Iraq and work your way up to the present.'

'Have you any idea how many entries that is?'

'I know how fast you work when you have the right amount of motivation,' said Makana.

The flow of traffic slowed to a halt as they approached Midan Tahrir, the sun glinting off the cars like molten iron, that locked solid in a matter of minutes. Makana climbed out of the Datsun as the horns began their unorchestrated keening and set off on foot. Skirting the side of the fenced-off area in front of the Nile Hilton, he found himself forced to walk in the road by the uneven pavement and the sheer weight of numbers. In the mid-nineteenth century this was the site of the Khedive's army barracks. The hotel was constructed in the Fifties, ushering in a new era of modernity with the promise of American luxury available right there on your doorstep. The gardens in front of the hotel, once popular for family gatherings, had since been fenced off – nobody really knew what for, which led most people to the obvious conclusion, which was that large spaces were unpopular with a government concerned about crowd control.

It took him ten minutes to reach Bab al-Luq and the building on Midan al-Falaki. The entrance was on a corner, and although the elegant staircase had seen better days it was kept neat and clean. On the third floor the door, as always, stood open. Makana wandered in through an unmanned reception area into the main office, which was illuminated by windows made grimy by the traffic. The space was divided by tables and desks that had been pushed into place to use the maximum floor space. They were all covered in heaps of paper and computers, although few people were in evidence. They seemed to keep irregular hours, coming and going according to their own schedules. Makana had no idea what they all did, or how it all fitted together. The sign on the door informed visitors that the office was occupied by something called the *Masry Info Media Collective*, MIMIC for short. As Makana understood it, a collective meant nobody was in charge. Sami Barakat had explained it to him. They gathered the news and fed it out to agencies around the world. 'In the old days every agency would have its own correspondent in every part of the world. Nowadays they can't afford it, so they depend on local sources, which is good for us.' Sami grinned. 'And gives us an outlet abroad, which means we can get around the state controls in this country.'

'Except that nobody here reads Japanese or whatever language your stories are published in.'

'It's true we have little influence locally, but that will come. Give it time.'

Sami and his wife Rania shared an area on the left-hand side of the L-shaped room. They had more space to themselves, which reflected a certain seniority. Over the years, Sami had become known as a voice of dissent. He was clever enough to be able to avoid trouble with the authorities most of the time, although a couple of short spells in prison were unavoidable for anybody in the sector. In recent years he had become something of a focal point for the younger generation.

Makana found his friend leaning back in his chair with his feet on the desk, talking on the telephone. You could never tell with Sami whether it was a social call or professional. There didn't seem to be much distinction. They were talking about the war in Iraq. When he saw Makana, Sami cut short the call and invited him to sit, which was a nice gesture except that all the chairs appeared to be taken. Makana leaned on the windowsill.

'Our brothers in Iraq are suffering terribly. This war is aimed not only at taking control of their wealth and natural resources, but destroying their past. The Ministry of Oil was the first place the US army secured. Big surprise, right? The last was the Baghdad National Library. The National Museum was looted. Thousands of antiquities vanished. Nobody cares. Apparently private collectors in the US are trying to persuade the Pentagon to relax legislation that prevents Iraqi heritage items being sold abroad. Can you believe that? They want less protection. Take my word, this is about erasing a people from history. Remove a nation's literature and history and what have you got left? Nothing. A people you can control. Within a generation the memory is lost.'

Over the years Makana had grown used to the way Sami became passionate about particular subjects. Nothing would deflect him. The only thing to do was ride out the storm. He lit a cigarette and agreed to a cup of coffee that Sami managed to order without breaking off his running commentary.

'The American soldiers built a camp on the site of the ancient city of Babylon. They actually filled their sandbags with fragments of priceless historical objects. Now it's all mixed up with Coca-Cola tins. Beautiful, right? The palaces of Nebuchadnezzar turned into a helicopter base. Now, of course, there's all this talk about recovery and prosecution of criminals, but we both know that's not going to happen. Seventy per cent of the manuscripts in the National Library were burnt by looters. You know what they'll do? They'll use some of that oil money to build a fancy new museum, and you know what it'll have in it? Nothing.'

As coffee arrived, Rania appeared, carrying breakfast: a handful of wrapped packages that turned out to be sandwiches. Her face broke into a broad smile.

'Sit down, join us for breakfast.'

A space was made on the table and chairs were found. The promise of food brought some of the others wandering over to join in. They were all fairly young. A mixture of men and women who ranged from their twenties to their mid-thirties, all of them clearly sharp, well educated and talented. The talk while they sat around and ate was of stories they were working on. Most of the details went by Makana.

'I saw you at Kasabian's opening the other day,' said one of the girls, a petite young woman with a mass of unruly black curls.

'Kasabian?' Sami frowned, his mouth full. 'I didn't know you'd taken an interest in art.'

'I was doing a favour for a friend. Do you know much about him?'

'Kasabian?' The girl's name was Nefissa. She wore a green canvas jacket, like the kind soldiers wore, and her fingernails were painted a matching colour. 'Well, he's pretty old school. Close to the big boys, ministers and so forth. A little out of touch. I mean, I wouldn't go to him to find out what's happening in the art world. Who's your friend?'

'Ali Shibaker. He had a couple of paintings exhibited there.'

'Oh, yes. Kasabian's very charitable in that way. Takes an interest in older struggling artists.' Makana made a mental note not to mention this to Ali when he next saw him. 'They're old-fashioned, part of a dying breed.'

'How so?' Makana asked, helping himself to a *taamiya* sandwich.

Nefissa had a spiky, opinionated character and no hesitation about expressing herself. 'They see themselves as some kind of elite and guard their space fiercely. Nobody new is allowed in.'

'Cronyism, it's called,' Sami said. 'It's a national sport.'

'Well, it's going to become ancient history,' Nefissa went on. 'New art spaces are emerging. That's why I was there. We're distributing leaflets about an exhibition.' Nefissa returned to her desk to fetch one. Sami took a look at it and handed it to Makana.

'If you're interested in art . . .'

'Just a passing curiosity, I'm afraid,' Makana smiled.

'So you're moving up in society,' Rania grinned, teasingly.

'I'm not sure they'll let me play with them for too long. Have you heard of someone called Dalia Habashi?'

'She's in a lot of trouble, I heard,' said Nefissa.

'What kind of trouble?'

'The financial kind. Basically, her gallery has been losing money for years. She can't afford to run it. She survives on bank loans, and the story is they're taking her to court. She's notorious for not paying artists when their work is sold.'

'Awful woman.' Rania screwed up her nose. 'Exploiting hard-working artists.'

'You can't say that,' Sami objected, 'just because you don't like her.'

'She's a snob. She flirts with men when she thinks she can get something out of them.'

'Don't look at me.' Sami held up his hands defensively.

'I am looking at you.'

'That was once.' Sami sighed. 'One time. Years ago. I'm amazed you still remember.'

'You mean, you were hoping I'd forgotten.'

'I'm not getting involved in this.' Nefissa raised two protective hands and retreated across the room.

'Nothing happened,' Sami sighed, appealing to Makana for sympathy. 'I was doing a piece on how cultural life in this country tends towards supporting the regime. We kid ourselves into thinking we're this great cultural reference point in the region but we have no critical faculties. We're world champions in the art of sycophancy. Kissing ass, as our American friends would say.'

'She's a manipulative bitch,' Rania threw back as she disappeared behind her desk. She glared at Makana. 'You notice how he changed the subject? She was born rich. Her father was some kind of businessman and politician. He was killed in Beirut. Some said it was political, others that he had fallen out with his criminal friends. In any case, she married a man twenty years older than her and set herself up here as a grande dame of the art world. Husband walked out on her naturally, when he finally realised what she was really like. Since then she preys on men, old and young, who she entices to buy her awful artworks. She's rumoured to be having an affair with someone high up in the National Democratic Party.'

'Qasim Abdel Qasim?' asked Makana. What he had seen of the two of them together at Kasabian's didn't suggest an affair. Perhaps they were good at disguising their feelings, or maybe there was something else between them.

Rania held up her hands 'You see?' She looked at Sami. 'Everybody knows.'

'It's unfair to malign the woman because she's made a success of herself. You of all people.'

'Actually, she's not the reason I came here,' said Makana, wondering what was going on between the couple.

'Just when it was getting interesting,' said Rania, then she sat down and started tapping away on her computer.

'Everything all right?' Makana asked quietly.

Sami shrugged apologetically. 'The usual. So, what do you need from me?'

'An Iraqi colonel by the name of Kadhim al-Samari. Ring any bells?'

Sami sat up and turned to the computer on a table beside him. 'I think he made it onto the deck of Most Wanted playing cards.' With a few clicks Sami had more information. 'There's a mention of him in a Human Rights Watch report. Looks nasty.' He reached for a cigarette absently as he read. 'Death squads. Torture. Not the kind of person you want to be on the wrong side of.'

Makana moved round the desk to take a look at the screen. Each playing card in the deck featured a member of the Iraqi high command, starting with Saddam and working down through his sons and advisers, politicians and military officers. All of them wanted. Most of them featured a photograph of the person in question, but in some cases the image was replaced by a black outline on a white background. The card featuring Colonel Kadhim al-Samari was one such.

'There's no picture?'

'No. I can try and find one somewhere else, but the CIA are pretty thorough.'

Makana perched on the desk and lit a cigarette. 'You haven't heard any rumours that he might be in this country?'

Sami leaned back in his chair to eye Makana. 'You're not telling me that you are actually looking for this animal?' Makana shrugged. Sami's eyebrows rose. 'You can't find something better to do with your time?'

'Do you think he could be here?'

'If he was a lot of people would be upset,' sighed Sami. 'The Americans to begin with. I mean, we're supposed to be on their side, right? Why would we be harbouring a wanted man?'

'Can you look into it for me?'

'Why not? My life is not worth living these days anyway.' He glanced in Rania's direction.

'But Sami, we need to be discreet about this.'

'Oh, don't worry. I don't want anyone to know I'm looking for this one.' Sami waved a hand to someone on the other side of the room. 'Ubay, want to earn a little money?'

The lanky figure strolling across the room had long, unruly hair and resembled a taller, slimmer, younger version of Sami, more like the Sami Makana had first met six years ago, before he had settled into the comforts of married life. At a distance Makana had taken him for a young man. He didn't realise quite how young until he reached them. He couldn't have been more than seventeen.

'Ubay is our resident computer genius. He's been doing this since before he could walk.'

'What do you need?' Ubay asked.

'See what you can find about a man named Kadhim al-Samari. One of Saddam's officers.'

'How soon do you need it?' asked Ubay, raising his eyebrows at Makana.

'As soon as possible, is the answer to that,' said Sami, ushering him away. 'Go, do it and keep it to yourself.'

'Isn't he supposed to be in school?'

'He finished school. He's already at university. The youngest ever in the Faculty of Engineering. His father wants him to get a proper job. He thinks computers is just a hobby.'

'It isn't?' asked Makana. Sami glanced sideways for a moment, not sure if Makana was trying to be funny. Something began to buzz in Makana's pocket and he pulled out the offending object and stared at it.

'I bought a telephone.'

'Congratulations, welcome to the twenty-first century.'

'I don't know why people keep saying that.' He was unsure what to do next. Sami took it from him and flipped it open before handing it back. Makana nodded his thanks.

'Hello?'

'We need to talk.' It was Marwan.

'Go ahead. I'm listening.'

'Not on the phone.' Marwan told him where and when and then the line clicked dead.

'Amazing,' said Makana, folding the telephone.

'The start of a new life, mark my words,' said Sami.

'One last thing,' Makana said. 'The man who came up in connection with Dalia Habashi.'

'Deputy Minister Qasim Abdel Qasim?'

'What can you tell me about him?'

Sami rolled his eyes. 'How long have you got?'

'Just give me the short version.'

'He's the original success story of this government, or one of them at least. Comes from good stock. Family of landowners who lost everything under Nasser and then got some of it back under Sadat and even more under our current president. Studied business in America, I believe. Then he went into politics. He's the perfect example of one hand feeding the other, or whatever the expression is. The state passes laws that benefit private enterprise which in turn takes control of public services. Everyone's happy and they all make lots of money.' Sami scratched his head. 'He's the sleazy end of the evolutionary chain. Word has it he's fond of gambling and women. Why the interest?'

'I'm not sure.' Makana sighed and got to his feet. 'It's probably nothing.'

'Whenever you say that, I know you're onto something.'

Chapter Five

Ali Shibaker's auto-repair business was not so much a workshop as a walk-in garage cluttered with machine parts and deconstructed vehicles. More cars were dotted along the narrow street, hoisted up on blocks, hydraulic jacks, wheels off, doors removed, engines stripped. The dust that skirted the road was stained black with caked engine oil.

Once upon a time, in the days when Ali had been a lecturer and Makana a police inspector, they had met through a mutual friend of his wife, Muna. It might have been centuries ago. Luckily Ali was not the type to reminisce. If he had been Makana doubted they would have remained friends for long. Despite the overalls, Ali was almost ten years older than Makana. On top of that he was an intellectual, a man of learning, a sensitive issue for a man who had dashed his schoolteacher father's grand hopes for him the day he announced his plan to become a detective.

There were around a dozen boys, the youngest about eight. All of them had been street orphans when Ali took them in. He gave them work and let them sleep in or around the cars for as long as they wanted to. He trained them, fed them and paid them what he could. It was a kind of life. And they looked happy enough wandering about, one rolling a tyre along, another stripping the plastic insulation off a piece of wire with his teeth, or swilling out a carburetter in a hubcap of kerosene.

'So, you've finally come around.'

'I think it's time.' Makana glanced in Sindbad's direction. The big man stood with his hands in his pockets, staring at the ground. Makana had overruled him. On the drive through Dokki the Datsun had protested, screeching at every turn. The clutch whined, the brakes squealed and there was something alarming happening to the steering.

'Good, good. Now, let's have a look.' Ali summoned a couple of his boys and they opened up the bonnet of the Datsun and peered inside. One of them went round checking the wheels, leaning his weight out and giving each a good shake. The Datsun protested noisily at the indignity of this examination. Sindbad bit his lip.

'Hmm,' Ali said. He stuck his hands in the pockets of his dirty overalls to feel about for his pipe, a relic from his days as an academic, when such things were still fashionable. He very rarely allowed himself to put tobacco in it, but he liked the feel of it.

'You'll need a car in the meantime.'

'Just a couple of days.' Makana noted the way Ali's eyebrows lifted. 'Perhaps a bit longer.'

'Perhaps.' The mechanic peered into the bowl of his pipe as if expecting it to talk. 'Let's see what we've got.'

Occasionally, when people brought a car in and found they didn't have the cash to pay for the repairs, they left their vehicle behind. A car might sit around for weeks, months and, in some cases, years. In the meantime, it was understood that Ali could try to earn back some of the money owed him by running an informal rental business on the side. In an empty space underneath a dull brown apartment building down the street, a collection of vehicles of varying ages was parked between the dusty yellow pillars. This was his vintage section. There was an old black Citroën with running boards, circa 1940, a long flat Chevrolet, a rounded Mercedes from the Fifties that lacked seats. In one corner, covered by a ripped tarpaulin, was an old whale of a thing. Sinbad helped Ali to tug off the dusty cover to reveal a faded green relic, the like of which Makana had never seen.

'How about this? It could do with a bit of exercise.'

'What is it?' Makana squinted warily.

'This, my friend, is a 1971 Pontiac Thunderbird.'

'Where's it been for the last thirty years?'

'Waiting for you, of course. It was the first of a series of sports cars. They got bigger and faster but personally I prefer the early models. The Japanese adopted the style for that thing you're driving around.' The upholstery was ripped and the interior was faded by the sun. Wires poked like thorny tendrils out of vacant slots in the dashboard.

'Where did you get it?' Makana asked.

'A rather fine old lady walked in one day and she just wanted someone to take it away. She couldn't stand the sight of it. It had been parked outside her house for years, ever since her husband had died.'

A raggedy boy of about eleven came scampering over, struggling under the weight of a car battery. The hood yawned up like the jaws of an extinct carnivore and he clambered onto the bumper and disappeared inside. When he turned the key the growl of the engine sounded like a jet plane starting up, deep and throaty. It grumbled and popped, the reverberations made the floor tremble under Makana's feet. Leaving the boys to prepare the car they retired to Ali's studio for coffee.

'How are you getting on with Kasabian's job?'

'It's too early to say.' Makana peered at a striking canvas leaning against a wall, trying to make out what it was. He saw a golden lion with wings flying through a dust storm.

'Just so long as you do right by him, I don't care.'

'I'll do my best,' said Makana, reaching into his pocket for his Cleopatras. He lit one and dropped the match into the ashtray, which was some kind of sculpture made of broken glass.

Ali stared at Makana for a while, puffing at his pipe, trying to get it to light. He set it down with a sigh. 'Look, the truth is, I'm not sure what I got you into.'

'I thought you trusted Kasabian?'

'I do. I told you, he's been good to me. Well, you may as well hear it from me. The truth is . . . There are rumours.'

'What kind of rumours?'

'Involvement in the black market. Trading in national heritage artefacts. There's nothing new about that. Tomb-robbing is almost as old as the tombs themselves.'

'How serious are these rumours?'

'You know how it is. A man like that creates enemies. People say things. He's successful. He has a lot of rivals. They all want to wear the crown.'

'You're thinking of Dalia Habashi.'

Ali shook his head. 'From what I hear she's in too much trouble to pose a threat to anyone. Look, all I'm saying is that you should be clear who you're dealing with.'

'I'll bear that in mind. What is that, by the way?'

Ali glanced over at the canvas set against the wall. 'Oh, that's Fantômas.'

'Who?'

'What can I say? Everyone wants a fancy artistic name nowadays, something to make them stand out.'

'Fantômas?'

'He got it from a film, I think.' Ali called out and a dark-skinned young man with stark features and long dreadlocks appeared. His prominent cheekbones looked like bruises under his eyes.

'Tell us about your work,' Ali said.

Fantômas stared at his canvas. 'It's a tetramorph.'

'A what?' Ali winked at Makana.

'The Greeks called them that. A combination of four forms, corresponding to the four corners of the world, the four elements of nature. The Assyrians had them, you know, on the walls of their palaces. A bull and a lion, with an eagle's wings and a man's head.'

'I see.' Ali was trying not to laugh.

'Are those real hieroglyphics?' Makana pointed to a vertical line of squiggles in gold.

Fantômas regarded Makana suspiciously, as though unsure if he was genuinely interested.

'Per-Hapi-On. The House of On, the sun god. What later became Heliopolis. The Romans said it wrongly and it came out as Babylon.'

'Babylon?'

'Sure, the word Babylon came to signify the power of the Romans in biblical times. Nothing to do with Mesopotamia.'

'So that's what it represents, the corruption of power?'

Fantômas shrugged. 'It's a comment on the times, on the war.'

'And there?' Makana indicated the wall of flame over which the lion appeared to be flying.

'The city of Babylon in flames.'

'Right.' Ali got to his feet impatiently. 'Some of us have work to do.' The young apprentice made himself scarce. 'Now, about the car. Do you really want to pay for the repairs on that wreck? I can give you a good price for the Thunderbird.'

Makana got to his feet and stepped to the window. Downstairs he could see Sindbad pacing about the big car as the boys gave it a quick wash.

'We'll borrow that monster for the time being. Can't you find a Datsun just like that one of his but in better condition?'

'It's an idea,' nodded Ali, sucking his pipe stem. 'I'll see what I can do.'

'Maybe we can fix it so that Sindbad won't know the difference.'

'Now you're asking for miracles.'

Chapter Six

On the phone Marwan had insisted they meet somewhere neutral. Makana suggested a roadside stall just off Maidan Sphinx, famous for its *ful*. The national dish. Mashed-up fava beans sprinkled liberally with olive oil and cumin were ladled into a couple of tin bowls and set on the narrow slanting shelf that served as a counter. A miniature television set had been ingeniously incorporated into the wooden structure of the cart so that diners could keep abreast of world events while they ate. The tiny black-and-white screen was no larger than a couple of packets of cigarettes and the image so grainy it was like staring into a rainstorm. None of it was good. A newsreel played out the unfolding disaster in Iraq. Resistance to the American occupation was gaining momentum. According to the rather excitable commentator the country was firmly on the road to civil war.

'Shia versus Sunni, it's the kind of thing the Americans have dreamed of for years. Muslims killing Muslims. Rid the world of them once and for all.'

Makana turned to find Marwan standing behind him.

'I wasn't sure you would find the place,' said Makana, scooping up a mouthful of beans with a strip of bread.

'Me? I've been coming here since I was a cadet.' He might have known the place, but he seemed to have other things on his mind than lunch as he stood there with his hands in his pockets waiting. Makana pushed his dish aside and pulled out his cigarettes as he followed Marwan a few paces away from the crowd.

'What's up?'

Marwan sized Makana up carefully. 'This man you're asking about.'

They stood under a small tree that was grey with exhaust fumes. The road alongside them was clogged with vehicles jockeying their way onto the roundabout.

'What about him?'

Marwan rolled his shoulders. 'I started looking into it, quietly.'

'And . . . ?' Marwan seemed reluctant. 'Look, if this is about money.'

'It's not that.'

'Then what's the problem?'

'This man is worth a lot.' Marwan leaned in close. A large man at the best of times, but close up it was easy to see why people might find him threatening. 'You understand?'

'A lot of money. I get it. There's a price on his head. That has nothing to do with this.'

'So you say.' A fat smirk spread across Marwan's lips. 'You wouldn't be trying to cut me out?'

Makana sighed. 'Don't tell me you're thinking of claiming the reward?'

'He's worth millions . . . of dollars.' Marwan's eyes widened.

'Before you can do that you have to find him.'

'I'm getting to that. I may have something.' Marwan looked away, suddenly coy.

'Have you thought how you are going to collect your reward?'

Marwan shrugged. 'Just deliver him to the American embassy. What could be easier?'

'Aren't you forgetting something?'

'Like what?' Marwan's brows knotted together.

'If he's in this country then someone has their hand over him. He's being protected.'

'Sure, I realise that.'

'If he suddenly disappears, his friends are going to want to know who sold him out.'

Marwan sniffed. For all the swagger and bluster he wasn't the kind of man who liked to go out on a limb. 'Are you saying you're not interested in the money?'

'You're welcome to it. If you want to go after him for the reward money, that's fine by me. Just let me get out of the way first.'

Marwan's head rocked from side to side as he weighed up the benefits.

'I just want us to be clear, that's all.'

'It's clear. I'll pay you for whatever you give me, and so far you've given me nothing.'

'All right. All right. I'll get something for you.' Makana stared at him. Marwan cleared his throat. 'There's a club, a private place, in Maadi. Apparently he goes there.'

Makana reached for his envelope and counted out a hundred dollars, then he changed his mind and added another hundred. 'That's just to be going on with.'

'Sure, I understand.' Marwan tucked the money away and handed over a slip of paper with directions. 'You sure you're okay about the reward? Money like that can change a man's life.'

'Be careful what you wish for.' Makana somehow doubted Marwan would go through with it, but you could never tell. Greed was a powerful motive. 'Just make sure you don't move without telling me first.'

'Don't worry about it.' Marwan grinned, back to his old self. 'I'm trying to do you a favour. Anyone would think I was cutting out your liver.' He turned and cheerfully kicked at a pink plastic bag lying at his feet. 'You see what this country is coming to?' A mountain of rubbish had collected along one side of the street. 'You think it's healthy to live like this, in a garbage dump?' Makana watched him walk away, still grumbling.

The conversation with Marwan put Makana off his lunch. Already he was getting a sense that this case could turn into something much more complex. That Samari had a price on his head was not going to make things easier, but Marwan wasn't the only person who would start to see dollar signs when talk of a bounty came up. On the other hand, Makana had nothing against a man whose crimes were clearly documented being brought to justice. Let Marwan hand him in. Once Makana had delivered him to Kasabian what difference did it make?

But there was something else bothering Makana. Why had Kasabian not been able to verify Samari's presence in the country? With people like Qasim around, it should have been easy. Unless Qasim had his own reasons for protecting Samari. He was beginning to wonder if Kasabian had been entirely frank with him. He asked Sindbad to drive him back to Zamalek. He had decided to pay an unexpected call on Aram Kasabian. He leant on the bell, stepped back and looked up at the high trees and the grand villa. It hadn't lost any of the charm it had possessed the previous evening. After a long delay the big white metal gate yawned open and the ageing gatekeeper let him in. His back was so stooped that as he followed him back up the path to the big villa Makana had to resist the temptation to reach out and stop the man falling flat on his face.

Kasabian's secretary was fretting at the top of the veranda steps. Jalal or 'Jules'. In broad daylight he looked older than he had the previous evening. Perhaps it had been an exhausting night. He was a pale, slightly plump man with thinning hair and a nervous disposition that caused him to fidget all the time, rolling his thumbs and clasping his fingers.

'You really ought to have called. As a rule Mr Kasabian doesn't see anyone without an appointment.'

'Well, I just happened to be close by, and there are a number of things that need clarifying.'

'Mr Kasabian is a very busy man.'

'I understand. It won't take a moment.'

Jules wrung his hands. 'Well, I can't promise anything.' He disappeared inside and Makana leaned on the balustrade and contemplated the lush scenery. A man could get used to this kind of peace. Yet all things came at a price. He wondered what that might be in Kasabian's case.

'Mr Makana, I didn't expect to see you so soon.' Aram Kasabian was wrapped in a white bathrobe, as if he had just stepped from the shower. A hint of irritation in his voice.

'I'm sorry to disturb you.'

'Quite all right.' Kasabian recovered his composure quickly. He gestured magnanimously at the garden. 'It's glorious at this hour, isn't it?'

'Delightful. Have you lived here long?'

'Forty years. It's been in my family for generations.' A wistful look crossed Kasabian's face, as if recalling a distant past. He snapped back to the present. 'Now, what can I help you with?'

'There were a couple of queries. I understand this is a delicate matter, but I think it might help if I could speak to your client, the American buyer.'

'I'm not sure why you think that would be of use to you,' frowned Kasabian, 'but I see no objection. He is obviously concerned with maintaining a low profile.'

'I understand that. It would just be for a few minutes.' Makana smiled. 'Just to help me get my bearings.'

'Interesting.' It wasn't clear that Kasabian entirely believed him. 'Well, I see no harm in it. As a matter of fact I was just preparing to go and meet him. We have an appointment for afternoon tea. Why don't you join me?'

'If it's no inconvenience.'

'Not at all,' Kasabian waved the matter aside. 'Let me finish dressing.'

Makana let Sindbad know what was happening and then waited on the veranda for another fifteen minutes. Turtle doves cooed in the trees. It gave him time to think. He recalled the conversation with Ali about enemies. It was quite possible that Kasabian was mixed up in something that he didn't quite understand. Dealing in stolen artwork or historical artefacts was a risky business. Was it possible that one of Kasabian's rivals was trying to set him up? Kasabian's mysterious American client seemed a good place to start.

When Kasabian finally emerged he looked his usual immaculate self, in a silver-grey suit with a powder-blue tie and matching handkerchief in his top pocket.

'We'll go in my car.'

The car was a Mercedes in fine shape and with a uniformed chauffeur at the wheel, although it was hardly worth getting into. The ride to the Marriott Hotel, which was around the corner, took about four minutes. The car slid smoothly up the ramp to deliver them to the door. Makana followed hard on the heels of Kasabian, who moved quickly for a man his age. The Marriott seemed to have been built with people like him in mind. The staff snapped to attention everywhere they went, as if royalty were among them. Money commands respect, as some great man might once have said. At the front desk the receptionist nearly fell over himself in his eagerness to be of service. His smile dropped when he had to come back after a lengthy interval to inform them that the man they were here to see was not in. Kasabian did not disguise his annoyance.

'That can't be. Are you sure? Mr Charles Barkley? Check again, please.'

'Yes, sir, Mr Kasabian. I've tried his room several times. I have also sent a bellhop to page him round the pool area and restaurants. I'm sorry, but he doesn't appear to be in the hotel.'

'Well, this is very strange. We had an appointment.' Kasabian glanced at his gold watch. 'Still, if he's not here, then there's nothing to be done.'

'Can I take a message?'

'No, I imagine I'll speak to him myself later. Thank you.' Kasabian was already heading for the exit. There seemed to be no point in staying longer. 'Quite ridiculous. A waste of time. I'm sorry about that. There must have been some misunderstanding. Can I give you a lift?'

'No, that's all right. I have my car coming to pick me up.' Makana scanned the hotel entrance hoping that Sindbad had parked somewhere discreet and out of sight.

'Very well. Let's speak when you have something for me.'

The two men shook hands.

Makana took a moment to look around the lobby before heading outside. As he did so he noted a man in a beige linen suit, rather crumpled and with stains around the armpits. A visitor unused to the weather, or a man who had come unprepared. For a second he wondered if this might be Barkley, but that made no sense. It was the way he was standing that struck him as odd; off to one side, reading a newspaper and wearing dark glasses. The rumble of the Thunderbird brought Makana's attention back to the front drive and he walked out to join Sindbad.

Chapter Seven

The Zerzura Gallery was set on the ground floor of a modern apartment building in Mohandiseen. A white horse that appeared to have wandered out of another century stood grazing in a patch of sparse yellow grass on the little square facing it. The gallery building was encased in grey marble and resembled a mausoleum. You might have expected to find a displaced head of state embalmed in the window, instead of carved lattice screens inlaid with mother-of-pearl.

To reach the window you had to clamber over piles of sand and broken brick. Construction appeared to have tailed off rather than come to a satisfactory conclusion, as if the builders had just lost interest. Despite this they were trying to preserve some sense of exclusivity. Chains prevented undesirable cars from blocking the entrance and a bored guard in a fancy uniform looked the Thunderbird over and decided to give them the benefit of the doubt. Tucked into the narrow gap between the next building were more leftovers: iron rods, timbers, more sand, heaps of broken breeze blocks and tiles, along with the tail end of a motorcycle: a yellow Yamaha.

Inside, a young woman wearing a headscarf sat behind a desk, her face illuminated by the blue glow of a computer screen. Makana murmured a greeting and moved on. Cases displaying jewellery in quaint rustic shapes evoked a city dweller's romanticised view of rural life. Table lamps inside clay minarets, ashtrays shaped like farmhouses in the *rif*. At the far end was a wall of canvases picked out by hot beams of white light. As Makana took a moment to examine these Dalia Habashi stepped out from an office at the far end of the room. She brushed away her surprise at seeing him with a flick of her hair and came forward.

'I wasn't expecting to see you so soon.' Her wrists jangled as she held out her hand.

'I just happened to be in the area.'

Dalia Habashi was elegantly dressed in grey trousers and a black blouse. She carried herself with style, although underneath it he detected a jittery nervousness. Her movements were quick and awkward and her pupils were dilated. He glanced towards the office with the drawn blinds from which she had emerged and she immediately gestured at the walls around them.

'What do you think so far?'

They strolled slowly around the gallery. 'I haven't really had time to take it in, but it all looks very interesting.' Makana glanced dutifully at each frame. 'How do you tell if something is valuable?'

'You can't, not really. I mean, you can, but there are no rules.' She pushed a hand through her hair nervously. 'It's all about whether someone else can see what you see.'

Makana nodded as if this made perfect sense.

'Many great artists never sold a painting in their lifetimes. Now their work sells for millions.'

'That seems unfair.'

'Did nobody tell you? Life is unfair.' She swivelled to face him. 'Why did you come here?'

'I thought I should devote more of my time to understanding art.'

Dalia Habashi examined him for a moment. 'You seemed a lot more charming last night. Now I have the feeling you are out to hurt me. You insult me by trying to appear more stupid than you are.'

'That's because I'm out of my depth.' He gestured around them.

'Not your sort of thing?'

'Not really.' Makana strolled on. Dalia Habashi followed. 'What was the name of your friend, by the way?'

'Which one?'

'The one on the motorcycle.'

She pulled up. 'So this isn't a social call?'

'I don't, as a rule, make social calls.'

'You must lead a very quiet life.'

'I'm not complaining.'

'What did Kasabian hire you to do?'

'I can't go into the details.'

'But you came here to ask me something. Why do you think I can help you?'

'Because you know this world.' Makana nodded at the walls. 'I need to understand how it works.'

'Why should I help Kasabian?'

'I get the feeling that whatever he's mixed up in might affect you too.'

Dalia Habashi considered this for a moment. 'Aram Kasabian is about as well established as you can be. He is the leading art dealer in the city. His grandfather started the business.' They turned along an aisle of glass cabinets containing jewellery. Makana peered at some gold earrings bearing pendants shaped like palm trees. A young couple walked in through the front door. It clearly wasn't their first visit. There was an air of confidence about them. The girl behind the front desk got up to greet them. These were the gallery's true customers. Young, wealthy and by the looks of them, recently married. Looking for something a little different but nevertheless familiar.

'How is business?'

'It's difficult for everyone,' Dalia answered glibly. 'Nobody is doing well.'

'I imagine there is a black market in valuable items – museum pieces, for example.'

'What makes you think I would know anything about that?' Dalia Habashi's chin lifted.

'You strike me as someone who makes it their business to know everything.'

'Nice try. I don't deal in stolen artefacts, if that's what you're after.'

'I didn't mean to imply that. I meant simply that you're an insider. You hear rumours.'

She studied him for a moment. 'All right. You don't get far in this business by sticking to the rules. There are too many grey areas. Clients are protective about their collections. They like to buy and sell with discretion, anonymously.'

'But there's a certain amount of risk involved. I imagine you have to invest quite heavily in a piece with no guarantee of a sale?'

'Where exactly is this leading?'

'I'm trying to get a feel for the art world. You are a leading reference, so it seems like a good place to start.'

'I'm afraid there isn't much I can tell you. This is a very

discreet business. Clients are fickle and easily scared off. You have to learn to instil confidence in them.'

'Is that what Qasim is to you? A client?'

Dalia Habashi smiled. 'Now you are fishing. I think you might learn more if you directed your questions to Mr Kasabian.'

'I intend to,' Makana nodded. 'By the way, how is your friend doing today?'

'Which friend?'

'The one you were defending last night. The motorcycle? I couldn't help noticing it outside.'

'Why does it always come down to this?' she sighed. 'Now if you don't mind, I have work to do.'

'Of course.'

Makana watched her go, switching on her charm to greet her customers. He left quietly. Outside he found Sindbad using an old rag to polish the car with all the loving care of an archaeological curator.

'Drive us around the corner and wait.'

Sindbad climbed behind the wheel and started the big engine. He seemed to have acquired a degree of formality since he had begun driving this car. The Thunderbird rolled around the uneven roads circling the square before turning off down a side road. Sindbad waved away a couple of boys who appeared to help with the parking process in return for a small tip and entered into a protracted discussion with them. Makana left him to it. He walked back to the corner of the road from where he could see the entrance of the Zerzura Gallery. It was less than ten minutes before the man appeared from inside the gallery. He rolled the Yamaha motorcycle backwards down to the road, climbed onto it and kicked the starter a couple of times before it came to life. Makana waved Sindbad forward, jumping inside as the Thunderbird rolled by.

'Turn right here.'

'But that's the wrong way, *ya basha*!'

'We'll lose him if we don't.'

They made it almost to the end of the street before a taxi turned in, blocking their way.

'Go around him.'

Sindbad swung the wheel and they lurched up onto a patch of broken pavement and rubble before lumbering by.

'This is no way to treat a car like this, *ya basha*.'

'Just go after him.'

With Sindbad muttering to himself, they rolled out of the square in time to see the Yamaha turning at the far end of the street.

'Stay with him, but don't get too close.'

Sindbad put his foot down and smiled as the big car surged forwards.

'*Wallahi*, this isn't a car, it's an F-16.'

The yellow motorcycle had reached an intersection and was already swinging round onto the opposite side of the dual carriageway. Sindbad spun the wheel and cut across three lanes of traffic. The lights were coming on in the shops on Ahmed Abdel Aziz Street. A plume of black smoke from the Yamaha's tailpipe sailed over the cars ahead of them like a banner. It felt as though following its movement was more a matter of faith than observation. Makana wanted to know more about the rider and his relationship to Dalia Habashi. Her dilated eyes suggested she was taking drugs of some kind, which added to the picture of her difficulties. This man, with his rough manners and motorcycle, seemed at odds with the kind of high-class environment in which Dalia Habashi's clientele moved.

The burr of the engine was audible as the Yamaha accelerated up the ramp.

'He's turning onto the bridge,' Makana warned, but Sindbad was already turning, forcing a small scooter bearing a family of four to weave erratically out of their way. They thumped over a pothole and the Thunderbird rocked like a boat as they curved up the ramp and onto the 6th October Bridge. They were lucky. The traffic was light and it was easy to keep the target in sight. 'Don't get too close,' Makana warned. In the distance green strip lights fluttered in the dusk, announcing mosques like flagships dotted on a sea of ochre. Towards the end of the bridge the vehicles began to coagulate, slowing to a halt. The rider flicked the Yamaha through the cars and veered right. He was taking the Gezira exit before they crossed to the east bank of the river.

'He's going towards the Qasr al-Nil Bridge,' Sindbad said.

The light was almost gone as they dropped off the bridge onto the Corniche. The single rear light of the motorcycle led them into Maadi, where finally they lost him. For a time they drove in circles, turning left and right, widening the net in the hope they would catch a glimpse of him.

'*Maalish, ya basha*, I'm sorry. It was my fault.'

'Not at all. We'll do one more circle.'

'But we can hardly see anything in this darkness.'

'Just once more round the block.'

They did one circuit and then another. Then Makana thought of something. He reached into his pocket and produced the piece of paper Marwan had given him.

'See if you can find this address.'

They drove round some more and finally turned into a quiet street, only to find, leaning up against a high white wall that surrounded a large villa, the Yamaha.

'Who said you can't believe in coincidence?'

Chapter Eight

Sindbad snoozed contentedly behind the wheel while Makana observed the building on the opposite side of the road. Over the high walls that fenced off the grounds from the street the crowns of a row of palm trees rose majestically. The languorous fronds dipped gently in the night air, a cool breeze wafting from the river. Beyond the trees he could see lights and his ears caught the faint sound of music. There was something not quite right about the gateway, which was made of stone and did not match the rest of the perimeter wall or the modern building behind it.

Makana sat and watched as people came and went. As the evening progressed more cars arrived, most of them expensive and chauffeur-driven. They pulled up and unloaded their passengers before driving off. The vast majority of these arrivals were male. They tended to be of a certain age and clearly comfortably off, as proclaimed by their clothes and bulging waistlines. Makana recognised a couple of television hosts, the odd journalist and businessman.

Inside, the party continued. By now there were figures leaning against the railing of the roof, strings of coloured lights over their heads and the movement of what might have been people dancing behind them. Makana's eye was drawn back down to ground level as a figure stepped into the street from the path leading up to the house. He paused to light a cigarette and Makana sat up. It took him a moment to remember where he had seen the man before. The Marriott Hotel, and wearing the same crumpled linen suit. This time the sunglasses were perched on the top of his head. He staggered on the uneven pavement. Makana nudged Sindbad awake. The big man yawned and rubbed his eyes like a baby.

'*Aiwa, ya basha.*'

'I need you to follow that man.'

'Man, which man, *ya sidi*?' Sindbad scrabbled about trying to right himself and straighten his clothes. Makana pointed to the figure retreating down the street. When he reached the end he would find a taxi and disappear. Makana opened the door and climbed out.

'Get going, and don't lose him. When you finish with that, go on home and get some rest. I'll see you tomorrow.'

Sindbad looked up at him. 'What about you?'

'I'll find my own way.'

Makana watched the big car surge away from the kerb. A beautiful thing to observe, but probably swallowed a fortune in petrol as well as drawing a crowd like a conjuror with a trick monkey. Crossing the street, Makana examined the entrance set into the modern wall. While the heavy metal gate was new, the stone archway that supported it looked out of place, flanked as it was by stones that had been carved with a motif. The structure didn't belong in this neighbourhood; it looked more like an architectural relic salvaged from the old part of Cairo.

The motifs on either side were identical: a lion with wings.

Before he had time to consider the significance of this fact the gate in front of him gave a slight lurch and began to swing inwards. An explanation was to be found in a security camera set high up to one side that angled down on whoever was standing outside.

A path led straight up from the gate to an open entrance at the front of the building where a small reception committee observed his progress. Three men. One enormously fat one sat behind the desk on the left watching a monitor. The second stood by the metal detector while the third man, who rivalled Sindbad in stature and had a shaven head, stood blocking Makana's path. He wore a tuxedo that fitted him the way a wedding gown might fit a water buffalo, but he knew his place and stood with both hands clasped before him.

'Good evening, *effendi*.'

'I'm not sure if this is the right place.' Makana struggled to light a cigarette, swaying on his feet for effect.

'What place were you looking for?'

'Well, it was recommended to me by a friend. Actually, I was supposed to meet him here, but I got delayed.'

'What was the name of your friend?' enquired the bouncer.

'You can't tell me he's not here because his motorcycle is parked right outside.' Makana swivelled and stabbed a belligerent finger in the direction of the gate. The bouncers exchanged a look. The fat one behind the desk grunted.

'Na'il? You're a friend of Na'il? Why didn't you say so?'

As they waved him through Makana noted the man behind the desk reaching for a telephone. The staircase took him up to the first floor, where an open gallery led to a white door. There was no sign of anyone about. He peered back down the stairwell to see the man in the tuxedo looking up. Stepping away, Makana turned to his right and began to walk. Before he reached the door it swung open.

The interior was illuminated by low lighting set around the walls. Plastic plants bloomed from every corner. Behind a high reception counter stood a tall woman with dyed blonde hair, fingernails painted blood red, and wearing a black-sequinned dress that sparkled and shone in the strange blue and red glow. She smiled as he entered.

'Good evening,' she purred. 'I am Gigi.'

'Good evening, Gigi. This is my first visit.'

'Welcome, *merhaba*. We ask guests who are not members to leave a deposit of a hundred dollars. No money is exchanged inside the club. An account is kept and all losses and wins are recorded. At the end of the evening we settle all accounts.'

Makana exchanged some of Kasabian's dollars for a handful of plastic chips. Then Gigi held aside a red velvet drape and invited him to enter. To reach the main casino you had to pass through the bar area, which had a long counter down one side and a number of tables scattered around. There were also curtained booths along the other wall for people who wanted more intimacy. A spiral staircase in the middle of the room led up to the roof terrace where the thump of music could be heard and coloured lights could be glimpsed against the stars. Beyond another archway the room seemed to expand and Makana saw several gaming tables. Small groups of people, mostly men, clustered around a handful of high semicircular tables. Behind each one a dealer shuffled cards and took bets. Exactly what they were playing Makana couldn't have said, but he saw plenty of money, both in chips and in cash, being exchanged for more chips. At the far end, along the bottom wall, a roulette table appeared to be the most popular attraction, perhaps because it required less experience to play. A stooped man wearing white gloves raked in chips from the green baize. Losing didn't seem to bother most people. Almost as if it was some sort of rite of passage: to be able to afford this place meant you had enough money to lose.

As she finished her tour, Gigi turned to him and beamed.

'Now, all our guests are invited to a free drink at the bar. Have you thought how you would like to spend the evening. Are you interested in gambling, Mr . . . ?'

'Makana.' There didn't seem to be much point in lying. 'A drink sounds good.'

He followed her over to the bar, where he asked for whisky, the only thing he could think of. The bartender, whose bow tie was askew, filled a glass with ice and trickled Scotch from a bottle with a worn label over it before wrapping it thoughtfully in a paper napkin. Makana circled the room, drink in hand, and studied the faces. The clientele were mostly businessmen of the self-made variety, aged between thirty-five and sixty. They wore flashy clothes and a lot of rings. They appeared to understand gambling as if roulette was a competition to see who could throw the most money away in the shortest time. There were some familiar faces, too – politicians, men with eager smiles and evasive eyes. He didn't see Na'il, the man on the motorcycle, nor did he see anyone who struck him as being a match for Kadhim al-Samari, although he hardly expected to find him that easily. Gigi's sparkling white teeth reappeared at his side. She leaned discreetly into him, engulfing him in heady perfume.

'If this is not to your liking, perhaps you would prefer to relax upstairs with one of our hostesses?'

'Perhaps.'

Gigi led him back towards the reception desk and the door alongside it. It was black, with a bronze replica of the winged lion on it that matched the one on the front gateway. She produced a key, and pausing only to look around her once, she opened the door and ushered him inside. A narrow set of stairs led to the floor below, where Makana found himself in another reception area, this time considerably darker and outfitted with a low sofa against one pink wall. The sofa was satin green.

'*Itfaddal.*' Gigi gestured for him to sit before vanishing through a set of lacy curtains.

Makana sat and decided the time had come for a cigarette. He took a moment to examine the décor more closely – not easy in the low lighting. On the walls were framed prints, mostly the work of European artists, depicting orientalist idylls. Naked women lying within their private chambers, frolicking beneath a waterfall or lounging in states of undress in a steam bath. Swarthy men in headdresses eyed them furtively, strummed lutes or counted prayer beads between their fingers.

The curtains opened and Makana came back to the present. Gigi reappeared, ushering in six women of various sizes and proportions. All of them were young and attractive. They wore variations on the kind of evening gown Gigi wore, though considerably less substantial. She paraded in front of them like a confident lion-tamer. To Makana things looked rather different. It had been a long time since he had been involved with a woman, and the sudden availability before him was somewhat daunting.

'Please take your pick,' said Gigi in her softest voice.

Makana, stalling for time, reached for his drink and was about to take a sip when he noticed something that caused his heart to stop.

'Number six,' he said, aware that his voice was no longer steady.

'A wise choice,' beamed Gigi. She clapped her hands and the other girls filed silently out of the room, leaving only one behind. 'Bilquis is one of our most popular girls. I leave you in safe hands.'

She was a tall girl with a slim, angular body and face. Her hair was pinned up to display an elegant neck. Her eyes were dark and quick. She spun on her heels and led the way down a corridor without a word. Makana followed along, his mind suddenly a blank. The corridor was so dimly lit he could barely see the person in front of him, which made the effect even more disconcerting. The long dress seemed to float along the floor, which made the figure striding away through the gloom feel all the more ethereal, as if he were following a ghost.

When they reached the far end the girl opened a door and gestured for him to enter. Makana stepped cautiously inside. Here, too, the light was low. The room was furnished in modern style. There were blinds on the windows and translucent drapes around the bed in some kind of mauve colour. It looked hasty and cheap. By this stage no doubt the client was meant to have other things on his mind than the furnishings. Apart from the bed there was a chaise longue, a chest of drawers, a small refrigerator, a television set. A door led off to a bathroom. When Makana had taken all of this in he turned around to find that the girl was busy undressing.

'Wait,' he said. The dress was already halfway off. She stared at him for a moment and then slipped the shoulder strap back into place.

'Would you like another drink?'

'No, no, I'm fine. Perhaps we could just . . . sit for a time.'

She stared at him as though waiting for the punchline of a joke, then she shrugged and went over to sit down on the edge of the bed.

'Would you like to watch a film?' She indicated the television. 'Some men find that sort of thing gets them ready.'

'No, not really.'

She watched him cautiously, wondering about this deviation from the usual procedure, then she crossed her legs and shrugged.

'It's all right. Some people like to talk, I know. We can sit for a while, but not too long. Gigi gets anxious if it takes too long.'

'I see.' Makana glanced around the room. There was a glass bowl with brightly coloured fish that rose and sank with mechanical regularity. 'Have you been here long?'

'Not so long.' Then she stopped herself. 'You mean in this country?'

'Yes.'

'Almost five years. And you?'

'A little longer.'

'How much longer?' She was watching him more carefully now.

Makana was trying to focus. How difficult could it be to conduct a conversation? 'I don't know, maybe thirteen years altogether.'

'That's a long time. I'm not planning on staying that long.'

'Neither was I.'

She tapped her nails impatiently on her arm. 'Look, I'm serious about time. We don't have for ever.'

'No, of course not. I understand. Actually, I didn't come here for this.' He nodded at the bed.

'Then what? We don't get paid to talk.' Then she was silent for a long time before a knowingness came into her voice. 'Who is it?'

'Who is what?'

She gave weary toss of her head. 'I've seen that look before. I remind you of someone. Everyone comes here looking for something or someone. A person, or a feeling, perhaps. Who is it?'

Makana was still considering how to answer this when there was a knock at the door, and without waiting for an answer, it swung open and Gigi stepped inside. She looked him up and down. It wasn't hard to see that something in her manner had changed. Gone was the smooth talk.

'I'm glad I caught you before it was too late.' Her smile was thin and mean. No sign of the pearly white teeth. She crooked a finger at Makana. 'Some people would like to talk to you.'

They were waiting in the reception area: two young men, both overweight, both dressed in blue jeans and shiny jackets. Both wore the dull expressions of hard men. The first one lifted his hand. It was a big hand, misshapen, as if the bones had been broken a few times. There were a lot of rings on that hand, big lumps of metal that could do a lot of damage if they hit you.

'Mr Zafrani wants to see you,' he said. It wasn't an invitation.

Chapter Nine

The driver, the shorter of the two men, drove in an aggressive manner, closing in on cars in his way and then flashing his lights for them to vacate the road. Makana had seen the same attitude in State Security drivers, only this man wasn't State Security. He kept snapping the wheel from side to side as he switched lanes. Most passengers might have felt a little queasy, but Makana hardly noticed being flung against the door time and again. He had the strange feeling that he had just fallen back through a doorway in time. When he'd first set eyes on the girl he had thought he was imagining things. Bilquis bore an uncanny resemblance to Muna. Not the Muna who had died that night on the bridge, thirteen years ago, but the young woman he had first fallen in love with long before that. She looked, in other words, exactly as he had imagined his daughter Nasra might look today. Of course, it couldn't be. It wasn't possible, or was it?

As they drove up onto the bridge, Makana could already see their destination, the old paddle steamer moored along the river, its outline sketched out in the darkness by red lights running up the square sides and around the upper deck. The name had been changed. Now the words, in English and Arabic on either side, spelled out the name *Al-Buraq*. The legendary animal of myth that had once carried the Prophet from Mecca to Jerusalem and back again in a single, fateful night. Laylat al-Qadr. It seemed like an odd symbol for the Zafranis to adopt, but then again, why not?

Makana's dealings with the Zafrani brothers over the years had been of an ambiguous nature. For a couple of gangsters with a nasty reputation, they had always treated him surprisingly well – or perhaps he had managed to avoid antagonising them enough for them to do him harm – but it was like playing with a pair of unpredictable and dangerous animals. You never knew when they might lose patience and decide to take your hand off, or worse. Of course, he should have guessed they might be behind the club. It was a cut above the *Buraq*, but they were nothing if not ambitious.

The car whipped down off the ramp and sped along the riverside to the brightly lit entrance. The boat had been given a facelift. Makana could remember the dark and gloomy restaurant on the upper floor that was always empty. Everybody knew it was just a cover for their more nefarious enterprises. Arches of white lights now greeted the visitor. The doormen still had faces like camel saddles, but now they wore uniforms and through the windows on the upper floor it was possible to see people actually eating. A group of overfed men stood around the entrance wishing they had something to hit. As Makana approached, they stepped neatly aside. Obviously, his escorts had some kind of seniority. The lobby and staircase were lined with tacky mirrored strips. A ball of rotating coloured lights played over them as they climbed. It was comforting to know that the Zafranis hadn't lost their taste for the cheap and gaudy.

The good life was beginning to show its effects on Ayad Zafrani. He had put on a fair amount of weight since the last time they had met. Makana had always thought of him as a small man, but he seemed bigger all round now. The suit was cut wide in the shoulders to disguise his expansive girth. He still had the same shaven head and steel-rimmed glasses. He got up from behind the desk and came round. Despite his bulk, he moved quickly, and it was easy to see how people might be intimidated. He looked Makana up and down as if this were a military inspection, then dismissed the two men with a wave and gestured at the sofa and chair arrangement on one side of the room.

'Please, make yourself comfortable.'

Everything was covered in synthetic black-and-white leather, so that the room resembled a scattered set of dominos. A broad window displayed the city skyline. Brightly lit minarets and fancy hotels reached for the heavens. If that didn't summarise this city, Makana didn't know what did.

'You've been decorating.'

'Renovation. You have to keep things new. People expect that.' Ayad Zafrani chuckled, fluttering a handful of rings in the air. Then his face grew sober. 'They didn't rough you up at all, did they, Didi and Bobo? They can get carried away.'

'No, they were perfectly civil.'

He rubbed a hand over his scalp fretfully. 'I swear to God, it's so hard to find decent help these days. All these kids think it's about driving fast and using your fists. I'm not saying that doesn't come into it, but you can't trust them to think for themselves. Not for a second. They're like children. You have to watch over them all the time.'

Makana's eye fell on the statue of Ramses that took up one corner of the room. It was about two metres high and painted in gold. He couldn't work out why the pharaoh's face looked so familiar, until he realised Zafrani was grinning at him.

'I see you haven't lost your sense of style,' Makana said.

Ayad Zafrani feigned modesty.

'That old thing? I've had it for years, just never had a place to put it. I heard there's a guy in London. Egyptian. Owns a big department store. Very fancy. I don't remember what it's called. He did the same, put his face on a pharaoh in the entrance. Now everyone thinks it was his idea. I can remember him standing right where you are now. Imagine that? No shame.'

'The world is filled with injustice.'

'Exactly my point. Speaking of which, what are you up to?' Ayad Zafrani settled himself heavily into the chair opposite Makana. Two old friends catching up. Air escaped with a loud hiss.

'I'm not sure what you mean.'

'You come to my club, naturally you're going to attract attention.' Zafrani was smiling. Never a guarantee that he was amused.

'Perhaps I like to gamble, spend a little time with the women.'

'We run a nice quiet place for men to relax in. They rely on our discretion. They don't like people coming around poking around.' Zafrani was grinning again, like a boy having fun. 'I bet you're wondering how I knew it was you when they called me.' He picked up a remote control and pressed a button. The television screen that dominated one wall of the room came to life. A few more buttons produced a grainy black-and-white image split into four parts. One showed the exterior of the house in Maadi. Makana noticed that the motorcycle was no longer there. Another image showed the view from the security area downstairs. The bouncers looked bored. The upstairs bar. The casino.

Ayad Zafrani clicked his way through one screen after another, each one producing more images.

'It's amazing, isn't it? We live in the age of miracles.'

'Don't tell me you have cameras in the rooms as well.'

Ayad Zafrani wagged a fat finger. 'You have a devious mind.'

'That doesn't answer the question.'

'You haven't answered mine yet. What were you doing there this evening?'

'Why all the drama? Those maniacs driving me here at breakneck speed?'

'I'm sorry about that. Look, I know you, remember? If you come snooping around it's not because you need a woman or you have money to throw away, which reminds me, how much did you put down on the tab?'

'A hundred dollars.'

'Dollars, eh? Sounds like you're moving into the big time yourself.' Zafrani went over to the desk and dug into a drawer. He came back and handed Makana a thick wad of Egyptian pounds in exchange. 'Let's call it even. I'll forget the chips they gave you.'

'What have I done to deserve such generosity?'

'It's not what you've done, it's what you're going to do.' He raised his hands to stem Makana's objections. 'You're going to tell me what you were doing at my club.'

'How is your brother, by the way?'

'My brother?' Ayad Zafrani examined the tip of his cigar. 'My brother has decided to devote himself to helping those less fortunate than himself.'

'Sounds like a noble gesture.'

'He's doing God's work. He spends all his time at a mosque helping the poor. He thinks it will help him in the next life. Me,

I'm more concerned with what happens in this one.' Ayad Zafrani gestured around them. 'This, he wants nothing to do with, except to finance his benevolent acts of course. What can I do?' Zafrani shrugged. 'He's my brother. Anyone else and I would have cut off his head and fed him to the fish.'

Makana had always found Zayed the more reasonable of the two brothers. Ayad was the more headstrong, less predictable.

'So . . .' Ayad Zafrani held out his hands. 'You're making me wait.'

'All right. I'm looking for someone. An Iraqi. A former colonel in Saddam's army.'

'Interesting.' Zafrani puffed on his cigar thoughtfully. 'Does this colonel have a name?'

'Kadhim al-Samari.'

'Where did you hear he was in my club?'

'You know how it is.'

'No, I don't, but I am interested about where you heard this story.'

'Are you saying it's true, he does go there?'

'I'm not saying anything of the sort. Look, you don't want to tell me, that's fine. I have nothing to hide. I'm just trying to run a decent club.'

'I heard you were trying to make your businesses legitimate.'

'You're thinking of my brother.' Ayad Zafrani threw up his hands in despair. 'And besides, in this country as you well know, there's a very thin line between one thing and the other.'

'So this casino is for a better class of customer?'

'You could say that. We've done it in style, you have to admit, right?' Ayad sniffed and reached for a cigar. 'Did you see the lions? I thought they were a nice touch.'

'They look old. Did you get them from a museum?'

'Almost. A house on Bendaka Street in the Mouski. It used to belong to some Venetian merchant back in I don't know when. But you're right, they probably should be in a museum for some dumb tourists to feel clever about, but who cares about them, right?' He sat back with a satisfied look and puffed clouds of smoke. 'All those old empires were built the same way. Sure, they legitimised themselves in time, but in the beginning? They just took what they wanted. The Romans, the Greeks, the Ottomans, even the British. They just walked in and took what they wanted.'

'And that's how you're building your own empire.'

'You see the beauty of it?' Ayad Zafrani grinned for a moment and then became serious. 'So why the interest in this Iraqi?'

'A client wants to make him a business proposition.'

'And someone told you I could put you in touch with him?'

'Can you?'

'You know how it is.' Zafrani splayed his fingers wide. 'If it's not of benefit to me I can do nothing.'

'I suppose you would be entitled to some kind of cut. I'd have to check with my client.'

'That sounds fair enough.'

Makana waited. 'So?'

'So I'll think it over.' Zafrani rolled a ring of cigar smoke next to his right ear. 'I heard you were asking about Na'il.'

'I might have been.'

'Don't tell me he's the one who brought you to the club?'

'In a way, yes.'

'Watch out for that one. He's a pest. He bribes my doormen to let him in. Peddles his pills to my clients. One of these days he's going to get what's coming to him.' Zafrani hauled his bulk to his feet. The interview was clearly over. 'I'll get the boys to drive you home.'

As Makana turned towards the door the gravelly voice caught him in his tracks.

'What about that girl, eh? What did you think of her? The one at the club. Sorry I had to break off your little meeting. She's one of your compatriots. Very popular girl.' Zafrani was watching Makana the way a cat might watch a sparrow for any sign of weakness. 'Feel free to go back and finish what you started. Any time,' he smiled. 'We all have our needs.'

Some time later, the car slipping through the silent streets like a dark knife through water, Makana's thoughts returned to the present.

'Where would I find Zayed Zafrani nowadays?'

'Try the Mustafa Mahmoud mosque in Mohandiseen,' grunted Didi, or perhaps it was Bobo.

Chapter Ten

The sun was bright on the upper deck the next morning and Makana sat with his feet up on the railing and his eyes closed. He'd tossed and turned for hours before finally giving up and sitting in his chair watching the world come to life. There was nothing more peaceful than the early hours of the morning when the city seemed uninhabited save for the birds and the wind rustling through the dry leaves of the trees along the river-bank. With his eyes closed he could almost imagine himself in Kasabian's immaculate garden.

'Morning, *ya bash muhandis*.' Aziza was her usual industrious self, rushing about tidying up the place, tucking notebooks and sheets of paper into neat piles, emptying overflowing ashtrays, picking up cups. Although still in her teens, she carried herself with the slow, careful movements of a somewhat older woman, avoiding the expenditure of energy, knowing that it was going to be a long day. She wore a light-blue gellabiya decorated with flowers. The hem that swept around her bare feet was grubby with mud from the riverbank. At home she never wore shoes, summer or winter. Without them she was light, even graceful, but if he ever bumped into her and Umm Ali on the street or in the market, Aziza would be wearing the ugliest plastic sandals that she bore as clumsily as if they had been horseshoes.

A glass of red tea stood steaming on the floor beside him, so Makana reached out to lift the glass. As he sipped, the hot sweet liquid seemed to drip life back into his veins. He was still in a strange state of mind. The heart-stopping moment when he first caught sight of Bilquis was still vivid in his memory. Perhaps he had never really fully accepted either of their deaths. Even though it was years ago, there was something about that episode that clung like a nightmare from which he one day hoped to wake.

Finishing his tea, Makana got to his feet and thought about the day ahead. He went downstairs, washed and dressed, and then called Fathi at the airport, followed by his real estate friend. Neither of them had come up with any information about Kadhim al-Samari. It seemed he had not come into the country by the normal channels, or somebody was covering his tracks. He watched a fisherman rowing his net patiently in a circle and called Sami.

'About our Iraqi friend. Is there any chance he might have contacts with anyone in the army here?'

'It's possible. I can make some calls.'

'Thanks. And I don't have to tell you to be discreet.'

'When am I ever not?' Sami laughed as he rang off.

Sindbad was parked under the big eucalyptus tree when Makana walked up the path to the main road. The big man was swatting away a group of curious schoolboys who were buzzing like flies around the Thunderbird.

'Let's move before someone decides to start selling tickets.'

'Sorry, *ya basha*.'

It was surprising that the car drew such interest. He had assumed that even a car as distinctive as this could only hold people's attention for so long. Elsewhere things might have been different, but here there was something new every couple of minutes – not so much a city, as a gigantic theatre of its own making. Apparently he was wrong.

'Tell me about last night. Did you follow the man?'

'Yes indeed, effendi. I followed him just like you said. A taxi took him to the Carlton Hotel. You know it? In the Tewfiqiyya, opposite the old Rivoli cinema.'

Makana knew it. Once upon a time it had been the European quarter, where it was like living in Paris. Nowadays it was a little less glamorous, but it still retained remnants of the old charm, largely buried under layers of concrete, iron and neon.

They were jammed in traffic which let them down off the 6th October Bridge at a pace that Kasabian's old gatekeeper would have managed to keep up with.

'We're not getting anywhere,' said Makana. 'I'll walk from here. You can catch me up later.'

Makana got out of the car and left Sindbad to his own devices. A vendor selling snacks marched smartly alongside him singing out his wares. Roasted melon seeds, peanuts, toasted corn. 'Hot, sweet and salty, get them before the Americans land on our heads!'

A century ago this area might have been described as cosmopolitan. Gentlemen wearing tarbooshes and European clothes would have strolled along or passed by in carriages. Armenians, Greeks, French, British, Syrians, Circassians, all lived there. Now it had a distinctly rural, feeling about it. The people of the land had moved into the city and they weren't interested in the least in becoming cosmopolitan.

The lobby of the Carlton was dark and discreet. Lined in

wood, it had a jaded but distinctive flavour to it. The old style had been whittled down by time and necessity to a dull everyday sheen. Behind the reception desk was a small man with a round head across which a few sparse hairs reached out optimistically towards the other side.

'One of your guests, an American, wears a linen suit. About this high.'

'Mr Frankie,' nodded the receptionist, briskly tucking papers away into corners.

'Mr Frankie. Does he have a last name?'

'Of course he has a last name,' the receptionist snorted. 'What's it to you?'

'I'm curious. He might be someone I need to talk to.'

The receptionist ran his eyes over Makana and leaned across the counter, lowering his voice. 'Don't be angry. I'm one of you. I checked his papers carefully, believe me.'

By 'one of you' the man meant he was an informant. A common enough occurrence in a hotel of this size. In his pocket Makana carried a laminated plastic card, purchased in its day from Barazil at an exorbitant price, that identified him as an agent of the State Security Investigations Sector. He bore little resemblance to the photograph, which was slightly water-damaged, but that didn't matter. Most of the time people were too nervous to examine it carefully once they recognised the insignia. On this occasion it wasn't even required.

'You checked with central headquarters?'

'I haven't had time. We've been very busy.'

'You'd better let me have a look.'

'Of course.'

The receptionist bent down and produced a photocopy of a passport made out in the name of Frank Cassidy.

A Japanese couple approached the desk. They were looking for the Egyptian Museum and refused to take a taxi. They had a map that unfolded like an umbrella. The receptionist shuffled about like a bull in the dark. Eventually, the Japanese took themselves off.

'Is he in his room?'

The receptionist didn't even need to glance at the rack of keys behind him. 'I take it as a duty to know exactly which of my guests are in and which not. You don't understand the service people like me perform. Mr Frankie went out twenty minutes ago. He will be gone for an hour or so. He likes to drink coffee and read the newspaper in a café not far from here.'

'I need to see his room.'

'It's more than my job's worth,' sighed the receptionist. 'I'm more useful to you people here than in the street, believe me.'

'I believe you. I'm trying to make this as easy for you as possible. I need ten minutes.'

'Nothing will be taken? I don't want to lose customers.'

'Nothing will be taken. Ring twice and hang up if he comes back.'

The receptionist snatched back the photocopy and set the key down. 'Ten minutes.'

Room 27 was on the second floor. It was small, surprisingly clean, and revealed almost nothing about its occupant. There was a single aluminium suitcase resting on a scuffed trestle in a corner of the room. Despite being equipped with an array of complicated locks, it was open. Makana lifted the lid and looked through its contents, which were few and in need of washing. Shirts, underwear, socks. A couple of books. In the sleeve were travel documents. An Egypt Air ticket in the name of Frank Cassidy which showed he had arrived in Cairo nearly two weeks ago from Amman, Jordan. There was no date of departure. The bathroom revealed a toilet bag, packed and ready to go. As he wouldn't need a change of socks, Mr Cassidy could be out of the door in less than two minutes. The glass in the bathroom smelled of alcohol. He found a half-empty bottle of rye whiskey concealed above the wardrobe. Hanging inside was a raincoat and a heavier blue suit. The cuffs of the suit were frayed and the elbows shiny from use. Whatever he was, Cassidy certainly wasn't rich, which begged the question of what he had been doing at Zafrani's club. He travelled light and he had travelled a lot.

There was something a little too familiar about this spartan existence. Whoever Frank Cassidy might be, he was not a simple tourist. The room added up to a portrait of a lonely man, a man who had come a long way for a reason. On the bedside table lay a well-thumbed guidebook to the city. As he flicked through the pages a photograph floated through his fingers to land on the floor. It showed a handsome boy with blue eyes peering out from under a mop of blond hair. Makana wondered who the boy was and what his relationship to Frank Cassidy was.

As he was replacing the picture inside the book he felt the buzzing of his telephone in his pocket. It was Dalia Habashi.

'I was wondering if we could meet? I think it might be in both our interests.'

Her voice had changed. There was something subdued about her tone now. Makana stepped to the window, which was shuttered. Through the slats he could see the street below. People came and went. A woman in black trudged along with a bucket in each hand. She walked as if she had been doing the same thing for a hundred years or more.

'What did you have in mind?' The telephone on the bedside table began to ring.

'Not over the phone. Shall we say Groppi's, around four o'clock?'

The phone on the table rang a second time and then stopped.

'Four o'clock. I'll be there.'

Makana turned to leave. In the doorway, he stood for a moment and studied the room one last time, wondering what it was he was not seeing. He took the stairs down to the lobby, moving quietly. The lift hummed up past him. Through the opaque glass he could make out the blurred shape of the American in the crumpled linen suit.

'Here he is,' said Sami as Makana walked in. 'Our very own favourite investigator of international renown. Have you had breakfast? I was just about to send someone out.'

Makana naturally had given no thought to eating. He reached into his pocket. Sami rarely allowed him to pay for any of the help he provided, and so in return Makana would try to contribute where possible. He came up with the wad of money Zafrani had given him. A reminder that if he wasn't careful he was going to wind up in debt to some very dubious people. Sami waved away the offer of money.

'Keep it, people might think you're trying to bribe me. And besides, you'll probably be needing it soon.'

'You know something I don't?'

'I was speculating.' Sami frowned. 'Don't tell me Kasabian fired you already? No, don't answer that or we'll never eat.' He shouted orders for one of the others to arrange a run to the nearby snack bar before slumping back behind his desk. 'So, are you out of the art business?'

Makana perched on the front of his desk. 'Not so far as I know, but I have an odd feeling about this.'

'What kind of odd feeling?'

'The kind where I'm in the dark and I can't see what's in front of me.'

'You don't trust Kasabian?'

'Kasabian has made himself a rich man by convincing people that what he is selling is of great value. He's a smooth talker.'

'You didn't have to take the job.'

'You always think you choose the case, but sometimes it's the other way around.'

'The case chooses you?'

'Something like that.'

It had started as a favour to a friend, but the truth was he had become intrigued by the story Kasabian had told him. Somewhere out there an Iraqi colonel who specialised in torturing people was selling fine art to collectors from New York. Something about that combination seemed to sum up what was wrong with the world. Maybe he thought he was trying to put the world right, and maybe that was the biggest mistake he had made. And then there was Bilquis. Makana wasn't sure he could explain what it was that drew him to her. He wasn't sure he understood it himself.

'Did Ubay come up with anything?'

'Let's ask him.' Sami put his fingers in his mouth and whistled. 'Your turn Ubay. Come and show him what you found.'

The youth gambolled over on legs as long and thin as the proverbial giraffe's. He was trembling with excitement as he carried his laptop over.

'This man is very, very dangerous,' he said gravely. The afro bobbed up and down like some exotic tree that had come to life as he sat and flipped open his computer. 'They call him the Samurai.' Ubay glanced at Sami, who nodded for him to continue. 'It appears to derive from his name – al-Samari, al Samurai – but actually it's a reference to his preferred method of torture. Several human rights sites carry the same story.'

'You mean he uses some sort of Japanese torture?' asked Makana.

'A knife. He makes a large number of cuts all over the body. None of them is fatal in itself, but as they add up the pain increases, causing the victim to die of blood loss or shock.'

'Sounds like the Chinese thing where you drip water on someone's forehead,' said Sami.

'It is a very slow and painful death.' Behind the large spectacles, Ubay's eyes were wide.

'Go on,' Makana urged gently.

'He is also accused of mass murder, of running death squads under Saddam. He is ranked lower than Chemical Ali, but is definitely linked to the Anfal genocide of 1988.' Ubay's knee was bouncing up and down like a sprinter itching to take off. 'Kurdish villages were wiped out with poison gas. Tens of thousands of civilians were killed, men, women and children.'

'What do we know about his background?' asked Makana.

'Colonel al-Samari made a name for himself during the Iran–Iraq war of Eighty-one to Eighty-eight, and later during the invasion of Kuwait in 1990. Originally he comes from the Sunni heartland around Falluja, so he was close to Saddam and the Baath Party. That is also where he was last based.'

'How much is the reward on that wanted card?' asked Sami.

Ubay squinted at the blue screen he cradled in his arms. 'Three million US dollars reward for information leading to his capture.'

'Is there any word of where he might be right now?'

Ubay rubbed his chin. 'He disappeared when the Americans arrived.'

'Three million for information. That's a lot of money,' said Sami.

'If I was looking for this man,' said Ubay quietly, 'I think I would be very careful.'

He could have been reading Makana's mind.

A commotion by the door announced the arrival of food.

'We'd better get over there before it's all gone,' said Sami.

Makana wasn't particularly hungry. Ubay got to his feet and stood there clutching the laptop to his chest. He was staring into space.

'Are you going to bring him to justice?'

Makana looked up. 'We'll see.'

Ubay remained where he was. 'Men like this,' he said finally, 'the world always finds a way of letting them off the hook.'

Makana watched him walk away.

Chapter Eleven

Makana knew about torture. He knew the helplessness that came over you after days of sustained suffering, about trying to hang onto your humanity. He recalled the humiliation, the loss of dignity, the desolation of the soul. For years he had told himself that he was over it, that the memory of that time had healed the way the physical scars had been absorbed into his body. He realised now that he was wrong. It never left you.

He was late for his meeting at Groppi's. Dalia Habashi had given up on him and was standing on the kerb trying to hail a taxi. Makana walked faster and managed to make it across the street without being run down. He arrived at her side just as she put her hand on the door of the taxi that had pulled up.

'*Maalish.*' He leaned down to address the driver. 'We won't be needing you after all.'

'Where did you spring from?' the driver demanded.

'Please, just move on.'

'Listen to me, *ya basha*. Let the lady make up her own mind. We all need work.' The driver hung on, hoping she would have a change of heart and climb into his cab anyway. '*Yallah, ya madam*, don't let a man rule your life. A lady should decide for herself.' It was a spirited try, but when she stepped back up onto the kerb he realised his chances of persuading her otherwise were non-existent. With a grumble the taxi crawled away, to a fanfare of horns from his fellow motorists.

Dalia Habashi pulled off her sunglasses and stared at him.

'Why must you make this harder than it is?'

'Perhaps we should just go inside.'

Groppi's was deserted at this hour. An air of despondency held sway over the gloomy interior. A waiter was busy trying to chat up the girl behind the sweets counter. She looked as if she was about to die of boredom. If she was entertained by his attentions she was doing a good job of hiding it. Neither paid any attention to the two potential customers as they walked by.

Dalia stalked to the far end of the room and settled at a table by the window. She fumbled in her bag for a pack of cigarettes and a lighter and lit one as he sat down.

'I'm not sure this is such a good idea.'

'I'm sorry, I was delayed.'

'You could have called.' She was staring out of the window but her hand was trembling. 'I don't feel safe, meeting you like this, in public.'

Makana realised she was scared. He tried to make light. 'I won't tell anyone if you don't, and besides, we have the place to ourselves.'

The table was scarred and bruised from years of neglect. Once upon a time this had been a handsome place, famous for its confectionary. King Farouk used to dispatch lacquered boxes of chocolates bearing the royal seal as lavish gifts to the princesses of England and France. Difficult to imagine the same thing happening today, just as it was too hard to envisage orchestras playing symphonies, or couples twirling across the mosaic floor in each other's arms. Another age, another dimension.

They smoked in silence. The waiters took no interest in them.

'Why did you want to see me?'

Dalia stubbed out her cigarette. 'I once did something very foolish.'

'Why don't you tell me about it?'

'It's not easy for a woman, you know.' Her eyes fixed on his. 'In this town, I mean, in this business. Men rule everything between them. They see women as a game, a conquest. Not as partners, not as equals.'

'Does this have something to do with the boy on the motorcycle?'

'Not exactly a boy. He's almost forty.'

'Na'il. You and he are . . .'

'Does it matter?' Her eyes narrowed.

'To me, no. But I think it matters to you a great deal.'

She looked at him for a moment and then reached for another cigarette. Makana leaned over to light it for her.

'My husband left me for a woman half his age. He gave me some money, but not all that much. I realised that the business would have probably folded a lot sooner if he hadn't been there to support me. I was naive, I suppose. Anyway, the point is that business hasn't been all that good.'

'You have financial problems.'

Her eyes flickered up. 'People love to talk.' She exhaled slowly.

'What happened at Kasabian's house the other night?'

'There was an argument. Na'il got into a fight. Well, it wasn't a fight really. But he said some things he shouldn't have said to one of the guests.'

'Qasim Abdel Qasim?'

Dalia nodded quickly. 'I shouldn't have told him, I suppose, but I did. When we first met everything seemed so perfect. I thought Na'il was the answer to my prayers. He had money. We lived a glamorous life. All over town, all the best places.' She sighed. 'By the time I found out he was as broke as I was, it was too late, I was in love.' Dalia gave a cold laugh.

'Where does Qasim come into this?'

Dalia Habashi took a deep breath. 'Some years ago, when I was at a low point, I asked him for money. Just a short loan, to tide me over. He had been coming to the gallery, paying attention to me. I knew he was married. I knew it wouldn't come to anything, but it was a distraction. He's a powerful man.'

'You had an affair.'

'Is that the word?' Dalia examined the tip of her cigarette. 'I don't know if that's what I'd call it. I suppose I went along willingly. I'm a grown woman. I knew what I had to do.'

'For the loan.'

'He used me. He used me the way he uses everybody.' Her face had darkened. She stared at the window and Makana saw her wipe away an angry tear.

A waiter lumbered up with all the enthusiasm of a man who had a date with his executioner.

'Go away,' snapped Dalia. 'We're talking, can't you see?'

The waiter was wearing a well-worn waistcoat that was buttoned up unevenly. He tried to straighten his bow tie, which stayed stubbornly lopsided, and turned to Makana, appealing to his masculine sense of order. Makana shook his head. The waiter trudged off dragging his feet, his soles brushing along the floor.

'You told Na'il about Qasim.'

'It was foolish, I know. We had a fight and . . . I don't know. I just said it.'

'And he confronted Qasim at the party.'

Dalia nodded as she fished in her bag for a packet of tissues to wipe her nose.

'Why are you telling me all this?'

'I had to tell someone. I can't cope with this on my own. You seemed, well, the kind of person who could help.'

'Help in what way?'

'Na'il is mixed up in something.'

'Does this have anything to do with drugs?'

'No, not like that. This is different.' Somewhere a door that needed oiling squeaked open and shut again. 'Na'il used to work for Kasabian. He did odd jobs for him. A little like you. He used to work with the police, you know.'

'Really? Then why did he come to me instead of going to Na'il?'

Dalia looked away. 'They had a falling out. Na'il is a little headstrong. He's a dreamer, really. Still thinks that one day it will all come his way and he'll never have to work again.'

Across the room, Makana could see the heavy-footed waiter talking to the manager, a nervous man with a moustache who draped one arm over the cash register as if it might just sprout legs and run off. There was some kind of discussion going on. The waiter pointed in their direction.

'Is that why you're worried?'

'He's always been the same but now he's mixed up with a different crowd.'

'What kind of crowd?'

'I can't explain. He's changed.'

'Changed in what way?'

'I think he's out of his depth.'

'What makes you say that?'

'I don't know. It's the small things.' She cast around looking for an answer. 'He started going to the mosque.'

'He wasn't religious before?'

'Not really. I mean, you know, he drinks and takes pills and smokes.' Dalia shrugged. 'No, he wasn't religious.'

'*Effendim?*' The waiter had resurfaced. His eyebrows drooped on both sides. He looked like a drowning man who knew he didn't have much longer. He glanced over his shoulder to where Makana could see the manager grinding his teeth. You had to order something to sit here.

'Coffee,' Makana said. 'For two.'

The waiter wandered off in a happy trance.

'Which mosque was this?'

'Does it matter?'

'Probably not.'

'The big one on the main road near the gallery.'

'The Mustafa Mahmoud mosque?' Makana frowned. It was the second time in as many days that name had come up. 'You think Na'il is mixed up in something he can't handle?'

'I don't know what he's involved in, but I'm afraid.'

'You must care about him a lot.'

'I'm scared.' Her eyes were filled with anguish. 'I'm afraid of what might happen. I don't know what I'd do without him.'

The rattle of porcelain announced the approach of the waiter. The cups hit the table with all the ceremony of a landslide. The coffee was lukewarm, served European style, a thin, grubby soup. The waiter retired to a chair a few tables away where, exhausted from the effort, he rested his head on his hand and closed his eyes.

'Look, I can see you're worried, but I'm not exactly sure what I can do.'

'You could talk to him. You could go to this mosque and find out what he's up to.'

'I could.'

Dalia stared at him for a moment. Her eyes seemed hollow, devoid of life somehow. Then she began gathering up her things, snapping cigarettes back into her bag.

'You're right. I'm sorry for bothering you. This was a terrible mistake.'

She got up without touching her coffee. Makana sighed. He watched as she put on her dark glasses and headed for the door. Through the window he watched her hail a taxi. In a moment she was gone. He took a sip of his coffee and pushed it aside. It tasted worse than it looked. He was the only person in the place now. The waiter was asleep, his head resting on his hand. Makana lit another cigarette. He wondered what it was that ever gave people the idea he could help them.

Chapter Twelve

The Mustafa Mahmoud mosque was set within the relative calm of a green or almost green barrier that broke the flow of Dowal al-Arabiya Street. The six-lane carriageway swept by, cutting a swathe through the modern district of Mohandiseen. The patch of yellowed grass deserved a medal for survival. Or perhaps a monument. Something modest and unobtrusive. The white-painted mosque could make no claims to belonging to a classical age of great architecture or having been built by one of the legendary figures that cluttered this city's history. The small building was dwarfed by the apartment buildings that surrounded it on all sides. It was a strange oasis in the midst of all that concrete and flying metal.

Back in the heady days of 1960s Nasserist socialism this had been open farmland allocated to young technocrats. It was named the *mohandiseen* after the engineers who were to bring the country into the modern era. As idealism faded and the city expanded, agriculture gave way to construction and yet more construction. By the 1970s comfortable villas had sprung up only to be crushed in turn by the flood tide of a population that refused to stop expanding. The fine houses were pummelled back into the ground to make way for rows of apartment blocks jammed one up against the next, twenty storeys high, to accommodate a growing middle class that demanded modern flats within striking distance of downtown.

To reach Zayed Zafrani, Makana first had to get past his henchmen, who sulked and stubbornly refused to let him by. Compared with his brother's guard dogs, Didi and Bobo, these men had an oddly spiritual aspect to them, like warriors from another age. They carried themselves with a certain reverence. Their beards and fixed stares suggested paramilitary training, very possibly in Afghanistan or Chechnya. Fighting the good fight for Allah. Eventually, when word filtered back, Makana was allowed through to the inner sanctum. At the back of the mosque an adjoining compound housed a clinic and a storeroom for donated clothes, medical supplies, food.

Inside stood a slim figure, dressed in traditional clothes. The light from the high window fell over him like a shroud. He was busy dispensing packets of pasta and rice to families in need. A woman with a child in her arms and three more in tow thanked him over and over, imploring the Almighty to bless him. He resembled a performer of miracles rather than an emperor of organised crime. To be fair, Zayed had always had a softer touch than his rather more unpredictable brother Ayad. He motioned for his bodyguards to fall back and invited Makana to stroll along with him on what felt like a rehearsed tour. He pointed out the stockpiles of food. Sacks of rice, enormous tins of oil and beans.

'For decades now the government has failed to help the weakest in society. There are millions in this city who are barely surviving. People are ignorant of this. They are blinded by newspapers and television that keep up a steady diet of new hospitals and factories being inaugurated by the Raïs and his heir apparent. Factories that close in a matter of weeks. Hospitals that remain empty because the contractor didn't do his job properly and can't be repaired because the money has vanished.' Zayed Zafrani lifted his hands in resignation. 'One day the people will wake up and realise that things should not be like this. In the meantime, we do what we can.'

'I ran into your brother the other day.'

'My brother and I have different interests. We are nine brothers and sisters and he took care of all of us. My father was useless. A weak man. He squandered his money on drink and other women. He abused his wife and children. In the end he got what he deserved.'

Makana was familiar with the rumour that the Zafrani brothers had driven their father out into the desert and buried him up to his neck in the burning sand. They left him like that for three days, and then ran over what was left of his head with a pickup. The brothers had been inducted into the life of crime by an uncle on their mother's side of the family, an ageing patriarch who was rumoured to be still alive somewhere, like Osiris ready to return from the tomb.

'Your brother says you're trying to go legitimate.'

Zayed Zafrani produced a modest smile – not a quality he was over-endowed with. 'Our retail businesses are successful. We give the people what they want at an affordable price. Modern appliances that free them up from daily chores. Women have an important role to play in society.'

'You mean when they know their place?'

Zayed Zafrani shrugged the distinction off. 'The people are the backbone of this country.'

'It sounds like you're thinking of going into politics.'

Zafrani laughed, 'I'm sorry, I forget that I am speaking to a cynic. We are trying to create an alternative society. Unlike the president's son and his coterie of bandits we do not seek to enrich a small elite of our friends. One day their heads will roll. I truly believe that. They represent the moral corruption of the West, the very thing that has placed us where we are now. They sell us out to big multinationals that come in and buy up this country for small change. A few men grow rich, the rest of us stay poor.'

'You're not doing too badly,' observed Makana.

'Yes, but at what price to the soul of this beautiful country?'

Makana refrained from comment. He was still having trouble believing this was not all part of an act.

'It doesn't sound as if you and your brother are reading from the same book. I visited his club and he seems to be making friends with a lot of those people you're talking about.'

'My brother has his own way and I have mine.'

'Still,' said Makana, looking around them. 'Talk like that can land you in prison or worse.'

'It would be a small price to pay for a part in history.'

'Now you do sound like a politician.'

Zayed Zafrani laughed lightly. 'The people yearn for justice, for fairness, for a chance in life. This government is too busy looking after itself to care about the common man. This is what the message of our prophet is to us.'

'That's why you're helping the poor?'

'We do what we can, with our limited resources.'

Not so limited, thought Makana as he peered into the clinic and saw a room full of high-tech equipment. Heart scanners. The latest technology. Bright and shiny new, as if they had been unpacked last week.

'Where does all of this come from?'

'Thanks be to God there are enough good Muslims in the world who know that wealth is nothing compared with doing the will of Allah.'

'Gulf Arabs? Oil sheikhs? And enough of them are friends of yours?'

'We have medical facilities that are the envy of hospitals in the West. We have doctors willing to give of their time and skills freely.' They had to step aside as a van was backed up to the door of the storeroom. 'Gifts from our wealthy brothers in the Gulf,' he smiled.

A chain of young men and women began relaying cartons inside with brisk efficiency. Makana read the logos printed on the sides of the boxes of medicines going by.

'It all sounds very noble.' Makana pulled out his cigarettes and lit one. Zafrani frowned.

'My brother believes in the old ways, in violence and intimidation. I can no longer be a part of that. On the Day of Resurrection the book on every man's soul will lie open. I saw the error of my ways. I hope one day Ayad will also. Perhaps even you.'

'Don't count on it.'

Zafrani smiled, a crinkling of the eyes. 'I believe that the way to change the world is through the hearts and souls of the people, not through their pockets.'

It struck Makana that he was looking at the more dangerous of the two brothers. Zayed was smart and devious. For all his swagger and bluster, Ayad Zafrani was easier to read.

'Between the two of you, you ought to be running this country.'

'Perhaps in a way we are.' The smile faded quickly. They had reached an open area behind the mosque where a row of tired-looking flowers had been recently planted. They looked grey and unhappy in this urban setting. Zafrani ordered one of his men to fetch some water. The guard looked unhappy at the prospect of getting his clothes dirty for the sake of a few flowers. Nevertheless, he wandered off and came back with a bucket.

'Actually, I came here to find someone.'

Makana watched the guard clumsily trying to keep his trousers dry and water the plants at the same time. He made what might have seemed a simple task incredibly complicated. Zafrani made a gesture and the bodyguard handed over the bucket and lumbered off, still shaking his leg.

'A man named Na'il? Rides a motorcycle. I believe he comes here sometimes.'

'A lot of people come here.' Zafrani's eyes twinkled behind his spectacles. 'Our doors are open to all, even those who do not yet know the meaning of belief.'

Makana left him there, trying to perform the miracle of bringing withered plants back to life.

Chapter Thirteen

That night Makana took a taxi back across town to Maadi and the house of the winged lion. The two doormen in shiny tuxedos looked him over and shook their heads as if he was wasting their time. Makana held out his telephone.

'Let's call Mr Zafrani and see what he says. Do you want to talk to him, or should I?'

The two men exchanged a long glance, then the fat one behind the desk nodded his consent and the shaven-headed one stepped aside.

'It's nothing personal, but we get paid to do our job.'

Upstairs, Gigi smiled as if greeting an old friend and he leaned on the bar and tried to behave as if he was. Just another lonely man in need of diversion. Having shown her the chips he still had from his last visit, he sipped the watery drink that was put before him and signed the chit. Ayad Zafrani was onto a good thing. A place like this encouraged people to be bad, reckless, and spend more money. For a time he wandered around the roulette table. Never having played before didn't seem like a disadvantage. None of the other players appeared to have much idea of what they were doing. They were more concerned with trying to outdo their friends. There was a lot of male camaraderie going on: middle-aged men grateful for a chance to leave their wives at home and play at being boys again. That about summed it up. The younger ones were trying to impress their elders. There was a lot of drinking and loud talking. If they got too loud or too boisterous, one of the wooden faces in a cheap tuxedo would step up and ask them quietly to tone it down. Ayad Zafrani ran a stylish establishment and Makana wondered how many of his clients actually knew who the owner was and how he made a living. To some it would only add to the thrill, a touch of danger.

One of the tuxedos was watching Makana from across the room. He had that fixed, canine stare that suggested he disapproved of something. Makana waved his glass at the bartender for a refill. It was basically iced water with a delicate hint of whatever the Scots had intended it to be. Makana held his glass up to the light. He understood the business of the paper napkin now; it made it harder to see the colour of the liquid inside.

'Where did you learn to pour a drink?' Makana tried to look like he was enjoying it.

The bartender mentioned a couple of places Makana had never heard of. Either there was a whole underground world of drinking clubs and clandestine bars or he had a lively imagination.

'Maybe you've seen a friend of mine in here. An American. Funny guy. Frankie. Wears a crumpled suit?'

'Mr Frankie?' The bartender had maintained a sour expression on his face ever since Makana had first set eyes on him. Now it lifted slightly. 'He's been here a couple of times. Jack Daniel's. Straight up. Likes to pour it himself.'

'I'll bet he does. Was he here with a friend?'

The sour face returned. 'I thought he was *your* friend?'

'Well, you know how it is. He owes me money.'

'I've never seen him with anyone. He comes in alone and he leaves alone.' The eyes narrowed some more. 'He's like you, he asks a lot of questions.'

'Give me another drink, and this time try to get some of that whisky into the glass.'

Makana turned his back on the counter. The place was quieter this evening. He decided to take a stroll around the card tables. Only three of them were occupied by solitary players, alone or in pairs. Some of Kasabian's hard-earned cash was deposited in the form of plastic chips on the green baize table, and the spinning wheel whisked it away into thin air and a dark pocket somewhere out of sight. There wasn't much excitement there. A drunken man who resembled the editor of a national newspaper was throwing his money away and pawing the girl next to him, who Makana recognised from the line-up on his previous visit. There was nobody in the place who answered to a description of Kadhim al-Samari. No Iraqis as far as he could hear.

Makana made a mental note of how much to add to his expenses and retired to the bar for another drink. He climbed onto a high stool, noting that the bartender's expression hadn't changed. He served Makana as if he'd never seen him before in his life. Perhaps he ought to be tipping the man more. He noticed that he did possess a smile, and that it came out with certain customers and not others, in particular a group of men at the far end who were deep in conversation. Makana recognised one of them as Qasim Abdel Qasim, which meant that Ayad Zafrani really was moving up in the world. Qasim wouldn't set foot in a place like this without assurances from the owners that they could be discreet. Makana wondered just what the connection was between the Zafrani brothers and Qasim.

'Hello.'

Makana turned to find Bilquis standing there.

'You weren't put off by your last visit?'

'I was just summoning up the courage to come and see you again.'

'Well, here I am.' She had a radiant smile, which he supposed was part of her job. Her hair was pinned back and she wore an elegant long dress. This time when he looked at her he realised that she was becoming distinct from the memory of his wife and the vision he had had of his grown-up daughter. It still hurt in a peculiar way to look at her, as if her existence somehow excluded that of Muna and Nasra, but he told himself this was some kind of compensation of the mind and heart for his confused emotional state. No doubt there were schools of psychologists who could explain it better than that, but for the moment Makana was happy to just sit here and contemplate.

'A drink for the lady?' Even the bartender seemed to have cheered up. Makana nodded and watched as some more of Kasabian's money was transformed into something that came out of a champagne bottle. Bilquis did a good job of pretending to sip it.

'Did you get into trouble the other night?'

'No,' said Makana. 'Just reacquainted with an old friend.'

'And now you're back.'

'Yes, indeed.'

'You must like the place.'

'Isn't that the idea?' When Makana offered her a cigarette she produced an elegant ebony holder from somewhere. He leaned forward to light it for her.

'Usually it is.' She exhaled a long stream of smoke into the air. 'But you're not usual.'

'The other day you said everyone comes here looking for something they already know. A person, a feeling. Something that reminds them of another time.'

'Who did I remind you of?' She blew smoke in the direction of the bartender, who got the message and shuffled away.

'Someone I once knew, a long time ago.'

'Who was she?' Bilquis wet her lips on whatever was bubbling in her glass.

'My wife, my daughter.'

She laughed. 'Which one is it?'

'When I saw you I imagined my daughter as a grown woman. The last time I saw her she was a small child.'

'You left them behind when you came here.' Her face grew still. 'We can't remember faces,' she said, 'not really. They fade in the memory. I tell myself I would recognise them if they walked into the room.' She gave a quick laugh. 'Sometimes I try to imagine that and it makes me happy for a time.'

'You came here alone?'

'Yes,' she nodded, her face growing serious. 'But I'm not alone anymore.'

'That's nice for you.'

'There are some things you wish you could leave behind, but you can't.' She studied him for a moment. 'There are faces I'd like to forget.'

'Yes,' he said. 'I think I know what you mean.'

'Is that why you came here, to get away?'

'I didn't have a choice.'

'That's what we tell ourselves, but it's not true. There's always a choice.' Her gaze had wandered away and now it returned, her eyes fixing on his. 'Why did you really come here tonight?'

'I was looking for somebody.'

'A friend?' She shook her head. 'Not a friend. You know the man who owns this place. That makes you a powerful man. Maybe even dangerous.'

'Or foolish.'

'If you had come here just to see me, now that would be foolish.' Her gaze moved beyond him and Makana looked over his shoulder to see Gigi standing in the archway tapping her watch. 'I have to get to back to work.'

'You have an appointment?'

'Sometimes we have special clients. They ask for one of us exclusively.'

'If you ever feel like talking about things.' Makana scribbled his new number on the back of one of his business cards.

She took the card and read it. 'I don't think that's a good idea, but thank you anyway.'

Makana watched her walk away. The waiter deposited a chit alongside him and asked for a signature.

Then he took himself home and tried to sleep. It was after midnight. The city was tucked up in bed dreaming its own dreams. He paced the deck, smoking until he had exhausted himself, then he dragged the big chair onto the open deck and sank into it. If he stared at the sky for long enough he imagined he could make out a few stars up there beyond the glow.

Something told him that Samari was here, in this city, very close. He had the feeling that he could almost reach out and touch him, as though he were slipping through the shadows under the trees on the embankment behind him. He would find him, Makana was sure of that. Eventually, he would find him. The question was what he would do with him once he did.

He must have fallen asleep for what felt like all of two minutes. He dreamed, but remembered nothing of it when his eyes snapped open, woken by an unearthly scream that turned out to be his new telephone. It was only when he was in the police car, racing over the bridge, that it came back to him.

He had been trapped inside a cage, falling through what felt like dense air which then turned out to be water. Sinking then, through water, but without fear. Not drowning. He knew he wasn't in danger. Someone else was in danger. Someone who was above him. Somebody he could not reach. He knew who it was. Nasra. And he knew what he had to do. It was simple. All he had to do was catch her. But the more he struggled to reach her the further she slipped away. He was moving too slowly. He was never going to be able to catch her. Then he woke up.

Chapter Fourteen

Okasha was talking urgently into a handheld radio when Makana arrived. The night air was bright with blue and red flashes from police cars and ambulances. Okasha indicated for him to stay where he was until he had finished. Then he moved straight on past him, towards the open gates.

'This way,' he said.

There were a dozen or so policemen milling around kicking their heels, ringed by curious onlookers, passers-by, tourists, all eager to know what was happening. It was almost dawn now and the sky was beginning to lighten above the high buildings surrounding them. In the garden the majestic trees were bowed over and still, waiting for air and light to lift the clammy touch of the night. More police officers were backed up inside the gate. Most of them appeared to have nothing to do. The crime scene was the usual chaotic jumble of people wandering in and out, happily trampling all evidence into oblivion. Those who weren't doing the trampling were yelling orders. That was the problem with orders. Everyone loved to give them but nobody liked to take them. Along with the police there was a crowd of civilians who had somehow managed to get through the cordon. Who they were and what they were doing here wasn't clear. Doormen, porters, household staff from the neighbourhood villas, apartment buildings and embassies up and down the streets. Everyone with an opinion. If you managed to get any uncontaminated evidence out of there, it would be a miracle.

'You'll have a fine collection of boot prints by the end of it,' Makana commented.

Okasha threw him a dirty look and snapped at a sergeant who was unlucky enough to be loitering nearby.

'Clear the area of anyone who is not essential to the investigation. I mean, right now. Everyone outside the gate.'

There were murmurs and mutterings, but slowly the crowd thinned out. Most of them looked half asleep, and they reluctantly tore their attention away from the object hanging at the top of the garden steps. Makana followed their gaze.

In the thin trace of grey light seeping downwards from the sky he could make out a heavy figure dangling from a rope. It was suspended from the central spar over the steps leading onto the veranda, right underneath the huge copper lamp, Makana had admired three nights ago. He moved closer, still not sure what he was seeing. An insistent buzzing announced that even at this early hour the flies were already feverishly at work. There was a lot of blood. It pooled in viscous streams that ran down the steps towards the garden, dripping down from one to the next, like creeping tendrils, forming strange patterns on the white stone, filling in the cracks, smoothing out the imperfections.

Kasabian was suspended upside down, his feet tied together by the same rope that held him in the air. The rope had been thrown over the wooden roofing timber and then secured to one of the pillars, wrapped around a couple of times and tied off. He was naked from the waist up.

'Who found him?'

'The old man who looks after the place.' Makana followed Okasha's nod and saw the hunchbacked gatekeeper. His ancient, skeletal frame was trembling all over.

'Nobody else in the house at the time?'

Okasha shook his head. 'He usually lets the staff off over the weekend. He has a place out of town where he goes for a couple of nights. Not bad for some, eh?'

'But he didn't go away this time.'

'Unfortunately for him.'

'Where is Kasabian's personal assistant, Jalal, Jules?'

'Away in Alexandria. He's on his way back now.'

Makana examined the way the rope was made fast to the veranda pillar. It looked like it was tied by someone who knew their knots. Okasha indicated a woman dressed in white overalls who was examining the body.

'Have you had the pleasure of meeting Doctora Siham?'

Makana knew of the forensic pathologist only by her formidable reputation. From what he had heard everyone who knew her was terrified of her. Even Okasha, drawing Makana behind him, seemed to treat her with great caution as he approached where she was kneeling before the body.

'Oh, Doctora Siham, this is the man I was telling you about.'

Doctora Siham cast a beady look up at Makana. He put her age at about fifty. Underneath her white overalls she wore a polo-neck jumper that reached up to her chin, vanishing into the folds of the traditional black scarf that covered her head. Her nose was pronounced and her eyes narrow and frowning. She said nothing but turned back to the case in hand.

'Any ideas yet?'

'Ideas?' She spat the word out like an unexpected fish bone. 'I deal in facts, Inspector. Ideas are for the birds.'

As if summoned by magic a black kite flapped messily down from the trees and settled on the feet of the corpse, where it began pecking. Okasha waved at it to enforce respect for the dead. One of his men came running to his assistance and managed to slip in the blood. Still, it achieved the desired effect and the crow took to the sky again. Doctora Siham was not impressed.

'Control your men, Inspector, or I shall take no responsibility for this corpse.'

As the officer, clearly in pain, hobbled away, Makana edged cautiously closer, aware that Doctora Siham's gaze was following his every move. Kasabian's torso was painted with blood. There appeared to be streaks of blood running down from here and there.

'Are those cuts?'

Doctora Siham carried on collecting samples from the floor of the veranda, sealing a glass phial and returning it to her case before getting to her feet to take a look.

'They appear to be shallow incisions, made with a very sharp implement. I shall need to get him into the lab to say anything more.'

'Is that what killed him?'

Doctora Siham considered the question.

'Hardly likely to be the cause of death. They appear too shallow to have caused any damage to the vital organs. The loss of blood appears considerable, however. I refuse to speculate at this stage.'

'Naturally.'

She gave Makana a wary look as if to decide if he was being sarcastic, and seemed to grant him the benefit of the doubt. Makana turned back to Okasha.

'How did you know to call me?'

'Ah, let me show you.' Okasha looked relieved to have something to do. He led the way up the steps, careful to avoid stepping in the blood. Doctora Siham watched them both with a look of despair. A police officer saluted briskly as they entered the house and went up the staircase. Saluting was just about all they were good for. There were policemen at every turn. One stood guard at the entrance to the office where Makana had sat not two days earlier. The room looked unchanged. Okasha indicated the desk where a diary stood open. Using a pen, he pointed out the entry for the appointment.

'That's three nights ago,' he said. 'Can you tell me what this is about?'

Makana gazed about him. He recalled the calm with which Kasabian had moved about the study, pouring himself a drink. It was the kind of room that had taken a lifetime to construct. Everything was exactly as he would have wished it, and all in the right place. Now it served no purpose save as a memory of the man, and a reminder of mortality.

'He asked me to find someone on behalf of a client. An American named Charles Barkley.' Makana opened the silver box on the table. The interior was lined with Dunhills, laid out in neat rows waiting for a hand to pick them up. Makana tried to imagine the box on the table on the awama. It might add a touch of style, though he couldn't quite picture it.

'I should bring in this Barkley.'

'He's at the Marriott.'

'You've met him?' Okasha asked.

'No. I went there with Kasabian the day before yesterday, but he was out.'

'I'll have him brought in to the station.'

'No,' said Makana. 'I think we should go to the hotel and see him.'

'We?'

'I want to see his face when you tell him.'

'Okay.' Okasha regarded Makana for a moment. 'Anything else you want to tell me?'

'Not just now,' said Makana.

'*Effendim*?'

Another saluting policeman appeared, this time a sergeant wearing white gloves.

'What is it?'

'We have located a potential witness, sir.'

As they passed him by, Makana took another, closer look at Kasabian. His face was almost unrecognisable; bloated and swollen and striped with blood, it resembled a hideous mask. Almost as if he had been turned into one of his artworks.

'How much would you say he weighed, Doctora?'

Doctora Siham looked the body up and down. 'Ninety-five kilos. Perhaps a little more.'

'So it would take more than one man to haul him up like that?'

'One strong man might be able to manage, but it would be a struggle, I would say.'

A rather dignified old man was waiting in the garden. The witness had the bearing of a military officer despite being dressed in pyjamas and what looked like an expensive paisley-green silk dressing gown. The neatly groomed moustache and hair perfectly in place lent him a passing resemblance to an actor who had stepped out of a 1950s film. He was in his seventies and presented himself with a little bow as 'The poet Ahmed Aziz'.

'Did you know the deceased?'

'The deceased? Give him a name.' The poet shivered – whether from cold, horror or age it wasn't clear. Eventually he gave a quick nod. 'Who would butcher a man like that, like an animal?'

'Did you know him?' Okasha repeated.

'Of course. We were neighbours. Mr Kasabian is a recent arrival, but he is a respectable man.'

'I understood Mr Kasabian had lived here for forty years.'

'Exactly. He's new.' The poet stuck to his story. 'His family had been here for generations, of course.'

'Of course,' Okasha sighed. 'I understand you claim to have seen something.'

'Claim? Do you think I would make such a thing up? Is that what happens now? The first witness is taken as a suspect? If you're going to charge me you may as well get it over with.'

'Nobody's going to charge you. Please, tell us what you saw.'

The dignified poet was happy to talk. Indeed, one might have been forgiven for thinking that he was even a little grateful to have found a captive audience. Arms clasped behind his back, he spoke as if standing on a podium; the bushy white eyebrows batted up and down as if they had a life of their own.

'Sleep is a rare luxury these days. And besides, it is in my nature to work at night. During the day there is too much noise and commotion. It disturbs the soul. Not like the old days.'

The sergeant leaned over to whisper something and Okasha cut the poet short.

'So, let's drop the poetry for a moment, shall we? A little bird tells me you are in the habit of spying on your neighbours, in particular a young lady who is a little careless with her bedroom blinds.'

The old poet glared at the sergeant. He did a good act of looking outraged. Then the fight went out of him. He looked confused for a second, then shrugged it off. 'What can I tell you? If our Lord places such a sight before my eyes, who am I to deny him?'

'Okay, uncle, so you like looking out of windows. Now tell me what you saw?'

'What I saw?' A tremor went through the old man's voice. 'I saw a bolt of lightning flying through the trees, like a yellow bird.'

Okasha was clearly not in the mood for flights of poetic fancy. 'A bird, lightning?' he snapped. 'What are you saying?'

'A motorcycle, ridden by the devil himself, voom!' The old poet's hand glided up into the air and away.

Chapter Fifteen

The terrace of the Marriott Hotel was a world unto itself. People wandered about in a happy daze. They were on holiday, recounting their adventures while ordering club sandwiches and French fries, ice-cream sundaes for their howling children. It might have been a terrace in Monaco or some other sunny resort. Waiters rushed to and fro bearing refreshments to keep them happy. Tall drinks, bottles of ice-cold beer and trays laden high with salads, hamburgers and pizza. A man wearing the tall hat and spotless white uniform of a chef strolled among the tables with all the ceremony of a pasha on a tight budget. The arches and elaborate ironwork of the original building were a lingering reminder that this had once been a palace. There was an irony in the fact that the opulence of the nineteenth century now survived only as a backdrop for tourists on holiday. The Khedive Ismail had built the place to impress visiting European dignitaries, including Princess Eugénie of France. Hard to imagine he would have approved of the travellers and traders who now thronged the place. The elegant lines were now dwarfed by squalid concrete blocks thrown up on either side to house more of them.

On the way over Okasha gave the order to start a search for Na'il's yellow motorcycle. Makana called ahead to warn Charles Barkley that he was coming to see him about Kasabian. The American sounded calm on the telephone. Detached, almost amused.

'How will I recognise you?'

'I'll be the one with a police inspector standing next to me.'

Okasha had asked Makana to make the call, claiming that his English wasn't good enough—

'I don't want to make a fool of myself before I even meet this fancy American.'

In the event, Barkley had no difficulty spotting them. He waved from a table close by.

'Mr Makana?'

Charles Barkley was in his early forties. A tall man, he was neatly dressed and wore a pair of wraparound sunglasses, jeans and a short-sleeved shirt. He looked lean, tanned and fit.

'I'm Makana, and this is Inspector Okasha of the Cairo police.'

They all shook hands. Barkley gestured for them to be seated.

'Can you tell me what all of this is about?'

'Well, I'm afraid we bring you bad news,' began Makana. 'It's about Mr Aram Kasabian.'

'Aram? Yes, of course. What has happened?'

'It appears that he has been murdered.'

Okasha cleared his throat. 'Very badly murdered.'

'But that's terrible!' Barkley leant forward, resting his elbows on the table. He stared blankly. 'I was speaking to him only yesterday.'

'What time yesterday?' Okasha produced a notebook and pen from his top pocket.

'I don't know. In the afternoon. Wait, I can tell you exactly.' Barkley reached for a telephone that rested on the table and scrolled through a list. 'Five-thirty p.m.'

'Can you tell us what you talked about?' Okasha's confidence in his linguistic abilities seemed to increase with every word.

'Well, it was about a confidential matter. I'm sure you understand that I am a little reluctant to discuss my business with Mr Kasabian in public.'

'I am familiar with your business with Mr Kasabian,' Makana said. 'I was hired by him on your behalf.'

Barkley regarded Makana more closely. 'I see. Well, in that case I imagine you can explain as well as I can.'

'It would be good if you could tell us in your words. I know you came to Cairo looking for a painting.'

'Is this relevant?' Barkley appealed to Okasha. Makana translated the last word.

'In murder all is . . . relevant,' said Okasha. 'Please, why you come to Cairo?'

'Very well, let me see. A few months ago I started to hear rumours of a certain painting. A very important piece of work, you understand. It has been missing for a long time, confiscated by the Nazis in Germany in the 1930s. After that it disappeared. It's been gone a long time. Now, apparently it has reappeared.'

'Where did these rumours come from?' Makana asked.

'Where do all rumours come from?' Barkley smiled.

'Excuse me,' Okasha interrupted. He turned to Makana. 'Can we stick to the murder here? I mean, if you want to ask more about this painting then by all means do so, but I'm trying to catch a killer and with every minute he is getting further away.'

A waiter bearing a broad smile and a heavily laden tray

appeared. He began to unload fruit, coffee, a plate of scrambled eggs and bacon. Barkley waved it all away.

'I'm sorry, I ordered breakfast. I didn't know.'

The waiter carried on smiling.

'Please, just take it away. Or leave the coffee. Would you gentlemen like coffee?'

Both Makana and Okasha shook their heads.

'No, take it away. All of it. I'll eat later.'

The waiter bowed and withdrew discreetly. Barkley turned to Makana.

'Perhaps we can talk in more detail after you've finished your questions. I'd like to hear your view of things.'

'Ask him if he can think of anyone who might want to kill Kasabian,' Okasha said. Makana relayed the question and the inevitable answer.

'No, I can't. I mean, I still can't believe he's dead. He was such a likeable man, and you say he was murdered?'

Okasha nodded. 'I am sorry to say so.'

Barkley took a deep breath and exhaled slowly. 'I always knew coming here was a risk. I was warned Egypt was a dangerous place. No offence.'

'Of course,' said Okasha. 'Mr Barkley, do you have family?'

'A family? Why, yes, a wife and two daughters. They're back in the States.'

'At this time a man must be with his family, but I ask you go nowhere without you are informing me first.' Okasha handed Barkley his card and stood. 'I take no more of your time.' He turned to Makana. 'Are you staying? Walk out with me. I want a word.'

Barkley picked up his telephone as they moved away.

'I want you to work with me on this,' said Okasha.

'As what?'

'I don't care as what. As my personal adviser, anything. This Kasabian is a big fish and a murder like this is going to bring the sky down on my head. We need to close it as soon as possible.'

'What choice do I have?'

'No, you don't understand.' Okasha jabbed a finger in Makana's chest. 'Back at the house you wanted to say something and you stopped. I know you, Makana. I don't want you going off by yourself. I want you to come to me, understood?'

Okasha invoked the wrath of Allah at the sight that greeted them when they took a wrong turn and found themselves on the steps leading down to the discreetly shielded swimming pool. Women in various states of undress, and men who paraded themselves in clinging loincloths that left little to the imagination.

'Barbarians,' muttered Okasha. As they turned away a man bumped into Makana.

'Sorry,' he said before going on his way. Makana caught a glimpse of a tall thin man with dark, unkempt hair that hung to his shoulders.

'Remember what I said,' Okasha called over his shoulder.

When he returned to the table Makana found Barkley smoking a cigarette and pouring from a pot of coffee. He got to his feet as Makana approached.

'I took the liberty of ordering a cup for you.'

'Thank you.'

Makana sat down, lighting a cigarette as he did so. It was easy to see how one might grow accustomed to such places. The hotel seemed a million light years removed from the city that lay beyond its high palatial walls. There were no crowds, no hustle, no hassle. The tooting of cars was a muted distraction, like distant birdsong. Waiters wandered discreetly and attentively between the tables. And it wasn't restricted to foreigners. A good number of the people sitting on the terrace were locals. Men with money, some here for meetings with hotel guests, others with families. All seemed to have wandered in for a reminder of what tranquillity felt like. Here was the reason why men like Kasabian, and Zafrani for that matter, strived to increase their wealth and power, so as to be able to afford this lifestyle, to raise themselves above the daily struggle.

Makana became aware that Barkley was studying him.

'Aram spoke highly of you. He said you were the best in the business.'

'He was very generous.' Makana wondered if this was what Kasabian had really said.

'I take it he explained the delicate nature of this matter?'

'Yes, he did. Mr Barkley, I'm not sure you're fully aware of the situation. Mr Kasabian was tortured. It looks as if somebody wanted information from him.'

'What kind of information?' Barkley snapped open his lighter and lit another cigarette.

'That's impossible for me to know at this stage, but I don't think we can rule out the notion that it might be related to the purpose of your visit to Cairo.'

'You think this has something to do with me?'

'That is a possibility we cannot ignore. Inspector Okasha is going to post extra guards outside and the hotel has increased its own security, but my advice is to avoid leaving the hotel.'

'I understand.' Barkley paused. 'That's terrible. To think he might have been killed because of what I asked him to do.'

'We don't know why he was killed. But it seems wise to take precautions.'

'Of course. I understand fully. Is there any way I can help?'

'Well, perhaps you could tell me a little more about your business with Kasabian. I know you came to Cairo because of a certain work of art, but what made you think that it was here? Can you tell me more about where you got your information? You mentioned that you had heard rumours.'

Barkley raised his hands. 'Who can say where these things start? Rumours are just that, but if they stick around for long enough it's usually because there's some truth to them.'

'Enough to get on a plane and come all the way here?'

'I'm an impulsive man, Mr Makana,' Barkley smiled. 'If there's something I want, I go after it. This is a very special piece of work.'

'I understand that, but you had very specific information connecting this painting to Kuwait in 1991 and Kadhim al-Samari. Now, where would you get such detailed information?'

Barkley exhaled and looked off into the distance for a moment, then he reached into his shirt pocket for another cigarette. He lit it and held his lighter across for Makana to light his.

'Look, you can call it coincidence or luck, but several things came together. Stories of what was taken out of Kuwait had been floating about since 1991. Legends, most of them. Nobody really knew what was in those private collections that Saddam's men broke open. I've been in this game long enough not to get too excited when people start talking, but then there was this Colonel Samari. His name started to come up.' Barkley clicked his fingers. 'At some point I just decided that was enough for me. So I came.'

'Where would information about Samari come from?'

'Come now,' Barkley grinned. 'You don't expect me to reveal my sources, do you?'

'I suppose I'm wondering how the name of an Iraqi colonel who is rumoured to be very secretive could come to circulate in New York.'

'It's odd, I agree, but that's the nature of the business we are in.'

'I had hoped to have this talk with you before this unhappy situation occurred. Kasabian brought me to see you the day before yesterday, in the afternoon, but you weren't in.'

'Well, I'm sorry I missed him.'

'I'm surprised he didn't mention it when you spoke on the telephone yesterday.'

'Must have slipped his mind.' Barkley spread his hands wide, then let them fall again. 'What makes you so sure that Kasabian's murder is linked to my business with him?'

'The method of torture used on Kasabian is that favoured by Samari.'

'So, that would suggest that he is in Cairo, after all?'

'It's possible,' conceded Makana.

'But you're not convinced?'

'I've seen nothing to prove it was actually Samari who carried out the torture.'

'But it could be him, is that what you're saying?'

'Kadhim al-Samari is a very dangerous man. If he thought someone was trying to find him he might have been trying to find out why.'

'Well, I'll be damned.' Barkley sat back in his chair. 'The way you put it very much suggests I could be in serious danger myself.'

'It would be wiser for you to go home, yes, but while the investigation is ongoing you will not be permitted to leave. As I said before, if you remain in the hotel you should be safe.'

'What about you? He might be after you.'

'Well, I have nowhere to hide,' said Makana. 'If he wants to find me, he can.'

'You say that almost as if you'd welcome the chance to meet him.' Barkley seemed intrigued. He cleared his throat. 'How does this affect the arrangement I had with Aram Kasabian? I mean, are you still willing to try and find Samari?'

'Under the circumstances, I'm not sure how wise that would be.'

'But you were paid to find him.'

'I was paid an advance, yes.'

Barkley placed his hands on the table. 'Let me try to be clear, Mr Makana. I'm not sure if you are aware just how valuable a find we are talking about. This one painting by Franz Marc is worth a great deal, but if it led to further discoveries then we are talking about a fortune.'

'A fortune?'

'And naturally, if you were to help me your share would be substantial.'

'How substantial?'

Barkley smiled and gestured around them. 'Life-changing. You would be eating here every day.'

'Supposing he's not interested in selling?'

'Everyone has a price, Mr Makana.' Barkley smiled, reaching for his sunglasses. 'I'm confident Mr Samari has his.'

'And you have no qualms about dealing with a man your country has declared a war criminal?'

'Mr Makana, let's not be naive. I'm as much a patriot as the next man, but we both know some of the worst war crimes in history were committed by the United States of America itself. Let history be the judge.'

'Samari has a substantial price on his head. Three million dollars. He's wanted for human rights abuses.'

'Believe me, these paintings are worth far more than that.'

'I take it that you've never been tortured, Mr Barkley?'

'No, I can't say that I have.'

'Well, I have. I don't care about the reward, but I believe he should be handed in to face justice for his actions.'

'Fair enough, if that's how you feel.' Barkley nodded his head slowly. 'I can see that I did Kasabian a disservice. When he told me he had hired the best I was in doubt. People tend to exaggerate these things. In your case I can see that he was right to put his trust in you.' Barkley got to his feet and held out his hand.

As Makana walked away he thought to himself that it all sounded fine except for the fact that finding Samari was not going to be easy. Add to that the chance that even if he did succeed he might wind up like Kasabian, in which case he wouldn't have much need for money ever again.

As he came out of the hotel a bellhop came hurrying after him.

'Sir, you dropped this,' he said, holding out the little silver object. 'A gentleman picked it up.' He turned to search for the person. 'Oh, he seems to have gone.'

'Never mind,' said Makana, taking the phone. 'Thank him for me when you see him again.'

Chapter Sixteen

In a taxi across town whose longevity would have put Sindbad's old Datsun to shame, Makana clung to the door with one hand to stop it from yawning open every time they went around a bend, and still managed to talk to Sami. The driver was amused, grinning as if he hadn't seen anything so entertaining in years.

'I just heard about Kasabian,' said Sami.

'I'm on my way over to you now.'

'Is it true that he was tortured?'

'Where do you get your information?'

'You know how it is, a policeman's salary these days is hardly enough to keep a family of cats alive. Is it any wonder there are leaks?'

Makana wondered what Okasha would say when he found out that details of Kasabian's murder were already being passed to the press.

'That would tie in with our friend, though, wouldn't it?' Sami was saying.

'It certainly looks that way.'

As he hung up he noticed the driver staring at him.

'The brother is not from here, is he?'

The curiosity Makana's accent provoked was not new. He gave his usual answer and got the customary assurances of being welcome. He had a feeling that wasn't going to be the end of it.

'It's not that I have anything against people coming here, you understand? I mean, it's not their fault that people can't find work. The old ways are gone. The factories, even the farms. Nowadays everything comes from China. One of them knocked on my door the other day. He had walked up eleven flights of stairs with a sack on his back.' Makana stared ahead, desperately hoping for a break in the traffic. Two young men were sitting in the open boot of the car in front of them, looking bored, their legs dangling over the back. As a method of transport it didn't look the most comfortable in the world, or the safest, but if it got you from one place to another what was the difference?

'Don't take it the wrong way. I'm only asking.'

'What are you asking?'

'Why would a man come all the way from China with a sack on his back to sell my wife a thing for taking the stones out of olives?' The car eased forward half a length. The driver was still talking. 'I've been eating olives since before I could walk and I never needed anything to take the stones out.' The more he talked the less progress they made.

When they arrived Makana waited for the driver to find change, resisting his usual tendency to tell him to keep it. In the end a pair of torn and dog-eared notes made their way out through the window and Makana tucked them into his shirt pocket making a mental note to give them to the first Chinese he came across. Once at the Info Media centre, Makana found Sami was not there. 'He went on a food run,' Nefissa, the woman with the curly hair, told him. Makana found him in a sanbusak place in Huda Sharawi Street. It took a while to push through the crowds. Was it Makana's imagination or did everyone do nothing but eat? Sami was perched on a stool beside the cash register reading a book, oblivious to the chaos around him.

'We're going to adopt him,' the club-footed man behind the cash register said. 'We'll change the logo to a picture of him sitting there with a book and a pastry. The students will love it. They'll think they'll get smarter just by eating here.' He chuckled like a locomotive running out of steam.

'No wonder it takes you so long to eat,' said Makana.

Sami looked up as a young boy in a plastic apron wearing a paper hat appeared with a warm bag full of freshly baked sanbusak for him. The two men pushed their way back out through the crowds thronging the doors. Outside a woman knelt on the pavement holding up a handwritten sign, itself something of a miracle in a country with forty per cent illiteracy. The shaky letters only added to the mystery: 'Where is Al-Baghdadi?' Makana handed her the change from the taxi.

'I can't go back to the office,' Sami was saying. 'Rania is annoyed with me again.'

'What have you done this time?'

'I don't know. I've lost track. I'm beginning to think it's something I did in a previous life.' Sami turned to look at Makana. 'Did you ever, you know, have doubts . . . ?'

'Doubts?'

'I mean, when you were married.' Sami hesitated. He came to a halt and stood there for a moment. 'Forget it,' he said, dismissing the subject with a wave. 'It's insensitive of me to even ask.'

They walked back in silence, Sami lost in his thoughts. In the spacious offices above Midan al-Falaki they found Rania beside herself.

'Where have you been?' she demanded.

'I went to get lunch, remember?'

Rania ignored Makana completely, an indication that she was not in the best of moods. The others in the room appeared to sense domestic strife and were keeping their heads down. She folded her arms.

'We have deadlines to meet, remember?'

'The good people of Holland can surely wait for us poor fellaheen to feed ourselves?' Sami edged past Rania and walked up and down between the desks distributing orders. The others, while glad to receive the food they had been waiting for, kept their thanks discreet. Rania turned her back and walked away as Sami retreated behind his desk. His old leather satchel and his battered laptop were dumped on a table loaded down with heaps of files. Makana found a chair that was more or less in one piece and sat down while Sami busied himself with his computer. He talked as he clicked away, one hand reaching for the opened bag of savoury pastries that lay between them.

'Help yourself,' he said, not taking his eyes from the screen. 'So are you out of work yet?'

'Not exactly. I met the mysterious American, Charles Barkley.'

'That's his name?' Sami frowned. 'Like the basketball player?'

'I don't know anything about that.'

'Don't tell me you're going to carry on looking for Samari? You must be insane. He's the number one suspect in the murder of your former employer, remember?'

'We don't know that for a fact.'

'How much fact do you need? I'd say one man cut to pieces is enough for most people.'

'How do you get all these details?'

'I can't tell you,' said Sami, biting into a golden pastry. 'Trade secrets. They're best when they're warm, by the way.' He pointed. 'See, I was right.' Makana moved round to look at the screen. 'The woman. You know, the one in the street just now, asking for money?'

'The one with the sign?' Makana remembered her. 'What about her?'

'She's been there for ages. It's only a matter of time before they take her away. Here, look at this.' He tapped the screen where a document headed *Egyptian Environmental Observer Agency* was displayed. 'It's one of those NGOs that you're never sure whether to trust or not. They produce reports that usually show what a wonderful and clean country this is. You get the picture.'

'Do I?'

'Well, that woman's husband lost his sight. You remember what her sign said?'

'"Where is Al-Baghdadi?"'

'Which, as I am sure you are aware, refers to Abdel Latif al-Baghdadi, historian and physician of the twelfth century. It's also a reference to a certain Al-Baghdadi Eye Clinic.' Hot sauce dribbled over Makana's fingers and he had to scrabble for a paper napkin. 'The other day you mentioned Qasim Abdel Qasim, remember?' Makana, his mouth full, bobbed his head. Sami looked despairingly at him. 'You know what your problem is? You're out of practice.'

'Go on,' Makana managed, trying not to make more of a mess than he had to.

'Well, I've seen that woman for weeks now. I always pass her and it seems such a sad case, you know? Husband promised an operation and then goes blind because the clinic never materialised. I mean, these people waited for years hoping for a cure, and then nothing. So I started looking into the clinic and discovered it had been halted because of this report.'

'The Egyptian Environmental Observer Agency?' Makana managed to clear his throat.

Sami rolled his eyes. 'Most of us eat every day. Let me order tea.' Sami called out and somehow it was relayed elsewhere. 'So, where was I?'

Makana swallowed. 'The clinic was halted.'

'Right. The report claimed that a scandal involving dumped chemical waste from a battery factory made the land uninhabitable. Obviously a clinic could not be built there.'

'Where's the catch?'

'Sounds suspicious, right? I looked up the group that produced the report. Once upon a time the Egyptian Environmental Observer Agency used to receive funding from the European Union. One of those nice little organisations that makes them feel they are making the world a better place.'

'Used to? You mean, they don't any more?'

'It happens, but with something like this, connected to the environment, you would have to do something pretty bad to make them cut back on their support.'

'Something bad like . . . ?'

'Like falsifying statistics or changing the outcome of a report.'

'You have evidence of that?'

'Evidence?' Sami frowned. 'They all want to keep it quiet. The Europeans for being duped and the rest of them for the usual reasons. Guess who's on the board of this particular environmental agency?'

'Qasim Abdel Qasim? Coincidence?'

'There's no such thing, remember? You taught me that,' Sami smiled.

'So what happened to the land where the clinic was due to be built?'

'Now you're getting somewhere.' Sami nodded at the screen and Makana moved round again. 'It was bought up for a fraction of what it's worth by Miramara Holdings. They are busy building a luxury housing complex even as we speak. The Isis Greens Resort.'

'Very nice, and who owns this little dreamland?'

'The usual grey people. A consortium, shell companies and the like. People in politics.'

'Including our friend?' Makana lit a cigarette and began to feel normality returning.

'Including Qasim Abdel Qasim, yes.'

Makana sat back. It occurred to him that there was nothing unusual about a figure like Qasim making money out of a deal that had been derailed for no apparent purpose other than making certain people rich. It was the opposite, in fact. It made you wonder if Zayed Zafrani didn't have the right idea. How did you put a stop to this kind of exploitation of the system? The answer was you didn't. You couldn't. Nobody could. It had evolved into a national pastime. This was the way things were done. Women sitting on pavements were fossils, ancient relics with their prayers and miracles. Ignore them for long enough and the earth would swallow them up.

Tea arrived and Sami leaned back, hands behind his head, his mind elsewhere. Makana sipped his tea. It was so sweet it tasted like some kind of embalming fluid, capable of preserving the body for centuries.

'Dalia Habashi has a friend called Na'il who seems to be in trouble. I think he deals drugs.'

'There's a whole circle of them,' said Sami. 'They live a charmed life, like characters in a soap opera of their own making. They dance the night away in exclusive clubs.'

'What kind of drugs are we talking about?'

Sami held his hands wide. 'The expensive kind. Uppers, downers, acid, Viagra, whatever. Nowadays I hear cocaine is in fashion. It seems the Colombians are using a new route. The fastest way across the ocean from South America to West Africa and then up by land, through Spain into Europe. Some of it finds its way in this direction.'

Makana was jerked from his thoughts by the sight of Sami getting to his feet.

'Where are you going?'

'I have to get out of here,' said Sami. 'Sorry.' He picked up his cigarettes and lighter and disappeared without another word. Makana sat there for a time. After a while he walked over to where Rania was sitting, typing on her computer from a printout next to her.

'What's up with him, Rania?'

She passed her hands over her face. She looked drawn and tired.

'I think he's having doubts,' she said.

'Doubts about what?'

'About our marriage, I suppose.'

'What makes you say that?'

Rania shook her head. 'I don't know. He's been like this ever since we started talking about children.'

'You want to start a family?'

'I don't have for ever. I'd like to get started as soon as possible.'

'And he doesn't?'

'He doesn't know what he wants,' she sighed.

It was getting on towards six o'clock as Makana arrived back at the awama. The day was almost done and he didn't seem to have made any substantial progress. On the way home he stopped off at a little food stall off the KitKat roundabout to buy himself something for supper. The sanbusak seemed to have awoken his appetite. He picked up a pot of koshary – lentils, meat and pasta, all drowning in a rich tomato sauce. Then he walked back towards the big eucalyptus tree that overhung the riverbank and the path leading down to the awama. The sun was sinking. Makana tried to call Kasabian's assistant. It was his third try. The first couple of times he thought perhaps he should give him a bit of time, considering that he was probably in shock. This time he hung on until someone finally answered.

'Hello?' said an old man's voice. For a second Makana wondered if he had dialled the wrong number, then he remembered the gatekeeper with the crooked back.

'I wanted to talk to Mr Jules,' he said, aware of how absurd it sounded using the assistant's Europeanised nickname.

'Mr Jalal is not available,' said the old gatekeeper drily, clearly not one for such frivolities.

'I understand, but this is urgent. Can you tell him it's Makana calling.'

There was a long pause and then, 'Let me see what he says.' Makana heard the heavy receiver being laid down on the table in the hallway and the slow slap of footsteps retreating. It took a while. He studied the elegant shape of the bark curling from the tree. He could see why an artist might find it interesting to try and reproduce the lines, but hadn't that already been done? Wasn't that why people began painting squares and faces shaped like guitars? There was a scraping in his ear as the old *bawab* came back on the line. He cleared his throat like a senator about to make a speech.

'I'm sorry, but Mr Jalal is not taking any calls today.'

'Did you tell him who was calling?'

'Certainly, sir.'

'I see. Well, thank you.'

'At your service, effendi.'

As he descended the path Makana waved to Umm Ali, who was scattering seeds of some kind to a collection of chickens that wandered along the riverbank behind her. The treetops swept back and forth in the wind and the sky was that strange ochre colour that usually heralded a dust storm.

'Looks like a *haboob*,' he said to Umm Ali as he went by. She straightened up and studied the sky before shaking her head.

'Not today,' she said, 'but soon.'

The chickens meant fresh eggs, which had improved Makana's diet somewhat. It seemed like the time to share some of Kasabian's money while he still had some.

'Umm Ali, I apologise for the delay,' he said, counting out most of the money Zafrani had given him in exchange for the dollars he had spent at the club. 'I've added a little extra for the inconvenience.'

She clutched the notes to her bosom, her face lighting up. 'I always tell people my tenant is as reliable as the sun. Even after a long night he always appears.' She bounced away up the incline with remarkable speed and returned with a large bag of her homemade pickles. 'These are made specially for you.'

Thanking her as graciously as he could, Makana climbed the steps to the upper deck with a veritable feast in his arms. He called Fathi at the airport. He still hadn't found any record of Kadhim al-Samari entering the country.

'Is it possible that someone might have deleted the record?'

'Not completely. Even if by someone you mean State Security or a high-ranking officer, Samari's name would still appear somewhere but the details would be blanked out. I went back over the last year and there is nothing.'

'So, if we assume this man is in the country he didn't come through regular channels?'

'He wouldn't be the first. There are plenty of other ways. Sea or land crossings. The desert. The military airports have their own system.'

Makana knew from his own experience that it was possible to cross the border illegally. The country's frontiers were long and porous, hard to seal completely. He gave Fathi a couple more names, Charles Barkley and Frank Cassidy.

'What are you looking for?'

Barkley was just Makana being cautious. Cassidy was a loose end. He didn't like loose ends. As a rule they tended to unravel any thinking that had gone before. He wanted to tie that one off before it got away from him. He gave Fathi the date of entry from Cassidy's airline ticket.

'Coming from Amman. Any information you have on him. And for Barkley everything also. Date of entry, port of entry, and where he was coming from.'

After that Makana settled down in the big chair out on the open deck, with his feet up on the railings, and lit a cigarette as he gazed out at the coloured lights playing on the water. In his mind he went back over the details of his conversation with Charles Barkley. Right now finding Samari seemed like a lost cause. If it was true that he had murdered Kasabian, and he seemed the most likely candidate, then he would hardly be inclined to sell a painting to the man that Kasabian had been working for. If he was the culprit then he would be busy disappearing back to where he had been hiding. Makana made a mental note to call Amir Medani, the human rights lawyer. He would know how to handle Samari legally.

It was always possible that it wasn't Samari who had tortured and killed Kasabian. That would mean there was another killer out there somewhere. But who? And what did they want out of Kasabian? The silence was broken by the sound of footsteps on the stairs. Makana looked round to find Aziza standing there. She wandered over and surveyed the pot of food by his chair.

'You're not eating,' she said, handing him the cup of coffee she had made.

'I'd forgotten about it. Help yourself.' Makana took the coffee gratefully and nodded at the bag lying on the table. He watched as she settled down on the deck with her back to the railings and began to eat. She was an odd girl in many ways. Curious and sharp-witted, she seemed at odds with Umm Ali's family.

'So,' she began, tucking into the heap of pasta and lentils with a plastic spoon. It seemed remarkable that she was able to eat such vast quantities of food without putting on weight. She still had the thin bony frame of a teenager. 'What are you working on?'

Aziza had appointed herself Makana's private assistant. She took an interest in his work and would answer the big black telephone that perched like an ugly crow on the desk, a prehistoric ancestor of the folding plastic shell that he now carried in his pocket.

'Do you know anything about art?'

'Art?' Aziza blinked and shook her head as another spoonful followed.

'Paintings. Some of them are worth a lot of money.'

'Sure, there's a man over by the mosque who paints signs. He's quite good. He did one of a man riding a horse. I can't remember what it was for.'

'Well, that's what I'm looking for.'

'A picture of a horse?' Aziza chewed thoughtfully.

'Something like that.' Makana realised he hadn't actually seen the picture in question. He wouldn't recognise it if it was standing in front of him. 'It's rather a special picture. Somebody has flown a long way to get hold of it.'

'Well, don't let that fool across the way hear about it. He already charges a fortune for painting his signs, and his horses look like dogs.' When she had polished off the food, Aziza collected the empty pots, along with various plates and cups distributed about the place, and left Makana alone with his thoughts.

He must have dozed off, because when he opened his eyes again several hours had gone by and he could feel the chill in the air. He knew at once that he was not alone. The night was quiet and still, the traffic reduced to the faint grumble of a lorry in the distance. As he began to swing his head towards the divan he heard the unmistakable sound of a gun being cocked.

'Okay, now let me explain how this works.' The voice was low and calm and spoke English with an American accent. 'Good. Now sit back in the chair. I want to see one hand on each armrest.'

Makana felt the barrel of the gun nudge against the side of his head. He lifted his arms slowly, one at a time, and placed them on the armrests.

'You're doing real good so far.' Makana felt the man behind him move. He turned his head slowly to see Mr Frankie, the American from the Carlton Hotel. Still wearing the same beige linen suit, more crumpled and stained than it had been, but still serviceable. The gun he held level in his hand was a large revolver with a stubby barrel. From that distance it seemed unlikely he would miss. The pistol was a disappointment. Makana hadn't found any gun when he searched his room. Either Cassidy carried it with him wherever he went or he was better at hiding things than Makana had given him credit for.

'Colt Python 357, in case you're wondering. Used to be standard police issue. This is my own personal weapon. You know how it is, old habits.' Cassidy shrugged his shoulders. 'What I am saying is that I am very familiar with this gun. I'd have no trouble hitting you from here. The bullet will go through you and that fancy throne you're sitting on and straight through the rest of this boat of yours.'

'It's not a boat.'

Cassidy made a throwaway gesture with his free hand. He didn't care.

'You followed me,' said Makana.

'Very good. Yes, I followed you from the Marriott Hotel. Bit of a roundabout route but here we are. A word to the wise: some of us don't react well to threats.'

'Threats?'

Cassidy reached into his jacket with his left hand and produced a folded sheet of paper that he tossed into Makana's lap. Makana opened it up and read what was written on it.

'Go Home.'

Cassidy was just below average height. A compact build. His hair was brownish, long at the back, hanging down to the nape of his neck. His face, like his clothes, had a lined, lived-in air about it. He wore a moustache that made him look older. Makana would have said he was around the same age as himself, in his late forties.

'You're making me feel very unwelcome.' Cassidy was shaking his head. 'Pushing notes under my door. I don't like being told what to do.'

'You don't need the gun.'

'I think I'm the best judge of that.'

'What do you want from me?'

'Well, that's an interesting question. I could ask you the same. You follow me to my hotel and search my room. I assume that was you, wasn't it? Why?'

'We don't get that many Americans around here.'

'Somehow that doesn't surprise me. You have a habit of killing them.'

'You shouldn't believe everything you read in the press.'

'I'd be a fool to believe any different.' Cassidy jogged the gun up and down. 'Now tell me about you. Why are you so interested in me?'

'I told you, I was curious.' Makana reached for his cigarettes and the gun jerked up. He pointed at his shirt pocket. Cassidy nodded. Makana lighted one and tossed the packet over when Cassidy gestured for him to do so. The cigarettes were not to the American's liking. He tossed it over his shoulder.

'Tastes like yesterday's newspaper.'

'It's an acquired flavour.'

'So is bullshit.' Cassidy reached into his jacket and produced a packet of Camels. The aroma of tobacco was so overwhelming Makana felt a twinge of envy. 'Tell me why you're after me.'

'I spotted you first at the Marriott. I didn't think much of it. But when I saw you outside the club in Maadi it seemed too much of a coincidence.'

'So you thought you'd search my room. Is that standard practice in this country?'

'You'd be surprised.' Makana turned over the note. The handwriting and the fact that it was written on paper from the Carlton Hotel suggested that it had been written hastily.

'I doubt it.' Cassidy smoked in silence for a moment, looking about. 'You live in this dump?'

Makana glanced around him. 'It has its charm.'

'If you say so. So who are you, state security? Some branch of the police?'

'Neither, I'm independent.'

'Don't make me laugh,' said Cassidy, his mouth twisting in a sneer. 'Nobody is independent in this country. Everyone is on the take. I've been here two weeks and already I've figured that much out.'

'Perhaps we're doing this the wrong way round.'

'How so?'

'Maybe if you tell me why you came here we can be of mutual assistance.'

'You want to help me?' laughed Cassidy. 'You live on a shipwreck. How are you going to help me?'

'Let me guess,' said Makana. 'You came to Cairo to look for someone, or something.'

'Very good. Maybe you want to read my palm next?'

'You're after the Franz Marc.'

Cassidy frowned. 'I don't even know what that means.'

'Why were you at the Winged Lion club?'

'There aren't that many places a man can get a drink in this town. The guy at the hotel told me about it.'

'What did you come to Cairo for, Mr Cassidy?'

'None of your damn business.' Cassidy had the smile of a man lost at sea, clinging to his life raft.

Makana got slowly to his feet. He held up the note.

'I didn't write this.'

'You don't mind if I tell you I don't believe you?' The gun followed him, but it was no longer really a threat and both of them seemed to know it.

'If I didn't do it, then somebody else did.'

'That's what you say.'

'Perhaps we are looking for the same thing,' said Makana.

'I told you I've never heard of this Franz guy. What say we try this my way?' The gun flicked upwards. 'Tell me why you're interested in me, and what your connection to Kane is.'

'Kane? Who is Kane?'

'This isn't what I call mutual assistance. Move over to the railing.'

'Is it something to do with the boy?' Makana asked.

'What boy?' Cassidy stared at him.

'The boy in the photograph.'

'That's right,' said Cassidy. 'I forgot you were familiar with my private possessions.' He got to his feet and moved towards the railing where Makana stood. 'What do they call you?'

'Makana.'

'That's it? No first name?'

'That's it.'

'Okay, let me spell this out for you. I don't know what your angle is, and I don't know what you want, but I'm warning you to stay out of my way. Understood?' He lifted the gun. 'Now I need you to sit down on the deck. Put your hands around that railing and bring them together.' Makana considered his options and decided to do as he was told. He watched Cassidy slip a plastic tie over his wrists and tug the loop tight. Then he stood up and tucked his gun away. He brushed his hands through his hair.

'I got to you once. I can do it again, any time I like. So this is the part where you need to pay careful attention. You stay out of my way, pal. Next time I won't be so gentle.'

Makana heard Cassidy walk away. He struggled to find a comfortable position and after a time gave up and slumped back to lean against the railings behind him.

Chapter Seventeen

Under the circumstances Makana did not pass too uncomfortable a night. He had known worse, he told himself. Aziza found him lying on the deck the next morning. The sun was coming up, the air still cool and clean. His bones felt as if he had been trampled on by a herd of buffalo and his wrists were chafed raw by the plastic strip. Aziza took it in her stride, taking one look from the top of the steps before disappearing to return carrying a large and very sharp knife.

'You had visitors last night?'

'I'm afraid so.' Makana sat up and rubbed his wrists.

'Why didn't you call me?'

Why hadn't he called? He had been lost in his thoughts. Cassidy was not after the painting. Then what? He was here in Cairo for quite another purpose. What that might be wasn't clear. At some point Makana had simply fallen asleep, and he was paying the price for that now. He tried turning his head to get the crick out of his neck and decided against it. Instead he got to his feet and sighed. As if reading his mind, Aziza disappeared down the stairs to boil water for tea. Makana lit a cigarette and slumped down into his chair. He turned the strip of plastic over in his hands. Cheaper and lighter than handcuffs, but typically designed to be used and thrown away. He'd seen them on the news. The American soldiers used them in Iraq.

A shower and a shave along with several cups of tea restored Makana's humour, and although his wrists still stung, his neck was loosening up. He climbed the path to the road, pausing to greet Umm Ali on his way. She was busy shredding a piece of sacking, to what purpose he could not imagine, but he was sure there was some benefit to the exercise.

'*Sabah al khair*, Umm Ali.'

'*Sabah al nour, ya bash muhandis.*' She would have bowed if she could.

There was a kind of cyclic nature to their relationship. During hard times common courtesies were kept to a minimum, but those times were balanced by the good days, when the rent had been paid and there were offers to do his laundry without his asking. Makana was aware that there lurked a furious temper inside her. He had heard it enough times, chastising her children, and more than one neighbour had felt the wrath of her tongue. Umm Ali's ferocity was legendary. In the local market he had witnessed her haranguing merchants for the accuracy of their scales. Somehow it mattered to her that they adhere to the social norms. He was the tenant and she the landlord. She would allow him a little leeway with the rent, on the understanding that when it finally arrived there would be a little extra for her – a gift, to buy herself something, which she would only accept on the premise that one or the other of the children needed new trousers or a shirt for school. He complied as if it was simply an afterthought and not an obligation.

Sindbad was waiting and twenty minutes later the Thunderbird circled the stern figure of Saad Zaghloul, aiming his bronze glare at a city in turmoil. In the 1920s, Cairo was ruled by a wealthy class that identified themselves more with London and Paris than with the fellaheen peasants who trod the muddy fields about them. As unrest spread across the region, eventually the British understood that their time was up. Independence was granted. Zaghloul was elected prime minister. So much of yesterday looks like today, thought Makana, as they pulled up outside the Opera House. Only the numbers on the calendar change.

'I want you to go back to that house in Garden City,' he told Sindbad, handing him a printout of the Most Wanted playing card of Kadhim al-Samari. 'Park where you can see the gate and keep an eye out for this man.'

'A playing card?' Sindbad looked amused. He could read well enough to make sense of the figures. 'Three million dollars is a lot of beans.'

'More than you and I could stomach. You call me if you see him.'

Sindbad was about to charge off when he noticed something. '*Ya basha*, there must be some mistake here. There's no face on this figure.'

'That's right. Because there is no picture. All you have is the description.'

The big man's brows furrowed. He started to speak and then stopped himself. Makana went on.

'He'll be cautious. Discreet. Around fifty years old. He's dangerous so don't go near him. Iraqi. A military man. He'll have an escort – guards, more than one, and maybe more than one car.'

Sindbad looked doubtful. 'I understand.'

'Call me if anything turns up, anything at all.'

Eager to prove himself worthy of the task, Sindbad gunned the engine and with a powerful singing sound the heavy car rumbled away. It was going to take some adjusting to go back to the Datsun after this.

The memorial for Aram Kasabian was held at the Opera House. Where else would be suitable for such a man? A solemnly dressed crowd hovered around the entrance to one of the art galleries that lay alongside the main building. The white dome and arches made it resemble, in this setting, a mosque. All it lacked was a minaret. Maybe that was the idea. A kind of secular defence held up against the superstitions of the encroaching masses. *Ces crétins*, as King Fouad once referred to his subjects. Educated abroad, he couldn't even speak their language.

The well-heeled set shuffled around one another inside the circular space. There was a subdued air. Uniformed waiters circulated bearing trays of fruit juice and soft drinks. Nobody asked who Makana was and he didn't offer that information. The guards on the door seemed to assume that anyone who could find the place was here for the express purpose of paying their respects. Guards generally knew to tread lightly when it came to stepping on expensive toes. Makana sipped what he discovered was guava juice and tried to mingle. As he slipped through the crowd he overheard snippets of conversation which confirmed that Okasha's leak was still running smoothly and freely into the press.

'To die like that, hung up like a sheep,' one woman exclaimed. Her earrings trembled, with indignation or excitement, it wasn't clear which.

'Butchered like an animal,' murmured her companion, a fleshy man with a bloated face. Nervously, he squinted sideways through thick glasses at Makana and licked his lips. Makana moved away. These people could scent an interloper the way a gazelle might a lion. He wasn't one of them.

'Ah, there you are. I thought you might show up.'

Ali was wearing some kind of Chinese-style suit. A relic perhaps of his Maoist days. It was buttoned up to his beard, which had been trimmed. He looked lean and, well, artistic, which was probably the point. Makana realised there was a streak of vanity in his friend that he had never noticed before.

'They're all here,' Ali said with a sigh, glancing around him. 'Friends and enemies. People he helped out over the years. It's all very sad.'

Makana let his gaze wander around the assembled mourners. Artists and their wealthy patrons, rubbing shoulders in honour of one of their own.

'Did he have a lot of enemies?'

'No.' Ali shut his eyes for a second. 'Aram Kasabian was a master at diplomacy. As smooth as silk. He could bring sworn enemies together and make money out of both of them. A gentleman.'

Makana listened with one ear. Across the room he spotted a tall, well-built man in his fifties, his hair dyed an unnatural shade of black. Qasim Abdel Qasim. Not a single grey hair in sight.

'What are you doing here?'

Makana turned to find Okasha standing next to him. 'I came to pay my respects, and to see what Kasabian's friends look like.'

'Take a good look,' nodded Okasha. 'He moved in powerful circles.' Makana duly looked. It was a male environment. A boys' club, as Dalia Habashi might have put it. No matter how cultured Cairo's elite liked to think themselves, some things remained as old-fashioned as ever. They did business with one another. Those who were in office smoothed the way for those

164

with the financial might to transform the country, to nudge the economy in ways that were lucrative for all.

'Any news of our friend on the motorcycle?'

Okasha shook his head. 'There are alerts out for him, but nothing yet.'

In a city this size putting out an alert was like throwing a stone from a minaret and hoping it would strike the right man. Finding one man on a motorcycle was beyond all realistic expectations. It would require more than vigilance, more even than luck. It would take something approaching a miracle for Na'il to be found if he didn't want to be.

'What I don't understand is why he would kill Kasabian,' Okasha said.

'We don't know that he did.' Makana felt a twinge of guilt at not having shared the information he had about Kadhim al-Samari with Okasha, but only a twinge. If the old poet was right then Na'il could be a very useful witness. 'Fleeing the scene of the crime doesn't prove him guilty of murder.'

'This is what I'm talking about.' Okasha squared up to Makana. 'Why do I have the feeling you're keeping something from me?'

Before Makana could speak somebody was tapping a microphone and the man with the badly dyed hair stepped onto an improvised stage on one side of the room. Qasim Abdel Qasim. Deputy minister. A man, as people liked to say, with a promising future.

'Here we go,' muttered Okasha. 'Now they will begin their nonsense.'

Qasim's address was delayed as a flutter of excitement went through the room. People were straining their necks to catch a glimpse of something happening over by the entrance.

'The president's son,' said Okasha.

'Now that we're all here . . .' the deputy minister began, which brought a few laughs. Everyone knew who he was talking about. And a comment came from that side of the room that Makana couldn't catch. The president's son was responding in person. It didn't matter what he said, everyone was delighted to be in his presence. It was hard to believe they were gathered to pay their respects to a man who had just been brutally murdered. Cheery pleasantries completed, Qasim turned to the matter in hand, managing quite neatly to switch from light banter to sombre reflection in the bat of an eye. The mark of a true statesman.

'Our dear departed friend, how often he brought us together in this very room to witness the latest developments in art. Aram Kasabian was a shining light in our little constellation and it was my honour to consider him among my personal friends.'

'He says that about everyone,' murmured Okasha.

'There are those of us,' Qasim went on, 'who believe that art plays a central role in our national culture. Our history sparkles with great artists and writers. Art is a brilliant light that, as we know, many would choose to extinguish, to return us to darker times. So let Aram Kasabian be remembered as an enlightenment figure. A man proud of his country, and whose country was proud of him. A man who strived every day to make this world a better place.'

'They make me sick,' said Okasha as Qasim droned on. He turned to push his way to the back of the crowd. 'They make out they are heroes, defending the values of their country.' Incensed, Okasha paced up and down. Makana lit a cigarette and waited. 'Meanwhile they're busy making themselves rich, at our expense.'

'What's bothering you?' Makana asked when he got a chance to speak.

'They want to shut down the case. That's why I'm telling you we have to close it.'

'Who wants to shut it down?'

'Who do you think?' Okasha nodded his head at the interior and the man on stage who was still talking. 'This is the kind of case where everyone is in the spotlight.'

'And they don't care who did it?'

'They want it sewn up neatly. No loose ends. In a case like this, that's all that matters. The whole world is watching.'

'I see.'

'I hope so.' Okasha scratched his head, an agitated man. 'And there's another thing. Na'il is one of us.'

'A policeman?'

'Ex-Central Security Force. A real lowlife. Apparently he went into business for himself, dealing in narcotics. They tried to throw him out but the case was dropped, so they kept him on off-the-record as an informant.'

'We still need to find him.'

'We will, and then you'll tell me what it is you're hiding from me.'

Makana turned away from Okasha to find Qasim standing in front of him with a bemused look on his face.

'Have we met before?' The smile was like a splash of olive oil across a sunny plate.

'At Kasabian's house, the night of the opening.'

'Ah, of course.' The smile faded. A case of mistaken identity. 'You're the investigator who was helping Aram. What exactly were you doing for him?'

'That's confidential.'

'I see.' Qasim turned to Okasha. 'Inspector, is this man helping you with your inquiries?'

'Yes, Deputy Minister, he is cooperating fully. We are working round the clock to bring the culprit to justice. Have no fear, it is only a matter of time.'

'Not too much time, I hope.' Qasim drew himself up to his full height. Already his eyes were roving the room looking for which direction to move in. 'Ah, Brigadier, perhaps you can tell us how the investigation is going? This is Brigadier Yusuf Effendi. Do you know Mr Makana, Brigadier?'

The stern man had a barrel-like stomach held in place by the brass buttons on his uniform. He leaned back and squinted at Makana. His voice was slurred and a slight twitch affected his rather impressive white moustache.

'Never seen him before in my life.' He snapped his fingers at a waiter and took a glass of something fizzy. 'Who is he?'

'Well, I was hoping you might be able to enlighten us. He is apparently helping Inspector Okasha here with the investigation into Kasabian's murder.'

'Really?' The brigadier turned his eyes on Okasha. 'What's this I hear about your looking for my nephew?'

'Your nephew, sir?'

'That's what I just said, Na'il Abdelkarim is my sister's child. He's an undercover operative with CSF. Now answer my question, is it true?'

'He was identified as a possible witness.'

'Who identified him?' demanded the brigadier.

'A motorcycle matching the description of the one your nephew owns was seen fleeing the scene of the crime.'

'Nonsense. Have you spoken to the boy?'

'We've been unable to locate him,' Okasha reported. The

brigadier muttered into his drink. 'Makana here also witnessed him being escorted out of Kasabian's house. It seems there was some bad feeling between your nephew and Mr Kasabian.'

'Now listen,' the brigadier addressed Okasha, 'I shall be taking personal charge of this investigation. You will report directly to me. Make sure you leave no stone unturned.' By now the brigadier's booming voice was attracting attention. Okasha shifted uncomfortably at being addressed in public like this. The brigadier wasn't finished. 'And as for this man, what did you say your name was?'

'Makana.'

'You realise it's an offence to impersonate a police officer?'

'I never claimed to be a police officer,' Makana said quietly. 'I was working for Kasabian.'

'Working? In what capacity?'

'I tried that already,' Qasim breezed. 'He says it's confidential.'

'Confidential?' The brigadier guffawed, spraying a good amount of spittle around him in the process. 'We don't know the meaning of that word. We have no secrets, and more importantly nobody has any secrets from us. Good luck with your investigation, Inspector. I shall have my eye on you. I want results.'

The guests were starting to file out of the gallery. Having done their duty and shown up, they now had better places to be.

Chapter Eighteen

The old gatekeeper got up from his chair when he saw the Thunderbird approaching. Sindbad climbed out, producing a rag to rub over the exterior. He seemed to have taken a liking to the car.

'Is he at home?'

'Mr Jalal? Yes, effendi, he is here, but as I explained on the telephone, he is not receiving visitors.'

'Then he'll have to get used to the idea. This is important.'

Like an old soldier the gatekeeper trailed along beside Makana as he walked up the path.

'Did Kasabian and his wife ever have any children?'

'No, effendi. They were never blessed with children.'

'Then who does the house go to?'

The gatekeeper was silent for a moment. 'It will go to his assistant, I suppose.' The sound of his leather slippers on the stone resumed. 'Things won't be the same without him.'

Jules was waiting for them at the top of the front steps. He was wearing a dark green robe over a pair of pyjamas and looked as if he had just got out of bed.

'I don't understand why you can't leave me alone at this difficult time. Have you no respect for the dead?'

'I'm sorry to disturb you. I just had a small query.'

He gave a sigh of exasperation. 'The press simply will not leave me alone. It's become quite intolerable.'

A part of Makana wanted to know just exactly what the relationship was between Kasabian and his assistant. Another, more old-fashioned side preferred to remain in the dark.

'It's just that the other day you mentioned that Na'il had worked for Kasabian in some capacity. I wondered if you could be a bit more explicit?'

'Look, I've told the police everything I know.'

'Well, I'm not with the police, Mr Jalal.'

'Obviously I understand that, but your business with Mr Kasabian is now terminated. It makes no sense, now that he's no longer around.'

'It makes sense to me,' Makana said. 'Look, Mr Kasabian may have been killed as a result of the investigation he hired me to do.'

'The police didn't say anything about that.' Jules looked suspicious. 'They're looking for Na'il.'

'Let me ask you, then. You know Na'il. Do you think he would have been capable of killing Kasabian that way?'

Jules shuddered at the memory, but then recovered. 'No, I don't believe so.'

'Neither do I. Look, it seems to me that the man I was paid to trace is the most likely suspect right now. I think that I have an obligation to find out if that's true, wouldn't you say?'

'Well, I think you're wrong. It can't be so.' Jules broke off and leaned over to address the old gatekeeper who was standing in the garden as motionless as a tree. 'Thank you, Amm Ahmed, I'll take care of our guest now.'

Muttering to himself under his breath, the old gatekeeper turned to wander back to his post.

Jules looked at Makana. 'You'd better come in.'

Makana followed him down a dark hallway behind the stairs and into a living room at the back of the house. It was a big room with a high ceiling but it felt small, crowded as it was with heavy furniture. There were statues and carved figures, glass cabinets whose shelves were arrayed with smaller items of a similar nature. There were wooden barges to carry the sun, complete with slaves to row them. Then there were animals – crocodiles, falcons, rams. Makana had visited the National Museum in Tahrir Square on occasion and it struck him that Kasabian possessed a collection that was worthy of comparison. Smaller in size, but the quality of the pieces was without doubt of a similar calibre. On the walls hung heavy, gilt-framed paintings of the country's former rulers, King Farouk and a collection of pashas, plump-faced and pale-skinned, all wearing the obligatory fez and rows of medals pinned to their swelling chests. They had bankrupted the country and hocked it to the European powers while sailing by on golden chariots drinking champagne. Those were the days.

'Aram was the last in a long line of art collectors. His great-grandfather first bought this house the year the Suez Canal was opened.'

'All of this is insured, I take it?'

'Oh, it's impossible to set a value on this collection in material terms.'

'I'm sure there are a few disreputable people who wouldn't mind trying.'

'The room is secured. The windows and doors are heavily barred and there is an alarm system. The most valuable pieces are in a safe. Of course, the best deterrent is simply secrecy. Very few people know about this room.'

'You mean he never showed it to anyone?'

'Only to a select few,' Jules smiled. 'People whose reputation would prevent them from speaking freely of what they had seen.'

'I take it that all these items were purchased legally.'

Jules gave a slight cough that might have been a laugh. 'Well, that depends on how you define legally.'

'How many ways are there?'

'They were all acquired through legitimate purchase, I can assure you. Please, there's no smoking in here.' Jules paused before going on. 'Naturally, there might be some debate as to how the seller came into possession of a particular piece in the first place. But the art world is full of such oddities.'

'Not so odd,' Makana said, strolling about the room. 'Let's talk about the not so legal pieces.'

'What do you mean?'

'I'm on your side, Mr Jalal, or as good as. I know in this business you sometimes stray over the line. Kasabian more or less told me that himself. Pieces are traded with no questions asked. Lost masterpieces and priceless artefacts that simply disappeared one day from a museum somewhere.'

Jules blinked a few times. 'What are you trying to suggest?'

'We're trying to find a reason why somebody wanted to torture and kill Kasabian, remember? He was tortured because someone wanted information. Now what kind of information could that be?'

'I really don't know what you are driving at.' Jules gave a half-hearted laugh.

'What was Kasabian dealing in? Either you tell me or we can call Inspector Okasha to join us. It's up to you.'

'Very well.' Jules took a deep breath. 'Items sometimes came to Aram, Mr Kasabian, by unconventional routes.'

'Unconventional routes?' Makana laughed. 'You people have a high-grade talent for sliding around awkward truths. Go on.'

'From time to time he would arrange extraordinary showings. Potential buyers would come, some flying in from the Gulf, or further afield. Aram adored these objects.'

'How many people know about this room?'

'Only Mr Kasabian, and myself of course. As I said, a few select buyers, friends.'

'What about Na'il, does he know?'

Jules looked at Makana and nodded silently.

'What exactly did Na'il do for Kasabian?'

'Well, Kasabian used him when he needed something done.'

'What kind of something?'

'Putting pressure on someone, that kind of thing. He had contacts in the security forces. He knew people. He was very useful in that way.'

'If he was so useful, why didn't Kasabian use him to find Kadhim al-Samari?'

Restlessly, Jules began to twist the cord of his robe into knots.

'Na'il got out of hand, didn't he?' asked Makana.

Jules nodded quickly. 'He started getting ideas. He was asking for money, big money, in exchange for silence.'

'Silence about what Kasabian was up to?'

'I don't really like to talk about this. I mean, especially here.' He glanced around at the walls of Kasabian's inner sanctuary.

Makana produced his telephone. 'Perhaps we should invite Inspector Okasha to join us.'

'Wait.' Jules held up a hand. He rubbed his temples. 'All right. Okay.'

'What did Na'il have on Kasabian? Was it something in this room?'

'I never liked the man.' Jules scowled. 'I tried to warn Aram but he just laughed. He said sometimes you need people like that to get their hands dirty for you.'

'Then one day, Na'il saw an opportunity that he couldn't resist.'

Jules hesitated and then relented. He moved Makana aside in order to reach a large glass cabinet filled with brass objects that looked African. The whole cabinet slid aside on wheels to reveal a section of wooden panelling. Jules pressed one side and a door clicked open to reveal a large grey safe, a metre and a half high by almost the same in width. He drew his robe tighter around him.

'If you wouldn't mind . . .'

Makana turned his back while Kasabian's former assistant bent to the combination lock. A few moments later there was a click, and the heavy door swung open to reveal a series of drawers. Using a key that hung on a chain around his neck, Jules unlocked one of these and opened it to slide out a tray that he carried over to a high table in the middle of the room.

'These are truly precious items,' he said in a low whisper. 'Of all the things Aram owned, these had a special place in his heart.'

The tray was covered in soft black felt and laid out on it in rows were a number of small flat objects. Makana saw broken tablets of stone bearing carvings. Most of them were incomplete, but he could make out what looked like a camel on one and a palm tree on another. Jules drew his attention to a small fragment, no more than six centimetres in length and about half that in width. On it was depicted a slender woman with a hand raised. The detail of the fingers was remarkable.

'Ishtar,' breathed Jules. 'The Babylonian goddess of love and war.'

'Exactly how much are these worth?'

'Oh, they're priceless. I mean, they date back more than six thousand years.'

Makana took a closer look at a figure of a bull with a human head as Jules went on.

'The Babylonian world was obsessed with darkness. The Underworld played a far more important role than in Ancient Egypt, for example. In the Babylonian universe only the gods inhabited heaven. Mere mortals were condemned to a house of darkness, to eat dust and live in silence.'

'Sounds familiar,' muttered Makana.

'One Sumerian fragment claims that a man with a righteous soul will live for ever.'

'Then we can all live in hope.' Makana pointed at the tray. 'Where did Kasabian get these, and don't tell me some round-about story about unconventional ways.'

Jules took a deep breath. 'Kasabian was selling these pieces on behalf of Kadhim al-Samari.'

Makana looked up. 'Are you saying that Kasabian was already in touch with Samari when he hired me to find him?'

'Yes,' Jules murmured, nodding his head.

Makana lit a cigarette. 'He already knew him.'

'He would be contacted from time to time. Aram had no way of contacting Samari directly himself. Samari is very paranoid. He changes telephones every few days.'

'That's why you think Samari couldn't have killed him.'

'It hardly seems likely, does it? I mean, Aram was working for him.'

Suddenly, the whole picture appeared to have changed. It was unlikely that Samari would kill Kasabian if they were partners, unless there had been a falling out.

'And they were on good terms – I mean, Samari was happy with what Kasabian was doing for him?'

'Absolutely. He had no complaints. Aram was discreet and efficient. He sold the pieces quietly and with little fuss. Kadhim al-Samari got his money, and that was all he wanted.'

That left Na'il dead centre, except that he had been blackmailing Kasabian. It would make no sense for him to kill him either. Makana paced across the Persian carpet.

'Okay, so let's go back to where I came into the picture. Why did he hire me?'

'It all went wrong when the American appeared.'

'Charles Barkley.'

Jules sat down in a high-backed chair close to the wall. 'When Barkley turned up, Aram got very nervous. He couldn't sit still. He waited for three days for Samari to call him. I don't think he slept for those three days.'

'What happened then?' Makana had found a tortoiseshell bowl containing coloured beads. He tipped them onto the windowsill and used the shell as an ashtray.

'When Samari finally called, Aram told him that an American buyer had appeared, that he was interested in a certain German Expressionist painting.'

'The Franz Marc.'

'Exactly. Barkley came with a reference from a decent dealer in New York, Norton Granger, whom Aram knew by reputation of course.'

'But Samari didn't trust Barkley.'

'Barkley had mentioned Samari by name. He couldn't understand where he could have got that information. He smelt a rat.

Aram was willing to take the chance. He trusted Barkley and there was a lot of money at stake.'

'Does Samari have these paintings?'

'As I understand it, he has some of them. But none of them had been put on the market. How could Barkley have heard of them? How could he connect them to Samari?'

'Kasabian had to get rid of Barkley, but he had to do it quietly.'

'Exactly. So he came up with the idea of hiring someone to find Samari, knowing that he would fail.' Jules shrugged apologetically.

'Go on,' said Makana. He didn't take offence. It was too late for that now. Kasabian had paid for his error with his life.

'The idea was to throw the American off the scent. Convince him somehow that Samari wasn't in the country. It wasn't hard, there is no trace of him. Officially, he never entered Egypt. He has friends in the military who took care of all that.'

Makana paced some more. He lit another cigarette from the butt of the first.

'I talked to Barkley. I asked him how he had come across the information that the painting was in this country, that Samari had it.'

'What did he say?'

'He said a lot of things about rumours, but nothing about exactly where they came from.'

'It happens all the time in this business.'

'Even if Barkley had heard the paintings were here in Cairo, how could he have connected them to Samari?'

'I told Aram it was a bad plan. A real investigator might actually find something, but he . . . well, he didn't think you'd get very far.'

'And now he's dead.' Despite knowing that Kasabian had set him up, the image of the torn and bloody body suspended from the roof beam remained vivid in his mind. Whatever Kasabian had done, he hadn't deserved to die like that.

'It doesn't make sense.' Jules hung his head. 'I mean, why torture him like that? What did he want from him?' He looked up, his eyes widening. 'The combination to the safe! You don't think they'll come after me?'

Makana had no answer to that. Somehow he thought whoever was behind this had their eye on a bigger prize. He nodded at the priceless artefacts.

'Hardly seems worth giving up your life for a pile of dusty old bits of stone, does it?'

'Rare objects from the ancient world.' Jules had a mournful look on his face. 'This is what fascinated him. Not modern art but the things from our past.' He looked up. 'But you're right, I'd trade it all in just to have him back.'

Makana left him there, surrounded by the treasures of past glory.

Chapter Nineteen

The first thing Makana saw when he opened his eyes was a crow perched on the rail of the deck a few metres away. It was completely motionless, so still that he wondered for a moment if it was real or something that had escaped from his dream. Then the breeze ruffled its feathers. It had grey wings and a jet-black head. It stared unblinkingly, apparently waiting for him to wake up, as if it had been watching over him. Then, in the wink of an eye, it flapped and was gone.

He had slept badly. It was becoming a habit. There was something about this case that seemed to be digging itself into him, sending him back in time. The torturer who haunted his dreams had now become Samari, a faceless creature who stalked the bleak hallways and yawning prison cells of his mind. It was a relief to open his eyes. He found a basket of fresh eggs placed in his kitchen by the ever faithful Aziza, a sign of the ongoing good feeling between himself and Umm Ali. He boiled a couple of them. A cupboard yielded a shield of dry bread that he dampened under the tap and warmed up over the gas flame. It felt like a civilised start to the day. As he was chewing away he looked up and saw the silhouette of a uniformed policeman appear at the top of the path.

They had come on Okasha's instructions to take him to the morgue. The two officers chatted idly in the front as they drove him at a sedate pace across to Manial Island, talking like old men in a café, discussing the cost of living and Ahly's chances of winning the league this year.

The Department of Pathology was located in a remote corner of the Faculty of Medicine at Qasr al-Ainy university. Makana was directed through a series of subterranean corridors following the familiar damp fug of scrubbing bleach and human decay, until he came to a white-tiled dissection room where Doctora Siham and Okasha stood waiting. Kasabian's body, or what was left of it, lay on a steel table between them. The skin was waxy and bruised. A rough line of stitches like mad calligraphy inscribed the Y-shaped incision running from groin to neck where he had been cut open. The thread was brown and resembled old-fashioned catgut. Doctora Siham looked wide awake and impatient.

'I thought we had dealt with this already.'

'This is for the benefit of Brigadier Yusuf Effendi, who is on his way here as we speak,' said Okasha. 'Did the blood and tissue tests come in?'

'Yes, I told you.'

'That's fine. All you have to do is take us through it all again. He insists on taking command of the case, so I need to show him that we are doing our work.'

'Why is he here?' Doctora Siham nodded at Makana.

'Because he's part of this investigation, whether the brigadier likes it or not.'

'This is ridiculous.' Doctora Siham folded her arms. 'Nobody trusts anybody. That's why this country is so far behind.'

'Please, spare me the political speeches at this hour.' Okasha gave her a withering glance.

No more than five minutes passed before the double doors flew open and Brigadier Effendi strode in. Even at that hour of the morning he cut an imposing figure, large in stature, his uniform immaculate, the brass buttons and gold braid gleaming fit for a parade ground. Okasha straightened up and saluted. The brigadier nodded back.

'Well, what have we got here?'

'Doctora Siham was about to take us through the results of her autopsy.'

'Very good. Proceed.' The brigadier snapped his fingers, eyes flickering round. 'Wait.' He stabbed a finger in Makana's direction. 'What is that man doing here?'

'He's here to assist in the investigation.'

'I don't need to remind you, Inspector, that civilians have no authority to be here.'

'Sir, I feel that in this case an exception could be beneficial to our investigation.' Okasha made a spirited attempt to stand up for himself. He cleared his throat. 'Mr Makana was working for the victim at the time of his death and I believe he might be able to shed some light on matters.'

'It's against regulations, Inspector. You are aware of that?'

'Yes, sir, but considering the circumstances . . . and the urgency of the case.'

'If you are prepared to take any possible consequences on your own shoulders then I have no objection.' The brigadier shot him a long look. 'Any luck finding my nephew?'

'I'm afraid not, sir.'

Doctora Siham made a noise that might have been a cough,

or a splutter of laughter. Heads turned towards her, but nobody had the courage to say anything.

'Perhaps we should get on, or do your regulations include me?' Doctora Siham asked. 'I am a civilian, after all.'

'Of course not. Your presence is indispensable.' The brigadier's moustache was pure white and betrayed a touch of vanity, now on display as he tried to turn on his charm, although clearly Doctora Siham was immune. His skin was a deep, jaundiced colour. It might have been the bright fluorescent light, or possibly something wrong with his liver. It gave him a slightly bronzed look, similar to the foetuses and organs that floated in formaldehyde in jars set along the far wall.

'Then, if you gentlemen have no objections perhaps we could proceed.'

'By all means, Doctora.'

Doctora Siham began to outline her findings. She gestured at the faintly bluish marks that adorned the corpse before them, which made Kasabian resemble a victim of some strange ritual sacrifice.

'I counted over a hundred and seventy cuts to the body, of varying degrees. These range from shallow to two centimetres in depth. It's hard to imagine how much that would have hurt.'

'Then the purpose of these cuts was to cause pain?' Makana wished he could smoke, if only to kill the odour of bodily decay and chemicals. He considered giving it a try, just to annoy the old brigadier, but he suspected that Doctora Siham would not have approved. She demanded their full attention.

'Yes. Cause of death was heart failure. None of these subcutaneous incisions in and of themselves was what killed him.'

'Is there a pattern to the way they were inflicted, a sequence?'

Makana wondered what order a torturer might use. Was there some kind of science to be applied in these matters? His own experience of torture had been of a more random and unplanned nature, the tried and tested method of continued beatings and isolation. Looking down at Kasabian, he imagined what he must have felt. The brigadier grunted something, but it wasn't clear what he wanted to say.

'I could not find any order or pattern,' said the pathologist, 'but the consistency of the wounds suggests a certain ... methodology.'

'A what?' frowned the brigadier.

'You mean, this wasn't the first time the torturer had done this?' asked Makana.

'Exactly.' Doctora Siham went on with her exposition. 'The ankles and wrists show contusions consistent with a long period of restraint with a rope. The victim was suspended upside down and remained that way for some hours after death, according to the discoloration caused by the settling of the blood. In my opinion, to do this properly, without risk of killing the victim too soon, requires some measure of experience.'

'Is there anything else you can tell us, *ya Doctora*?' Okasha felt it was time to weigh in, acutely aware of the brigadier's presence. He shifted from one foot to the other uncomfortably. The brigadier stood with his hands clasped behind his back and wore the expression of a man who has more important things to do with his time. 'I want to know why this was done to this man. He was a good, decent, upstanding man and he didn't deserve this.'

'Why do men do these things?' asked Doctora Siham, arching her eyebrows. 'You might be better suited to answering that question than myself. What I can say is that the murder weapon was big. Some of the later wounds are deeper and less straight.' She ran a gloved hand over some of the longer gashes. 'So, either the perpetrator was getting tired or running out of patience. Or . . .'

'Or what?' demanded the brigadier.

'Or he was beginning to enjoy himself.'

'Can you say what type of weapon was used?' Makana asked. She gestured for him to move closer. He leaned in over her shoulder.

'As you can see, the knife is moved from left to right in some cases and from right to left in others. This would suggest a slashing movement.' The doctor was thoughtful. 'Up and down. A smooth, practised action.' She straightened up and drew interconnected circles in the air with her right index finger. 'High to low on both sides.' Her eyes came to rest on Makana. 'The knife is very sharp on one side and with serrations on the other, which cause tearing.'

'What kind of knife are we talking about?' Okasha queried.

'Not very common, is the answer. Long blade, wide and with a serrated tip,' Doctora Siham said. 'A fancy hunting knife or a military survival knife.' She stopped speaking as the brigadier cleared his throat. He was clearly moved. It must have been a while since he had attended a post-mortem.

'Inspector Okasha, I cannot stress how important it is that you solve this case as soon as possible. This man was a personal friend, my wife bought paintings from him and now someone has tried to carve him up like so much chopped liver. We have to clear this up and we have to do it now. And that's an order. Before I am demoted, heads are going to roll.'

'Of course, sir.' Okasha even managed a snappy salute.

'We're looking for a maniac. Someone who is a menace to society. The sooner we have him behind bars the better. I shall be making a press statement this afternoon. Is there anything I can give them, anything at all?'

'We are following a number of leads.'

'That's it? Well, you'd better have something better than that soon or you'll be joining your friend here as an investigator.' The brigadier glanced at Makana. 'I intend to keep a tight hold on this case.' He was already heading for the door. 'Allow nothing to deflect you from your path.'

When he had gone Okasha gave a sigh of relief, removing his cap and pushing a hand through his hair.

'Now all we need to do is find the killer,' he said, looking at Makana. 'And you need to tell me what you know.'

'Na'il was blackmailing Kasabian about his dealing in stolen artefacts.'

'You think that's a reason to have killed him?'

'Perhaps they argued. But we still need to speak to him.'

'I agree. We're doing our best, but you know how it is. What about you?'

Makana had the nagging sense that an essential piece kept slipping out of his grasp. He couldn't escape the feeling that Charles Barkley was not being entirely frank with him. Why had he really come to Cairo? How had he known about Samari and the painting? The more he thought about it, the more he was convinced that somehow Barkley held the key to all of this.

'Me? I'm going to have another talk with our American friend.'

Chapter Twenty

Hamid Bostan, assistant manager at the Marriott Hotel, was a worried man in an impeccable blue suit. The real manager was a bright-faced blond man from Switzerland with an unpronounceable name and a big smile revealing rows of perfectly aligned white teeth. His face filled an enormous framed portrait in the lobby where he welcomed new arrivals as they entered with a cheery gaze. Almost as convincing as the portraits of Mubarak that graced government offices everywhere. Naturally, he was too busy to actually take part in the day-to-day running of the hotel, which was left to Bostan, the thin man in the blue suit. He wore a pencil moustache that somehow matched the fine layer of hair combed across the top of his head. It wasn't the first time he had had dealings with Makana, which perhaps explained why, the moment he caught sight of him, he spun and walked in the opposite direction. Makana followed him to the reception desk, where Bostan proceeded to studiously ignore him while engaging with a young man on the other side of the counter. The effect was undermined by the receptionist, who kept trying to draw his manager's attention to the fact that someone was waiting to speak to him.

'Sir . . .'

'Yes, yes. I can see.' With a sigh Bostan finally turned to Makana. 'I am not blind, I would just prefer not to see you in my hotel.'

'I haven't come to cause you any trouble.'

'That would make a change.' Bostan abruptly turned away from the counter and began walking. Makana fell in beside him.

'Would it surprise you to know that I am actually working for one of your guests?'

'Nothing about you would surprise me.' Bostan paused to reprimand a bellhop whose uniform needed straightening. It seemed to cheer him up. 'Who is this fortunate individual?'

'Mr Charles Barkley.'

The name brought the hotel manager to an abrupt halt. As it happened, right beside the life-size photograph of his superior. The contrast between the confident Swiss smile and the harried, nervous Egyptian could not have been stronger. He resembled a lean, underfed greyhound. He couldn't have done a better job if his tongue had been hanging out.

'Barkley?' Bostan echoed, steering Makana by the elbow to one side. 'I should have guessed it. Are you really working for this man?' He dropped Makana's arm and stepped back for a moment, before drawing closer. 'I should have you arrested.'

'Any particular reason?'

'Mr Barkley and his associates have gone. They left the hotel overnight without checking out. Do you know what that means?' Without waiting for a reply, he tugged Makana back to the reception desk and began issuing orders. Behind the counter people tripped over one another in their haste. Finally, a sheet of paper was set on the counter. Bostan scrutinised it for a moment and smiled, as if in disbelief. 'The bar bill alone comes to almost three thousand dollars.'

'What associates?' Makana asked. Bostan stared as if facing an idiot. 'You said he had associates?'

'Five of them.' Bostan slid another sheet of paper forwards. 'Four Americans, Raul Santos, Randy Hagen, Cody Jansen, Eddie Clearwater, and one Iraqi, Faisal Abdallah.' He tapped the names on the list as he read them out. Makana took the sheet.

'Don't you take photocopies of guests' passports when they check in?'

'Naturally. Standard procedure. You can't just allow anyone to walk in.'

'Heaven forbid.'

Bostan snapped his fingers a couple of times. 'Show me this Barkley's papers.' There was more agitation behind the counter. The receptionists seemed to be drawing lots as to which one of them would break the bad news. He looked from one to the other. 'Well, what is it?'

'Sir, we have photocopies of four of the Americans but not Mr Barkley.'

'I see, and how do you explain that?'

'I can't.' The girl twisted her fingers into a knot. 'There was some confusion when they checked in.'

'Really? Well, believe me there will be no confusion when I find out who is responsible. Who was on duty?'

'I was, *effendim*. I remember that Mr Barkley said his passport was at the bottom of his suitcase and he would bring it down later.' She gave a shrug. 'He was very convincing. Since we had all of the others . . . I was trying to be accommodating.'

'We'll see how accommodating you find it without a job.'

'Yes, *effendim*.' She lowered her eyes. 'And . . . there's something else.'

'What? Don't keep me waiting, girl!'

'There's a problem with Mr Barkley's credit card,' she said. 'We tried getting in touch with American Express but they were very slow.'

'What about the others?'

'It all went on Mr Barkley's Gold card.'

'All of it?'

'Oh, yes. It was meant to be a temporary measure. Mr Barkley assured me personally that he would rectify the situation.'

'Who authorised that?' Bostan glared from one to the other of his receptionists. 'Who was the idiot who gave permission for this to happen?'

'Well . . . actually, sir, it was . . . you.'

'Me?' Bostan began to massage his temples. 'Check again with American Express.'

'We already did that. They say that the card was not issued by them.'

'You hear that?' Bostan turned to Makana. His eye caught that of his superior hanging on the wall. He sighed. 'Get me the manager of American Express on the line. If it was one of their cards they have to honour it.'

'They believe it to be false, a counterfeit card.'

'I want to speak to him. Get me the director on the telephone immediately,' Bostan raged. The receptionists collided with one another in their haste to reach the telephone.

'Can I have copies of these papers?' Makana interjected.

Bostan's face was livid. 'You can have whatever you want if you think you can recover our money. You find that man Barkley and you have my personal permission to wring it out of his neck.'

'I have American Express.' The receptionist held up a telephone like a trophy.

'I'll take it in my office.'

'He's upset,' Makana said as Bostan stalked away.

'I don't understand it,' fretted the woman receptionist. 'Everything seemed to be in order.'

'How was the reservation made?'

'By fax from the Grand Hyatt in Amman.'

'Did you check with them?'

'I called them myself,' the receptionist sighed. 'They have no record of a Charles Barkley staying with them.'

Chapter Twenty-one

Makana faxed all the papers through to Sami's office and then called him several times but couldn't get through. He rang off to find Dalia Habashi had been trying to call him. An icon that was new to him told him he had a message. After several failed attempts he managed to enter the correct combination of keys and suddenly found Dalia's voice speaking to him.

'I need to see you. Please call me back, I'm scared.'

Makana tried to call but was rewarded only with an engaged tone. After that he tried Sami again, still without luck. He managed to reach Rania, who told him that the faxes had come through but that Ubay was not around.

'Do you have any way of reaching him?'

'He's a bit unpredictable, our boy genius, I'm afraid. I'll let him know you called.'

'Any idea where Sami is?'

'Sorry, that's even harder to say. He went out on one of his strange errands.'

'Rania, are you and Sami okay?'

Makana heard her sigh. 'I told you we've been talking about having children. The problem is that Sami doesn't think he's ready.'

'Maybe he just needs time to get used to the idea.'

'How much time can he need?' Rania asked. 'I'm not getting any younger. Sometimes I just don't understand him. He's so negative about the future, and I know what he's thinking: what's the point of bringing children into the world when you know they will never have a chance of making something of themselves?'

'You and Sami didn't do too badly.'

'Things were different then. It's getting more difficult every year. So many people work hard to give their kids an education. They go to school, study hard for ten years and get into university, another five years maybe and then what, join the eighty per cent of graduates who are out of work? We don't have the contacts to find our children a job.'

'Things can change.'

'On good days that's what I'd like to believe too,' she said. 'On bad days, I just think that nothing is ever going to change. Look, I'm sorry to unload all of this on you. You know what he's like. As soon as he grows up and accepts that this is his life, and that there is no perfect moment to start a family, then we'll be fine.'

Rania rang off and Makana lit a cigarette. He wandered down the hotel ramp to the river's edge and stared out at the sun gleaming on the water. It was a welcome moment of tranquillity. No sooner had the thought passed through his head than the telephone in his pocket began to buzz. He reached for it with a sigh. There were advantages to not being available all the time. It was Dalia Habashi.

'I've been trying to reach you for hours. Where have you been?'

'I got your message. What's happened?' Makana asked.

'I don't know. I don't know,' she repeated the words over and over.

'Listen, Dalia, I need to speak to Na'il. Have you any idea where he is?'

'No, that's the thing. I've heard nothing. Before I was worried. Now I'm scared.'

'Scared of what?'

'I know something is wrong. I can feel it. He never disappears like this.'

'When we talked the other day, there was something you didn't tell me.'

She gave a loud sniff. 'What do you mean?'

'About Na'il and Kasabian. You knew about that, didn't you?'

'Look, he didn't kill him, if that's what you're thinking.'

'I didn't say that he did. But he was blackmailing him wasn't he?'

There was silence at the other end.

'Where are you now?'

'I'm at home. I can't go out, I daren't leave, I'm afraid,' she whimpered.

'What are you afraid of?'

'I don't know,' she moaned. 'What if he's dead?'

'Who would want to hurt him?'

'I don't know. I don't know!' She sobbed for a while and then it came. 'Those gangsters.'

'The Zafranis?'

'I warned him. I told him not to get mixed up with them. But that's the thing about Na'il, he always thinks he can find a way where nobody else can. He's like a big kid, with that motorcycle of his.' She fell silent. 'I can't bear it any longer.'

'If you're afraid then perhaps you should go away for a while.'

'I can't. I couldn't just abandon him. He needs me.'

'Just until this blows over. Na'il can take care of himself. Wherever he is, you can't help him.' Makana listened to the sound of her breathing. 'He'd want you to think about yourself, wouldn't he?'

'I suppose so.' A sob escaped her. 'I could go away, just for a bit. Now. Tonight.'

'The sooner the better.'

'I'll go to the Hilton. They're always kind to me there. I'll get a room and catch the first plane out tomorrow morning.'

'Sounds like an idea. And Dalia?'

'What is it?'

'You need to tell me everything you know.'

'Yes, yes, I will. I promise. But not now, not over the phone. At the hotel. We can talk there.' Another long pause followed. Then she gave another sniff and was gone.

The offices in Bab al-Luq were deserted when he arrived. In the far corner sat Ubay, chewing what looked like a stick of wood and turned out to be sugar cane. The big eyes blinked slowly when they lifted to find Makana standing in front of him.

'Where is everybody?'

Ubay spat out a wad of pulp into a waste bin by his side and bit off another chunk to resume chewing in that slow, deliberate manner that Makana had come to realise was characteristic of him.

'Some kind of meeting. I don't know. Politics. They're trying to start a movement or something.' He gazed around him as if he had only just noticed that everyone had gone.

'How are you getting on with what I sent you?'

He sat up. 'I ran a general search for Charles Barkley and came up with a total blank, apart from the references to basketball, of course.'

'Basketball?'

'Sure. Charles Barkley is a famous basketball player. Didn't you know?'

'How would I know something like that?'

'Everyone knows.' Ubay shrugged as if these things were obvious. 'Anyway, I started with the other names, thinking, you know, that it was probably the same story, and then I hit something.'

He talked without taking his eyes off the screen as he clicked through one window after another until he came to what he was looking for.

'What am I looking at?' Makana leaned down and squinted at the screen.

'This is Friendster.'

'Which means what exactly?' Makana asked, reaching for his cigarettes. It was going to be a long business if he was going to have to ask for an explanation of every term that came up.

'It's a networking site.' Makana just looked at him. Ubay elaborated. 'It's a space where people can hang out. You know, to meet? There are a few of them around and they seem to be catching on.'

'How does something like that work?'

The long fingers twitched as Ubay fished for words. 'It's like a room, except it's not real. I suppose it's like a noticeboard, but it's interactive.'

Why not call a room a room? 'You mean they don't actually meet, in person?'

'Not necessarily. I mean they can do, but they don't have to.' Ubay shrugged. 'It all happens in a kind of virtual dimension. You go in. You set up an account and you tell people about yourself.'

'What's the point?'

'The point?' Ubay stared blankly at Makana.

'Why would anyone do something like that, telling people about themselves?'

'I suppose because they want to meet people.'

'People they don't know?'

'Sure. People anywhere in the world. Lots of people do it. Millions, in fact.'

The concept of millions of people signing up to a room that didn't exist to meet like-minded souls made Makana wonder what he was missing.

'So what is this?'

'This is Raul Santos.' Ubay clicked the mouse and brought up the page. A stocky Latin American man in his thirties with a broad face and floppy bangs of shiny dark hair hanging over his brow. 'From Honduras originally, but on Friendster he's busy telling everyone how he became an American citizen.'

'I thought that was meant to be difficult.'

'It is, for most of us. But there are a few exceptions.' Ubay clicked his way through. 'One of them being when you join the army.' As he scrolled down the page more images of the same man appeared, this time in olive-green fatigues, his hair shaved to a bristle, proudly holding up an M16 rifle. Another showed him on a dusty track wearing a heavy pack. 'Raul signed up to the US Marines. He thanks his buddies.'

'Is that Iraq?'

'Afghanistan in 2002.'

'So, he's a soldier?'

'Well, that's the interesting thing. It seems that soon after he got his citizenship, Raul's contract ran out and he dropped out of the Marines.' Ubay brought up another page. 'He decided to make some money.' In the next image Santos had exchanged his uniform for a less regular outfit. He was posing casually with another automatic weapon balanced on his hip. Now he wore a pistol in a holster on his thigh, wraparound sunglasses and a black bandanna tied about his head.

'What's changed?'

'He became a private contractor. A soldier for hire. It's the new thing. There are thirty thousand of them in Iraq, more than all the other so-called allies combined.'

'What's this?' Makana indicated the logo on Santos's sleeve.

'The company logo. Let me zoom in.'

Magnified, it showed a jackal's head in green superimposed on a pair of crossed bones.

'Green Jackal Securities,' Makana read the lettering that capped the image.

'They're a private security firm engaged by the Pentagon for special missions.'

'In other words, mercenaries.'

'Uh huh. It got me thinking, so I started looking for the other names under the same company.' Ubay clicked the mouse with his right hand and then leaned back in his chair and chewed away at his stick of cane. 'Two more came up. Hagen and Clearwater.'

'What about the fourth one, Jansen?'

'No luck with that.' Ubay shook his head. 'After that I did some background checking on them individually. It turns out there was something on both of them. Eddie Clearwater has a criminal record. He's been to prison several times, always short stretches. He specialised in burglary and pickpocketing.'

'Any pictures?'

'Not for him. I had more luck with the other one, Randy Hagen.'

Makana found himself looking at a newspaper article. *USA Today* and a picture of a crime scene. An overweight police officer stretching a strip of yellow tape across the entrance to a shop.

'A man was killed while trying to rob a supermarket in South Dakota. It's not clear what he was after. Turns out he was on day release from a mental institution and was living on the streets. He was armed with a child's toy pistol. One of the other people in the shop shot him dead.' Ubay tapped the sheet of paper with the names on it. 'Randy Hagen. It was considered self-defence. Hagen proved in court that he felt his life was in danger and he had to react quickly. He was charged a small fine for carrying a concealed weapon.'

'Hagen became something of a local hero.' Ubay pulled up several more pictures of a smiling Hagen celebrating his victory outside what appeared to be a courthouse.

'Did you find any more pictures?'

'Not really. These are exceptions. Santos celebrating with his friends online and Hagen shooting someone.'

'And no images of a Charles Barkley in the art business?'

'I have lots of them, if you're looking for a basketball player. Other than that, no.' Makana started to get to his feet. Ubay leaned back and cocked one enormous and very worn shoe on the edge of the desk. 'I get the impression they try to avoid publicity, apart from Kane, of course.'

'Kane?'

'Zachary Kane, the founder of Green Jackal Security. He appears to be something of a strange bird.'

Makana sat back down again. 'Tell me about him.'

'Well, Green Jackal was started up about three years ago. Right after the attacks on New York and the Pentagon. Somebody spotted an opportunity. It's a small outfit. They had about thirty operatives in Afghanistan when they began, most of them ex-marines and Special Forces.'

'How did you find all this out?'

'Oh, there's no end to stories about him. Kane loves publicity.'

'What were they doing in Afghanistan?'

'They began providing protection for US and Afghani officials, and then graduated to running a detention centre in Helmand. They got the jobs nobody else wanted.'

'Tell me about Kane.'

'Well, like I said, there are lots of stories about him. It's not clear what his military history is. Some versions say he was in the Green Berets, that's the American Special Forces, but it's a claim that has been disputed. I can't find confirmation either way. In any case, he got himself involved with a television film crew in some hotel in Kabul. He told them he was in charge of a mission to capture Osama Bin Laden. They paid him a huge amount of money for permission to go along.'

'He made it up?'

'American military sources deny he was ever part of such a mission and said it was certainly not their policy to turn a manhunt for the most wanted terrorist in the world into a television show.'

'So he made a lot of money out of it.'

'Not just money. Kane became a celebrity. He appeared on television talk shows. For a time he was a hero, something like a modern-day John Wayne.'

'They never found Bin Laden?'

'No.' Ubay laughed in great hiccups, like a cartoon character. 'They drove around for a time, but never found anything.'

'What happened to Kane?'

'The army couldn't discipline him because he wasn't a soldier. They couldn't fire him because of some technical problem about who actually employed him. But they didn't like him. They didn't approve of his methods.' Ubay brought up another document. 'This is a Human Rights Watch report on the treatment of prisoners. There's a whole section devoted to Kane's outfit. They were torturing people.'

'I thought they all did that.'

'Sure, but they don't get caught. Kane was out in Helmand province, executing people in public squares. He was acting like some kind of warrior king, calling tribal leaders to vow their allegiance.'

'That must have damaged his image.'

'Not at all. When the case came up you had celebrities on Fox News defending his actions, saying he was giving the Taliban a taste of their own medicine and there should be more like him.'

'He was never charged then?'

'No. Mercenaries, or contractors to give them their proper title, fall into a grey area as far as the law is concerned. You can't charge them as civilians and they can't be disciplined as military officers.'

'In other words they are free to do as they like.'

'Pretty much.'

'So what did they do with him?'

'They moved him out of the way, transferred the whole outfit.'

'To another part of the world?'

'To Iraq. Kane's unit was given a new task, providing support for forces around Falluja.'

'And since then?'

'Nothing. It seems he learned his lesson. Kane vanished from the front pages. He was in enough trouble. He was sued for breaching all kinds of contracts, owed money to publishers and movie producers. It seems he just dropped out of sight. Just got tired of it all, I suppose.'

'Do you have a picture of him?'

'Here you go.' Ubay pointed at the computer. Makana leaned forward to look at the grainy image. 'That's Zachary Kane.'

Although somehow he had been expecting it, Makana still felt a jolt of recognition as he stared at the face of the man he knew as Charles Barkley.

Chapter Twenty-two

The early evening traffic was in full swing as Makana threaded his way across the underpass between the maze of fast-moving cars. It meant taking your life into your hands, but there was no other way. When he reached the relative sanctuary at the middle, the fading light illuminated a battlefield of potholes, twisted iron railings and broken kerbstones. The rush of a bus going by whipped at him with a blast of hot, combustible air as the driver mercilessly triggered a three-tone party horn designed to provoke cardiac failure in all but the most sturdy-hearted.

Learning that Charles Barkley the art collector was actually Zachary Kane the mercenary felt like a light going on in Makana's head. It filled out the landscape with new shapes and forms. The complexity of what lay ahead of him was growing clear. Kane had come to Cairo with his associates, other soldiers of fortune, to seek out Kadhim al-Samari. They had flown in from Amman, carrying a false credit card and at least one fake identity. Kane had registered as Charles Barkley and contacted Kasabian. He had persuaded Kasabian that he was after a price-less painting. Was that what he was really after, or was it Samari he wanted? Why not both? There was always the possibility that this was some kind of American hit squad, here in some kind of semi-official capacity.

At the Ramses Hilton, Makana asked for Dalia Habashi and they called up. He spoke to her briefly. She told him to come straight up to room 719. She was standing in the doorway waiting for him, looking the worse for wear, when he stepped out of the lift. Her clothes were crumpled as if she had been sleeping in them and her hair was a mess. A glass dangled in one hand. A half-empty bottle of vodka stood on the table next to a television set that showed American soldiers patrolling in some desolate corner of Iraq.

'What took you so long?'

'I came as fast as I could.'

Her eyes were red from crying and drink. 'You don't seem to take this very seriously. My life is in danger.' She crossed unsteadily to the table and poured more vodka over a handful of melting ice cubes. Then she sank down onto the bed with a sigh. 'I don't know. I was doing really well, and then, boom! I just couldn't deal with it any more. I couldn't stay at home for a moment longer. I booked myself on a plane and got myself this room and everything is packed. Then suddenly it hit me that I'd never see him again.'

'You don't know that for sure.'

'A woman can tell,' she insisted. Her eyeliner had run in monochrome streaks down the side of her face.

'I think you're doing the right thing,' he said. 'You should get out.'

'I feel like I'm running away.' She took a gulp of her drink.

'And still no word from Na'il?'

She shook her head wordlessly, then lay down on her side and clutched the bottle to her. 'He's dead. I can feel it. And that means I have no one to protect me.'

'Protect you from whom?'

'Who do you think?' She mumbled something to herself that he couldn't catch. 'Once they've had a taste, they just keep coming back. I should never have gone to him. Why does it always have to be about money?'

Makana realised she was talking about Qasim.

'Is that why Na'il was trying to blackmail Kasabian? To get the money to pay off Qasim?'

'The police came to ask me questions. They think he killed Kasabian. That makes no sense. He was getting money from him and he was going to get more. Why would he kill him?'

'He was seen fleeing Kasabian's house on the night of the murder. It's possible he saw something.' Makana sat down on a chair facing the bed. 'Are you sure he didn't tell you anything?'

'Why would I lie? Look at me, I've got nothing left to lose.' She rested the vodka on the bedside table to light a cigarette, ignoring the sign on the table that asked guests not to smoke.

Makana lit a Cleopatra. One more wouldn't matter. He got up to open the window, which moved twenty centimetres and then stopped. The building was sealed like a glass box for the air-conditioning. The sounds of traffic and horns far below filtered through the gap.

'The last time we talked you said Na'il was mixed up with the Zafrani brothers. Was that Ayad Zafrani?'

'I don't know. How would I know something like that?' She scowled at him, her eyes out of focus. 'You don't listen to half of what I say,' she grumbled, and reached for her vodka.

'Did Na'il ever mention an American named Charles Barkley, or Zachary Kane?'

'He mentioned a lot of names. He was always bragging about how many important people he knew and how they were all going to be his ticket to the stars. He was a dreamer.' Her glass was empty. She reached for the bottle again and slipped to the floor. Makana tried to help her up. She giggled and wrapped an arm around his neck.

'Why don't you stay here tonight and keep me safe.'

'I don't think that's a good idea.'

'Why not?' She pulled him down and kissed him.

Makana said nothing. He held her at arm's length until she slumped back with a sigh and pushed her hands through her hair.

'You're right. I know. I'm just going to pieces.' She lay back and closed her eyes. 'What does any of it matter? Tomorrow I'll go to the airport and be in another country by noon. I probably won't be back for a while.'

'What about the gallery?'

'It can take care of itself. Besides, it's not as if people are stampeding through the doors.'

In a few moments he heard her gentle snores. He got to his feet. Night was falling. He saw his reflection in the glass, a shadowy presence against the brightness of the room behind him. The woman on the bed seemed to be shrouded in a halo of light. Below him Cairo surged in constant anxiety, a seething mass of light and movement. An enigma, as ancient as the Sphinx and just as incomprehensible.

His telephone rang as he walked down the ramp from the hotel entrance.

'I'd been hoping to hear from you,' said a familiar voice.

'Mr Barkley.' Makana drew to a halt. 'I'm sorry, I've been busy.'

'Not so busy surely to make time for a client?' A hearty chuckle came down the line.

'Of course not. Where are you?'

'I'd rather not say.' There was a long pause. 'The situation has changed slightly. I don't have as much time as I thought I had.'

'I'm sorry to hear that. These things have a pace of their own.'

'I understand. I think it's better we meet in person.'

'Shall we say the Marriott like last time?'

'No . . . no, that's no longer an option. Why don't we try somewhere different? I think I really need to get out and see a bit of the town. You can't hide behind high walls all the time.'

'If you're sure.'

'I hear there's a great café inside the old bazaar, the Fish bar or something.'

'Fishawi's.'

'Yes, that's the one. Shall we say three o'clock tomorrow afternoon?'

Makana tucked his telephone back into his pocket and stood for a moment in the midst of the whirling turmoil. Cars rushed past him, lights flashing, horns screeching. The city felt as if it were about to implode.

Chapter Twenty-three

Walking past a supermarket Makana's eye caught the glitter of light on glass. It gave him an idea, and he retraced his steps. When he reached the Carlton Hotel, the man behind the desk was not the person he had met before. This one was half asleep, his face squashed out of shape by his upturned palm. He jerked awake as Makana walked in.

'What is it?' He was a large man with a loose, jowly face and red eyes that cried out only to be allowed to close once more. Makana fished in his pocket for a slip of paper and squinted at what was written there.

'Mr Frank, Room 27?'

'What about him?'

'Special delivery.' Makana held up the supermarket bag containing a bottle of Butler's gin. 'He called from his room.'

'You can leave it here.' The receptionist licked his lips.

Makana drew back. 'My life wouldn't be worth living. He's American, you know.'

'You don't have to remind me. May Allah spare us from them.'

'I'd be out of a job tomorrow. I can't afford that.'

The receptionist rubbed his bleary eyes. 'I don't think I've seen you in the shop before.'

'I'm standing in for my brother-in-law, he's having a baby.'

'Really, the short one, Abdelhadi?'

'That's the one.'

'I didn't even know he was married.'

'The world is full of mystery. Shall I go up?'

'Sure, go ahead. But the lift isn't working. You'll have to take the stairs.'

'Just my luck. What floor is it?'

'Second floor. No need to complain.' He put his head down again. Makana started off in the direction of the staircase, stopped and returned to the counter. The receptionist forced his eyes open again.

'Now what?'

'I just thought. What if he's asleep? You know, he sounded like he'd already been through one of these. You know what these Americans are like.'

'So leave it here. I told you, I'll make sure he gets it.'

'On my eyes, I swear, I can't do that.'

'What do you want me to do?' The receptionist got to his feet to hobble a couple of steps, just enough to demonstrate that he was not only bulky and moved with difficulty, but that he also had a club foot. 'I told you, the lift's not working. I can't go up there.'

'I can see that.' Makana tapped his fingers on the counter and waited. The two men looked at one another. There was no point in rushing these things. Finally, he said, 'Look, why don't you just give me the pass key? I'll go up, knock on the door. If he doesn't answer, I'll leave it on the table.'

'I can't do that.' The receptionist toyed with his keys.

'What difference does it make to you? I'll be back in no time.'

'What happens if something goes missing from the room?'

'Look, I'm just like you. I'm just trying to do my job. I want to get this over with as fast as possible and get back to the shop.'

The receptionist looked unconvinced. 'Seems like a lot of trouble. How much does a bottle like that cost anyway?'

'I'm just taking care of things, you understand? Abdelhadi wouldn't be happy if he found I'd lost his customers while he was away, would he?' Makana thought the matter over a little more. 'I'll tell you what, we'll split the difference.' He placed a ten-pound note on the counter. It wasn't much, but it was a concession of sorts. In the blink of an eye the note was replaced by a pass key.

Outside the door of Number 27 Makana listened to the sound of a voice droning on in what he took to be English. He realised that it was the television. Slipping the key into the lock, he turned it quietly and went in.

Cassidy was lying asleep on the bed still wearing his clothes, or most of them. The jacket lay in a heap on the floor, over an upturned chair. The boots had been kicked off in different directions. One stood in the hallway while the other sat on top of the television set, which was tuned to a debate between two American men and a woman who were all getting very excited about Iraq, a country they had probably never heard of until their president decided to invade it. Makana switched the volume up. Behind him, Cassidy stirred, turned over on his side and went on snoring, the almost empty bottle of Jack Daniel's still gripped in his right hand. The gun was hanging in a shoulder holster off the far bedpost. Lying on the dresser was a bag of plastic ties identical to the one Cassidy had used to secure him to the railing of the awama.

Makana slipped one of the ties around the American's left wrist and pulled it tight against the bedpost, stepping back as Cassidy began to stir. Removing the gun from the holster, he lifted the chair upright and sat down to wait. Cassidy came awake slowly, dropping the bottle, then rubbing his face and trying to move before he found one hand was restrained.

'What's going on?'

He tugged hard and the bedstead screeched in protest. Eventually he wriggled upwards and looked around him.

'I brought you some supplies.' Makana nodded at the bottle of gin on the bedside table.

'Thoughtful of you,' mumbled Cassidy. 'What is it, I'm not paying the right person downstairs?' He gave the bed a kick.

'Don't take it personally.'

'You're in my room and you're holding my gun. How is that not personal?'

Makana waved the Colt in his hand. 'This is only a gesture. I don't intend to shoot you.'

'You need to work on your bedside manner.' Cassidy tried to sit up again, found he couldn't and tugged at his bound wrist again.

'You'll hurt yourself if you go on like that.'

Cassidy closed his eyes and rubbed his face with his free hand. 'I'd like to know what I'm doing wrong here.'

'People are always suspicious of foreigners in this country.'

'Then they shouldn't invite so many damn tourists.' The malevolent look on Cassidy's face made Makana all the more glad he had taken the precaution of restraining him. 'How about a cigarette?'

'I would not object.' Makana reached into his pocket.

'No, not those things. There's a carton in the wardrobe.'

There were three cartons of American cigarettes. As he moved back Makana picked up the jacket off the floor and went through it. In the inside pocket he found a wallet that folded open to reveal an identity card and a gold shield that announced his prisoner as Detective Frank Cassidy, Los Angeles Police Department, Homicide Division. Makana opened a fresh pack of Camels and lighted himself one before throwing the packet across. The taste of the tobacco felt as rare as fine caviar. Not that he'd ever tasted caviar, but he imagined it as similarly exotic.

'You're a long way from Los Angeles. What are you doing in Cairo?'

'I thought I warned you to stay out of my business.' Cassidy lit a cigarette and dropped the lighter on the bedside table. 'Why are you here, in my room in the middle of the night?'

'That's an interesting question.' Makana flipped off the television and sat down in the chair again. 'I find myself in a . . . how do you say, a predicament?'

'You're not going to start using fancy words now, are you?'

'What I mean is that this is a difficult situation.'

'Don't come crying to me, buddy.' Cassidy gave Makana a hostile stare. 'How about untying this and we can talk like gentlemen?'

'In a moment, perhaps. I need to ask you some questions first.'

'I'm all ears.' Cassidy jerked his arm like a gorilla on a chain. Makana wondered how long it would be before the bedstead came apart.

'I saw you in the Marriott Hotel. You were looking for a man named Kane.'

'Full marks. Go to the top of the class.'

'Why are you after Kane?'

'I told you, mind your own business.'

Makana cocked the revolver. 'I wouldn't push my patience too far, Mr Cassidy.'

'I thought you said you weren't going to use that.'

'This is Cairo. Things happen. A tourist is robbed at gunpoint in his room. Nobody will make a fuss. It's the kind of thing they like to keep quiet. Bad for the trade.'

'Something tells me you're not kidding.' Cassidy relented with a heavy sigh. 'All right, Kane killed my son.'

'The boy in the picture?'

Cassidy nodded. 'Is there really gin in that bottle?'

Makana squinted at the bottle of Butler's. 'It's a local brand. I can't guarantee it.'

'I'm asking for a drink, not a guided tour. Jesus, what's wrong with you people? There's a glass somewhere around here. Try the bathroom.'

Makana placed the gun on top of the television set, then fetched the glass and poured raw gin into it. He winced as he handed it over.

'Are you sure you want to drink it like that?'

'It's my liver, or do you have an opinion on that too?'

'Just watch out with that cigarette, the whole place might go up.'

'Help yourself to one, or is that against your precious beliefs?' Makana passed on the drink but took another Camel. Cassidy sipped his drink and pulled a face. 'Ouch. That would take the paint off a Sherman tank. Just leave the bottle where I can reach it.'

'Can we get back to Kane?'

'By all means. Zachary Kane is a very dangerous man.'

'You say he killed your son.'

'How about we take turns answering questions. What is it you do for Kane?'

Getting to his feet, Makana crossed to the window and smoked his cigarette. Across the way a woman was hanging out her washing. Who does their laundry at this hour, he wondered. He turned back to the bed.

'I don't know about your jurisdiction as a police officer, but I'm pretty sure it doesn't run to carrying a concealed weapon in this town.'

'How would you know?'

'I know that you're out of your depth.' Makana pointed at the telephone. 'I could make a few calls that would turn your life upside down.'

'If you were going to do that, you'd have done it already.'

'You're in a foreign country. You don't speak the language. Have you ever seen the inside of an Egyptian prison?'

'No, thank you, and I don't intend to either. Maybe we should start talking turkey.'

'Turkey?'

'Money. How much do you want?'

'I don't want your money.'

Cassidy laughed coldly. 'Everybody in this country has a price. It's just a question of picking the right number.'

'I want you to tell me about Kane.'

Cassidy considered the question for a moment. 'All right. In Afghanistan Kane passed himself off as Special Forces, but he never made it through the programme. He's a fraud. He's more interested in making a career for himself in the media.'

'American television?'

'That's right, buddy. Americans would believe Kane was the Messiah if it came out of the mouth of one of those wax dolls that read the news. Anyway, Kane is smart. He strung them along with his story about hunting down the world's most wanted man.

Once the network figured out what was going on they had to see it through or they would all end up with egg on their faces. Don't ask me how he got away with that.' Cassidy drew on his cigarette and flicked ash onto a bedside table that already showed burn marks in the wood. 'Kane is a strange man. I ran every kind of trace on him and came up with nothing. It's like he didn't exist before he joined the army.'

'You say he killed your son. How do you know this?'

Cassidy reached under his vest to produce a medallion on a chain. 'St Christopher. Patron saint of travellers. His grandmother gave it to him when he went away.'

'And you found it, where?'

'In a palace outside of Falluja. The place had been torched. Kane and his men had gone off the map two months earlier. They survived the mess in Afghanistan and were reassigned contracts in Iraq. It's a goddamn scandal, but things were getting out of hand with in Falluja. In March of this year Iraqi insurgents killed four security contractors. They dragged them from their cars, beat them and set them on fire. They hung the bodies from a bridge.'

Makana recalled the incident. That was the first time he had heard of mercenaries operating in Iraq as private contractors.

'The point is the US military needed all the help they could get. They got Kane. My son was also in the area. His unit was ambushed. A roadside bomb, but his body was never recovered.' Cassidy stared into the bottom of his glass. 'I was never satisfied with the army's answers. They didn't know where he was. I'm not the kind of guy to settle for that. Ask any of my ex-wives. They'll all tell you. Old Frank never knows when to quit.' He drained the glass and reached for the bottle.

'So you went to Iraq to look for him.'

Cassidy nodded. 'I went to his base, Camp Volturno.'

'It sounds like a place in Italy.'

'Nice guess. Actually they named it after a river in Sicily. The Marines won an important battle there back in World War Two. Camp Volturno my ass. Before that it was a holiday resort for Saddam's sons. They called it Dreamland.' Cassidy shook his head in wonder. 'Two pictures of the same scene, and neither of them make any sense.'

'You said your son was caught in an ambush but he didn't die?'

'The whole story stank.' Cassidy squinted as he drew on his cigarette. 'The army couldn't explain what they were doing out there that night. They had been on a routine mission searching for weapons, but that was miles away. The explosion happened way out in the desert, on a back road, not much more than a track. I went out there to take a look. Nothing but the burned-out wreck of their Humvee. It looked like a set-up by local insurgents. The other soldiers in the car were killed. Their bodies were recovered, but not Virgil's.'

'Virgil? The boy in the photograph?'

'Virgil Cassidy. My son.'

'I see. Please go on.'

'Anyway, it turns out there was an incident involving a hotel owner in Falluja. Faisal Abdallah. Before the war, this hotel manager had been a driver for one of Saddam's officers. Once it was clear the war was over he did what most people did. He took off his uniform and blended in.' Cassidy straightened up in the bed as best he could. 'The way I see it, Kane had something on this guy. There were rumours the insurgents were getting support from old Baath Party members and former army officers. They picked him up, along with four others. The reason I know this is there was a complaint made against Kane's outfit by Abdallah's

216

family when he disappeared. A week later Kane goes off the grid.' Cassidy gave a grunt of annoyance. 'I don't know what the hell we thought we were doing going into that country. The say Iraq was one of the most developed countries in the Middle East before the war. Hell, I'd hate to see the rest of it.'

'The invasion, you mean.'

'Have it any way you like.' Cassidy reached for his glass.

'As I understand it there was something to do with oil reserves,' said Makana. 'Tell me how you connected Kane with your son.'

'I told you, the army's story didn't make sense. I've been a homicide detective for over twenty years and I know a cover-up when I see one. I know when I'm being lied to. Old habits. If the facts don't add up . . .'

'Then you don't have all the facts,' finished Makana.

'Something like that,' nodded Cassidy. 'Anyway, I started nosing around but nobody knew anything. It was like my son had vanished into thin air. Of course there was always the chance that he'd been killed and dumped, or kidnapped by insurgents, but those guys are after ransoms. They're not interested in soldiers, they want drivers, engineers, people connected to some big company with money. I came across the story of the hotel guy and that led me to Kane.'

Cassidy paused for a drink.

'Have you any idea how much a private contractor costs the US government? A Blackwater operative is paid six to nine times the amount a US army sergeant earns for the same services. Does that make any sense to you? Nor me. Kane had taken over one of Saddam's old palaces. Legend had it he was living like Kublai Khan out there. When I arrived I found the place had been torched. They'd been running some kind of torture chamber in the basement. It was full of bodies.' Cassidy stared into the bottom of his glass. 'One of them was my son. That's where I found the medallion. It had been burned. He went missing around the same time as Abdallah. Coincidence? I don't think so. The way I figure it, my son stumbled onto something and Kane took care of him.'

'You said this man Abdallah, the hotel manager, he worked for one of Saddam's officers before the war. Do you know the name of this officer?'

'No.' Cassidy shook his head.

'And he was never found. You said he disappeared.'

'That's right. His family were convinced he was murdered, but the body was never recovered. It's not unusual,' Cassidy shrugged. 'Bodies disappear all the time over there. He might have been one of those poor bastards I found in the basement.'

'A man named Abdallah was staying at the Marriott with Kane and his men.'

'Is that so?' Cassidy struggled to sit up and push his hair back from his face. 'How many men does he have with him?'

'Five. Four Americans and the Iraqi.'

'I only saw a couple of them. They were careful not to be seen together. Wait a minute, you said *was* staying. Past tense. You mean they're no longer there?'

'Apparently not. Maybe you scared them off. How did you know Kane was in Cairo?'

'Old-fashioned police work. I asked around and picked up his trail.' Cassidy reached for a cigarette. 'He drove out of Iraq and across the Jordanian border to Amman. I hired a car and did the same. I was taking a chance, but it panned out. He was staying in some dump downtown. I found out he reserved a room at the Cairo Marriott in the name of Charles Barkley. So here I am.'

'You did pretty well for a man who doesn't know the region.'

'People are pretty much the same wherever you go. You give them the right incentive and they'll tell you what you want to know. I think that makes it your turn to talk.' Makana took a deep breath and got to his feet again. His back felt stiff and the room was stuffy and airless. He fiddled with the window until it finally swung open, letting in the fetid night air. He wasn't sure which was worse.

'Two weeks ago, Kane approached Aram Kasabian, a local art dealer. He claimed to be an art collector from New York named Charles Barkley, said that he'd come across rumours that pointed to a very valuable painting being on the market here in Cairo. This particular painting has not been seen since the Nazis were in power. According to Barkley it was in the hands of a man named Kadhim al-Samari, a former colonel in Saddam's army.'

'How would an Iraqi colonel get hold of a painting like that?'

'Samari was in the Republican Guards when they invaded Kuwait in 1990. It's possible this painting was in one of the private collections they looted and drove back to Baghdad with them when they retreated.'

'Zachary Kane wouldn't know a work of art if it was served to him in a cocktail bar with a paper umbrella in it.'

Makana didn't try to pursue the logic of this argument. 'Three days ago Aram Kasabian was tortured and murdered using a method favoured by Samari. He cut him to shreds.'

'Charming.'

'Samari is a specialist in torture. He's wanted for war crimes. There's a reward on his head.'

'And you think he killed Kasabian?'

'That would make no sense. Kasabian was working with him,

selling his artworks and making him a fortune. There's no reason he would torture him.' Makana shook another Camel out of the packet and lit it. 'Kasabian hired me to keep Samari happy. He wanted to put Barkley, or Kane rather, off the scent, make him think they weren't in touch. Samari is a very cautious man.'

'Wait a second.' Cassidy frowned. 'The way you tell it makes Kane the most likely suspect.'

'I agree.'

Cassidy scratched his chin. 'Kane is an impulsive psychopath. If he thought Kasabian was trying to take him for a ride he would turn on him in a heartbeat.'

'If he felt Kasabian was holding back he might torture him to find out where Samari was,' said Makana. 'The problem being that Kasabian couldn't tell him because he didn't know.'

'Which is why he died.'

The question remained as to how Kane could have known that Kasabian was deceiving him.

'Why does Kane want Samari so bad?' Cassidy asked.

'There is a reward on his head. Three million dollars.'

Cassidy clicked his tongue. 'Three million dollars is nothing to someone like Kane. You split that between him and five others and you come up with peanuts and change. No, he's after something else, and whatever it is, it has to be big. My guess would be this artwork you're talking about. There's more than one painting, right?'

'According to Kasabian, if there are more it would be one of the finds of the century.'

'That sounds more like it.' Cassidy reached for the bottle of gin again and then decided he'd had enough. He set the bottle down on the bedside table and settled back on the bed. 'Still, it's a big move. If he goes into the stolen art business what happens to his military career?'

'Maybe he's thinking of retiring.' Makana snapped open the revolver and emptied the bullets into his pocket. 'One last question. When you find Kane, what are you planning to do?'

'I'd like to arrest him and take him back to the States to stand trial for Virgil's murder, but I don't think there's much chance of him coming quietly, do you?'

Makana tossed the Colt down onto the bed and headed for the door. 'Take my advice, Mr Cassidy, go home. There's nothing for you here.'

'Hold it just a minute. You are going to untie me before you go, right?' Cassidy jerked the plastic tie and the bed shook. 'Hey, you can't leave me like this!'

'Call room service.'

Chapter Twenty-four

Down the street Makana had to wake up the driver of a taxi who was sound asleep under a sheet of yesterday's newsprint. He was a young man with several missing front teeth and a wayward look about him that said he was as honest as they come. The radio played old love songs that floated out of the open windows and lost themselves in the night air. When they reached Maadi he asked him to wait. Sindbad had nothing to report. The front seat of the car looked like the aftermath of a cockfight, with bones and grease-covered paper strewn about. It seemed that Sindbad had been staving off boredom by eating. Makana gave him some money and told him to take the night off.

'Take the taxi. Go home and get some rest.'

'Whatever you wish, *ya basha*. I wouldn't complain but my wife tells me she should have married the baker, as she sees more of him than she does of me. You know how it is.'

There was a time when Makana would have nodded understandingly and dismissed the subject. Now he found himself wondering what he actually knew about domestic life. It seemed so long ago that he had lived in a family, with people around him that he loved and who loved him in return. Now he was surrounded by people who struggled almost every day to maintain relationships. First Sami and Rania, now Sindbad.

Once he was alone, Makana opened all the windows to get rid of the smell of fried food before settling himself behind the wheel and lighting a cigarette. Sindbad had chosen the spot well. Without moving his head he could observe the entrance to the villa. The light over the gate and the stone lions with wings on either side were all the advertising there was. If you didn't know it was here you wouldn't stumble upon it. The windows on the upper floors were shuttered and the glass painted over. Nobody could see what went on behind them.

Makana smoked another three cigarettes as cars came by, dropping off passengers in twos or threes. Some came alone. The night dragged on. The party upstairs showed no signs of abating. Cars arrived to carry people away. Then, Makana saw the headlights of a car turning into the quiet street ahead of him. It stopped at the far end. Its headlights raked overhead and Makana peeped up to see a large BMW with dark glass. In itself this wasn't so unusual. Nowadays even lowly NGO consultants drove SUVs with smoked glass in the hope that potential terrorists and assassins would be put off by not knowing whether the vehicle's occupants were Westerners or not. What did it tell you about a country where invisibility was a sign of privilege? Everyone wanted to disappear.

Without warning the SUV began reversing out of the street and round the corner. Makana started the engine and was just pulling out to follow the first car when another identical SUV cut in front of him from behind, blocking his escape.

Two men jumped out, from front and rear. They came round to Makana's door and pulled it open. He found himself looking into the barrel of an automatic pistol.

'Out!'

Raising his hands to show they were empty, Makana stepped out of the car. Hands pressed him to the side of the Thunderbird and searched him carefully. The bullets from Cassidy's gun were weighted up and tossed aside. When they were satisfied they turned him round and held him as the second BMW slid up. The rear window slid down smoothly. The gun pressed hard into his spine urging him forwards.

'No false moves,' whispered the bodyguard.

Inside the rear of the second car sat a man wearing a dark suit. His grey hair was cut short. He wore dark glasses even in the night, but perhaps they performed another function. A jagged scar ran across the front of his face from above his left eye and down to his right cheek. The glasses covered up some of the damage. He leaned forward to examine Makana from top to toe. When he spoke his voice was low.

'Do you know who I am?'

'Kadhim al-Samari.'

'Very good. Now tell me, why are you so interested in me?'

'Kasabian hired me to find you.'

'Kasabian is dead.'

'That doesn't mean I'm not supposed to finish what he paid me for.'

'A loyal employee.' Al-Samari removed his glasses. His eyes were hidden in shadow, but Makana could feel them scrutinising him. 'Why was Kasabian killed?'

'I thought you might be able to help me with that.'

'You think perhaps I had something to do with it?'

'A man calling himself Charles Barkley came here looking for you. Kasabian hired me to find you, or rather to prove to this American that you are not here.'

'You know who this man is, the one calling himself Barkley?'

'An American mercenary by the name of Zachary Kane.'

Samari's lips drew into a thin smile. 'A bounty hunter.'

'I believe he's the one who tortured Kasabian.'

'Why?'

'He wanted Kasabian to lead him to you.'

'Why should he be after me?'

'I can think of a million reasons. Several million in fact.'

'The price on my head?' There was something slightly off about the Iraqi. He had clearly been badly wounded at some stage. It looked as if the bones of his face had been broken and then reset themselves slightly out of shape, so that the two halves didn't quite match up.

'Either that, or a fortune in stolen artwork, beginning with the German Expressionists.'

'You've done your work well.' Samari smiled. 'Would you say that he was a dangerous man?'

'Yes, I think it's safe to say so.'

'And would you say that he intends to do me harm?'

'I can't say, but from what I've seen I would think that was a possibility.' Makana kept his eyes fixed on the man inside the car.

'You don't need to be afraid of me.' When Samari smiled it had a strange effect on his features. 'I'm not going to hurt you.'

'What makes you think I'm afraid?'

'I know your story. Kasabian told me who he was hiring for the job. I know everything there is to know about you.'

'Not everything.'

'Don't be too sure. I have my sources.' He leaned forward and lowered his voice. 'It never leaves you, ever,' he whispered. Makana breathed in. The street was quiet and deserted, so silent that you could hear the light wind shifting the leaves of the tall neem trees. Then Samari signalled and the guard behind Makana stepped back a pace. 'Don't bother looking for me here again, I shall not return.' Samari looked at Makana again. 'But I wish to make a proposition.'

'I don't work for people like you.'

'You already are working for me, in a manner of speaking. Why don't you listen to what I have to say?' Samari rested one ringed hand on the window frame. 'I will pay you ten times what Kasabian paid you.'

'That's a lot of money. What do I have to do?'

'Lead me to Kane. That's all. I will take care of the rest.'

'I don't see why you need me. You have contacts here, in the government, in the army. They can get State Security involved.'

'You forget who you are talking to,' Samari said softly. There was no trace of the smile this time. 'Not many people turn me down. Will you do it?'

'Do I have a choice?'

'A wise decision.' The smoked glass slid smoothly back into place. The goon holding the gun pushed him aside and jumped into the front seat. Both SUVs sped off.

Chapter Twenty-five

Back in the Thunderbird Makana sat and smoked, considering his situation. He appeared to be caught between two very dangerous men. Kane and Samari had already killed and would no doubt kill again. He was wondering how he was going to extricate himself from this mess when the front gate of the house across the street opened and a slight figure appeared. He recognised her at once. Bilquis was dressed in such a casual fashion that he might have mistaken her for one of the domestic staff, but somehow he knew it was her. Her head was covered and she wore a long skirt and coat. The clock on the dashboard said it was almost midnight. Maybe it was the end of her work shift. It was a weekday night and maybe things were a bit slow. Or perhaps she had been waiting for someone; a certain special customer who had just called to cancel.

Makana stayed low in his seat. He didn't start the engine until she had turned the corner, then he pulled out. The Thunderbird rumbled slowly along the street. He reached the corner in time to see her climbing into a taxi cab. Swinging the wheel, he followed at a distance. The traffic grew heavier as they approached the centre of town. Despite the hour, people were busy, going from one social engagement to another, or in most cases, just cruising around looking for something interesting.

They swept by the bronze lions that stood guard over the Qasr al-Nil Bridge and crossed to Dokki. The taxi driver seemed to prefer the backstreets and he cut left and right until they came out on Sharia Sudan, almost by the railway station, where Bilquis got out and crossed the street. Makana parked the car a little way off and hoped it would be still be there when he got back. He continued on foot. Oil lamps hissed around stalls where *taamiya* was frying in thick brown oil, the bean rissoles floating in a furious golden froth. She walked fast, with her head down, ignoring the hawkers and the all-night purveyors of snacks, boys selling boxes of perfumed tissues, plastic roses, flashlights, lanterns that played the national anthem, alarm clocks shaped like mosques that woke you with the sound of the azan. She climbed the stairs to the footbridge. The moan of a horn announcing a passing train afforded Makana a brief flash of the side of her face caught in the headlight beam from below her, and then she was down the other side and slipping through the crowd.

Considering the time of night it was remarkably lively in al-Dakrur. Crowds milled around as if the concept of sleep was unknown to them. Three-wheeled rickshaws churned up the dust. Minibuses sounded carnival tattoos, festive lights spinning. Where they were all going was a mystery, as were the reasons for their haste. Following Bilquis was now simply a question of keeping her in sight. There was so much distraction it would be almost impossible for her to see he was behind her.

She cut down a side street, less an alley than a gully slashed through the rough brickwork. The light from the main road dwindled with each passing step. Makana felt the uneven ground beneath him rather than saw it. He stumbled along through a flurry of smells – rotting vegetables, coal smouldering in a brazier, stagnant water. Then, unexpectedly, the inviting warmth of a bakery. A group of men gathered in the shadows around the orange hemisphere of the oven where a sinewy man toiled, sweat glistening on his neck as he shuffled blackened trays containing rows of soft domes of pliant dough, and pulled out golden loaves.

Makana hurried on. At the next corner he almost lost her, catching just a glimpse of her coat as she disappeared through a doorway. The night was cool and still. He stepped back to watch the windows, waiting for a light to come on. He was leaning back, looking upwards, when somebody shoved him in the back. Hard. He stumbled forward to recover his balance before turning.

'What do you think you're doing?'

The young men from the bakery. Apparently, watching dough rise wasn't enough excitement for them tonight. They moved around him to form a loose circle.

'We don't take kindly to people who spy on our womenfolk.'

'I wasn't spying.' It wasn't much of an argument. 'I'm a friend. I just wanted to make sure she got home all right.' As he spoke a light came on above them. The third floor. A rickety window. The glow illuminated his face. Makana beamed. The picture of innocence. 'Looks like that's my work done.' He turned to walk away but they blocked his path. One of them leaned in.

'We look after our own around here. You should remember that.'

Makana studied the little group, trying to pick out the leader. In this case a plump, bow-legged man whose trousers were falling down. Challenge the leader. If he backs down the others will follow suit. If he was going to have to fight his way out then this was the one he would have to hit first. He stepped towards him.

'You should be proud of yourself, taking care of women like that. I feel safer just knowing you're around.'

Makana pulled out his cigarettes and placed one in his mouth. At the same time the leader flashed a smile. There was a look of delight on the flabby face, as though anticipating the fun he was going to have. Makana moved to step past but one of the others blocked his path. Behind him he heard the snick of a switchblade opening.

'You seem to be in a hurry to leave.'

Makana turned back to the leader. Now that he looked more closely he realised that they were all a lot younger than he had at first thought. Still in their teens. Where were the men, the fathers, older brothers? In prison, gone abroad or to the other end of the country in search of work? Leaving these youngsters to roam the neighbourhood, to run it as they saw fit, their own little kingdom.

'You have a better idea?'

'Yes, we're going to check your story.' The big one lumbered forward. 'And if you're lying . . .'

Despite the dull eyes and clumsy gait there was something commanding about his presence. It was clear that he did this all the time. His reputation was founded on swaggering about these streets dealing with troublemakers. For the moment it seemed to make sense to go along with them. Makana followed him with the two others bringing up the rear. They entered the building and climbed a dusty, uneven staircase. Something brushed against Makana's leg. A cat, he told himself, but then again maybe not. On the third floor the big one knocked. After a time footsteps could be heard approaching.

'Who is it?'

'It's Adly from downstairs. I have to ask you to open the door if you don't mind.'

There was a long process of bolts being pulled and locks being turned before the door finally swung to. Bilquis stood there, her head covered by a loose shawl. Underneath it Makana could see that she had let her hair down. Adly signalled for Makana to come forward.

'This man was following you. He claims he is a friend.'

For a long moment, she stared at Makana, before finally nodding her assent. The boys muttered their apologies and disappeared back down to the street to look for more suspects. As their footsteps clattered away, Bilquis looked at him in silence. Then she stood to one side.

'You'd better come in.'

The flat was small. A couple of steps in from the front door brought you to the middle of the living area. A threadbare sofa and a low table stood on a cracked linoleum floor. Against the wall at the back was another table. This one was covered with newspaper on which a pale green plastic bowl was surrounded by potato peelings and a knife. To the left a curtain of coloured beads led into what looked like a kitchen. Another door to the right looked like a bedroom and a dripping sound from a third door promised a bathroom. The paint on the walls was stained in places where a leaky pipe had left its trace. Makana saw cracks in everything. A broken windowpane patched up with tape so old it looked petrified.

Strangely enough, now that they were alone there seemed to be nothing to say. They circled around one another awkwardly. Bilquis retreated to her heap of potato skins and began wrapping them in newspaper as if they were precious relics. It wasn't clear what she was going to do with them once she had finished, and at some point the absurdity of the task seemed to overwhelm her, so that she sank down into a chair and covered her eyes with a hand.

'You have no right to follow me.'

'It's what I do,' he said. 'I follow people.'

'That's not a particularly honourable way of making a living.'

'No, I suppose it isn't.'

She made no attempt to reply. Her surroundings said more clearly than words ever could that everyone did what they had to do to get by. She fished around on the table and came up with a packet of cigarettes and a lighter. Lighting one, she inhaled deeply. No sign of the ebony holder she had used in the club. The scarf slipped off her head and fell around her shoulders.

'I lived in a place much like this, years ago. When I first arrived in this city.'

'You're welcome to have it back.' She blew smoke into the air.

'It belonged to a friend of a friend.' Makana hadn't thought about that time in years. 'There was a cat that used to climb through the window into the kitchen and help itself to anything it could find.' He peered through the doorway into the kitchen, which smelt faintly of gas and burnt oil, as if perhaps he might find the same cat staring back at him. 'She was smart enough to open cupboards, even the high up ones. I always wondered how she did that.'

'Why did you come here?'

It was a reasonable question, and one to which Makana had no answer, reasonable or otherwise. His silent admission seemed to satisfy her.

'I was curious.'

'To see how I lived?' She passed a hand around the room. 'Now you've seen it.'

'Yes, now I've seen it.' He examined the picture of the Kaaba on one wall and tried to straighten it. As soon as he took his hand away it slipped down again on one side.

'They let you leave early tonight.'

'I was expecting a client who didn't show.'

'Your special visitor? The one from the other day?'

'It often happens. People make appointments, other things come up.'

'Of course.'

She inhaled again. 'Why did you really come here?' She got to her feet as Makana reached the bedroom and peered inside. A small boy was sleeping in the middle of the narrow bed. Reaching past him she drew the door gently closed. This was what she'd meant that night in the club when she said she was no longer alone.

'My son is sleeping,' she said.

'How old is he?'

'Hadi is five.' She nodded to herself. 'He's all I have.'

'His father?'

She stepped away and turned. She was standing under the light in the middle of the room. She looked him firmly in the eyes.

'I don't know which one of them he was.' She held his gaze.

'A security officer.'

'There were five that I can recall. After that I passed out.'

'You were active politically?'

'Not at first.' She laughed bitterly. 'I knew nothing about politics. My father was a small-time merchant in the Souk al-Araby. He sold sesame seeds and oil. I was the first person in the family to get into university. I was going to be a doctor. I think I would have made a good doctor.'

She sat down again, stubbing out her cigarette, grinding it into the heap of skins. An acrid smell filled the room. In the watery light her face seemed to age, as if the telling of her story reminded her of what she carried within her.

'I went on a demonstration. That was all. It was supposed to be fun. Everyone was excited. We thought we could change the world. It wasn't politics, it was . . . a belief in ourselves, in the future of our country. Our future. Then the police came for us. They beat us, boys and girls, it didn't matter. They treated us worse than you would treat an animal.' Her eyes lifted to meet his. 'I was so badly bruised I couldn't stand up for three days. I started to get involved, organising meetings. Setting up more demonstrations, distributing leaflets, painting banners. I suppose you would call that politics. To me it was common sense. We had to stop these people. Someone inside the group must have betrayed us. They picked us up one night in a faculty building.' She reached for another cigarette. Over the flame from the lighter she shot him a cold look. 'The first time I set eyes on you, that's what you reminded me of, one of those bastards.'

'I was one of them, once. A police officer, I mean.'

'Is that why you're here?'

'Things were different back then.'

'Now you just follow people.'

'Yes.'

'Interrogation is a fancy word for what they did. They weren't interested in information. I didn't know anything of value anyway. I was just a student who had decided enough was enough. It was intimidation. They wanted to scare us into stopping. Well, they did a good job of it, that much I can say.' She silent. A long trail of ash smouldered at the end of her forgotten cigarette.

'They took you to one of the ghost houses?'

She nodded. 'An ordinary house in a nice urban neighbour-hood. The garden had been converted into sheds. There's no other word to describe it.'

'I was held in a similar place.'

She stared at him. 'Why did you really come here tonight?'

'I thought I could help.'

'What?' She laughed drily. 'You wanted to just turn up and save me from all of this? Did you believe that you were the only thing standing between me and freedom? You have no idea about me, about my life, about what I have been through. You can't save me from something you've never seen.' She broke off and covered her eyes with a hand. A choked-off sob escaped her. 'Look around you, this is it, the story's end. There's nothing be-yond this.'

'There's your son,' he said quietly.

'You think it's that easy to go back?' she sniffed, shaking her head from side to side. 'I can never go back. It's better my family thinks I am dead.'

'Is that why you came here?' Bilquis said nothing. She reached for another cigarette. Her hair had come loose from the ribbon that held it at the nape of her neck. 'When you found out you were pregnant?'

Her hand trembled as she held the flame up. 'I knew that no matter how far I went, I would still feel their eyes on me, their filthy hands. But there is no way back. Not now . . .' A long sigh escaped her. 'And now, he's what I live for.' She took a long drag and looked up. 'I don't want him to know what I do. He's still young but soon he will start to ask questions.'

Makana looked around the room. The cracks in the walls, the flaking paint. The sound of voices raised in the next room.

'How did you get involved with the Zafrani brothers?'

'They own a lot of property. I had no way of paying the rent and one day someone came to make me an offer. One thing led to another. It's not so bad. I'm an investment. They look after me for now, but one day I will be no good to them any longer. What do you want from me?'

'Your special customer. He's an Iraqi named Kadhim al-Samari.'

'He's the one you're looking for?'

'You know he's a dangerous man.'

'All men are dangerous in their own way.'

'There's a reward on his head.'

'That's why you're after him? It must be a lot of money.'

'What makes you say that?'

'There aren't many like him.' Bilquis examined the tip of her cigarette.

'He's worth a lot, but he's very dangerous.'

'What if I help you?'

'Why would you help me?'

'A reward like that . . . It could change someone's life.' She flicked ash onto the heap of potato skins.

'You need to think about your son. What will he do if something happens to you?'

'I am thinking about him. Do you think he will thank me for not acting when this opportunity was in front of me? This could be my ticket out of here.'

She lit another cigarette and stared at the wall. 'If I don't do this I will think about it for the rest of my life. Every time I can't afford something. Every time there's a rat on the stairs. Every winter when we are freezing, and every summer when we can't sleep for the heat. Every time he asks me for something I can't

236

give him.' She turned her head to look at Makana. 'Let me help you. We can split the money.'

'I'm not interested in the money.' Makana scratched a flake of paint on the door frame. 'If something happened to you . . .'

'So what? I'm not your responsibility. If I decide to do this it's for me.'

From where he was standing Makana could look out of the window and across to the other side of the street. Two women were chatting as they hung out their laundry. The streets around here were so narrow you could reach across and borrow a clothes peg if you needed to. Somewhere a couple was arguing. It sounded real, but then again it might have been coming from a television set.

'How often does he come to visit you?'

'Once a week, sometimes twice.'

'Does he always call ahead?'

'No calls. We agree a day and that's it. He's always on time.'

'Do you know where he stays? I mean, does he ever mention a place in Cairo?'

She thought for a minute. 'No. He comes further than that. I don't know where, but there is dust on his clothes and in his hair from the road. Not city dust. He's a very neat man. Immaculate.'

'You mean he might have come a long distance?'

'The sea. He smells of the sea.' She sniffed and rubbed a hand across her nose. 'He carries a knife. A long one, which he keeps here, strapped to his arm.' She indicated her left forearm – the sort of detail that you might learn from seeing a man undressing. 'He travels everywhere with bodyguards. Two men are with him all the time. They check the room before he comes in. They wait outside the door while he's with me. Two more wait in the car.'

'You need to think about this very carefully.'

'Look around you. Do you really think I have any choice?'

Makana turned to leave and again stopped. 'About the other night,' he said, not sure why he felt the need to explain. 'It's not that I don't find you attractive.'

She met his gaze evenly. 'It's because of what I do. You don't have to explain.'

'No,' he said. 'It's not that. It's that you remind me too much of what I've lost.'

She stared at him for a moment. A fleeting expression crossed her face. He wasn't sure what he read there – the shadow of a former self perhaps. For a brief moment he imagined he saw her as she might have been six years ago, before her fate took an unexpected turn. Then it was gone and the flat, coldness of her eyes came up to meet his.

'Then perhaps you should start thinking of me as who I am rather than who you would like me to be,' she said, and closed the door gently in his face.

Chapter Twenty-six

Makana opened his eyes to find the sun high in the sky. The river in the early morning always seemed like something of a small miracle. A cool breeze ruffled the water.

Although he had slept it felt as if he'd spent most of the night thinking. The grizzled face of Mek Nimr, his old sergeant, had risen out of the shadows to haunt him once more – a small man who had transformed himself into a monster. Makana blamed himself for never having seen it coming, until it was too late. Mek Nimr had spent years quietly building up a grudge towards the world, cultivating his own envy of those in society who had been more fortunate than himself, including Makana. Mek Nimr had no loyalties, no moral code. All the years he had worked alongside him, Makana had never fully understood him, which made the betrayal, when it came, all the more shocking. But it was the vehemence of it that had surprised him the most. Mek Nimr changed according to the way the wind was blowing. If they said be a pious man of God he could become that at a click of his fingers. It made no difference to how he behaved. What he craved was power and money, anything else was just a means to that end.

239

Makana felt the familiar twinge of guilt. At having got out of there, leaving people like Mek Nimr in charge. What else could he have done? Perhaps the world would have been a better place if he had thrown himself on the pyre and sacrificed his own life. Who knew?

When Bilquis told him her story he had understood what she was talking about. He knew the world she had escaped from. He had seen the inside of those torture chambers. And he knew the man whose narrow eyes would have been on her while she was being abused. Mek Nimr. He was sure of it. It was impossible for Mek Nimr to have engineered their meeting – even he was incapable of that – still, irrational though it was, Makana couldn't help feeling there was some kind of message in all of this, a message meant for him alone to grasp.

Aziza's voice calling from down below brought him back to the present.

'*Ya bash muhandis.* Wake up, there are men here to see you.'

'Good morning,' he said, yawning. Looking past her, he was surprised to recognise the two somewhat overweight men standing at the top of the embankment looking down. He even remembered their names. Didi and Bobo. They wore cheap imitation leather jackets and had acquired sunglasses somewhere along the way. They stood with their hands clasped in front of them and their legs apart like men who had watched too many gangster films. Neither of them spoke, but it was clear why they had come: their master had summoned him again.

Makana washed and dressed and made his way up the path to meet them. The man behind the wheel of the Toyota Land Cruiser was wearing the same type of sunglasses. Someone must have stumbled over a lorryload of the things. Makana got into the back as indicated. They drove fast. Neither man spoke.

When Makana asked where they were going, the one sitting next to him just grunted and said nothing. He had assumed they would be returning to Zafrani's riverboat and so was surprised to find the car heading in the opposite direction. Makana looked out of the window and watched the city flying by. The driver applied his customary skills, intimidating other road users and racing up behind anyone who got in his way, flashing his lights and leaning on the horn until they shuffled aside. It was effective enough and they made short work of the traffic and were soon skirting around the hills east of the city.

Ten minutes of fast driving through barren brown landscape brought them to a series of compounds set behind high walls and wire fences. Giant billboards announced them as Greeneland, Homeland Estates, Regal View and finally, Isis Greens Resort No. 1. They skirted the perimeter and Makana spotted a piece of faded cardboard blown by the wind up against the fence. On it were the words 'Where is Al-Baghdadi?' and Makana recalled the woman sitting on the pavement downtown. Then the car slowed and they spun through an open gateway.

Construction was still under way. Clouds of fine dust in the distance testified to work in progress. An unsurfaced path that might one day become a road curved around the outside of a row of unfinished houses. The style suggested some kind of meeting of a Spanish hacienda topped with icons from the ancient world – the architectural equivalent of a car crash. Statues of the falcon god Horus were set into niches in the walls, while figures of Isis lay around on pink marble pedestals.

The driver took a fork away from the main track that led over a hump to reveal an almost surreal explosion of green. Isis Greens, as in golf greens. Clearly a priority in a country unable to produce enough food to feed its population. What self-respecting Egyptian would purchase a home in the desert if it wasn't equipped with a golf course? He was gazing upon a gaudy miracle, a promised land for the modern age. Beyond the undulating green veldt the earth resumed its usual dull brown hue, broken and without a hope.

As they slowed to a halt, Makana could make out a man standing on a ridge swinging a club: the large, now familiar, figure of Ayad Zafrani killing time. Didi and Bobo followed him over. The grass was damp and springy underfoot, like a lush carpet. Zafrani stood and waited for him, king of all he surveyed.

'Ever try your hand at this game?'

It wasn't the kind of question that demanded a serious answer, but then Ayad Zafrani wasn't interested in opinions. All he needed was an audience.

'It relaxes the soul.' Zafrani spread his broad chest and sucked air into his lungs. He was beaming like a boy with a new toy. 'Out here I can breathe. It's amazing, isn't it? Five minutes from the city and we are in another world.'

'They'll be storming the gates to get in.'

'Oh, it's going to be very exclusive.' Zafrani raised a gloved hand. He was all decked out for the occasion. A pink shirt and chequered trousers with a matching cap. It was a little disconcerting, watching a man struggle to transform himself. 'Only a select few will be allowed in.'

Makana allowed himself a moment to survey the estate behind them. 'Are there really that many wealthy people in this country?'

'You'd be surprised. Land is the greatest investment of all. It's where the real wealth of Egypt lies, in the earth. Construction, that's what it's all about.'

'Why have you brought me here?'

'I thought you'd like a little fresh air, some exercise.'

'Didn't this use to be government land?'

Zafrani waggled his hand. 'You've been investigating. I wouldn't have expected less.' He indicated the way down the grassy incline. 'If you were to take an interest in the business side of things I might be worried, but I know these matters hold no interest for you, which is why we make such good partners.'

'Partners?'

'Certainly. After all, we're doing what partners do, are we not? We help one another in ways that can be mutually beneficial.'

Ahead of them was the skeleton of an unfinished clubhouse. Concrete walls had been erected on the sides and back. There was a roof also, but the front appeared to be open.

'When it's finished, there will be windows all the way up to the sky. When you sit down to eat it will feel like you're flying over the course. We're bringing in a chef from Italy. One of the best.' Zafrani chuckled to himself. The golf club swung loosely in his hand. They stood for a moment and contemplated the building. 'I'll let you into a secret. I have a dream that one day presidents and heads of state will be seated in there, discussing great plans, signing treaties that will change the world.'

'Everyone's entitled to dream,' said Makana. And perhaps it wasn't such an unlikely prospect. The Zafrani brothers had their sights set on increasing their political influence. 'And I suppose it helps to have business partners like Qasim to help turn a plot of land designated for an eye hospital into a golf course.'

'It all depends on how you look at things.' Zafrani pressed a hand to his chest, the picture of honesty. 'I myself don't believe a clinic would ever have been built here. It's all about keeping the wheels turning.' He circled a finger in the air to illustrate his theory. 'Someone wins a contract to build a hospital but then decides that it's too much of an expense anyway, so they sit on the land until someone else comes along to take it off their hands.'

'And everyone makes a profit.'

'Naturally,' Zafrani smiled.

'I expected to see you at the memorial service for Kasabian.'

'Not my thing, funerals.' He pulled a face. 'I'm a very private man, as you know. I knew there would be a lot of people there. The press. It's not good for me to be too much of a presence.'

'Sure, that must be a worry.'

Zafrani wasn't listening. He stepped up onto the ground floor of the clubhouse. A chill wind blew through the open frame of the unfinished shell. He pointed out the details as they would materialise. A bar here, a television screen there, showing live golf from around the world, naturally. It was a marvel to Makana that there were people who had the time for such pursuits. Wasn't there a Roman emperor who played his fiddle while the city burned around him?

On the far side of the open space, Zafrani gestured for him to go through a doorway. A staircase led down into the basement. There wasn't much light and Makana edged his way down, one hand on the wall, acutely aware that Didi and Bobo were a few paces behind him. He stepped into what Zafrani explained would eventually become the kitchens. The latest technology. All the gadgets needed to produce world-class cuisine. It was hard to see. In the faint glimmer of light that filtered through a row of narrow slits high up in the outside wall, Makana could make out something moving at the far end.

'Why *have* you brought me here?'

'Call it an invitation to the truth.' Zafrani was still swinging the club as if it were a walking cane. 'You see, I'm not sure how involved you are in all that's going on, and I need to know how much I can trust you.'

'What is it you're worried about?'

'What I'm worried about?' Zafrani gave a meaty laugh. 'You're the one who should be worried, and yet you ask me. I like that. It shows character.' He tightened the straps on his gloves and grasped the golf club with both hands. He took several steps into the gloom. 'Now, this one understands, or at least he is beginning to.' There was a whistling sound as the club flew through the air and a thud as it struck something heavy and soft, like a human body. Makana glanced back at Didi and Bobo and was relieved to see they hadn't moved. He stepped forward.

Hanging from some kind of hook in the ceiling was a man. His torso was naked and covered in blood. He spun lightly in a circle, revealing long weals and bruising on his back and sides. Makana could not see his face clearly. Zafrani grasped him by the hair and lifted.

'Remember this one?' It took a few moments for Makana to recognise Na'il. 'He doesn't look like much, but take my word, he's a slippery one. Selling drugs where he shouldn't be selling, and telling stories to the police. Now, if there is one thing I cannot abide, it is dishonesty. A man you cannot trust.'

A gangster with principles, thought Makana. If a moment ago he had been wondering where this was all leading, now he had his answer, and it wasn't one he liked. How long had Na'il been here? What had Ayad Zafrani done to him in that time? By the smell and the state of his clothes, Na'il had been tied up here for several days. He wondered if Dalia Habashi had managed to get out of the country. He sincerely hoped she had.

'You brought me here to see this?'

'I want you to realise how seriously I take my work.'

245

'Believe me, I don't need any more convincing.'

Zafrani nodded. 'You understand, I'm a civilised man. I'm trying to do this in the most civilised way I can think of.'

Makana refrained from comment. He lit a cigarette.

'You're mixed up in something,' Zafrani went on. 'I'm not sure you know how big it is.'

'Why don't you tell me?'

'Big, small, what's the difference? It's all about cooperation. Nothing gets done in this country without that.' Zafrani's face twisted into something resembling a smile gone wrong as he stepped back and swung the club again. This time the sound was different, sickening, as if something inside the body had snapped. A rib or two. It sounded like hitting a sack filled with fruit.

'He's not going to tell you anything he hasn't already told you.'

'That's right, I'd forgotten. You're something of an expert in this field, aren't you?' Zafrani held out the club. 'Care to have a go?'

Makana ignored the offer. 'What is it you think he knows?'

'He's been hanging around my club, selling his drugs, asking questions.' Zafrani cocked an eye. 'A little like you.'

'I told you what I was doing. Kasabian asked me to find someone for him, an Iraqi.'

'Yes, yes. An Iraqi colonel. Everyone wants to find this Samari, and they all come to me.'

'He was seen at your club.'

'Did you ever ask yourself how, in this wonderful city of ours, someone like that, a foreigner, would find his way to my club?' Zafrani reached down and grabbed a handful of Na'il's hair and jerked his head up. 'He doesn't look too good, does he?' Na'il was barely conscious. He opened one good eye and stared at

Makana. Zafrani let his head drop, and rubbed his hand on his trousers. Na'il groaned and spluttered blood through broken teeth.

'You see how hard it is to get cooperation these days?' Zafrani changed his grip and brought the club down hard on Na'il's shoulder. There was a snap of breaking bone and a wild scream that echoed through the empty rooms around them.

'You want me to ask. All right, who brought Samari to your club?'

'Who do you think? Go ahead, take a wild guess.' Zafrani produced a cigar from his pocket and stuck it in his mouth.

'Your partner?' asked Makana. 'Qasim Abdel Qasim?'

'You see.' A broad grin broke across Zafrani's face. 'You do know more than you let on. One of Qasim's early victories was as a broker in a big arms deal in the 1980s when we were supplying weapons to Iraq. He's known Samari since then.'

'And when Samari found himself in trouble he called on his old friend to give him shelter.'

'One good turn deserves another.' Zafrani leaned down to address Na'il again. 'Do you know what happens when I break both your knees? You'll never walk like a man again. You will be crawling the streets begging for scraps for the rest of your life. Is that what you want?' Na'il moaned and cried some more.

'So you're all working together,' said Makana.

'What?' Zafrani was breathing heavily.

'You're working together. I don't see why one small-time drug peddlar should be a threat to that. You're all much bigger than him.'

'That's what I'm trying to explain to you.' Zafrani took a moment. He loomed over Makana in the dark. 'It's about co-operation. We all have to protect our interests. Now, if there is a breach of that trust in either of our separate houses, we are obliged to clean it up. Understand?'

'You're saying Na'il has broken some kind of bond between you.'

'Your American friend. Remember him? Somebody talked to him, and by doing so he put our partner in danger.'

'That's what this is about?'

'That and other things.'

'Like what? He's a small-time hustler who makes money selling drugs to high-class party people.'

'Exactly my point. Now where would a small-time rat like this get his hands on all those drugs? I supply the drugs. I know where they come from.' Zafrani surveyed his handiwork and sighed. 'I really didn't expect this much resistance from such a little shit.' Tucking the cigar carefully into his shirt pocket, he turned and began swinging the club, again and again, slamming it into Na'il's already battered body. Makana glanced over at Bobo and Didi. Even they seemed to be wincing.

'That's enough,' Makana said quietly.

'What?' Zafrani turned on him. He was breathing heavily. Sweat was pouring down his high forehead in glistening beads. He put a hand to his ear. 'What did you say?'

'There's no point in killing him. It's not going to change the facts.'

'Facts? Really? Now that I find interesting.' Zafrani snapped his fingers and Bobo, or was it Didi, hurried forward with a small towel. 'Now why would you want me to stop? Is it because you're afraid of what he might tell me?'

'Why would I be afraid of that?'

'Okay, let me ask you something.' Zafrani took the towel and passed the bloodstained golf club over in return. Bobo took it gingerly, holding it at arm's length, not sure what to do. Something nasty slipped off the end of the club onto the floor. 'He's not telling me what I want to know. Now what does that tell you?'

Makana regarded the slumped mass. A spasm went through Na'il's body, causing his left foot to twitch. He was still alive. Whether that was a good or a bad thing Makana couldn't decide.

'It means that he's more scared of someone else.'

'Exactly.' Zafrani dabbed at his face and rubbed his neck. 'Now don't you find that interesting? I find it more than interesting. I find it very worrying.'

Na'il was coughing and spluttering. Blood dripped from his battered face to the floor. His jaw hung slackly. He probably couldn't have talked even if he'd wanted to. Zafrani took back the club and poked him with the end of it for good measure. 'This is a small fish. Someone else is feeding off him.'

'Killing him is not going to solve anything.'

'It'll send a message.'

'Try using the post office. Assuming you're trying to reach someone in the land of the living.'

'I have a reputation to protect. A man loses his reputation and he is finished. Dogs turn on the weakest in the pack and tear him to pieces, even their own siblings.'

'There's something else to consider. The police are looking for him. They like him for Kasabian's murder.'

'This one?' Zafrani snorted. 'He couldn't kill a kitten.'

'Maybe, but the police are still after him.'

'I don't see how that solves my problem.'

'Dump him. Kasabian had a lot of friends in high places. The police are not going to give in until they pin his murder on someone. They'll find out who Na'il was working for. You have enough ears inside the police to find out what he tells them.'

Zafrani was silent for a moment. 'Not bad,' he said. Handing the club back to Bobo, Zafrani took a moment to light his cigar with a fancy gold lighter, squinting out of the corner of his eye at Makana. 'Not bad. I like it. But what's in all of this for you?'

'I have my own interests to protect. I'm supposed to be helping the police catch Kasabian's killer. The sooner this case is wrapped up the better for everyone.' Makana counted on Zafrani not knowing that the police were looking for Na'il as a witness, not as their prime suspect. At some stage he might discover the truth but Makana would cross that bridge when he came to it.

Zafrani puffed rings of grey smoke into the air. 'You must learn not to take these things personally.'

Sound advice coming from a man who had just beaten someone half to death on suspicion of sullying his reputation. Makana lit another cigarette. The basement felt damp and reeked of blood and death. He didn't like being here, didn't like feeling he was an accessory to Zafrani's crimes. The golf club swung lightly between them. Makana wondered what it would take for Zafrani to turn on him.

'My brother tells me you are interested in the girl at the club. The dark one.'

'Leave her out of this.'

Zafrani smiled awkwardly. 'It's complicated, all of this high-class stuff. I mean, in the old days I just did what I wanted to do. Now, I have partners here, partners there. It's not easy.'

'It's the price for moving up in the world.'

'I don't even like this one they call the Samurai. Apparently he's got plenty of money and he's eager to invest. But these Iraqis.' Zafrani was wagging his head in dismay. 'He comes to the club, likes to gamble, to spend time with the girls. He likes your friend, by the way. While he's up there in heaven his bodyguards are drinking whisky, the expensive stuff, and throwing money at the roulette wheel like cowboys.'

'Isn't that the idea?'

'Sure, but because they are friends of the house they think they don't have to pay their debts. I explain this to Qasim and the others, but they look down on me like I'm an idiot. Without me they would have nothing. All of this.' He gestured expansively. 'I did this. They just put the money in. They're hypocrites, the lot of them. They like to have fun at the club, but the next day they're in parliament vowing to defend Islamic values and all the rest of it. What happened to this country, that we're in the hands of a bunch of two-faced cowards?'

'Don't expect me to answer that.' Makana sensed deep resentment in him. In a way he felt sorry for Qasim and anyone else whom Zafrani might be building a grudge against.

'The point is that now we have the Americans looking for this Samurai snake. Any day now a ton of rockets is going to come falling on our heads when they decide to get rid of him.'

'I thought you were partners.'

'That's what I'm trying to tell you. I can't move against him. My business with Qasim would be over. Those two are old army buddies. No, this has to come from somewhere else.'

'I'm not sure I follow. What exactly are you asking me?'

'I'm not asking you anything. I'm saying, if you want to help this girl, she's yours. All you have to do is get this man off my back.'

'How do you expect me to do that?'

'Turn him over to the Americans. Collect the reward. Let them take care of it. I don't care about the details, I just don't want it anywhere near me. I don't want the club involved.'

'And then you'll let her go?'

'All her debts will be cancelled.'

'What are you going to do with him?' Makana nodded at Na'il.

'Like I said,' Zafrani swung the club, 'I'm going to send a message.' He nodded and his men came forward to lead Makana away. 'Keep me informed.'

Makana turned to walk away. Behind him he heard a scream and the thud of the club. He began walking towards where he thought the exit was. Didi and Bobo fell in behind him. As he walked up towards the light, Makana felt his heart judder back into life again. He didn't look back.

Chapter Twenty-seven

It had all started with Na'il. Makana could see that now. He must have gone behind Kasabian's back to Kane and told him that he was working with Samari. There was no other way that Kane could have found out. Na'il. Trying to help the woman he loved, or trying to make a profit out of other people's business? Always playing both sides to his own advantage. Only somehow it had gone wrong. Kasabian was dead and now, well, Makana didn't think it looked good for Na'il himself.

The ride back into town proved just as hair-raising as the journey out, with heart-stopping moments roughly every sixty seconds. The driver raced into narrow spaces, braked and jerked the wheel at the last minute. Either he was a very good driver or an idiot who lived a charmed life, Makana couldn't decide. Sindbad was leaning up against the Thunderbird when they arrived at the awama. Didi and Bobo sized him up through the car window as if he were a potential opponent.

'Who are your new friends?' Sindbad was using the roof of the car as a table to eat his snack. A sandwich the size of his forearm.

'Ayad Zafrani's men,' explained Makana.

They stood back as the SUV lurched out into the afternoon traffic and sped away. Makana looked at his watch.

'We'd better go,' he said.

The Khan al-Khalili was the familiar mix of the quaint and the gaudy. Some of the shops were no larger than wardrobes. Shelves crammed with artefacts of every shape and form. Semi-precious stones alongside painted wood. The eyes of innumerable gods gazed out in astonishment at the people who wandered by in droves, like pilgrims flocking to an ancient site of worship. Kids followed tourists as doggedly as puppies looking for a home. They waved painted papyrus sheets desperately in the hope that they might wear down their resolve. Some succeeded, others were swatted away like flies. In the cafés the visitors tried to look like old hands as they suckled waterpipes or sipped sweet mint tea.

Between the two sides there was a mutual recognition that neither would ever really understand the other. To the tourists the locals represented a way of life they were happy to view from a distance, so long as it was temporary and they had a seat secured on a plane out of here in the not too distant future. The local vendors on the other hand were content to smile and play the jester if it encouraged sales. Beyond that, and the universal sexual appeal of the occasional beauty, the Europeans, Americans, Japanese and all the rest of them might just as well have landed from another planet. It wasn't just the way they dressed or talked, it was the mere idea of having enough time and money to travel the globe at leisure to see how other people lived. To them it was a crazy idea. Why bother to travel when you already lived in the greatest country in the world?

Fishawi's was an icon of the bazaar. Though not much more than a shortcut, an alleyway with sagging divans and run-down furniture, it had a touch of the old Arabian Nights about it and drew the tourists in like hungry flies, eager to soak up something of the 'genuine' atmosphere they had come so far to savour. That is if they happened to believe that Old Cairo was occupied by backpackers and middle-aged travellers in cargo pants, every one of them born with a camera and a knapsack strapped to their bodies.

Zachary Kane was dressed likewise, still in character as Charles Barkley, art dealer, or so it would seem. He was seated alone at a table halfway down. The waiter was setting out coffee for him. He looked up as Makana approached.

'Ah, perfect timing,' he smiled, gesturing at the chair opposite him. 'Will you have something? I just ordered one of those water-pipes.' Makana asked the waiter to bring him coffee with little sugar. 'What a great language. Just the sound of it.'

'I called your hotel only to learn that you are no longer staying at the Marriott.'

Kane gave a theatrical sigh. 'What can I say? I'm afraid I was so disturbed by the tragic death of our mutual friend. Your words of warning hit home and I decided to change my location with-out delay. I'm sure you understand. After all, that is what you and your inspector friend were saying the other day, was it not? To take precautions? To be careful.'

The waiter appeared to set up the shisha. He unwrapped the pipe and set glowing coals onto the bowl before handing it to Kane.

'As I understand it you left so fast you forgot to pay your bill. The manager is a very worried man.'

'A misunderstanding. The money should have been wired from our New York office. It really wouldn't surprise me if there was a delay. Frankly, I am astonished at the way things are run in this country.'

'These are hard times,' said Makana, wondering how long Kane would keep this up.

'I consider myself a prudent man, Mr Makana, and since I have no idea how long this trip is going to be drawn out, I felt it made sense to move somewhere a little more modest.' Kane blew clouds of perfumed smoke into the air. 'This country seems to feel it is open season on tourists. Costs are prohibitive, even by New York standards.'

Makana watched him carefully.

'Perhaps it would help if we dropped the games.'

'As you wish. Have you made progress?'

'I believe so, but perhaps not in the way you had hoped.'

Kane cocked his head to one side. There was a slight hardening in his eyes. He set down the long pipe stem on the table.

'Perhaps you'd care to tell me what you mean.'

'I'll get to that, but there are a couple of things that we need to straighten out first.'

'I see.'

'This may not mean much to a worldly man like yourself, but I have certain standards. I don't like being deceived. In other words, I like to know who I'm working for.'

'That sounds perfectly reasonable.'

'That's how I feel.' Makana took a moment to glance casually up and down the narrow lane. He spotted two of them. The blond one, Hagen, and the Latino, Santos. They were seated at a table in the back, trying to look like tourists. They even had a guidebook they were pretending to study. Out of the way, but close enough to arrive in a hurry if needed. 'So, in this case, as I say, we seem to have a problem.'

Kane folded his arms. 'What exactly is it you think you know, Mr Makana?'

'Well, first of all I know that your name is not Charles Barkley. It's Zachary Kane. I know that you didn't come to Cairo alone.' Makana nodded in the general direction of the two other Americans. 'And I have a fairly good idea that you're not an art dealer.'

Kane sat back and smiled. 'I hope this isn't some elaborate strategy to try and raise the value of your services?'

'It's not about the money.'

The waiter paused as he went by to deposit the coffee. Kane waited until he was out of earshot. He held up his hands.

'Look, we seem to have some kind of misunderstanding here. I can see how you might feel a little ticked off that I haven't been entirely honest with you, but there's a reason.'

'Well, I'm happy to hear it.'

'There's always a reason.' Kane's smile faded. He leaned forward and spoke urgently. 'Okay, cards-on-the-table time. You've obviously done your homework, so I'll level with you. But I must warn you that what I have to tell you is confidential. You cannot breathe a word of this to anyone. Is that understood?' Kane paused to make sure Makana was following him. 'We're on a special mission, to extract Samari and take him back.'

'Back to Iraq?' Makana raised his eyebrows.

'I know how it looks and I apologise for having deceived you. It's a grey area. He's wanted for human rights abuses. But officially, the US cannot operate in this country without the government's permission. Egypt is an ally. That's why they hire us for this kind of job. We're cheaper, partly because we rely on local operatives like yourself.' Kane allowed himself a smile.

'Quite a story.'

'It's a delicate business. We're flying low, under the radar so to speak.'

'So the Egyptian government doesn't know what you are doing?'

Kane shook his head. 'We can't just come storming in. People here are touchy. There's a lot of opposition to the war. You've seen the demonstrations on the streets. The Egyptians aren't too happy about the US presence in Iraq. We have to tread carefully.'

'So what happens to him once you get him back there?' Makana sipped his coffee.

'Well, the usual things. I mean, he'll be processed and tried.' Kane gave Makana a stern look. 'He's not a nice man.'

'It's a fine story, but it doesn't explain why you killed Kasabian.'

Kane said nothing for a moment. He reached for the shisha and sucked on it, blowing clouds into the air for a time.

'What makes you think I killed him?' He had a crooked grin on his face. 'I mean, don't you need evidence before you start throwing accusations of murder around?'

'There is one witness, a man named Na'il. Maybe you remember him? He rides a yellow motorcycle.'

'If you say so.'

'Well, you'd remember him because he's the one who came to you and told you that Kasabian was taking you for a ride. He worked for Kasabian, which is how he found out about what was going on. He was probably a little annoyed that he hadn't been given the job of finding Samari. Who knows? Maybe he thought he could make more on the side selling that information to you.'

'Why would he do something like that?'

Makana held his hands out wide. 'Rich Americans come to town and everyone expects to get paid.'

Kane nodded. 'Never underestimate people's capacity for greed.'

'Kasabian tried to cheat you, and I have a feeling, Mr Kane, that you're not the kind of man who likes being cheated.'

Kane returned the pipe stem to the table slowly.

'I don't know how it works in this damn country, but you were hired to provide information. Where I come from, if a man takes an advance for a job he's obliged to see it through. It's an unwritten contract, if you like. You can't just turn around and start asking questions. You were hired to find Samari.'

'Mr Kasabian hired me. I don't know what happens in your world when the person who hired you is brutally murdered, but over here we tend to take that kind of thing personally. Loyalty to our masters. It goes back a long way.'

Kane laughed. 'You're not kidding are you? That's why you're stuck in this dump making chump change finding lost souls.' He weighed the long padded stem of the waterpipe in his hands. 'Do you really think anyone cares about who killed Kasabian? Look around you. This is a city of eighteen million people. Most of them don't have running water or toilets that flush. You think they give a damn about the death of some fancy art dealer? I don't think so.'

'The police are very keen to find out who murdered Kasabian. I'm sure they would be most interested to know that it was a private contractor hired by the US government.'

'You're persistent, I'll give you that.'

'There's too much at stake for me,' said Makana. 'You can leave when this is over, but someone around here is going to have to pick up the pieces. I don't want that person to be me.'

'I understand, believe me, I do.' Kane kept his eyes on Makana. 'But I have to tell you, you're making a classic mistake.'

'What mistake is that?'

'You're not seeing the big picture.' Kane fell silent as a group of tourists wandered by, led by a high-voiced woman holding up a red umbrella and speaking what might have been German. 'How do you think Samari has survived so long in this country? He has protection.'

'Samari had no reason to kill Aram Kasabian. They were partners. The art world is not an easy place to understand. Samari needed someone who could sell the stolen pieces he had. He needed Kasabian.'

'Maybe he got tired of him.' Kane shrugged. 'Maybe they had a lovers' quarrel. It happens.'

'I am curious though,' said Makana. 'Why do you want him so badly? This isn't about the reward. It isn't about museum pieces or stolen paintings. It's personal.'

Kane seemed momentarily distracted by the noise around him. The boys going from table to table with their trinkets, the waiter whisking through, tapping out a rhythm on his metal tray, even the tourists trudging by in their practical shoes and sensible clothing. Through the bands of light that filtered down through the covered screens high above, tiny birds chirped as they fluttered by.

'You need to get things in perspective,' said Kane finally. 'You're a smart man. There's a lot of money at the end of this rainbow. Now, I don't know what your plans are for the future, but charming as it is, me, I wouldn't want to grow old and poor in this city. I'd want enough to lift me up out of the horseshit and give me a comfortable life.'

'You're talking about a deal?'

Kane leaned across the table, a gleam in his eye. 'Do you have any idea how much Samari is sitting on? It's a once-in-a-lifetime collection of stolen art. A king's ransom and then some. When Samari marched into Kuwait with a unit of Republican Guards they turned the place upside down and shook its pockets. They came up with all sorts. Gold bullion, silver, diamonds and art, lots of art. They loaded it all up and drove it back across the border. Most of it they could get rid of, but the paintings, that's not so easy, especially when your country is under UN sanctions.

A Picasso in Baghdad is about as valuable as a pair of Prada shoes. There's nowhere to go.'

'How is it that you know so much about Samari?'

'I've been following this guy's progress for longer than you can imagine. I know everything about him there is to know.'

'So this is not just about delivering Samari to justice. It's personal.' Makana sat back for a moment to think. 'You must have known that killing Kasabian would stir everything up. There's a manhunt going on, looking for the wrong man, but still. What did you think would happen? Did you really think Kasabian would lead you to him, just like that? Samari has a formidable reputation. Kasabian was more scared of him than he was of you. He didn't know who you were.'

'Well, he knows now.' Kane's face was set in a grim mask. It was the first admission of guilt, and Makana felt the palms of his hands grow damp. He reached for a cigarette and found the packet was empty. He raised a hand to summon the waiter. 'Careful,' said Kane quietly. Makana held up the empty packet. 'Just cigarettes.'

The waiter came over with a packet of Cleopatras and Makana paid him. He unwrapped the cellophane thinking about Cassidy's Camels. A rich man would be able to smoke Camels every day.

'Tell me about what you had in mind.'

Kane eased up slightly. He rolled his shoulders as if to relax them.

'The war has helped Samari. He's richer now than he ever was. People come to him with items from the museums. Old, very old stuff. The great Iraqi heritage. We're talking Ali Baba's cave of wonders. Modern art, treasures of the ancient world, Mesopotamia, the riches of Babylon.'

Makana recalled the delicate shape of the palm tree on the

tablet in Kasabian's little treasure trove. Priceless fragments of a forgotten history. The world was always happy to buy up the past.

'Added to that, I can show you a list of some of the paintings: Marc, Matisse, Chagall. A king's ransom on today's market, hundreds of millions of dollars.' Kane talked with the zeal of a prophet and the charm of a sorcerer. A purveyor of flying carpets and miracle cures.

'And how do you plan to get hold of these things?'

'Well, that's where you come into it. You lead me to Samari and you'll get a cut.' Kane took a moment. A shoeshine boy clicking tin caps on his fingers like castanets paused by their table. The American gave him a dirty look and the boy took himself off.

'Don't tell me your conscience is bothering you. Just remember that Samari helped gas the Kurds in 1988. He's a war criminal. He's going to stand trial.'

'Along with George Bush and Tony Blair?'

'You're a laugh a minute, you know that?'

'I don't see anybody laughing,' said Makana.

'Don't tell me you're not interested. I've seen where you live. I know the kind of life you lead.' Kane seemed to tire of the shisha and instead produced a packet of cigarettes and snapped the brass Zippo lighter open, producing flame and the high organic buzz of naptha fumes. 'You're almost there. All you have to do is point us in the right direction and get out of the way.'

Makana glanced back to see if the two other Americans were still in place. He wondered where Jansen and Clearwater were, and the Iraqi, Faisal.

Kane grinned. He reached down to a pocket and produced a thick envelope which he placed on the table between them.

'There's ten grand there. Call it an advance. You lead me to him and you'll get double that.'

Makana contemplated the envelope. 'It doesn't seem like all that much compared with the millions on his head.'

'Ah, now I think we're getting somewhere.' Kane wagged a finger at him. 'You strike a hard bargain, Mr Makana, but I'm sure we can come to some arrangement. Take this as a down payment against, shall we say, a five per cent cut?'

'Ten per cent.'

'Five per cent of at least twenty million? That's an easy one million dollars. Don't get greedy my friend, a million dollars still buys a lot of falafel.' Kane glanced over towards Hagen and Santos and a signal seemed to pass between them. The American glanced at his watch. 'Time's up,' he said. 'You're almost there. All you have to do is lead me to him.'

'What makes you think I know where he is?'

'You wouldn't be sitting here if you didn't have a pretty good idea of how to find him.' Kane got to his feet. He handed Makana a strip of paper with a number on it. 'Don't take too long about it. I'm not known for my patience.'

'How do I know I can trust you?'

Kane smiled. 'We all have to have a little faith.' He looked over his shoulder. 'I'm going to leave now. Don't try to follow me. Stay here, enjoy your coffee.'

Makana watched Kane walk away down through the lane and turn left. When he looked back the two other Americans had disappeared.

Chapter Twenty-eight

The awama was quiet. The dying sun was warm on the soft ground and the smell of mud and growing plants conjoined in a rich mixture that seemed timeless. It reminded Makana that he was getting older and one day he would be dead and this ground would still be here, just as it had been in the last days of Akhenaton.

The rumble of the big engine announced Sindbad's arrival. Makana made a mental note to call Ali and find out how the repairs were coming along. He was beginning to miss the old Datsun. Cramped and unreliable as it was, it had a certain modesty that he preferred over the brash showiness of its American counterpart.

A few moments later Sindbad appeared on the upper deck, his face sombre, as it always was when he had to deliver a report. He took his work very seriously.

'Well, *ya basha*, I did what you asked. I waited until the American came out of the bazaar.'

'Was he alone?'

'Not for long. Two other men came out of the Khan al-Khalili behind him and followed him down to the road. A car arrived.'

'What kind of car?'

'American. Cherokee Jeep. Black.'

'Egyptian registration?'

Sindbad produced a greasy scrap of paper, torn from a food wrapping. 'Egyptian, *ya basha*. I checked it personally.'

'Very good.' Makana wondered where the Americans would have got hold of a car. Rented? Stolen? Perhaps it was not so difficult to explain. 'Did you see how many people were in the car?'

'First only the driver, Arabic, then two others arrived.'

That was all of them. Faisal would be doing the driving. Clearwater and Jansen must have been in the bazaar somewhere in case they were needed. Kane certainly didn't believe in taking chances.

'Where did they go?'

'I followed them, *ya basha*, to a hotel on the Pyramids Road.'

On the paper Sindbad had scribbled the car registration and the name of the hotel.

'Five Seesons.' Makana squinted at the letters, printed in clumsy fashion, dotted around the paper almost as if they had no relationship to one another. He glanced up at Sindbad. 'Was it really written like this?'

'Yes, *ya basha*. Exactly like that.'

Makana paid Sindbad some money for the day's work and sent him home. Then he sank down into the big chair with a sigh and watched the sunset ripple on the water. Two white egrets flew by, flying in tandem as if they had plans, somewhere to go. He was caught at the centre of a hazardous constellation. Samari. Kane. The Zafrani brothers. If he wasn't careful he was going to end up torn to bits between them. The brutality of the attack on the golf course came back to him and he called Dalia Habashi's number. When he got her voicemail he hoped it meant she was out of the country. He didn't leave a message.

His phone rang. It was Bilquis.

'I tried calling you earlier,' she said.

'Sorry, I was caught up with something. I had the phone switched off.'

He could hear noises in the background. A child talking to someone. 'Is that your son?'

'Yes. He's here with me. I'm at home.'

'You're not working tonight?'

'No, not tonight.'

Makana put his feet up on the railing and stared out at the river. A calm seemed to come over the city just before nightfall. That magical moment that would be gone in a handful of minutes.

'I was thinking about you last night,' he said.

'You mean you were thinking about your wife and daughter?'

'No, it was you I had in mind. The story you told. It made me think about how much I left undone behind me. I ran away.'

'Did you have a choice?'

'We always have a choice.'

'To die for nothing, that is not a choice.'

'Perhaps. But by turning my back I left the place to those who abuse their power.'

'There is a lot of evil in the world,' she said. 'It takes more than one man to put it right.'

'Who is there with you?'

'It's the neighbour who stays with him until I get back from work.' She paused. 'Don't you get lonely living there all alone?'

'It doesn't feel as though I'm ever alone.' Makana looked up at the bridge loaded with cars that rumbled by off in the distance. There was the bustle of the street behind him. Muffled by the embankment and the low wall and the trees, but still there. And perched halfway up the bank was the little shack that seemed to have been nailed to the earth where Umm Ali and her little family lived.

'You've made this country your own,' she said. 'I admire that. Me, I will never be at home here.'

'You have your son with you, at least that's something.'

'Yes, and one day he's going to be ashamed of me. How will I face him then?'

The light was almost gone, a thin film over the river, a strip of sodium orange above the bridge. He lit a cigarette.

'Why did you call me?' he asked.

'What we talked about. Will you really help me?'

Makana sighed. 'I think it's a bad idea for you to get involved.'

'What choice do I have?'

'Samari's a dangerous man.'

'All men are dangerous.'

'Not like this one.'

'This is my chance to get out. I don't want to live this way for ever.'

'Someone could get hurt. You could get hurt. Your son.'

'You're afraid.'

'I'd be a fool if I wasn't.'

'You're a man, you don't understand what it's like. To have to do what I do every night.' Her voice was trembling. 'I know what you must think of me, but you have to believe me. I just want to make a new life for myself and my boy. Is that such a bad thing?'

'No,' he said quietly, 'of course not.'

Her voice was low, whispering in his ear. The water below was dark now, so thick and viscous it could have been blood. There was a long pause, longer than the last. Makana almost thought she had gone.

'If you don't help me then I will have to do something myself.'

'Bilquis, listen to me. You don't need to get involved.'

'One of these days I won't be able to hide from him any longer. If my son ever finds out what I do, I will die of shame. It's as simple as that.' There was a pause. 'He called me.' She hesitated. 'He wants to see me.'

'When?'

'Tomorrow afternoon. He's visiting his tailor in town. He wants me to go away with him.'

'Does he normally do that – I mean, arrange his times with you?'

'He's always very exact about when he comes to visit. He's not interested in the other girls.'

'I understand.'

'Don't you see? This is our chance to get him. Inside the tailor's shop he will be unguarded, vulnerable and alone.'

'What are you suggesting I do, knock him out and drag him to the embassy?'

'I thought you wanted this as much as I did. I thought you cared, that you understood, or was all that stuff about losing your wife just small talk?' Makana said nothing. 'With this money we could have a chance of a life.'

'We?' Makana felt his heart twist in an unfamiliar way.

'Why not? We're so much alike. You understand what I've been through. What it's like.'

Makana said nothing.

'Think about it, please, for me?' She gave him a description of a tailor's shop that was situated in the downtown area. Makana knew the area. On Sharif Basha Street, off Kasr al-Nil Street. 'Don't disappoint me,' she said, and the line went dead.

Makana sat and listened as the night came down. He wondered if Zafrani meant it when he said he would release Bilquis in exchange for getting Samari off his back. Was it ever possible to trust a man like Ayad Zafrani? Trying to apprehend Samari was like writing your own death warrant. Perhaps there was another way. Above him the bats turned arcs through the shadows as the trees drew close and the darkness came to life.

Chapter Twenty-nine

The sound of the wailing sirens ought to have alerted him, but Makana was tired. After another long, restless night, he had only just fallen into a deep sleep. Even the sound of heavy boots was not enough to get him to open his eyes. It was only when he was dragged to the floor, handcuffed and hauled to his feet that he realised what was going on.

There were five of them. Two held him up while three others ransacked the room, making a point of going through his things. They pulled open drawers and tipped the contents on the floor, they pulled books down from the shelves and then trampled over them in their haste. He could hear others downstairs, the crash of plates and cups breaking.

'What is this all about?'

'Quiet! Speak when you are spoken to.'

A lull fell over proceedings when it was announced that the brigadier had arrived. He took his time, roaming around the lower deck with an entourage of yapping assistants. Finally, after a long wait, he emerged at the top of the steps. The look of triumph on his face was only partially concealed by apparent outrage.

'I always wondered how a creature like you lived,' he sneered. 'Now I have my answer.'

'Are you going to tell me what this is all about?'

'I'll tell you when I'm good and ready.' Brigadier Yusuf Effendi tipped a pile of papers onto the floor with his swagger stick. 'Bring him along.'

They allowed Makana to dress quickly and then marched him up the path.

'Don't worry, Umm Ali, it's all going to be cleared up.'

'May the lord have mercy on you,' she implored. Her teenage boy bared his teeth at the policemen and then quickly ducked a blow aimed at his head. Aziza stood in the doorway and watched him go. Makana flashed her a smile that she did not return. Up on the road the cortege of vehicles moved off with all the ceremony of a presidential motorcade, with Makana tucked into the rear seat of a squad car between two uniforms.

'Where are we going?'

'You'll see,' grunted one of them.

It soon became apparent. As the dull brown pillar of the Ramses Hilton rose into the sky before them like a pagan monument, Makana felt his heart sink. He had a bad feeling about this.

The hotel lobby was busy with people coming and going. The procession of policemen cut a swathe through tourists and staff alike. When they arrived at the seventh floor the lift doors opened to reveal more people. The brigadier was standing by the door to room 719.

'Go ahead,' he invited Makana.

As he pushed the door open slowly Makana had the feeling he knew what he was going to find. The sound of laughter came from the television set on the far side of the room. Adil Imam rushing about a stage in a performance that was about a hundred years old. The audience laughing in fits at his antics. Makana stopped at the threshold of the main room.

She might have been asleep. But there was something wrong about the way she lay. Dalia Habashi was wrapped in the sheets of the unmade bed. She was lying face down, her head hanging over the far side of the bed. Instead of fleeing the country she had decided to leave this world. There was something terribly sad about the whole scene. The rumpled bedclothes, the television set with its inane racket.

'Can't you switch that off?'

There was a forensic technician standing by the bed. He looked up and stepped aside as Makana drew closer.

'Don't touch anything.'

Makana could hear the brigadier tapping his swagger stick behind him. He ignored him and flipped off the television. Then he knelt down and looked into her open, sightless eyes. They were staring off into the empty void. Her pale skin had already turned grey.

'How long?' he asked, without taking his eyes from her.

'Difficult to say,' mumbled the technician. Makana glanced at him. Either the man was an idiot, or he was waiting for someone to tell him exactly what time would suit them for death to have occurred.

Already the blood had drained downwards, forming dark patches of lividity around her neck and chin. He lifted the sheet slightly. She was wearing a nightgown. The lower part of her arms and shoulders displayed the same blue colour, which indicated that she had been lying there for at least twelve hours.

'When was she found?'

272

'She left a Do Not Disturb sign on the door, so hotel staff didn't come in until this morning.'

On the bedside table was a bottle of vodka with the cap beside it. The bottle was almost empty. Next to it lay an array of smaller bottles, different sizes and colours. Pharmacy bottles. A collection of drugs. Some of Na'il's products perhaps. Makana read some of the names. Seconal, ketamine, sleeping tablets, tranquillisers. There was enough to put a busload of rowdy football fans into a coma. Certainly enough to push one unhappy woman across the threshold from life to death. Makana remained there for a minute, staring at the side of her face. In death, Dalia Habashi seemed more beautiful than in life, as if the burden of chasing dreams and ambitions she could never achieve had loosened its hold on her features, allowing the real woman to rise to the surface and show her face one last time before she sank into darkness for ever.

Makana straightened up. He turned to face the brigadier. The look of satisfaction on his face was now easier to understand.

'You've got some explaining to do. Murder is a serious charge.'

'This was a suicide. Any fool can see that.'

'Still trying to teach us our business, eh? Well, we'll see how that works out for you. As far as I can see it's a simple case, really. You developed a fixation on this woman. You pursued her, so much so that she had to seek refuge in a hotel. Still you refused to relent. You followed her here and forced yourself upon her. Then, to cover your shame you made her swallow pills to make it look like suicide. Let's see what the medical examiner says about sexual assault.'

'They won't find anything because there isn't anything to find. This is ridiculous, and you know it.'

'Do I?' The brigadier shook his head. 'We have witnesses who saw you going up to her room. It's as plain as the sun. You're a demented and perverted man. When she wouldn't give you what you wanted you killed her.'

'You've spent so much time with politicians, you can't tell fact from fantasy any more.'

The brigadier hit him across the face, hard enough to draw blood.

'You forget who you're talking to. Perhaps you think that because this little whore was busy corrupting my nephew I think she deserves this? Well, think again.' He moved closer. 'I'm going to enjoy observing your interrogation. When we've finished you'll be only too happy to tell us everything.' He signalled to his men. 'Take him away, and if he makes one move to get away you have my personal permission to shoot the dog.' He smiled at Makana. 'This isn't the jungle here. We'll see how your fancy tricks fare against good Egyptian justice. Take him outside to the van and keep him there for me,' he ordered.

There was an audience of equally shocked faces gathered to watch as they dragged Makana out of the lift. Despite the early hour the lobby seemed to be packed with slack-jawed tourists who were being afforded more entertainment than they had bargained for. Some were even taking pictures. You could see it on the brochures: 'A city of danger and excitement!' Two sets of hands grabbed hold of Makana's shoulders and dragged him along, heels sliding on the polished floor, until he was outside. There was a police prison van parked at the bottom of the ramp. A high lorry with metal sides and tiny windows covered with wire grilles close to the top. Makana was led up the steps and thrown inside. He landed in a heap on the beaten iron floor as the door slammed shut behind him and the bolt screeched into place.

In the half-light Makana could make out benches on either side. These were occupied by three men who appeared to have been detained overnight. A fourth lay on the floor without moving. Despite the early hour, the inside of the prison van was airless and hot. It stank of unwashed men, the acrid stench of stale sweat and urine mixed with oxidised metal. Someone shuffled aside to allow Makana a place to sit. Getting up slowly, he examined himself cautiously and decided that nothing was broken. There would be plenty of bruises by tomorrow, but he would survive.

Somehow in their haste they had overlooked his telephone. When he pulled it out the man sitting opposite him said, 'Don't let them see you using that.'

'Don't worry, I'll be quick.' Makana dialled Okasha's number only to be rewarded by the engaged tone. He had a feeling even Okasha was not going to be enough this time. He was going to need a good lawyer. He slipped the phone inside his sock for safety.

'What did they pick you up for?' The man opposite was staring at him.

'I'm not sure,' sighed Makana. 'Trying to help them with their work.'

'It doesn't matter what you did.' This from a young man further down who was nursing a nosebleed. 'They don't care what they charge you with.'

'We were minding our own business when this big car rolled up,' said the third man. These two seemed to be friends. 'The driver told us to move on. We told him we had just as much right to be there as he did. So he called the animals out and that was it.'

'What happened to your friend?' Makana gestured at the man on the floor.

'He was concussed. They were taking him to hospital when they got a call to come here.' The young man thumped his fist

275

into his thigh. 'I don't see what gives these people the privilege to walk all over the rest of us.'

'What are you, students?'

'Faculty of Architecture,' he nodded. 'Soon as I graduate I'm leaving this country.'

'Shame on you,' said the first man. He was older and clearly not one of the group. A rubbery-faced fellow with scabs all over his chin and the shifty eyes of a habitual offender. 'As soon as you get your education you leave. How can you not think about helping?'

'This country doesn't need my help. It needs a miracle.'

'Easy for you to say.'

'Who was in the big car?' Makana asked, if only to break the deadlock.

'One of those fat crocodiles who sit on the president's knee.'

'You mean a minister?' asked the man with the scabs. 'If you mean a minister then you should show him the respect of his post.'

'Listen to you,' the young man laughed. 'What have they done to deserve respect?'

'Anyone in this country can rise to a government position. Where would you be if you were elected and people talked about you that way?'

'Well, there's not much chance of that happening, is there?' the younger man retorted, ignoring the pleas of his friend with the bloody nose to desist.

'People like you make me sick,' the scabby-faced man whined. 'You have all the privileges but all you can do is talk your country down.'

They were interrupted by a thumping on the door. A face peered through the grille.

'Which one of you is Makana?'

'I am.'

'Say *Alhamdoulilah*, you're being transferred.'

The scabby-faced man thought this was too much. 'Why the hell is he being transferred? He only just got here. I've been here all night.'

The guard rapped his baton on the grille. 'You carry on and you'll stay there all week.'

There wasn't room to stand up properly in the back, so Makana had to stoop as he went towards the door. He nodded to the young man as he went by.

'Do you want me to call someone for you?'

'No, it's okay.' The student sounded weary. 'They do this all the time. They'll drive us around until they get tired and then they'll let us go. Processing us would be too much trouble.'

'Why are you getting so friendly with him?' snapped the scabby man. 'He's a snitch. They just put him in here to get us to talk.' He started to laugh, as if he was losing his mind. The man with the bloody nose threw himself forward.

'If anyone here's a snitch, it's you, so shut your mouth old man, before it's shut for you.'

Makana stepped up to show his face at the grille. After a time he heard the bolt squeak and then he was climbing down the steps to the street.

'You don't remember me, do you?' said the man who let him out. He had a single stripe on his sleeve and his round face strained at the strap on his helmet, distorting his features. He glanced around furtively as he undid Makana's handcuffs. 'I used to drive for Inspector Okasha in the old days. I gave him a call. He sent a car for you.'

'What about the brigadier? I don't want you to get yourself into trouble.'

'I can say I was only obeying orders. He can take it up with the inspector, but you can't stay here.'

Makana needed no encouragement.

'One thing, the brigadier said something about his nephew. Do you know anything about that?'

'That's where you're going now.'

Slipping some money into the man's hand discreetly, Makana climbed into the back of the police car. The rising sun was now an orange ball of flame. There was no reason for Makana to feel as sad as he did about Dalia Habashi's death. It just seemed so pointless. What had pushed her over the edge? Was it Na'il? Had she heard from him? Or was it worse than that? Makana wondered where they were taking him.

They were driving in the direction of Giza. Light flared though the gaps between the buildings, a blinding dazzle. It was still early and the traffic was heading in the other direction, which meant they made fast time. They were almost at Giza station when he saw the flashing emergency lights up ahead, a constellation of them clumped together under the dark wing of an overpass.

It seemed that Ayad Zafrani had taken his suggestion a little too literally. He had dumped Na'il all right. The yellow motor-cycle had been transformed into a tangled mass of chrome, burnt metal and blackened paint. An infernal machine that seemed to serve no recognisable purpose. Okasha was standing off to one side giving orders. An area had been roughly cordoned off by wooden barriers and a crowd had gathered to watch proceedings. The body was already loaded onto a stretcher. Doctora Siham was moving around it making a preliminary examination, no doubt spurred on by the urgency of the case.

'Ah, there you are.' Okasha looked up and dismissed the men he was talking to. 'How could I have guessed that you would be getting yourself into more trouble?'

'Dalia Habashi is dead. The brigadier seems to think it was murder.'

'And you naturally disagree with that assessment.' Okasha's face looked drawn. The strain seemed to be getting to him.

'I do, particularly since he seems to think I am the prime suspect.'

Okasha rolled his eyes. 'Brigadier Yusuf Effendi has a career in the force that dates back forty years.'

'You'd have thought that in all that time he might have learnt something.'

'I'm not going to debate this with you. Once he finds out that his nephew is dead he's going to get a whole lot worse. And that's nothing compared to when he discovers you're no longer in custody. So I'm counting on you here.'

'How did it happen?'

Okasha pointed with the aerial on his hand radio. 'The motorcycle came over the edge up there. Must have been going pretty fast.' Two police technicians were leaning over the parapet looking down at them. 'There's a gap in the railings where a bus apparently hit it six months ago and it hasn't been repaired properly. He went straight through.'

'So, you think it was an accident?'

'What else? He comes round the bend too fast, loses control. It happens all the time.'

They moved over to look at the motorcycle. A group of excited boys were pointing and trying to climb under the barrier. A policeman was doing his best to hold them at bay, rushing back and forth like a shepherd with a flock of wayward sheep. Considering the fall the Yamaha had acquitted itself fairly well. The front wheel and forks were twisted out of place and it must have caught fire. The petrol tank was ruptured and the seat was a charred mass.

Na'il's battered and broken body lay on a stretcher behind an ambulance from the forensics department. Doctora Siham looked up as they appeared.

'Ah, there you are,' she said, running a wary eye over Makana. 'And I see you brought your unauthorised friend.'

'How does a man get a cup of coffee around here?' Okasha grunted. He beckoned to one of his men and ordered him to send someone to fetch coffee. The order was passed along the line. A young policeman in big boots jogged away.

'Sure you're up to it? You might want to wait.'

'I grew up in the *rif*,' said Okasha. 'Slaughtering animals was an everyday matter.'

Doctora Siham tilted her head back. 'Interesting you make no distinction between a sheep and a human being.' She pulled back the sheet and leaned over the body.

Na'il had been in bad shape the last time Makana had seen him, in the basement of Ayad Zafrani's clubhouse, but now he looked infinitely worse and very much dead. The face had been caved in and the jaw detached. He didn't resemble a human being so much as a broken and battered piece of meat. Makana was glad he hadn't eaten that morning and even managed to resist the urge to reach for a cigarette.

'He wasn't wearing a helmet?'

Doctor Siham shook her head. 'Doesn't look that way. People think they are indestructible. They fly through the air like gods with wings until they hit something.'

'Very poetic,' muttered Okasha. 'Is there anything you can tell us?'

'Not much that you'd care to hear,' said the pathologist. 'The wounds seem consistent with what we know. A high-velocity impact. The head in particular. His mother would have trouble recognising him.'

'We're sure it's him,' Okasha said. 'He had a driving licence and identity card in his wallet.'

'There are no signs of burns,' Doctora Siham went on, 'even though the machine caught fire. He was found some ten metres from the motorcycle.'

'There's an old guy who sleeps under here,' grinned Okasha. 'The body missed him by about this much. He woke up with a shock.'

'Did he see anything?' Makana asked.

Okasha shook his head. 'I talked to him myself. Nothing he says makes sense.'

Doctora Siham cleared her throat.

'Sorry, Doctora, please continue.'

'It's too early to say for sure, but there's something odd about the injuries.'

'What do you mean by odd?' Makana asked.

'Well, if you look at the lower back and ribs, particularly the sides, you can see haematomas.' She indicated the yellow and purple weals. 'In this case, death would have been instantaneous, or as good as. In a fatal traffic accident the trauma occurs at or immediately before or after the moment of death. There isn't time for bruising to occur. The heart is no longer pumping the blood. The blood tends to pool according to gravity, but that takes a different form.'

A boy carrying coffee cups on a tray was let through the barrier and made his way over. Okasha's face lifted.

'Ah, finally.' He turned and began spooning sugar into a glass.

The others declined. The boy looked at the corpse with open curiosity. Makana declined the offer of coffee. Doctora Siham tapped her foot.

'When you're ready.'

'Sorry, Doctora,' Okasha apologised and paid the boy for his coffee. The boy held his hand out for the money without taking his eyes off the body.

'Off you go, boy.' Doctora Siham shooed him away. 'As I was saying, his superficial wounds appear consistent with the kind of trauma associated with what we see here; high-velocity vehicle collision with static objects. There is shearing, abrasion, broken legs and arms, but then there are other signs. Bruising, even cuts that show signs of healing.'

'Meaning what?' Okasha frowned as he sipped his coffee.

Doctora Siham gave him a curious look. 'Meaning that some of this damage was inflicted before the accident. Perhaps several days before.' She glanced at Makana to see if he was following. Okasha sipped his coffee and brushed a hand over his moustache. 'Let me see if I understand this . . .'

'He was tortured before he was killed,' said Makana.

'You should keep this one close,' said Doctora Siham. 'He could save you a lot of time.'

'Tortured?' Okasha glanced at Makana, who looked back at the body. It would be true to say he felt a certain degree of complicity, guilt even. He had witnessed Na'il being beaten. Could he have saved him? It seemed unlikely, but still. It was a bad feeling, this helplessness, and the sense that he should have tried harder. It was possible that Na'il had been a key witness. He was the only person to have been on the scene when Kasabian was murdered or shortly afterwards. He would have been invaluable if it came to putting any kind of legal case together. Makana's thoughts turned back to Dalia Habashi. Had she known Na'il was dead? Had she just guessed it? Makana would never know for sure.

Doctora Siham was speaking. 'The picture is distorted by the high-impact trauma produced by the fall.' She shook her head. 'But there's no doubt in my mind.'

'You're saying he was tortured and then pushed off the overpass?' Okasha was incredulous. 'On his motorcycle?'

'It's a novel twist.' The pathologist shrugged. 'Usually it's a long fall from a high building. This is a more imaginative variation on the theme. Don't tell me this is the first time you've heard of it, Inspector.' The doctor pulled the sheet up and gestured for them to load it into the ambulance. Then she peeled off her rubber gloves and reached into her coat for a cigarette. Makana lit hers and one of his own. She crossed her arms and looked down at her shoes.

'I'll be able to tell you more when I get him into the lab, but right now I'm inclined to believe that somebody beat him over a period of hours, perhaps days, and then, when death occurred, decided to hide the evidence by making it look like he rode over the edge of the road on his motorcycle. Not bad, but obviously not too smart either.'

'So he was beaten. Any idea what with?'

Doctora Siham tugged at her ear. 'I can't say, but it looks like a long instrument. A metal bar, but fairly thin. Perhaps an iron rod. I'll be able to tell you more when I can do a more thorough investigation. All that I'm telling you now are simply my preliminary thoughts on the subject.'

'We appreciate all your efforts, Doctora,' Okasha said stiffly. It was a reminder of the authority the pathologist exerted. She had a reputation for tearing strips off bigger men than Okasha.

Now she dropped her cigarette to the ground and walked towards her car. 'I'll let you know as soon as I have more.'

'A formidable woman,' Okasha said, with an admiring shake of the head. 'Of course you know what they say, that if she had a husband she wouldn't be as devoted to her work.'

'Maybe you should be thankful,' said Makana.

'Oh, believe me, I am.' As the ambulance pulled away, Okasha turned his attention to Makana. 'So, what do you think? Why would anyone torture and kill our friend?'

'You mean our best witness?'

'Possibly.' Okasha shrugged. 'We don't know what he might have seen or not seen.'

'Na'il was mixed up in a lot of things.'

'And this woman at the hotel, what is her connection?'

'They were involved.'

'Involved as in they were sleeping together?'

'Dalia Habashi was in trouble financially. Na'il was trying to help her, in his own way.'

'There are times I almost think I understand you,' Okasha eyed Makana suspiciously. 'We've known each other a long time. I'd like to think you would tell me if you knew anything about this.'

'Believe me, there's nothing I'd like more than to finish this before the brigadier gets a chance to lock me up again.'

Okasha's eyes were heavy and swollen. 'The brigadier wants me out. That's how he works. He wants those loyal to him close by. He probably already has somebody lined up for my job.'

'I've always told you, if you want to get ahead you need to make friends in politics.'

'Well, I would if I could stomach them. Nowadays it's all about having your photograph taken with a minister, or an actress, or some other damn fool.'

'It's about a lot more than that and you know it.'

Okasha motioned to the wrecked motorcycle. 'Tell me what this is about.'

'Na'il was blackmailing Kasabian. He knew Kasabian was selling antiquities on the black market. Some Egyptian pieces, which nobody seems to care too much about, but also Iraqi, which has become a hot issue since the Americans moved in. Na'il threatened to expose him and wanted money to keep quiet. Money he was planning to give to Dalia Habashi.'

'Where would Kasabian get hold of Iraqi antiquities?'

'From an Iraqi officer named Kadhim al-Samari. The man I was hired to find.'

'What you're saying makes no sense. He hired you to find someone he was already dealing with?'

'That's where it gets complicated.'

'Get to the point, Makana. We don't have a lot of time here, and bear in mind you've just accused the brigadier's favourite nephew of blackmail.'

'Na'il was an enterprising man. He had another deal going for him. When he found out why Kasabian had hired me he went straight to Kasabian's client.'

'The American? Charles Barkley?'

'Exactly, only it turns out his name is not Barkley, it's Zachary Kane.'

'You're making me dizzy. I need more coffee.' Okasha tossed the dregs from his cup to the ground and cast around frantically for the boy, who was nowhere to be seen. The crowd on the barriers had started to disperse. Now that the body was gone there didn't seem to be much of interest.

'Na'il told Kane that Kasabian was trying to deceive him. Kane is not someone to take being crossed lightly. He must have been furious. I think he took Na'il along with him when he went to confront Kasabian. Here was Na'il's chance to prove he was not to be messed with, only things got out of hand. Kane hung Kasabian up and started cutting strips off him. That was too much for Na'il, so he fled, probably thinking he might be next.'

'What you're saying suggests that this man Barkley, or Kane, is the one who did this.' Okasha indicated the mangled remains of the motorcycle.

'No, that's not exactly what I'm saying.'

Okasha swore under his breath. 'You'd better tell me everything or I swear I will throw you to the brigadier and his dogs.'

'I'm getting there,' said Makana as he lit another cigarette. 'Kane is after Samari. He doesn't care about Na'il. He tortured Kasabian to get him to talk. The only problem was that Kasabian couldn't tell him what he wanted to know, because he had no idea where Samari was – nobody did then or now.' Makana fell silent. They were loading the remains of the motorcycle onto a lorry to take back to the police compound. 'If you're serious about catching Kasabian's killer then we have to move quickly.'

'Nothing would give me more satisfaction than closing the case without the brigadier's help.' Okasha shook his head gravely. 'Now that his nephew has been killed there'll be no stopping him.'

'Do you think you're up to arresting an American?'

'You mean this man Kane?' An unhappy look came over Okasha's face.

'Can you do it?'

'We'd have to have a pretty solid case against him. A thousand kinds of trouble are going to come down on our heads if we arrest an American.'

'Come on, you'll be a national hero. The man who arrested an American mercenary for killing an Egyptian. They'll put a statue of you in Tahrir Square.'

'We'll need evidence. The murder weapon.'

It was a possibility. Kane might be that confident of his position to hold onto the knife he used. It was slim but it might be enough.

'Or a confession.' A light appeared in Okasha's eyes as he began to glimpse a way forward. Signed confessions were something of a police speciality, after all. Anyone could be made to confess to anything. All it took was time.

'We'll need to move quickly.'

Okasha reached for his radio. 'Is he still at the Marriott?'

'No, but I know where he is.'

'So let's go and get him.'

'We can't just walk in there. Kane is not alone. He's got five others with him. At least four of them are trained mercenaries and most probably armed.'

'We can bring in the CSF, no problem.'

Chapter Thirty

As with everything, it was easier in theory than in practice. There was a lot of standing around with Okasha barking orders into the car radio with one hand while making frantic phone calls with the other. It was made more complicated by the fact that Okasha was trying to avoid involving the brigadier or any of his cohorts.

'We'll meet the other units along the way. We haven't much time. Brigadier Effendi's informers will be tripping over themselves to let him know what's happening.' Okasha waved Makana into the back of his car. They swept off down towards the Pyramids Road. Even with sirens wailing and lights flashing the going was slow. The heavy mid-morning traffic could only respond sluggishly and they seemed to crawl at times. The longer it took, the more time Makana had to think of what the consequences might be if they didn't get hold of Kane.

The Five Seesons Hotel proved to be an unsightly building, a cracked lump of concrete that once upon a time must have been painted a mint-green colour. A white stripe ran around the outside edge like piping on a cake. Time, intense sunlight and traffic fumes had faded it to a dusty off-white. Rain streaks ran like tear tracks down the pockmarked façade where dull patches of plaster had fallen off here and there. A dusty light-box sign ran down one corner of the building, each painted letter worn partially away.

It stood directly on the Pyramids Road, a dual carriageway swamped with traffic running into and out of town at high speed. The noise and vibrations alone would have put paid to any ideas of rest and tranquillity. They approached from the wrong side and had to go half a mile down before effecting an illegal U-turn and coming back up. Makana managed to persuade Okasha to switch off the sirens. By now everyone in Cairo must know they were on their way.

The procession of police cars, CSF vans and a prison lorry much like the one Makana had been locked in few hours ago all swept into the hotel forecourt. The interior had an abandoned quality to it, as if the place were about to be condemned. A few visitors sat huddled together looking bored as they waited for something to happen. The sight of some thirty-odd police officers charging in off the street in riot gear certainly created a stir. Some clutched one another in panic while one red-faced man cheered like a supporter at a football match. Behind the desk an unhappy woman in her twenties, wearing thick lipstick that glistened the colour of pomegranate juice, took a step back as they approached.

'There's a group of Americans staying here,' Okasha snapped.

'Take your pick,' she said, clicking a stapler nervously.

'A man named Charles Barkley, or Zachary Kane?'

'We don't have anyone by that name.' She was watching the men in riot gear moving around the lobby. 'What's this all about? We don't have terrorists staying here.'

'Americans,' Makana explained. 'They are trained soldiers. There are six of them altogether. Zachary Kane, along with Clearwater, Santos, Hagen, Jansen and an Iraqi named Faisal Abdallah.'

'Does that description make any sense to you?' Okasha demanded.

She turned coy, eyes darting from one to the other. 'We might have a group of men like that.'

'They would have checked in sometime in the last couple of days,' said Makana.

The receptionist's eyes were on the computer screen as she tapped a couple of keys.

'Don't you normally examine passports when people check in?'

'We have to, those are the regulations.' Her eyes remained on the screen.

'But sometimes you don't.'

'If it's very busy. You know, they're tourists. They have nothing to hide.'

'You're saying these men checked in without any documentation?' Okasha waded in.

'Oh no, we would never do that.' She smiled again. 'Usually it is arranged in the first day or so.'

'How did they pay?'

'In cash. American dollars.' The receptionist held up a handful of newly painted fingernails. The colour matched her lipstick. Makana wondered how much extra Kane had given her to keep her happy. 'Anyway, they've gone. They checked out about an hour ago.'

'An hour ago?' Okasha thumped a hand down on the counter. 'Where did they go?'

'Back to where they came from, I suppose.' The receptionist shrugged. It was nothing to do with her. 'They paid in full.'

'I'm sure they did.' Okasha pulled Makana aside. 'You'd better get out of here, because it won't take long for the brigadier to get wind of this operation. He'll be calling any second to tell me he's on his way. It's going to be hard enough to explain this without you around. We're going to search their rooms and then I'm going to leave a car here in case they decide to come back.'

'They may have left town or simply switched hotels.'

'We'll find them, wherever they are,' Okasha said, before turning away.

Chapter Thirty-one

Some two hours later found Makana and Sindbad sitting in the Thunderbird. The downtown area was calm and almost deserted. Most people were at home with their families on a Friday afternoon. The shops and businesses were shuttered and padlocked. In the evening it would come to life again as people strolled about beneath the buzzing lights looking for diversion, but for now it was tranquil, almost unnaturally so. The occasional toot of a horn sounded plaintively in the distance and for a time it was possible to imagine these streets as they might once have been, when the volume of traffic and people still fell within the parameters of what city planners might have had in mind for it. A solitary vendor made his way up the middle of Sharif Basha Street, an enormous net filled with footballs on his back. The brightly coloured globes rose up over his head. They resembled mysterious planets and lent his figure an air of myth: a god of other worlds keeping the universe in motion.

While Makana studied the street for any signs of movement, Sindbad yawned and grumbled about there being none of his favourite snack bars anywhere near. It wasn't that he minded sacrificing his day off. To hear him talk it sounded as though he was glad of the opportunity to get away from home and his expanding brood of growing children.

'The little ones are two years old now and I swear by our lord above I have never heard such a noise. They could waken Sayidna Hussein himself from his tomb. If it's not one it's the other.'

Makana had lost track of just how many children Sindbad had. He suspected there were five, but it was possible he might have missed a couple along the way. Sindbad never tired of reminding him that a man's pride was in his family, as if to underline the fact that Makana had nothing around him in the way of spouse or offspring.

'A man needs children. It's in his nature.' Sindbad's understanding of philosophy was as a means of endorsing his way of life. His voice rang with the wisdom of centuries. Two minutes, or whatever the average time for the act of procreation might be, and suddenly he was an expert on all things human.

As he listened with half an ear, Makana considered the wisdom of not bringing Okasha in on this. But right now it made more sense for Okasha to be dealing with the brigadier while Makana focused on tracking down Kane and his men. Makana also felt that it would be hard to explain to Okasha what exactly he was trying to do.

Another twenty minutes went by without change. Sindbad's head lolled back against the door frame. His mouth hung open and he snored softly to himself. Makana shook him awake.

'They're here.'

The tailor's shop was an old-fashioned place on a small square set back from the street and tucked under a row of arcades. The name *Awad Suleiman & Sons* was hand-painted across the glass in flowing gold script both ways, in Arabic and English. The square was dotted with a few palm trees and some grey blocks that must once have been meant for some other kind of vegetation that had either perished or never arrived. Pigeons drifted down and waddled across the paving stones.

The two black BMW SUVs rolled up to the kerb in tandem. The tinted windows hid the occupants but Makana was sure they were the same vehicles he had seen outside Zafrani's club. There was a moment's lull. On the far side of the square was a branch of Bank Misr, its doors barred and a guard in a white police uniform lolling in an old chair by a sentry box. Across his knees rested a battered AK47. To the left of this, directly opposite the tailor's shop, was an old apartment building. It looked as though it had been neglected for years. The windows were covered with brown wooden shutters, many of which were cracked, half-open or closed and missing slats.

From where they were parked Makana had a view of the arches and the door to the tailor's shop. The car doors opened and three men climbed out of the lead vehicle. They were dressed in grey suits. Probably not the kind made by Awad Suleiman & Sons, but respectable enough. They spread out. Two of them walked back to the second vehicle and took up positions on either side. The third man opened the rear door. None of the guards was holding a weapon, but the way they stood, protecting one side of their jackets, suggested they were armed. The sentry outside the bank pushed back his beret and scratched his head, wondering perhaps if the car's passenger was a famous singer or actress.

When he appeared, Kadhim al-Samari was dressed in black. He wore a polo-neck shirt that went up to his chin, a black suit and dark glasses. He buttoned his jacket calmly before moving off. He carried himself with the confidence of a man who was comfortable with money and power. He wasn't a big man: all the bodyguards were taller than him, which made sense if their job was to shield him from attack. As the little procession made its way over the square towards the tailor's shop, Makana climbed out of the car.

'Stay here and keep your eyes open.'

'*Hadir, ya basha.*' Sindbad sat up and rubbed his eyes, suddenly anxious. All thoughts of children and food were gone.

As Samari went inside two bodyguards took up positions outside, one close by the door, the other a few metres away in the middle of the square. They each took up an angle to watch; one to the left, the other to the right. The third man remained by the cars. A fourth and fifth man were presumably behind the wheel of the cars. A team of five for one man. Samari didn't like to take chances. He knew he had enemies. No doubt there were plenty of people who would like to see him dead, as well as others who would be more than happy to collect the reward for turning him in.

Makana walked across the square. From the entrance to the tailor's shop the bodyguards watched him approach. One of them stepped forward as if to block his way, but the second put a hand out to stop him. He recognised Makana from outside Zafrani's club.

'I need to talk to him,' said Makana.

The guards looked at one another, then one of them stepped forward and gestured for Makana to raise his arms before running his palms over him to search for weapons. Then he stepped aside. Makana pushed open the door and heard a bell ring to announce his entrance. The tailor's shop smelt of freshly spun cloth. Yards of it lined the shelves on three sides of the interior.

Behind the counter a white-haired man with a tape measure around his neck was writing something down in a ledger. To his left a boy of about sixteen, slim and well dressed with his hair oiled and combed, was perched on a ladder replacing a bolt of cloth on a high shelf. Kadhim al-Samari was nowhere to be seen. The tailor looked up at Makana. He assumed that the guards wouldn't let anyone by who wasn't welcome. He nodded in the direction of a narrow doorway covered by a curtain. Makana stepped through and found himself in a large fitting room. There were racks of clothes along one side and a full-length mirror on the other in which Kadhim al-Samari stood admiring himself and his new suit, which was still waiting for the finishing touches. He glanced at Makana before going back to his reflection.

'So, it is perhaps time for me to change my tailor.'

'Please don't do it on my account.'

Makana crossed the room to another doorway and a curtain. Beyond, a long dark corridor led to a workshop where he could see a couple of sewing machines. He drew the curtain closed.

'For man of few habits you make a surprising number of exceptions.'

'A weakness, I know,' Samari shrugged. 'It's hard to find a good tailor, but I suppose you know all about that. As for the girl, well, perhaps I don't have to explain that to you.'

Makana reached for his cigarettes. Samari returned to examining his suit in the mirror.

'I'm serious. You should try improving your wardrobe. The quality of your clients will increase infinitely.'

'I'm not sure that's all there is to it.'

'I'm just saying you should consider it. Clothes make an impression.'

'Thank you, but I'll manage.'

'Mr Suleiman is a maestro. In my view he's the best tailor in the Middle East. You ought to let him try.'

'Some other time, maybe.'

'Then perhaps you'd care to explain what you are doing here.' Samari's eyes were small and dark. They fixed unwaveringly on Makana's reflection.

'I came to tell you that Kane is on the move.'

'You came to warn me?'

'The police are searching for him as we speak. When they catch him he will be charged with murder.'

'I see, you have been busy.' Samari watched Makana carefully. 'And why come to me?'

'Because Kane will be in a panic now. If he's going to make a move against you it will be soon.'

'Interesting. Your concern is touching. Tell me, how did you find me?' He tugged the cuffs of his new jacket. 'It was the girl, I suppose. Is she the one you're really concerned about?'

'She wants to make a life for herself and her child.'

'And you think you are the one to provide her with that?'

Makana said nothing. It occurred to him that striking a match in here would be a good way of seeing the whole place go up in smoke, but he did so anyway.

'You had a family once, didn't you? You know what it's like.'

Samari's face hardened. 'If you're going to appeal to my human instinct, you should make sure your research is complete. My wife and three children were killed by an American air raid in 1991. They were in the basement of the house. A two-thousand-pound bunker-buster brought the whole building down. What they call surgical strikes.' Samari ran his fingers along the unfinished lapel of his jacket. 'Since then, well, once a man has lost a family he is reluctant to begin again, but I don't need to tell you that, do I?' Samari held Makana's gaze in the mirror. 'Yes, I know all about you and where you come from and why you are stuck in this city trying to earn a few piastres in your own way.'

'I don't think you appreciate how dangerous Kane is.'

'On the contrary.' A smile crossed the Iraqi's face, 'I'm not sure you appreciate how dangerous I can be.'

'Take the opportunity, leave Cairo. Things are going to get very uncomfortable here in the next few days.'

'Why the sudden concern for my well-being? I asked you to bring Kane to me. I offered to reward you handsomely, and now you appear without warning, telling me to leave town.' Samari turned sideways to study the cut of the jacket. He spoke without lifting his eyes. 'Why are you really here?'

'You're a wealthy man. You have millions. You could buy Bilquis her freedom.'

'That would suit you.' Samari snorted. 'I pay Zafrani for the girl and disappear. What then? Are you planning to take care of her and her bastard son? Somehow you don't seem the type.'

'Your time here is up, I think you know that. Kasabian's murder has stirred up a lot of trouble and it's not going to end there. When they get hold of Kane the whole story is going to come out, and then even your old friend Qasim is not going to be able to protect you.'

Samari's eyes glittered as he turned on Makana. 'What if I cared for the girl? Did you think of that? What if I wanted her for myself?'

'She's just a whore to you. That's all she'll ever be.'

'And she's more to you?' Samari fell silent for a moment. 'You didn't come here for the girl, did you? I see it in your eyes.' He stepped closer. So close Makana could feel his breath on his face. 'You don't approve of me. You think I should be brought to justice perhaps? To pay for my crimes?' Samari's voice dropped to a whisper. 'If I thought for a second you had come to try and claim the reward I would kill you without hesitation.' He remained like that, motionless. Then he snorted. 'You don't have the guts to try and kill me,' he said, turning back to the mirror.

'Have you asked yourself why Kane would go to so much trouble to find you?' Makana asked. 'This is not just about some paintings. I don't even think he's interested in the money. No, this is personal.'

Samari shrugged. 'A lot of people have tried to kill me over the years, and as you can see, none of them has managed to succeed. I've been avoiding assassins for a long time, and I intend to go on doing so. Anyway, I have invested too much here to just leave. Kane is nothing. A small-time mercenary. I am curious though as to how he found me.'

'He went to Falluja to find you, but you had already left. He met a man named Faisal Abdallah.'

'Faisal?' Kadhim al-Samari frowned. 'Yes, he used to drive for me. A herdsman's son and a coward. You think he betrayed me? It doesn't surprise me. It is natural that a man should take care of himself.'

'You had contacts here. Qasim Abdel Qasim, an old military comrade who had turned himself into a successful businessman and politician. And Ayad Zafrani, a big-time gangster and club owner.'

'We all need friends,' shrugged Samari.

'Yes, but not many of them seem to stay loyal, do they? How long do you think Qasim and Zafrani will be able to protect you?'

'You have to trust people.'

'You trusted Kasabian and now he's dead.'

'I believe that was my fault,' said Samari quietly. 'I probably alerted Kane to Kasabian's existence. The Ishtar piece. I knew it was a mistake to sell. Too distinctive, but there was a buyer nosing around, a German. Kasabian assured me we had a unique opportunity. It would never be as valuable as it was then. So we sold it. I had two. One is still in Kasabian's hands, or was.'

'The Babylonian goddess of love and war. Yes, it's still there. I saw it. Kane was already on your trail. That sale told him someone was selling stolen Iraqi antiquities in Cairo.'

'Stolen?' snorted Samari. 'These pieces are part of our heritage. Is it better for them to be crushed by American tanks, or wind up in the pockets of Rumsfeld and Cheney?'

'Kane told Kasabian he was looking for the Franz Marc painting to put you off your guard. If he had come around asking about antiquities you might have become suspicious.'

'It's true. The talk of *The Tower of Blue Horses* put me at ease. An American buyer might have known of its existence. I asked Kasabian to look into him.'

'Kasabian tried to hire Na'il, who saw an opportunity he couldn't resist and decided to go into business for himself.'

'Kasabian was a poor judge of character. It's a weakness.'

'Perhaps. Na'il threatened to expose Kasabian's dealings in stolen antiquities. That would have brought attention on you. Attention you were keen to avoid.'

Samari had given up fiddling with his jacket.

'You gave the order to Zafrani to get rid of Na'il, didn't you?'

'If you leave these things unchecked they catch up with you one day.'

'Then you effectively killed another person, too, Dalia Habashi.'

Samari pulled a face. 'A meddler. A gossip with no head for business.'

'She took her own life.'

'Take my advice, you can't save all of them. Don't try. You'll avoid a lot of heartache.'

The tailor stuck his head through the curtain. Noting the smell and spotting the ash and stubbed-out cigarette end on the floor, he gave Makana a dirty look.

'How is the fit?' he asked Samari.

'It could be taken in a little in the shoulders.'

'Let me have a look.'

While the tailor fussed around moving pins and making adjustments, Samari went on: 'You've made your case, Mr Makana, now you have all the pieces. But you're making a mistake. The girl is not worth it. Take my word for it, they never are. Forget your noble task and go back to your dull life. If you won't help me find Kane, my advice is to stay out of my way.'

The tailor finished his work and slipped the jacket off and helped Samari on with his own. He held the curtain for Samari and Makana.

'I'll send someone to collect it next week. For now I'll take the shirts.'

'As you wish, sir.' The tailor gave a slight bow. The shirts were already wrapped in brown paper. The apprentice picked them up and followed the Iraqi as he moved towards the door. Outside the two guards straightened up. There was a moment's hesitation and then a nod to indicate it was safe for him to come out.

In the doorway, Samari paused to address Makana.

'Don't try to follow me and don't, not even for a second, think about trying to claim the reward. Believe me, you won't get far.'

The square was still quiet. An old man in a grubby gellabiya was wandering through examining the dead plants in the ornamental pots that had been abandoned to their own fate. A former gardener, thought Makana, or perhaps a poet in search of inspiration. Catching sight of a group of pigeons picking their way between the plants, the old man clapped his hands to shoo them away and a small flock of them took to the air.

It was at that moment that the sniper decided to take his shot. If not for the scattering of pigeons he might have killed Samari on the spot. Instead the bullet went wide. The glass shopfront shattered and the young apprentice crumpled to the floor at Makana's side. Blood spilt out of him over the brown paper package of shirts he had been holding.

'You!' Samari turned on Makana just as another shot rammed into the door frame. The Iraqi ducked left. Makana moved in the opposite direction. The bodyguards had produced weapons from underneath their jackets and were spreading out. They were looking upwards, trying to spot where the shooter was. Another shot, silent, like the first one. The rifle had a silencer. Makana felt rather than saw the bullet slamming into the wall beside him, sending a puff of plaster into the air.

One of the guards shouted and fired across the square. A man stepped from behind a pillar and fired back. The guard's body jolted as three bullets hit him squarely and he crumpled to the ground. Again, the weapon must have been silenced. Outside the bank the sentry scratched his head, more mystified than alarmed, the Kalashnikov still resting on his splayed knees.

With his head down, Makana had almost reached the next pillar along in the arcade when a man stepped out in front of him. Makana's first reaction was surprise that he recognised him. He had seen the tall skinny man with long, unkempt hair before. It was at the Marriott Hotel the day he had gone there with Okasha to meet Charles Barkley. Unconsciously, he realised that this had to be Eddie Clearwater, but there was barely time to register the fact. Clearwater was levelling a pistol at Makana's chest. He was trapped with nowhere for him to go. Two loud shots sounded from Makana's left and Clearwater was thrown back against the wall. He slid to the ground as Makana turned to see Frank Cassidy stepping from a doorway, his Colt Python in hand. He joined Makana behind the pillar.

'Thank you,' said Makana.

'Don't mention it.'

The noise from Cassidy's revolver reverberated through the small square. The sniper had fallen silent. It took Makana a moment to locate Samari, who had ducked down and was partially hidden behind one of the rectangular plant troughs. He was staying put, waiting for his men to do what he paid them for. The second bodyguard was firing now as he advanced across the square in the direction of the man who had shot his partner. He was too far away to be accurate, but that didn't stop him firing off five or six shots. The old man in the gellabiya went down with a cry.

The police sentry had finally figured out that something was up and now did what came naturally, which meant jumping behind the metal shield alongside the bank door. In his haste he fumbled the Kalashnikov and it clattered to the ground. He managed to retrieve it and scurry behind the protective shield, where he remained out of sight. Makana wondered if he was equipped with a telephone or radio.

Two of Kane's men were now advancing across the square from either corner. They came at the second bodyguard from different angles. Before he could make up his mind which one to go for they had taken him out. They advanced in tandem, firing carefully placed shots that kept the third bodyguard pinned down behind the cars.

'They want to take him alive,' Makana heard Cassidy say next to him. 'The sniper wasn't aiming to kill Samari, just to take out his guards.'

It made sense. Of course they wanted him alive.

The driver of the second car leapt out. He let off a burst of automatic fire that caused Kane's men to pause. Makana recognised them from the café in the bazaar: Hagen and Santos. The nearside window of the first BMW shattered, reminding everyone that the sniper was still in position. Kane's men drew level with Samari. Makana wondered if Kane was the shooter with the rifle.

'They don't need to take out the other two,' Cassidy said.

It was true. If their objective was Samari, then they almost had him within their grasp. That was when Samari changed the game.

Santos addressed the Iraqi. When Samari did not respond he leaned over to pull him to his feet. In one smooth motion Samari came up, his arm flying out. Even at a distance, Makana could see the scarlet arc of blood as it fountained into the sunlight. Santos screamed and staggered back, both hands to his throat as he sank to his knees. Samari slipped back into the shadows beneath the arcade while Hagen tried to help his friend. The bodyguards renewed their efforts. Over by the cars, the driver had located the sniper and sent a long burst towards the first-floor windows where the wooden shutters threw off splinters as bullets smashed into them. The second man loosed off several wild shots at Hagen while advancing to protect his boss. Hagen ducked behind a pillar. Santos was dead on his knees. Blood still poured out of him in spurts. Then his hands dropped and he fell onto his face and was still. The driver had paused to reload. Hagen threaded his way through the arcades as he jogged away.

By now shouts were coming from nearby. People peered cautiously from windows and doorways. Makana watched Samari hurrying towards the second BMW. One of the two bodyguards made a move towards his fallen colleagues, but Samari waved him back. They all climbed aboard and both cars sped off. People began to come forward to examine the dead and the wounded.

'It's time for us to go,' Makana said to Cassidy. Sirens in the distance were drawing nearer.

Chapter Thirty-two

When they got back to the Thunderbird, Makana told Sindbad to drive away slowly.

'No sudden moves and keep your foot light on the accelerator.'

Sindbad edged into the road and cautiously rumbled through the crowds now spilling into the street in front of them. Even the police sentry had reappeared and was trying to take control of the situation. He waved at people to stand back. Little attention was paid to the Thunderbird.

Samari's cars had taken off at high speed and disappeared from sight. Following him was now out of the question. He would be fully alert and intent on making a clean getaway. More sirens were converging from every direction. The city was in turmoil, as if the attack had somehow triggered off a series of shocks that rippled outwards.

'Thank you,' said Makana to Cassidy as they moved off.

'Lucky for you I decided to follow you.'

'Yes,' agreed Makana. 'Lucky for me.'

'You can thank me when you get me Kane.'

'I didn't see him back there.'

'Kane's too smart to be caught in the middle,' Cassidy said. 'He would have been behind the scenes, coordinating things.'

There was something else bothering Makana. 'How did Kane know about the tailor's appointment?'

'Perhaps he just followed you, like I did.' Cassidy sank down in the back seat and lit one of his Camels.

It was possible that Kane had followed him, but Makana thought it unlikely. It wouldn't have given him enough time to set up the ambush. It had all been carefully planned. Kane and his men had studied the location well. They had weapons and transport in place. They had worked out their escape route.

As they drove Makana realised that he was going to have to trust Cassidy in some way. He had saved his life, after all. Perhaps an American could help him to understand how someone like Kane thought. Whatever the explanation for Kane's appearance, he knew it wouldn't take Samari long to work out who had betrayed him. He dialled Bilquis only to be rewarded by the engaged tone. A police car, lights flashing, cut across their path, causing the Thunderbird to screech to a halt.

'Where are we going, *ya basha*?' Sindbad asked. His voice was trembling. Makana could see that his hands were gripping the wheel tightly. The shooting had upset him.

'It's all right, Sindbad. We'll be okay.'

Without a word, Sindbad pulled up, opened his door, leaned out and vomited quietly into the gutter. After a moment or two he straightened up and plucked a scented paper tissue from the box he insisted on keeping on the dashboard.

'Where did you get the help?' Cassidy asked.

They drove first to the club in Maadi, where Makana leaned on the buzzer until the door opened. The house was sleeping the day away. None of the bouncers was in sight. Upstairs Gigi herself opened the door. Wearing a housecoat and with her hair in curlers, it took him a moment to recognise her without the make-up and the glamorous clothes.

'What do you want at this hour?'

'Is Bilquis here?'

'Control yourself. What do you think this place is? A twenty-four-hour supermarket? We need our rest just like everyone else.'

'I need you to tell me if she's here,' said Makana slowly.

Gigi pouted. 'She hasn't shown up yet, and I won't be surprised if she doesn't.'

'Why do you say that?'

'Because she's trouble. Always has been, right from the start.' Gigi folded her arms. 'She used to do her job and not answer back. Then all of a sudden she thinks her life is going to change. Somebody needs to teach her a lesson.'

Makana was already heading for the stairs. On the way down he tried Bilquis again. As he reached the ground-floor veranda, a wall fell on him. As he flew sideways and tumbled to the ground, he watched his telephone come apart as it skittered across the floor. When he looked up he saw the fat bouncer. He looked bigger from this angle. He was chewing something and was frowning so fiercely his eyes seemed to meet in the middle of his forehead. Perhaps he was angry at having his lunch disturbed.

'You should know better than to come around here annoying people when they are trying to rest.'

Makana tried to sit up and felt a sharp pain in his ribs.

'Look,' he began, holding up a hand. 'I don't have time for this.'

'Oh yeah? Well, let me tell you what I don't have time for.' Underneath the fat there was clearly a lot of muscle. He hauled Makana to his feet with as much ease as a normal person might scoop up a kitten. Then he hit him again, in the stomach this time. Makana folded over.

'I don't have time for liars. I don't have time for people who pretend to be invited guests when they aren't.' He wasn't even breathing heavily. Makana saw the foot coming up towards his face and managed to turn away so that the blow struck his shoulder. It was still powerful enough to send him flying backwards into the wall. The bouncer lumbered closer. Makana wasn't convinced of the wisdom of getting to his feet at this point, but he knew that if he stayed down he would be kicked senseless in a matter of minutes. He feinted left and moved right. The fat man laughed. Makana managed to get in a low kick to the man's right knee which stopped him in his tracks. The fat man's expression hardened.

'Now you're starting to really annoy me.'

'Any trouble, *ya basha*?'

Makana was never so glad to see Sindbad. The bouncer turned to face him.

'Who are you?'

'I'm the one who teaches you a lesson.'

The fat man weighed Sindbad up and grunted to himself in satisfaction, or perhaps it was anticipation. On a normal day Sindbad looked fairly big, but next to this man he seemed to have shrunk. Makana wasn't too concerned. He had witnessed Sindbad's skills on a number of occasions and had never failed to be impressed by how lightly such a large man could move. If you watched him carefully you realised he carried a lot of his weight in his shoulders and arms. His waist, despite the years of married life, was relatively slim. But it was his legs that were the most impressive, because they were actually quite slender. He moved on his toes, slipped to his left with effortless ease, closing in on the bouncer with speed. His hands flew out, delivering a combination of blows

309

that stopped the fat man in his tracks. A look of bewilderment came over him. He threw a punch that Sindbad swatted aside as he stepped in to deliver a body blow that brought the bouncer to his knees. It hardly seemed like a fair match. Makana retrieved the pieces of his telephone as the bouncer crashed to the tiles face first with a crunch that made him wince. Sindbad was rubbing his knuckles. He seemed to be enjoying himself.

'I really need to start training again. You know how you can let things slip? What with the job and the family, I never seem to have the time.'

'You're doing fine, Sindbad, believe me.'

Cassidy was waiting for them by the gate.

'Okay, so I can see how he can come in useful at times.'

'We have to get across the river. I can't reach her on the phone.'

The traffic was sluggish. They crawled slowly towards the river, then onto the bridge, edging their way up. It felt like a monumental task, like building a pyramid. Off on the horizon the sun glowed a fierce red.

Makana was making no progress with putting his telephone back together. It was as if he had too many pieces. Feeling his frustration mounting, he dumped the whole collection in a heap on the seat next to him.

'Having trouble?' Cassidy asked.

'See if you have better luck than me,' said Makana, passing the pieces to the back seat.

After a time, Cassidy sat back and whistled. 'Well, now we know how they found out about the meeting.'

'What have you found?'

Cassidy was holding up a strip of plastic with a circuit printed on it.

'That's the bit I couldn't fit in,' said Makana.

'That's because it doesn't belong there. It's an audio bug. They were listening in on your conversations.'

'They heard Bilquis telling me about the tailor. How could they do that?'

'Well, they must have taken it off you at some stage. A bar or lift. Someone standing too close to you? Notice anything like that? Or they might have bumped into you by accident.'

Makana remembered the man in the Marriott. The man who had stepped out in front of him and had been about to shoot him.

'Eddie Clearwater.'

The bellhop had handed him back his telephone. Makana gave the instrument a malevolent glare. It seemed to have borne out all his misgivings. He turned it over in his hands, fighting the urge to fling the thing out of the window and be done with it.

When they finally reached Sharia Sudan, Makana left Sindbad and Cassidy in the car and crossed the footbridge by himself. Remembering his last visit, he decided it would be wise not to draw more attention than was necessary. As it turned out there was no one around to block his progress. The boys who hung about outside the bakery must have been sleeping the night off.

The door to Bilquis's flat was wide open.

Makana walked cautiously inside, fearing the worst. It was too quiet. He could hear the sounds of the street, someone selling bottles of kerosene for stoves. The main room held the first signs of trouble. One arm had broken off the sofa, a chair had been overturned, broken glass crunched underfoot. The picture of the Kaaba now lay shattered on the linoleum floor. Wisps of smoke drifted from a smouldering cigarette that lay in the tin ashtray on the table. Makana moved into the boy's room. The bed was unmade. He turned as someone came in through the front door behind him.

'Who are you?' A stout man in his fifties, with greying whiskers and wearing a gellabiya. In his right hand he held a length of metal pipe.

'Where is she?'

'Are you a friend of hers?' Makana nodded. The pipe lowered a fraction. 'We live next door. My wife usually fetches the boy around this time. We look after him while his mother works.'

'What happened?'

'It was about the time when my wife usually goes over to fetch him. Suddenly we heard all this noise. We thought maybe they were playing a game. Banging and crashing. We began to grow concerned. My wife tried to go in, she was knocked aside. They took them both, her and the boy.'

'Did you see who they were?'

'They were dressed like businessmen. They took her. That's all I know.'

Makana moved to the window and looked out. Nothing was out of the ordinary. At the far end of the street he could see a group of people gathered at the corner.

'How long ago was this?'

'Just now. My wife came screaming. I went back to fetch this from under the bed.' He brandished the pipe. 'By the time I got here they had disappeared into thin air.'

'Did you call the police?'

'The police?' The man jerked back as if stung, a deep frown of incomprehension on his face. 'Now why would I do that? I don't want to cause problems for anyone.' The man scratched his chin. 'She's a nice girl, I guess she's just mixed up with the wrong people. It happens all the time. Take my brother's son . . . Hey, where are you going?'

When he came out of the narrow doorway Makana looked

both ways and then began running down the uneven alley towards the main street. The crowd he had seen from the window was gathered at the corner. People were offering their opinions, pointing at the moving traffic. A young man was picking up guavas and replacing them in a heap.

'What happened here?'

'What happened?' The boy glared at Makana. 'They came out of nowhere, knocked the whole corner down. Who do you think is going to pay for all that fruit?'

'What kind of car was it?'

'Who knows? Big and black and driven by a donkey.'

Makana made his way slowly back through the crowds and over the footbridge. Cassidy was leaning against the side of the car smoking.

'Samari's men have taken her and the boy. We need to find out where they went.'

'Does it occur to that maybe you're taking this a little personally?'

'You're here to avenge your son. If anyone can understand it ought to be you.'

'I'm just saying, I thought we were looking for Kane.'

'It's the same thing. Kane can't stop now. After this afternoon he'll be on Samari's trail. Find Samari, and sooner or later Kane will show up.'

'But you don't know where Samari has gone,' Cassidy pointed out. 'You haven't a clue.'

'No.' Makana thought for a moment. 'But maybe I know someone who can help us with that.'

They drove back down the Dowal al-Arabiya Street. Outside the white mosque Makana told Sindbad to pull over.

Zayed Zafrani was busy supervising the unloading of a van

full of old clothes. On a row of tables heaps of them were being sorted through by a legion of women dressed in black.

'More aid for the needy?'

'Our work is never done.' Zafrani clasped his hands together and allowed himself a little smile. The women rushed back and forth moving things from one trestle to another. Hard at work, they resembled a crowd of furious birds, pecking away. 'What can I do for you today?'

'Do you remember that the last time we met I asked you about a young man, Na'il Abdelkarim?'

Zayed Zafrani lifted his hands in a confession of ignorance. 'I'm sorry. I have so many things to concern me. Why do you ask?'

'I saw him this morning. He was quite dead. Someone tried to make it look like a road accident, but he had been beaten to death.'

'Such a line of work.' Zayed Zafrani shook his head in despair. 'Allah willing, you will be rewarded in the next life.'

'I wouldn't count on that.'

'I don't understand why this concern brings you to me.'

'The last time I saw that young man alive he was on the receiving end of your brother's wrath.'

'I'm sorry to hear that. I wish I could teach my brother to be patient, but he has a troubled soul.' Zafrani struck a tone of lament. 'If I could change him I would do so in an instant.'

'Ayad is mixed up with some important people. He's trying to gain political interest.'

'He's an ambitious man, in his own way.'

'He has some powerful friends, people he does favours for. Eliminating Na'il was partly that. A favour. But he also had his own reasons. He suspected Na'il was working for a rival, someone who was trying to muscle in on his territory. That's why he beat him to a pulp.'

'He has a furious temper.' Zayed shook his head like a man dismayed.

'The thing is, I can't think of many people who would dare to go up against your brother. His reputation is rivalled by few. Of course you had a fairly formidable reputation yourself, before you took an interest in charity.' Makana smiled.

'Always a pleasure to talk to you, Makana, but as you can see, I am rather busy.' Zafrani made to move away. Makana raised his voice.

'I kept asking myself, who would dare to go up against a man like Ayad Zafrani?'

Zayed Zafrani pushed his spectacles back up his nose. Light glinted on the glass. Some of the women were now looking in their direction.

'Na'il peddled recreational drugs. Amphetamines, Prozac, ecstasy, Viagra, the kind of things that allow the beautiful people to party all night, to indulge their lusts and float through this world on a happy cloud of chemical dust.'

'Why is this of interest to you?' Aware of their audience, Zayed Zafrani lowered his voice.

'I'm trying to help someone who I believe is in danger.'

'What has any of this to do with me?'

Makana produced his telephone. 'Pharmaceuticals are produced in batches. They have serial numbers to help trace them. The police are searching his property now. I imagine they would be interested to know where he got his supplies. They might like to try and match them to the stocks you have here.' Makana tilted his head towards the warehouse.

When Zafrani spoke again there was a hard edge to his tone. There was no trace of the old benevolence.

'I shall give you some advice, Makana, as an associate, if

not a friend. Do not interfere in matters that do not concern you.'

'Perhaps I should have a word with your brother before I talk to my friends in the police. He might be more receptive.'

'You are treading on dangerous ground. Better drop the matter while you still can.'

'You're the only person who is capable of challenging your brother. You said yourself that he steers his own course. You wanted to bring him back to the true path, didn't you? You set up Na'il as your emissary, to peddle his drugs in order to convince Ayad that someone was trying to muscle in on his business. Then what, an anonymous call to the police? Perhaps close the club down for a while? It wouldn't last long because he has powerful friends, but maybe it would encourage him to take your ideas about legitimising the business more seriously.'

'Think what you are saying.'

'I have thought,' said Makana. 'This was all about the two of you and Na'il paid the price. And he's not the only one. Indirectly, it caused the death of a woman. What happened about showing benevolence to others. Isn't that written in the Quran?'

Zafrani was quiet for a long time. Behind him the women carried on working, apparently oblivious to the conversation.

'I don't want any unpleasantness with my brother.'

'I understand.'

'What are you asking for your silence?'

'Information.' Makana struck a match. 'The Iraqi Kadhim al-Samari. I need to know where he is. You have networks at your fingertips. You have people who work the streets, politicians, policemen, and you have those outside the law. If anyone can do it, you can.'

Zayed Zafrani thought for a long time and then he nodded. 'I will do this for you on one condition, that you never speak of this matter again. The trust between brothers is sacred.'

'Like so many things,' said Makana, 'only when it suits our needs.'

Chapter Thirty-three

Light was fading as the three of them gathered on the upper deck of the awama. Sindbad picked up the telephone to order food. Cassidy leaned on the railings and smoked a cigarette. Makana joined him.

'There's no chance you have anything to drink around here, is there?' Makana looked at him but said nothing. 'I should have guessed,' Cassidy sighed. 'Okay, what happens now?'

'Now we wait.'

'That's your plan?'

'If Samari is in this country, Zayed Zafrani will find him.'

'How do you know he'll come through?'

'It's in his interest. He wants to buy my silence. It's just a matter of time.'

'Time is the one thing we don't have a lot of.'

'We have no choice.'

'We're giving Kane a chance to get ahead of us.'

'If you have a better plan I'd be happy to hear it.'

Cassidy grunted something unintelligible and turned to gaze moodily down at the river.

Makana eased himself down into his big chair. He was in some pain. The thumping the bouncer had given him, along with general wear and tear, left him feeling battered and bruised. He seemed to have gone beyond normal fatigue and was floating through the world on a haze of cigarette smoke. His thoughts were with Bilquis. Why had Samari taken her and the boy? Revenge? He could have had her killed on the spot. Taking her with him suggested he had something else in mind. He could be planning to spend some time on her with his knife – not a thought that bore dwelling on. There was also the possibility that they were already dead and lying by the side of a road somewhere. Things were moving swiftly and Makana knew that Cassidy was right. They didn't have time to spare. There was also Kane to consider. There was no telling what his next move might be. Another reason to find Samari fast.

Somewhere upstream there was a party going on. Far enough away thankfully for the noise to be negligible. From time to time a purple streak would fly up into the night sky and burst into thousands of starry fragments that glowed for a moment or two before falling to earth, extinguishing themselves in the darkness.

'They're pretty aren't they?'

Makana turned to see Aziza standing beside him in the gloom. She put her elbows on the railing and gazed upwards at another rocket.

'Did you solve the case yet?'

'Not yet,' said Makana.

'But you will.'

'You sound more sure of it than I am.'

'You always do.' She pushed herself away from the railing just as another gigantic fireball exploded into orange-and-green shards that floated dreamily down. 'They're pretty,' she decided, with the kind of logic that makes a child so self-assured, 'but they're just a distraction.'

As she disappeared Makana checked his telephone again. It wasn't that he thought it might suddenly have stopped working so much as that he felt the need to do something. A boy on a noisy motorcycle turned up carrying bags full of fiteer, pancakes topped with cheese and meat and all manner of things. It was a mistake to let Sindbad order, he realised. He assumed everyone had the same gargantuan appetite as he did. Cassidy wandered over to take a look.

'What is that, some kind of local pizza?'

'*Bizza*? Yes, yes, bizza. Very good.' Food was a universal language as far as Sindbad was concerned. He held up a box for the American to try one. 'Bizza, Egyptian style.'

Cassidy chewed and gave it his approval.

'Not bad.'

He sat down alongside Sindbad, who was delighted. Having endured Makana's general indifference towards the business of sustenance, he was overjoyed to finally discover a kindred spirit. When his phone rang Makana got to his feet and stepped towards the railings, only to discover it was Sami.

'Tell me you weren't involved in that Wild West shoot-out this afternoon.'

'Only as an observer.'

'I knew it.' Sami cursed under his breath. 'You need to be careful who you trust.'

'You found something?'

'Your American friend, this man, Frank Cassidy. He was there also?'

'Why do you ask?' Makana glanced back to where Cassidy

and Sindbad were cheerfully engaging in some kind of culinary exchange using sign language.

'Someone claims to have seen him in a café near the Carlton. Did he shoot someone?'

'He saved my life.' Makana recalled the moment just before Cassidy shot Eddie Clearwater, when he had expected to be shot himself.

'Well, he needs to stay low, the police have an alert out for him. I take it you have a plan?'

'I think so.' Makana paused. 'We're going after Samari, to get the girl back.'

'Are you sure you that's wise?'

'Ask me that in twenty-four hours.'

'I hope so. Take care, Makana. If there's anything I can do to help . . . Oh, and by the way, Rania and I have decided to have a child.'

'Well, that's progress.'

'I don't know whether to laugh or cry,' Sami said. 'I'm not ready for this.'

'You're probably more ready than you think.'

'Why am I taking advice from a solitary man who lives the life of a hermit?'

Makana rang off and turned to face Cassidy, who was still chewing enthusiastically. 'What is it?'

'This may seem obvious, but do you happen to possess a gun by any chance?'

'I don't like guns,' said Makana.

'I'm not asking you to adopt one. I just think it might come in handy.'

'I'll take my chances. Carrying a gun is usually a good way of ensuring you get shot.'

'You must have a different outlook here.' Cassidy gave Makana a long stare. 'Look, if it's any consolation, if he'd wanted to kill her he would have done it straight away.'

Makana studied Cassidy for a moment. 'Tell me again about your son.'

'My son?' Cassidy stopped chewing.

'The one in the picture. You said Kane murdered him?'

'We've been over all of this. Virgil must have figured out what Kane was up to. Maybe he threatened to talk. Kane was already on thin ice after Afghanistan. If Virgil reported him for torture abuses that might be enough to put a dent in Kane's plans.'

'How close were you to your son?'

'What can I say, he was my son.' Cassidy wiped his mouth carefully with a paper napkin. 'The truth is, after we got divorced he stayed with his mother. I didn't see him that much. I had problems of my own, I guess. I was a homicide detective with a drink problem. What do you want me to tell you?'

'Nothing. I was just curious.'

'Look, my son is dead. That's why I'm here. That's why I'm going to find Kane.' Surprised, perhaps, by his own anger, Cassidy ran a hand through his hair and stared at the floor for a moment.

'We should try to get some rest,' Makana said finally.

They arranged themselves as best they could. Cassidy lay down on the divan and closed his eyes. Sindbad stretched out on a rug on the floor and was snoring instantly. Makana sat back in the big chair and smoked in silence. The night was unusually quiet. As the sounds drifted away and a cold breeze chopped at the river, Makana could hear the water slapping against the side of the awama. His eyes must have closed for a moment or two, because when his telephone began to vibrate in his hand he jerked awake in an instant. It was Zayed Zafrani.

'I am told you must try looking east. The Sinai Peninsula.'

'A little more detail would help.'

'He has a villa along the coast from Sharm el-Sheikh, outside Santa Katerina.'

Makana listened as Zafrani outlined directions, kicking a snoring Sindbad awake as he did so. Cassidy was already on his feet. Together the three of them made their way up the path to the road. The big eucalyptus tree swayed back and forth in the night air as if troubled.

Chapter Thirty-four

The Thunderbird rumbled contentedly over the smooth tarmac as Sindbad put his foot down and they raced along the open road leading east from Cairo. It still took a while to get out of the city. A minor accident blocked one carriageway. A huge lorry had collapsed on its side, spilling its load of sacks and barrels across the road. Then they were clear, driving through wide open landscape, surrounded by darkness. It was a relief to leave all of that behind. The only lights visible came from small towns in the distance, or cars that flashed by in the opposite direction. There wasn't much traffic. Long-range taxis and lorries, the occasional bus.

'What do you plan to do once we get there?' Cassidy asked from the back.

'I haven't actually thought that far ahead.'

'Great. What is this place we're going to?'

'Santa Katerina. It's a monastery.' Makana handed a map over. Cassidy produced a flashlight from his pocket. 'There's a small town nearby.'

'How long to get there?'

Makana estimated another six or seven hours at the rate they were moving, so long as they didn't run into more traffic. He rolled down the window and let the cool night air in. There was nothing visible beyond the strip of the road. The world seemed to hover just out of reach of the headlights.

'I have to say it's kind of peaceful out here, once you get away from it all.'

Makana wondered at the wisdom of bringing the American along. In part he felt he owed it to him for saving his life. On the other hand, Brigadier Yusuf Effendi would probably have a field day to know that he was in the company of a man wanted for shooting another American in broad daylight, that he was helping a fugitive and a murderer. In the back seat Cassidy folded his arms and closed his eyes as he sat back and tried to sleep. Makana looked out at the darkness ahead of them and wondered what he would do when he found Samari.

After four hours they were running low on fuel. Sindbad pulled off the road beside a petrol station in the middle of nowhere. It was still early and they would have to wait for it to open, but it wasn't worth the risk of driving on. There was no telling where the next fuel stop might be. Makana closed his eyes for a moment and the telephone in his pocket began vibrating. He got out of the car to answer the call.

'Where are you?' Okasha asked.

'I'd rather not say.'

'Don't play games with me, I don't have time for this.'

'Any luck with tracking down Kane?'

'No, our mysterious American friend has disappeared from the face of the earth, apart from a curious incident that happened yesterday afternoon and now has us on high alert.'

'An incident?' asked Makana.

'Don't try that with me. A car that sounds suspiciously like that museum piece you're driving around was identified.'

'Kane went after Samari.'

'Downtown Cairo turned into Baghdad. Do you have any idea how much pressure there is to bring the culprits in?'

'I can only imagine.'

'That's right. You'd better stand well clear of this when it goes down.'

'I'll bear that in mind.'

'I'm serious. There are questions in parliament. They want people to hang. The American embassy has become involved. This is an international incident.'

'As soon as I have something I can give you, I'll call.'

'You'd better, for your sake.'

Makana hung up and stared at the distant hills. He turned as he heard Cassidy come up behind him.

'Where did you learn to speak English anyway?'

'I watch a lot of movies.'

'I bet you do.' There was a long pause, then Cassidy said, 'You asked me about my boy.'

'Virgil.'

'At heart he was a good kid, but he got himself into a lot of trouble when he was growing up. Part of that was my fault, I guess. Too busy trying to put the world right, fighting my own demons. I had my problems and in the end, well, I guess that's why people break up. That was hard on him. I read somewhere that divorced kids always blame themselves in some way. You ever married?'

'A long time ago.'

'Well, it sticks with you. Anyway, 9/11 had an effect on him. I mean, he started to straighten out, began to ask himself questions, about being an American, things like that. The way people live in other parts of the world. He wanted to do good. I think that's why he signed up to go to Iraq.'

'You mean he joined the army because he wanted to help the Iraqis?' Makana was thinking that he would never really understand the Americans.

'Sure, that and the family tradition. I was in the Marines and my old man was in Vietnam. My grandfather fought in France during World War Two. Still, surprised the hell out of me, I can tell you. I was proud of him. You won't remember this, but right after 9/11 President Bush made a speech. He said this was not a war on Islam, that this was about helping people to free themselves of a tyrant, to bring them democracy. Well, I guess Virgil was young enough to believe some of that stuff.'

Cassidy lit a Camel and offered one to Makana. 'That's why Kane killed him. Virgil was an idealist. He joined the army because he wanted to make the world right. It was only once he was in Iraq that he realised he'd joined up for all the wrong reasons.' Cassidy paused to look out at the light spreading over the barren landscape. 'He said his sergeant had told him not to think about all that negative stuff, how the fat cats in Washington were turning this war to their own profit, how they were getting rich on the blood of young men like himself and his buddies. The Iraqis didn't seem to care for their help either. They threw stones and cursed them. War is an ugly thing, but a war without honour is worse than hell.'

The air was cold. The sun seared its way out of the earth on the eastern horizon. There was something reassuringly ancient about the sight, a ritual that kept repeating itself over and over. Some days it seemed to Makana that they had forgotten the things that wise men once knew. Cassidy was still talking.

'He only had a few months to go. I tried to encourage him to keep his head down and just get through it. All he had to do was come home and everything would be all right.'

'But it didn't work out like that.'

'Kane murdered him, and for that he's going to pay.' Cassidy's impatience spilled over and he kicked the dust and turned away. Makana watched him go, marching across the grey sand in a wide circle, trying to work off his frustration.

Makana wasn't sure how Cassidy would react when he came face to face with Kane, but he was glad to have the American along. He leaned against the side of the car and watched the light spreading on the eastern horizon. The prospect of going up against Samari was not one that he relished, but he couldn't see that he had any choice in the matter. Bilquis didn't know about the listening device in the telephone. She knew nothing about Kane and his men, which meant that she would deny everything. Samari would not believe her and in all probability would then set about torturing her, or her son.

'Kane may be ahead of us up there,' Cassidy said when he came back.

Makana had the same feeling. He wasn't sure how, but he had the feeling that Kane was always one step ahead of them. The audio bug in the telephone explained how he had learned of Samari's visit to the tailor's shop, but how many other tricks did Kane have up his sleeve?

Off in the distance a faint light caught his eye. A fierce, insistent blink far back on the road.

'Kane doesn't give up. He's come this far, he's not going to stop now.'

Makana tore his eyes away from the road to examine the American. Cassidy stepped closer.

'I know what you're thinking. You're thinking I'm too emotionally involved. It's affecting my judgement. Well, that's bullshit. I'm a cop, just like you were.'

The lights were red and blue and they were approaching at high speed from the west, the direction of Cairo. Makana went over to the Thunderbird and nudged Sindbad awake.

'Find the attendant and wake him up. Get him to fill the tank.'

Sindbad did as he was told. Three dark-blue armoured Land Rovers. They were heavy and slow, their windows protected by metal grilles. A big screen across the front windscreen was tilted back onto the roof to allow the driver to see where he was going. Makana watched them draw close and drive straight by. He shivered involuntarily at the cold and wished he was wearing more than the thin windcheater he had pulled on, although in a couple of hours he knew he would be too hot. The lights carried on into the distance. Makana was hoping they would keep going, but he saw them slow and come to a halt. Then they wheeled around and came back.

The three Land Rovers crunched off the road and spun in a circle across the stony dust until they were roughly arranged around them in a semicircle, their long radio antennae whipping in the air. The passenger door of the lead vehicle opened and a large, baggy figure of a man descended and hitched up his uniform trousers. When he waved, the doors of the other vehicles opened and men poured out. There had to be over twenty of them in all. Dressed in black, they wore body armour and helmets and carried an assortment of weapons.

'What a magnificent sunrise, eh? Don't you think?' Marwan lifted his arms up to the sky and stretched. 'Makes you feel proud to be Egyptian, doesn't it?' He moved closer. 'Well, in your case, maybe not, right? What are you doing out here, Makana?'

'You were following us?'

'Now why would you think a thing like that?' For a man who spent most of his nights drinking himself into a stupor, Marwan looked surprisingly alert at this early hour. An eager executioner anticipating a good day's work ahead of him.

'You were just driving this way?'

'We're stationed out here. The CSF is running things in this part of the Sinai now.'

'I'd like to believe this is a coincidence.'

'I'd like to think the same, but we both know it isn't true. Cairo was turned into Falluja yesterday afternoon, or maybe you hadn't heard?' Marwan glanced over Makana's shoulder. 'Who's your friend?'

'Somebody we picked up along the way.'

'That's interesting. He wouldn't happen to be American, would he?'

'Why do you ask?'

'No reason.'

'Where are you headed?'

'The same place as you, I imagine.' Marwan studied Cassidy for a moment longer before turning back to face Makana. 'I don't know what to make of this, to be honest. There we are driving along and what do I see?' Marwan nodded at the Thunderbird. 'You really ought to get yourself something a little less conspicuous.'

'So everyone keeps telling me.'

'There were reports of a strange old car in connection with the shoot-out.'

'You know how unreliable eyewitnesses are. One day it's blue, the next it's red.'

'Yeah, I suppose you're right.' Marwan scratched his neck. 'But then there's the other thing.'

'What other thing?'

'You remember that person you asked me about? High-level Iraqi officer? Well, you're not going to believe this, but it seems he's no longer welcome in our country. In fact, I have orders to put him on a plane out of here as soon as I can find him.'

'What about his friends in powerful places?'

'You know how it is with friends.' Marwan shrugged. 'When people start getting gunned down in broad daylight nobody is safe.'

'He's not alone. Samari has a woman and her child with him.'

Marwan's big head shook in dismay. 'When are you going to learn?' He stared off at the rising sun for a moment. 'I understand, I really do. You lost your wife and kid. But you need to learn that you can't save the whole world.'

'All I'm asking for is twenty minutes, that's all. You know what happens. If you go in with your guns drawn a lot of people are going to get shot.'

'I'm touched by your faith in our skill.'

'You know it's true.'

Marwan said nothing. Instead he helped himself to one of Makana's cigarettes. Makana cupped a match for him. For a few moments the two men stood and smoked in silence.

'Even if I wanted to help you, I don't think it's worth it.'

'She has a young son by our people back home. She was raped and tortured.'

'I hear what you're saying. This is personal. You want to do right by her.'

'Twenty minutes to get her out. That's all I'm asking. Then you can go in and get him.'

Looking Makana in the eye, Marwan took three quick puffs

and dropped the cigarette to the ground. He stepped on it with his boot heel.

'I warned you. You can't say I didn't. I told you not to get involved.'

'I've been involved for as long as I can remember,' said Makana.

They took off with the Thunderbird sandwiched between the first two Land Rovers.

'What exactly is happening?' Cassidy asked.

'We're cooperating.'

'You sure that's wise?'

Makana looked back at him. 'We don't have much choice.'

They drove along the coastal road, past row after row of houses, chalets, hotels with names like Sea View and Blue Bay, all unfinished, the empty doorways and window frames facing out at the sea optimistically, as if awaiting the return of a vanquished fleet. Eventually they turned off and started climbing into the hilly interior. The advantage of having a police escort, Makana learned, is that you don't waste time at checkpoints. The men on duty recognised Marwan and waved them straight through. They swept past barriers of old oil drums filled with sand and strips of traffic spikes that were dragged aside. The narrow, winding road cut through the stark landscape. Slabs of rock jutted out of the barren grey dust. The Thunderbird creaked and groaned in protest, the underside scraping the ground as they bounced along the uneven road.

Santa Katerina barely qualified as a town. A scattering of disconsolate buildings ranged over a rising slope hemmed in by rocky pinnacles including, somewhere among them, the blunt hill that was Jebel Musa, where Moses received the Ten Commandments, if you happened to believe in that sort of thing.

There was an air of serenity in the valley, and it was easy to imagine this as a sanctuary, a place of refuge from the world. One of the most sacred places on earth according to the old books of prophecy and legend; certainly one of the most desolate. The convoy swept past a solitary camel being led by a figure wrapped up from head to toe and came to a halt in a cloud of grey dust on an unclaimed space somewhere in the middle of it all. The air was cool when Makana climbed out. Marwan was marching around making sure everyone remembered who was in charge. He came over and rested a boot on the front bumper of the Thunderbird. He pointed over Makana's shoulder.

'The monastery is up there, to the south. That's where God spoke to Moses from inside a burning bush, so if you hear any voices you'll know someone is trying to tell you to turn around and go home, forget about this *sharmuta*. If you go up there it's at your own risk. I'll give you fifteen minutes, then I'm coming after you.' Marwan crunched back across the stony ground to his men.

'*Ya basha*, it's not my place to question, but would it not be wiser to leave this girl to her own fate and return to Cairo?'

'It would be, undoubtedly, but that's not what we're going to do.'

'I thought as much,' said Sindbad with a sigh as the engine coughed into life. 'May Allah watch over us,' he muttered as he thrust the gearstick into place and put his foot down.

Chapter Thirty-five

They drove east, up a rising curve that cut into a narrow rocky cleft. On the last bend, Makana indicated for Sindbad to pull over. He turned around to address Cassidy.

'There's no reason for you to risk coming in. You may as well stay out here and keep an eye open for Kane. If all goes well we'll be back in less than fifteen minutes.'

Cassidy thought it over and got out of the car. They left him standing by the side of the road as they drove on. Makana felt a degree of relief. The American was an unknown quantity and therefore something of a liability. He didn't want to complicate negotiations with Samari any further than was necessary.

It wasn't hard to spot the place. A couple of men standing around the entrance, wearing the headscarves of the Bedouin and nursing machine guns, reported their arrival. Makana counted the minutes as they consulted someone on a small radio. To his surprise, they waved him through. The short drive leading off the track rose steeply, winding through a tight corner and out onto a flat plateau. A high brick wall and a solid metal gate protected the villa. Beyond it the view was spectacular. A commanding vista of the little town below and the rocky land-scape surrounding it, dotted with lumpy hills that stretched off into the distance.

The iron gate slid aside to reveal a modern villa set in the shadow of a rocky outcrop. A couple of armed guards, one of whom carried his arm in a sling, sauntered across. They looked the car over before waving them through. Everyone was a little jumpy, no doubt as a result of what had happened in Cairo. Inside the compound were a number of vehicles including the two BMWs Makana had seen. Over on one side was a pickup truck. Next to it a man wearing a khaki overalls was wiping engine oil off his hands with a rag.

'This way.'

'Stay here,' Makana told Sindbad as he climbed out of the car.

The guard gestured with his good hand. He had an automatic pistol hanging in a shoulder holster under his bad arm. A second guard carrying an M16 followed behind Makana.

The villa was perhaps twenty years old and two storeys high. A functional structure of metal, glass and concrete, clearly it had been chosen more for its remote location than for its design. Apart from the view there wasn't much to recommend it. Wide steps led up to a long open terrace of cracked tiles that extended across the front of the house. A sliding glass door gave onto a lobby furnished with a long dining table. More steps led up to a living area that was starkly furnished with ugly sofas and a glass coffee table. A stone fireplace to one side did its best to add a touch of style and came up short. The room was cold and un-attractive. Above it a gallery with iron railings ran along the upper floor with a spiral staircase on one side for access. Beneath this an archway led further into the interior of the house.

'Sit there.'

Makana sat. The guard took up a position by the door, so that the light was behind him. The M16 was trained on Makana and his finger was on the trigger. The wounded guard went slowly up the spiral staircase and disappeared through a doorway. Makana resisted the urge to reach for a cigarette. He didn't want to make the guard any more nervous than he clearly was. The ambush in town must have scared them all. They weren't taking any chances. The question was why they had let him in so easily. Time was ticking by. Any minute now Marwan would come charging in with his boy soldiers and people were going to get hurt.

'You are either very brave or very foolish.' Kadhim al-Samari stood by the railings on the upper gallery. He came slowly down the staircase. 'First you try to kill me and then you walk in here calmly as if nothing had happened.'

'I didn't try to kill you.'

'Where is your mercenary friend?'

'I told you, I don't work for Kane.'

'You told me, it's true.' The Iraqi moved closer. He reached into his sleeve and produced a knife. It was black and had a short, square blade – the same knife Makana had watched him slice across Raul Santos's neck in the square. He was wearing a dark blue suit and smelled of expensive cologne. He leaned closer to rest the blade flat on Makana's shoulder. 'You know what this is?'

'A samurai knife.'

'Very good. It's known as a *kaiken*. It's so sharp it would cut through your jugular without your feeling a thing, until it was too late, that is.'

'I've seen how it works.' Makana stayed very still.

'The smartest thing you did today was to arrive unarmed. If you had been armed you would be dead by now.'

'I believe you.' Makana tilted his head in the direction of the gunman. 'Since I'm not a threat, perhaps you could ask him to lower that?'

Samari considered the situation and then stepped back from Makana and signalled. The gunman unclamped his finger from the trigger and lowered the gun to hang on its strap from his shoulder. Makana decided a cigarette at this point was well deserved.

'Okay, Mr Makana, now tell me why you're here.'

'I came to propose a deal. A way that both of us can profit and at the same time eliminate a common problem.'

'A deal?' Samari folded his arms and considered Makana for a moment. 'I warn you, if you are lying to me I shall kill you myself.'

'I'm not lying.'

'Very well, let's hear it.'

'There are three cars full of CSF troops waiting for me down in the valley. Soon they'll be on their way up here. They plan to put you on a plane and get you out of the country.'

'I don't believe you. They would never do that.'

'You've overstayed your welcome in Egypt. After that shoot-out yesterday your friends are no longer all that interested in protecting you.'

'It was regrettable, but I am still a useful partner to them.'

'No doubt, but this is politics. It's all about appearances. Kane lost a man yesterday. The Americans are asking questions. It's only a matter of time before they discover that the Egyptians are harbouring a man on their Most Wanted list. You.'

'So far I have no problem with your reasoning, but what exactly are you proposing?'

'If I'm right, Kane is on his way here. He may already be in the area.'

'How can you be sure of that?'

'Because you're his only objective. He's not going to give up now.'

Samari's face hardened. 'He's persistent, that much I will give him, but even supposing he could find me, he wouldn't dare come after me here.'

'Why not? He attacked you in downtown Cairo in broad daylight. There's not much that puts that man off.'

'He killed two of my men. He almost killed me. What is he after?' Samari's voice was tense. He too was shaken.

'My feeling is that it's personal.'

'But why? Who is this Kane?'

'I can't tell you that. All I can say is that he won't stop until you're dead.'

'So what do you propose?'

'We hand him over to the CSF. Dead or alive. He's all they want. He killed Kasabian and caused a scandal in the middle of Cairo. Kane is an embarrassment to the Egyptians and the Americans will want to end the whole affair as quietly as possible. You would be able to stay on in this country.'

The Iraqi considered the logic of Makana's argument.

'And you, what do you get out of this?'

'You let the girl and her son go.'

Samari laughed. He seemed genuinely amused. 'I didn't think people like you still existed. You belong in the history books, an extinct species.'

'Don't hold your breath.'

'Tell me, you really have no other ambition? You want to help the girl. That's it? You aren't after money?'

'I get paid for doing my job. Kasabian paid me to find you. Kane paid me more.'

'Yet here you are offering him to me.'

'Kane will want to cover his tracks. He'll kill me as soon as I'm no longer of use to him.'

Samari's eyes glittered. 'You don't trust Americans. You would rather take your chances with me.'

'At least with you I feel that I know where I stand.'

'A rational man. How interesting.'

'Then we have a deal?'

Samari stared at Makana for a long time. 'You are a strange one. Strange enough to be telling the truth. It would be inconvenient to have the CSF arrive now. Can you really stop them?'

'I'm the only chance you've got.'

'I'll tell my men to prepare themselves.' Samari went over to the door and called his lieutenants to him. Makana lifted his telephone and called Marwan. He wasn't happy.

'This isn't what we agreed,' he grumbled.

'This is better. You get the man who started the shooting and Kasabian's killer. On top of that the brigadier doesn't lose face. He can keep his friend and business partner around. They'll shower you with decorations.'

'How can you be sure this man Kane is going to show up?'

'He hasn't let me down yet. Just keep your men out of sight.'

Makana could hear Marwan mulling over the possibilities.

'All right, you have twenty-four hours. But you'd better not try anything else.'

'Don't worry about me,' said Makana and hung up. He wondered what to do about Cassidy and decided that the homicide detective was resourceful enough to take care of himself.

'You're wasted in this job of yours.' Samari squared his shoulders and produced a silver cigarette case and a gold lighter. 'You could be making a fortune. Why don't you come and work for me?'

'I have enough trouble sleeping as it is.'

Samari chuckled. He squinted through the cigarette smoke at Makana. 'Do you know where I made my name as a military officer? The war with Iran was coming to a close and we were losing. Our generals were threatening to rebel against Saddam. We had fought the Iranians for six long years and still they were not defeated. A new strategy was devised, a flexible defence force. I was part of a unit of the Iraqi Republican Guard.' He strolled about. It was a big room, with long leather sofas in black and glass coffee tables. The walls were whitewashed and bare. A hideaway for a man who moved around a lot.

'One night we came under attack, a massive offensive around Basra. Our situation was critical. We were outnumbered and could expect no reinforcements for twenty-four hours. I knew we would not last the night, so I came up with a plan. We flooded the Iranian trenches with water. Not too much, up to about knee height. A discomfort but nothing more. Then we dropped a high-tension electric cable into the water and switched on the power. We killed over a thousand of them that night. I was promoted and decorated. My career was made, as one general told me.'

Lighting another cigarette with the lighter, Samari sat down on the sofa opposite and contemplated Makana. 'We are not so different, you and I. I too have lost my country. The Americans will redraw the map of the region to serve their interests. Civil war will make it easy to divide the country into three manageable parts, and do not imagine they will stop there. Secure

Israel's control of the West Bank, push the Palestinians into Jordan? In the end we will have a toothless, docile Middle East, a client state to American interests, begging for Western aid, much like Egypt.' Samari smiled. 'For a time we stood up to them. We defied them, that is something I am proud of.'

'Your view of history is a little selective,' said Makana. 'You forget the repression, the prisons and torture chambers, the gassing of the Kurds, draining the marshes. Anyone who was suspected of not being loyal was killed or thrown into prison.'

'You disapprove.' Samari smiled as though indulging a feeble relative. The long scar rigidly divided his face into two uneven halves. 'You think we need more idealism and justice. Well, let me tell you, we are not ready for democracy. You cannot end centuries of feudalism at the stroke of a pen. We are tribal. We don't understand the idea of voting for someone who is not one of us, not of our family, or clan, or tribe.'

'Tell it to the Americans.'

Samari laughed. 'You think the Americans are in Iraq to spread freedom and equality, to bring us the light of democracy? Don't be stupid. They want oil to drive their cars, water for Israel and land to control the region. Democracy is just a formality, a game they are asking us to play. Saddam's big mistake was defying them, firing missiles into Israel. I'll always admire him for his courage and despise him for his foolish vanity. You cannot defy a giant.'

There was a sound from above as the wounded guard appeared on the upstairs gallery. He held a pair of field glasses in his good hand.

'The CSF are withdrawing.'

'Very good,' Samari nodded, turning to Makana. 'You've done well. It looks like I shall let you live.'

'What about Kane?'

341

Samari shrugged. 'If he appears my men will deal with him. Yesterday he had the advantage. He took us by surprise. I have his measure now. The next time we will be ready.'

Samari pushed his hands into his pockets. For a man who had a price on his head and a group of professional soldiers after him, he looked relaxed. He snapped his fingers and the guard upstairs disappeared back through the doorway behind him. Samari strolled over to the wide glass window that looked down over the high wall and the long drop down into the valley. The house was in shadow, but the valley was bright with afternoon sunlight. At this distance the town looked like a toy model. A moving dot marked the passage of a vehicle along one of the roads. It was quiet. Marwan and his men were out of sight. The only tourists around would be up at the monastery looking at the burning bush, or whatever they had found to mark the spot.

'I shall miss this place,' Samari was saying. 'You can feel there is something special about it, a spirit from the times of the prophets.'

'What is it about men of violence that they yearn to be seen as wise and knowledgeable?'

Samari snorted his disbelief. A movement caused him to turn. 'Ah, here she is.'

Makana turned to see Bilquis standing on the upper-floor gallery. She was dressed in a way he had never seen before. A pair of blue jeans and a white blouse. Expensive, fashionable. She looked elegant and modern in a way that surprised him. She descended the spiral staircase and went over to sit down on the leather sofa vacated by Samari.

'So you decided to come after all?' she asked. She wore make-up, a layer of powder on her face that lightened her skin colour, and blue eye shadow along with a dark lipstick. Makana wasn't sure who he was looking at.

342

Bilquis reached across the table, helping herself to a cigarette from the silver case which she lit with the gold lighter. She seemed entirely at ease, completely familiar with her surroundings.

'I was worried. I assumed you had been taken by force.'

Her eyes narrowed as she blew a plume of smoke in his direction.

'Your son?'

'Upstairs, sleeping.'

Makana wondered where this new-found confidence had come from. She sat back on the sofa, crossing her legs, her feet neatly fitted into a pair of shoes with slender gold straps. Samari moved around behind the sofa to rest his hands on her shoulders.

'I made Bilquis an offer, which she has accepted.'

'An offer?' asked Makana, glancing at her. Bilquis didn't meet his eyes.

'As soon as the mechanic has finished we shall fly out of here,' Samari explained.

'Fly where?'

Samari made a throwaway gesture, as if it hardly mattered. 'Beirut, or Libya, maybe the Gulf for a time. Just until things blow over.'

'What about Kane?'

'I pay my men for that. No need for me to stay here and wait for him.'

'You're going with him?' Makana asked.

'What did you expect?' Bilquis regarded him coolly.

'Don't be cruel to him, *habibti*, he came all this way to rescue you.'

Makana saw that he had misjudged the situation. Bilquis wasn't in need of rescuing. That moment had passed. He had effectively had his chance and had failed to take it. Instead of helping her to claim the reward he had tried to talk her out of it. Now she had made her move.

There was a knock at the front door and the mechanic appeared. Samari went over and stepped out onto the terrace, sliding the door to behind him.

'What has he promised you?'

Her eyes flickered towards his. 'A new life in a new world.'

'Of course he has.' Makana lit a cigarette and glanced over at the terrace where Samari and the mechanic were still talking. He could see now that it wasn't overalls but some kind of jump-suit, like the kind pilots wore. He wondered where it was possible to land a plane around here.

'And the reward?'

'I'm reconsidering.' Bilquis leaned forward. A whiff of expensive perfume floated across the room. 'This way I have something at least.'

'You'll always be at his mercy.'

'What choice do I have?' Bilquis glanced towards the door, her voice low and urgent. 'It's not as if you have anything better to offer. Scraping by on the change you make?'

She was right, of course. Compared with the life of luxury Samari was offering, what did he have? She stared at him for a moment longer and then stubbed out her cigarette and got to her feet. Without another word she left the room. Makana watched her climbing the stairs as Samari returned, followed by the guards, who ushered Sindbad in ahead of them.

'I'm afraid that until our departure we are going to have to take some precautions.'

Makana got to his feet and looked at Sindbad.

'Sorry about this.'

'*Maalish, ya basha.*' Sindbad seemed to take it in his stride.

The archway under the stairs led into a corridor that brought them to a large open kitchen where a man was busy chopping vegetables. In the far corner there was a storeroom sealed off by a heavy wooden door. Makana hesitated.

'Wait a minute.'

The guard prodded him in the back with the barrel of his M16.

Samari was apologetic. 'We can't risk having you wandering around. I'm sure you understand.'

'At least let Sindbad go. You only need me as insurance.'

'I'm sorry, that would be imprudent.'

Sindbad and Makana were told to sit on the floor with their backs to a metal pillar in the middle of the room. Their hands were bound behind them with chains and padlocks. The door was closed and Makana leaned back against the pillar.

'Did you see the American out there?'

'No, *ya basha*. No sign of him.'

Makana hoped that Cassidy would remain out of sight. He leaned his head back and closed his eyes, glad of the silence. There was enough to think about.

Chapter Thirty-six

As afternoon turned into evening and the light coming through the tiny window faded, Makana listened to the sound of Sindbad snoring to himself on the other side of the iron pillar. He wondered how close Kane and his men were and when they would make their move. There was no doubt in his mind that they would be coming. How or when he did not know, but soon, he was sure of that.

'*Ya Allah*,' yawned Sindbad as he came awake. 'Why do they have to keep us next to the kitchen? It's torture. Can you smell that? What do you think it is?'

'I have no idea,' said Makana, although he had to admit that after five hours he too was beginning to feel hungry.

'I could smell aubergines frying, I swear it.'

'You were dreaming. Go back to sleep.'

'Do you think they will feed us?'

'I wouldn't count on it.'

Sindbad slumped back into a dismayed silence. The rattle of pots and pans from next door was a distraction. Makana was trying to hear what else was going on. Several times he had heard the sound of the gates being opened and a heavy vehicle going out. A van of some kind, or a small truck. A while later it could be heard returning. Then the sound of men being ordered around. The truck passed by their little window, which indicated that the track twisted round and descended behind the house. Makana was wondering how Samari planned to make his getaway. He was sure now that the man in the jumpsuit who had spoken to Samari was a pilot or flight mechanic. The only airports Makana could think of were down on the coast, at Taba or Sharm el-Sheikh, at least an hour away by road. Would they make for there, or was there an airstrip close by?

To take his mind off the issue of food Sindbad had turned his attention to the chains that bound them. He rattled and heaved.

'Save your strength.'

'Don't worry, *ya basha*, I'll just give it a try.'

It looked like a hopeless case, but Makana didn't have the heart to tell him. Sindbad strained and struggled until sweat beads popped from his forehead but to no avail. He finally slumped back.

'I haven't eaten all day. Now, if I wasn't working on an empty stomach, it would be another matter.'

'Don't worry about it,' said Makana. But the truth was that he was worried. If Kane arrived and found them chained up they would make very easy victims.

The hours went by and the house grew quiet. The noises from the kitchen died away until there was only the hum of the refrigerator. Outside, through the high window, Makana could hear the cry of some kind of nocturnal predator, an owl perhaps, warming up for the evening's hunt. That was when he heard footsteps. The door opened to silhouette the last person in the world he expected to see. Bilquis. Dressed in a silk gown, she knelt beside him, fumbling with a set of keys.

'Don't make a sound. You have to go now. The guards won't notice if you leave by the back way. Follow the track down. Eventually it will bring you to town. Wait there until we have gone.'

'Come with us,' Makana said.

She avoided his gaze. Her eyes were deep shadows in the dark.

'I can't,' she said.

'You're not safe with him.'

'You don't know that.'

'What happens when he tires of you? Think about the boy.'

'I am thinking about him,' she hissed angrily. Her head dropped and for a moment she was still. 'Hadi is the only thing I think about.'

'Come with us now. I'm sure there's another way.'

'Why is this so important to you?' she asked. 'Why do you care?'

He wanted to say something, something that would appease her anger, that would convince her that she was making a terrible mistake, but he couldn't. He wanted to tell her that it had something to do with another mistake, one that he had made years ago, the consequences of which he had to live with every day. But the truth was that he had no answers, not even for himself. Bilquis nodded to herself as if this was what she had expected. She stood up and drew the gown more tightly around her. Makana massaged his wrists to get the blood flowing again.

'He'll make you pay for this.'

'We'll be gone before he finds out.'

Makana caught her wrist as she turned to go. 'If he finds out, he'll kill you.'

She pulled herself free. 'You must go now.'

They moved through the kitchen and along the corridor past the archway that gave onto the main living area. Through it Makana could see two of the guards sitting at the dining table playing cards. Beyond, through the glass, he could see two others smoking on the terrace as they stood guard. Bilquis pointed down the corridor.

'At the end you go down a set of steps to a doorway,' she whispered. 'It's not locked. It'll bring you straight out onto the hill track. Turn left and follow it down. Be quiet and move quickly.'

'I . . .'

She cut him off by placing a hand over his mouth. In the dim light he looked into her eyes, searching for something he was no longer sure he had ever seen. She took her hand away slowly.

'If things had been different,' she whispered, 'who knows?'

Then she turned and was gone.

Makana led Sindbad along the corridor and down the short flight of steps to the outer door. As she said, it wasn't locked, only bolted from the inside. Makana pulled back the bolt and urged Sindbad out ahead of him. As he stepped out he could see the stars over the town and a thin strip of street lights along the road. He was drawing the door quietly to behind him when he felt a gun barrel pressed to the back of his neck. A hand grasped his shoulder and spun him round, pushing him hard up against the wall. In the moonlight he recognised the blond American, the one with the beard who resembled General Custer. Randy Hagen. He held a finger to his lips and Makana could see no reason to object. They were all there, four shadows, silent in the dark. They were heavily armed and communicated only by hand signals.

Out of the corner of his eye Makana saw Kane approaching. He signalled for Hagen and the Iraqi, Faisal, to go round to the front of the house. Then he addressed the youngest member of the group, a man in his twenties with a scruffy beard, his head shaved to a bristle. This had to be Jansen, the last member of Kane's group.

'Keep an eye on these two, kid. Either of them makes a move, shoot them.'

Jansen prodded Makana in the side with the barrel of his gun. They moved back inside, following Kane up the steps and along the corridor. At the archway leading into the main living area, Kane signalled and Jansen pressed Makana against the wall, the gun to his neck.

Perhaps Samari's arrogance was such that he had never believed Kane would be able to find him, or else he expected to be gone before he turned up. In either case the Iraqis were caught napping. Makana counted nine silenced shots. A moment or two later, Makana and Sindbad were dragged into the living area to find the lights on and everyone assembled, the living and the dead. Makana recognised the guard who had held a gun on him that morning when he had arrived. He was face down on the steps leading down to the front door, his shirt pockmarked with bullet holes. The one with an arm in a sling lay in a heap beneath a bloody smear on the wall by the sofa where Samari sat with his head bowed. Hagen and Faisal came in through the front door. The two men on duty out there were face down on the terrace. The only people missing were Bilquis and her son, Hadi.

Chapter Thirty-seven

Kane strolled about the room with a theatrical air, enjoying his moment. He was dressed all in black, cargo pants and a vest over a black T-shirt, a black bandanna tied over his head. A compact machine pistol was slung over one shoulder while a chrome-plated automatic rested in a holster on the other. He gave orders to search the villa, then he turned to address Samari.

'You are one difficult animal to rope, I'll give you that.' Training his weapon on Makana and Sindbad, Kane signalled to Jansen, who hauled Samari to his feet, bound his hands, and dragged him to the centre of the room. 'Search him good.'

Jansen tossed a knife across. Kane weighed the *kaiken* in his hand.

'So this is what you used on Raul? Nice piece.' He tested the blade with his thumb.

'What do you want from me?' Samari was staring at the side of Kane's face.

'I'll come to that. You just have to be patient.' Kane moved past Samari towards Makana.

'How did you find us?' Makana asked.

Kane beamed. 'Well, the wonders of modern technology and all that.' He reached into his vest and produced a little device. 'It's called a lo-jack tracker. Easy to follow as a trail of bread-crumbs. Yesterday when you were all in the tailor's shop I managed to slip it underneath one of those nice BMWs out there.'

'How?' Makana asked. 'The cars were occupied at all times. There was a driver in each one.'

'I didn't say it was easy, but it was certainly not difficult. You wear a disguise. You find the blind spots in the mirrors.' Kane leaned over Makana, the *kaiken* in one hand. 'You know, I am a little disappointed in you. I thought we had a deal.'

'You shouldn't have killed Kasabian like that.'

'You could have been a very rich man. But that's the thing, some people just don't know what's good for them. Just like Kasabian. I don't like it when people lie to me, but he could simply have told me how to find this place.'

'He didn't know.'

'I'd like to believe you, I really would, but the thing is I've just about lost faith in there being anybody in this part of the world who knows how to tell the truth.'

Makana turned as he heard Samari start to swear. His face had drained of blood.

'It can't be.'

The Iraqi was staring straight at Kane.

'You're dead.'

A look of satisfaction came over Kane, as if this was a moment he had been anticipating for a long time.

'You're not Kane,' Samari whispered. 'I know you, and your name is not Kane.'

'Somebody once said there are no second acts in American lives,' Kane smiled. 'And maybe that's true. All I know is that in the land of opportunity everyone gets a chance to reinvent themselves.'

Samari must have panicked, because he made a move to get past Jansen, who neatly sidestepped and clubbed him with the butt of his machine pistol. Samari fell to the floor.

'Now that's a disappointing development, and not a good one from your point of view.' Kane circled Samari where he lay sprawled on his side, one hand clutching his head. He looked over at Makana and grinned. 'Perhaps I should explain. Let me see. Well, we have to go all the way back to February 1991, Kuwait City. Saddam is under delusions of grandeur. He thinks he's invincible, that the United States will never touch him. So he has invaded his next-door neighbour, a country that he believes should by rights belong to him. The Kuwaitis flee, taking themselves off to London and Paris to sit out the war in luxury. Of course there isn't enough time for them to take all of their valuable possessions with them, so they leave most of it behind, thinking they'll be back in a couple of weeks. Wrong.

'Meanwhile a crack unit of the Iraqi Republican Guard is roaming the city, relieving the wealthy Kuwaitis of their incalculable riches. They break into numerous private art collections and gather up a fabulous haul of pearls, diamonds and gold, not to mention priceless works of art the world hasn't seen for decades. Nobody has any idea of what these vaults contain, except the owners of course, who are far away and helpless. The only problem is that the Iraqis are losing the war. Operation Desert Storm is moving in fast. Land forces are on the outskirts of the city and the airspace is controlled by coalition fighter planes. There is nowhere to run.'

Samari sat up and shook his head to clear it. Kane continued with his story.

'As you can imagine, quite a situation. You've got your hands on one of the greatest hauls of war booty since the Nazis rolled into Paris. More wealth than King Midas, but no way out. The road to Baghdad is a death trap. A turkey shoot. The airport is under siege. The port is sealed off. The oil wells are on fire. And then' – Kane spun on his heels and paced across the floor – 'then you had a stroke of luck. Why don't you tell us what happened?'

'We ran into you,' murmured Samari.

'That's right, Colonel. You remember that.'

'I remember,' nodded Samari, his head lolling.

'You thought you were going to die, didn't you? When you saw the Bradley closing in, you thought the end had come.'

'Yes. Yes.' Samari was gasping and coughing. 'The end.'

'And you would have died, wouldn't you? Out there in the desert. Without our help.'

'We would be dead.'

'But you didn't die. You were saved.' Kane patted Samari on the shoulder. 'I saved you.' He was grinning now. Samari looked unsure of himself.

'You saved us.'

'If it wasn't for us, you'd be dead and none of this would ever have happened. Right?'

'Right.'

Kane was still smiling. Samari tried to smile back. He seemed to think it was expected of him. Kane began to chuckle and Samari followed suit. In a few moments they were both laughing like lunatics.

Then, abruptly, Kane struck Samari across the face with the barrel of his gun. When he straightened up, Samari's mouth was bloody. He spat out a tooth.

'I'm glad you remember,' Kane said soberly. 'I can think of a few guys who would be glad to know that you haven't forgotten them. Hinks and Mason, for example. Those names mean anything to you?'

Samari whimpered. Kane signalled to Hagen and Jansen, who dragged Samari to his feet. A rope was thrown up over the railings of the gallery and clipped to the plastic tie around Samari's wrists.

'Two fine men. Charlie Hinks was a driver and Tommy Mason was my gunner. Remember them?'

Samari wailed as they hauled him into the air until his feet no longer touched the ground. The thin band of plastic cut into his skin and he groaned, gritting his teeth against the pain. Kane swung the machine pistol behind his back and pulled the shiny automatic out of his holster and held it up.

'Do you know what this fine piece of weaponry is?'

'Desert Eagle, 50-calibre,' Samari whined.

'So you know what a bullet this size can do to a man's leg, right? The doctors won't find any pieces to put back together.' He swung the gun from one leg to the other. 'Which knee would you rather do without?'

'Please, you don't have to do this,' Samari murmured. 'We can make a deal.'

'A deal?' Kane arched his eyebrows. 'Really? What did you have in mind?'

'There is enough to make all of us rich.'

'Did you say rich?'

'Yes, yes,' muttered Samari.

'Paintings? Is that what you're talking about?'

'Paintings, works of art, antiquities. Diamonds. Lots of diamonds. Rubies, pearls. Gold bullion. I have it all. I give it to you.'

'Sounds like you're a rich man. Where is all of this stuff?'

'I have it, all loaded up into a truck, ready to ship out.' Samari was spitting blood.

'You're forgetting one thing,' Kane smiled. 'I trusted you once before.'

The guard lying on the floor beside Makana chose this moment to groan. He wasn't dead after all. Kane seemed to welcome the distraction.

'Hey, a volunteer!'

Without moving, without bothering to look, Kane swung the automatic and pulled the trigger. The man's body jerked once at the impact and he was silent. The shot was deafening in the narrow space, and when he looked again Makana saw a hole in the man's chest big enough to bury a fist in.

'Not pretty.' Kane shook his head. He moved closer to Samari and rested the barrel of the pistol against his cheek. 'You don't seem to understand. I didn't come here to make a deal. I came to kill you and take everything you've got.' Samari murmured something that was drowned out when Kane fired again. The bullet seared a furrow across the side of Samari's face and took off most of his right ear. He gave a screech of pain.

There was a shout and Faisal appeared on the upper floor dragging Bilquis along behind him. Her eyes were wide with fear and she held her son in her arms. The boy was crying. Dressed in pyjamas, Hadi was small for his age and obviously terrified. She was trying to comfort him, though clearly he could sense his mother's fear and clutched fiercely at her. Faisal herded her towards the stairs, prodding her in the back with the barrel of his gun.

'My, my, what have we here?' Kane went over to meet them at the bottom of the stairs. 'Who are you, darling?'

'I . . . I'm . . . nobody,' she stuttered.

'No, somehow I think you must be somebody. And who is this?' Kane pulled Hadi from his mother's arms and flung him aside in the direction of Hagen, who grabbed him and held him still. The boy screamed for his mother.

'No, please, I beg you.'

Kane ignored Bilquis's pleas. He struck her hard across the face.

'Leave her alone,' said Makana. 'She's just a girl he picked up in Cairo.'

'You know,' Kane turned his attention to Makana, wagging the automatic, 'I really wish I understood what your game was. Why are you trying to protect her?'

'She has nothing to do with any of this.'

'I'd be inclined to believe you,' Kane said, 'except that I don't. Nobody takes a whore and her child along with them. That just doesn't make any kind of sense.' He tucked the automatic back in its holster and addressed Samari. 'So, I'm assuming this woman means something to you. And her child.' Kane snapped his fingers and Hagen handed him another plastic loop which he slipped over the boy's head and pulled tight. The boy squirmed, struggling for breath. Bilquis cried out. Hagen dragged her back. Kane held the five-year-old boy firmly by the nape of his neck as he tightened the tie notch by notch. Hadi squirmed, grabbing at the thin band of plastic around his throat, trying to free it. His eyes bulged and he began coughing and spluttering.

'You see how easy it is to kill a child?'

Bilquis was screaming by now. She managed to slip free from Faisal's grip. Kane backhanded her. This time the blow was hard enough to send her flying to the floor. She stayed there, both hands to her face, and began to weep. Makana got to his feet. The young man turned on him.

'Where'd you think you're going?'

'My knees hurt,' said Makana. He reached into his pocket for his cigarettes. Kane seemed to find this interesting. He waved to Jansen.

'It's all right, Cody. I've got this.' Kane turned to Makana. 'What do you think you're doing?'

'You're wasting your time. You need to hurry up.'

'Oh, and why's that?'

'Because Central Security Forces will be coming through that door any minute and you won't stand a chance.'

Kane grinned. 'No offence, buddy, but why the warning?'

'There's no need for anyone to get hurt. Take what you want and leave, but you need to do it quickly.'

'Nice try.' Kane jerked the plastic loop a notch tighter. 'But somehow I have the feeling that my approach is more efficient.' The boy's eyes rolled up in his head as he began to lose consciousness.

'You don't understand, he doesn't care if you kill the boy.'

Kane jabbed a finger at Makana. 'You keep on talking and you're going to start to annoy me.' Nevertheless, he took a moment to consider the situation. Pushing the boy aside, he picked up the Japanese knife again. Hadi writhed on the ground as Kane dug the blade into Samari's shoulder and cut a line across his back from top to bottom.

'I have to admit, this is a lot more satisfying.'

Samari's shirt came away in tatters and a scarlet stream sprang up in its wake. Kane stepped back to admire his handiwork. The Iraqi gritted his teeth, allowing barely a whimper to escape. Kane dragged the knife back across Samari's body in the opposite direction. Now his torso was marked by a cross of blood. Kane wiped the blade on a strip of Samari's shirt.

'What I remember about that war was the confusion. Thousands of guys running around out in the desert with no idea of what was up or down. We were just a bunch of rookies, cut off from our unit, about forty miles from the Iraqi border. Our Bradley had mechanical problems. We were trailing along at a snail's pace, trying to reconnect with our boys, when lo and behold we come across them. Just him and a driver in the middle of nowhere. They weren't expecting to see us.'

At Kane's feet Hadi was kicking feebly now, losing strength. Bilquis threw herself forward, but Faisal cut her off, putting an arm around her neck and jerking her back.

'You remember Faisal?' Kane grabbed a handful of Samari's hair and lifted his head up. 'He used to work for you. Used to drive your car, used to kill people for you. Remember him?'

Samari spat deliberately on the floor.

'No love lost between you, huh? Well, that's too bad, because Faisal here has been very helpful. He's the guy who brought us to Cairo. Now, just imagine you had treated him a little better. Just think what loyalty you might have earned with a little generosity. But that's not you, is it? No, you don't believe in sharing. But you know what? I think he's a good man and deserves a reward.' Kane nodded to Faisal. 'Take her upstairs, do what you want with her.'

Faisal struggled up the stairs dragging Bilquis behind him. She was still crying, pleading with them to let her son go. Hadi appeared to have passed out. Makana thought he could see the boy's chest rising and falling. Blood was running down Samari's body in rivulets, pooling on the floor beneath him.

'We should have killed you there and then, but we were young, still wet behind the ears. The war was a joke. All that training and for what? We hadn't even seen any Iraqis up close and now we had the drop on two of them.' Kane turned in a circle to make sure his audience was still with him.

'Then we opened up the crates in the back of the truck and I saw the most incredible sight I had ever set eyes on in my life. Paintings so beautiful, right there in that barren desert sun. It was like water, like a vision of an oasis. It felt like a religious moment, you know? Like Michelangelo or some shit. I don't know anything about art but I knew right then those things were valuable.'

Samari swung limply on the end of the rope. He mumbled something. Kane leaned in and cut him again. 'I'm not done talking. Show a little respect.' He wielded the knife like an artist with a brush, slashing here and there, over and over until Samari's torso was running with blood. He stepped back to examine his handiwork, then he reached into his vest pocket and produced a couple of cigars. 'Here, soldier,' he offered one to Jansen, who declined, and instead tossed it over to Hagen, who grinned and ran it under his nose to sniff it.

'Soon this war will be over and we'll all go back to our regular lives. Well, I for one do not plan on going back to mine. Wars make men. We're going home as heroes, and we're going home rich.' He took a moment to light his cigar, puffing smoke into the air. 'We're going to take your head back in a box, but before that we're going to take your treasure and put it in a safe place.' From upstairs Makana could hear Bilquis scream. Kane nodded to Jansen.

'Go see what he's up to. I don't want him to kill the bitch. Not yet, anyway.'

Jansen went up the staircase. Light was beginning to break outside. Flies were starting to buzz. Makana sank down onto the sofa. The body of one of the guards lay in a heap to his left. He hadn't even had time to draw his pistol, which still rested in its holster. Makana could read the name Browning on the side of the pistol grip.

'I'm beginning to tire of this game.' Kane stepped up to Samari and cocked his pistol. Then he turned and pointed it at the boy's head. 'Let's start with the little guy.'

Casually, Makana let his hand drop down the side of the sofa. Without looking he felt around blindly, touching wet cotton. Blood. Then the webbing of a holster. The gun was almost within reach when a voice behind him spoke:

'I wouldn't do that if I were you.'

Kane had frozen. The barrel of the Colt Python was jammed against his left ear. Frank Cassidy stepped out from the corridor. Kane laughed.

'Who the fuck are you?'

'The last person you expected to see. Frank Cassidy, LAPD.' Cassidy stepped aside and looked around him. 'You're a hard man to track down, Mr Kane.'

'A little off the reservation, aren't you, Frank?'

While Kane was talking Hagen started to lift his weapon but the Colt swung towards him.

'Don't even think about it.'

Cassidy knew what he was doing. Hagen lowered his gun and raised his hands. Cassidy took a step to his right, where he had a better angle.

'Drop your weapons and kick them away from you.'

Kane smiled. 'What are you going to do, Frank? You have six shots in that Colt. You think you can take all of us out with six shots?'

'Maybe not,' Cassidy smiled. 'In which case you'll have to decide who goes first.'

Kane sighed. He made a big show of placing his weapons on the floor. Hagen did the same. Makana got to his feet, pulling the guard's Browning from its holster and checking it was loaded. He signalled for Sindbad to retrieve Kane and Hagen's weapons.

'Keep him covered,' Cassidy said to Sindbad, using his hand to make his point. 'If he makes a move, you shoot him.'

Sindbad indicated that he understood.

Kane was looking at Cassidy.

'You're the guy who shot Eddie. Why don't you just tell us what you want, stranger, and we'll find some way of accommodating you.'

'I didn't come here to make deals.'

'Then what did you come here for?'

'I'll get to that.' Cassidy moved up the steps. 'Why don't you finish your story.'

'I'm not sure I can,' said Kane.

'No, I'd really like to know how all of this started.'

'You're calling the tune.' Kane took a long drag on his cigar. 'Where was I? I guess you'd call it my moment of revelation. St Paul on the road to Damascus. Whatever. When I looked at those paintings I saw what the war was really about. In a way I'd seen it for days. It was written out there in the desert. The horizon was black with the smoke that poured from hundreds of oil wells the Iraqis had torched on their retreat. Huge burning towers of billowing black smoke. I'd never seen anything like it. It looked like the gates of hell. I understood then that this was a war about profit, about protecting your interests. Nothing more. And we poor grunts would never amount to anything more than foot soldiers and pawns working for the giant corporation that is the United States.'

'So what did you do?' Cassidy prompted.

'I didn't do what I should've done, which is to kill him right there and then. Instead I persuaded my men that this could work out well for us. We couldn't haul that stuff back to base and we couldn't hide it anywhere nobody was going to find it. We had to trust him. We had to make a deal.'

'He agreed to share what he had with you?' Makana asked.

'That's what made it so perfect. We needed each other. He couldn't get anywhere without our help.'

'You trusted him,' said Makana.

'The war was over. The Iraqis were done. Once we were finished with Kuwait it was a straight ride into Baghdad behind General Schwarzkopf. I mean, why stop there? The whole country would be under our control in a matter of days. That's what we thought.' Kane jerked a thumb at Samari. 'He knew that even if he went back to Baghdad, he would be finished. But he wasn't going back, he said. He was going to get the stuff out. He had contacts, people who would sail the booty away into the Persian Gulf and out across the Indian Ocean. I thought we were partners.'

'But that's not how it turned out,' said Makana.

'No.' Kane shook his head. 'I told our friend here that we would guide him through the American lines. We had charts. We had satellite positioning. He knew about Iraqi minefields and troop lines. Between us we could make it to the border.'

'He turned on you,' Makana said.

'No. Fate lent a hand. We were close to the Iraqi border when a Tomcat flew over one evening. On its way back from a mission, I guess. There weren't supposed to be any Americans in that zone. He saw the truck and the decommissioned Bradley and drew his own conclusions. Anyway, he took a run at us, emptying his guns on his way home. In the confusion our friend here

363

managed to get hold of a weapon. I was inside the Bradley when it was hit and I was left for dead. When I crawled out they were dead, all of them. Butchered, cut up into pieces. He fed their tongues to the birds. There were vultures feeding on their guts.'

Kane studied the glowing end of his cigar.

'He drove back into Iraq anyway?' Makana asked.

'I don't think he ever really believed Iraq would lose. He knew Saddam would never surrender.' Kane smiled wistfully. 'And things changed on our side too. Turns out we had other priorities. The Saudis were worried that taking out Saddam would bring in the Shias, who they hated worse than beer and barbecued ribs. President Bush decided it wasn't worth going to Baghdad. So we sold out the Iraqi people to keep our allies happy. Hundreds of thousands died in that uprising, thinking we were coming to help them get rid of Saddam.'

'So Iraq remained intact and Samari could go home,' said Makana.

'Exactly. I should have died out there in the desert. But I didn't. If there was one thing that kept me going it was the thought of getting even one day.'

'Who is Zachary Kane?' Samari spluttered.

'You don't remember, do you?' Kane gave a hollow laugh. 'Zachary Kane was the last member of my crew. A young kid of nineteen who hailed from some one-horse town in Iowa. Funny thing is he was dead set against the deal, said I couldn't trust you. I should have listened to him.'

'You took his name?' Makana asked.

'I'd had a few problems with the law and I knew Zach didn't have any family, so at a certain point it just made sense. I'd kept some of his papers – driving licence, Social Security card, stuff like that. I reinvented myself. I brought Zachary Kane back to life.' He turned to regard Samari, who seemed barely conscious by now. 'It doesn't seem like much, does it? The life of one man? But he was a good kid and he died because he trusted me. So I carried him with me all these years. I swore that one fine day I'd get my revenge.' Almost as an afterthought he pressed the glowing tip of the cigar into Samari's armpit and smiled as he screamed.

The noise brought Faisal back onto the upper gallery. He was busy trying to button his trousers and raise his gun when Cassidy shot him cleanly through the neck. As he did so, Hagen moved, diving to one side and pulling a long thin knife from his boot which he threw. It hit Cassidy just under the left shoulder. Makana fired and Hagen went down clutching his thigh.

Makana swung the Browning back towards Kane who raised his hands and smiled. A swift burst of automatic fire swept across the room as Jansen opened up from the gallery above. The table kicked and spattered splinters into the air.

'Everybody stay put and no one gets hurt.' The young soldier swung the barrel of the rifle to take in all of them. Bilquis was shielded behind him. Makana lowered the Browning. Sindbad put down his guns. The only one who didn't move was Cassidy, who held the Colt aimed up at Jansen.

'You'd better be sure of your aim,' said Cassidy. 'I don't usually miss at this distance.'

Something about his words must have struck home because Jansen seemed taken aback. He lowered the automatic rifle a fraction.

'Dad? Is that you?'

Chapter Thirty-eight

'Virgil?' Cassidy was looking up at Jansen.

'Jesus, Dad, don't call me that. How many times do I have to tell you?' Jansen started to descend the stairs. 'What the hell are you doing here anyway?'

'You're alive.' Cassidy lowered the Colt. 'I can't believe it.'

Kane stirred, lowering his hands. Makana swung the Browning back in his direction. Jansen didn't notice. Kane raised his hands to show he wasn't going anywhere.

'Sure I'm alive,' Jansen said. With a glance at Kane he went over to his father and examined the wound. 'It's in deep. If we try to move it we could rupture an artery.'

Cassidy didn't seem to care. Clearly in pain, he squeezed his son's shoulder.

'You're alive.'

'You'd better believe it. Now let's take a look at you.'

'How touching.' Kane rolled his eyes. 'A real family reunion.'

'My son,' Cassidy said to Makana. 'I can't believe it.' He leaned against the wall and slid down slowly to the floor, one hand clutched to his shoulder.

'I thought your son's name was Virgil Cassidy?' said Makana.

'I've always hated the name Virgil,' the young man explained as he reached for a first-aid pouch in his pack. 'Anyone in their right mind naturally would. When they got divorced I took my mom's family name, Jansen. Cody's my middle name.'

Sindbad retrieved the weapons he had set down and took over keeping Kane and Hagen covered. Picking up the *kaiken*, Makana carefully sliced the plastic loop from around the boy's neck. He was relieved to see Hadi jerk awake. He hadn't been sure he was still alive. Now he sat up and began to cry. Bilquis came down the stairs unsteadily. Her blouse was torn and her hair was a mess. She avoided Makana's gaze as she bent to take her child in her arms.

'Take him to the kitchen,' Makana said. 'Clean him up, give him something to eat.'

He turned to cut Samari down. Bilquis paused and helped to support him. The Iraqi looked too weak to stand. His hands were still bound together. He resembled a wounded animal. His back was bowed and his eyes were lowered. He swayed and almost fell. Makana watched him hobble away, dragging his feet, leaving a trail of blood on the tiled floor.

'Who said America isn't a great country?' Kane was grinning. 'Anyone can become anything they please.'

'Sit on the floor,' Makana indicated. 'Put your hands on your head.'

Kane sat cross-legged on the ground. Hagen groaned. Jansen glanced over at him but ignored him. His attention was on his father.

'I saw you, in Cairo, at the Marriott,' said Cody. 'I thought I was seeing things.'

'You saw me?'

'The last person in the world I expected to run into. And there you were snooping around the lobby, doing your detective thing.'

'But you didn't say anything?'

'I couldn't, Dad.' Cody sighed. 'I wasn't alone. I figured you were there for me, or for Kane. I didn't know how you'd found us, but I knew that if I identified you they would kill you. I held back and hoped you would just go away. I even left a message at your hotel, telling you to go home.' He gently removed his father's hand from the knife wound. 'You shouldn't have got involved, Dad.'

'I'm your father, of course I'm involved.'

'This is going to hurt.' Cody held a dressing pad to the wound and pulled the blade out slowly. Cassidy groaned. He looked as though he might faint. 'Keep talking.'

'I followed you,' gasped Cassidy. 'They said you were killed in action.'

'And you just wouldn't take the army's word for it.'

'I had to know,' insisted Cassidy. 'I couldn't just leave you out there alone.'

'So what did you do?' Cody taped the dressing down and added another.

'I went to Falluja. I followed the trail.'

'Once a cop, always a cop, isn't that what Mom used to say?'

'Something like that.' Cassidy was smiling. Then slowly the smile faded. 'What happened, son?'

'It's complicated, Dad.' Cody stared down at the ground.

'What the hell are you doing with these guys?'

Cody stood up. 'We need to get you to a hospital, Dad. You need surgery.'

'I don't get it,' Cassidy said. He was watching his son.

'Like I said, it's complicated.'

Kane slow-clapped from across the room. Grinning, he held his arms out wide. 'Here we all are, one happy family.'

'This is between me and my son,' growled Cassidy. 'Stay out of it.'

'I hear you,' laughed Kane, 'but you have to admit, it's a touching scene.'

Hagen, who had been clutching his leg, decided to make his move then, throwing himself sideways. He announced his move with a growl. Cassidy leaned past his son, raised the Colt and shot him. While Makana was distracted Kane threw himself forward and rolled, ducking out through the doorway. Sindbad went after him. He came back a moment or two later.

'He's gone, *ya basha*.'

'He can't have gone far,' said Makana. 'Can you use that thing?'

Sindbad looked down at the M16 he was clutching. 'I think so, *ya basha*.'

'Then get outside and keep your eyes open for anything. Kane might be back.'

'*Hadir, ya basha*.'

Outside dawn was breaking and the sky was clearing. Sindbad stepped out onto the terrace and began pacing from side to side like a good sentry. Cassidy was slumped against the wall with his eyes closed.

'How's he doing?' Makana set down the Browning and knelt beside Cassidy.

'He's losing a lot of blood,' said Cody. 'He needs to get to a hospital.'

'Do the best you can. Help will be on the way.' It seemed something of a miracle to Makana that his telephone was still working. He called Okasha, explained where he was and something of what had happened.

'I can be there in an hour with a helicopter,' Okasha said. 'We'll need as many men as we can get if we are to catch Kane. You'd better call Marwan and let him take care of Samari.'

Makana hung up. Cassidy looked pale and exhausted. He looked up at Cody.

'Talk to me, son.'

Cody nodded to himself a few times. 'Okay, I'm just going to get this off my chest and then we'll be done with it, right?' He glanced up at his father. Frank Cassidy nodded.

'It all started when we hit an IED. I must have been out for a while. When I woke up everyone was dead. I thought I was finished too. I was wounded and I was out in the desert. Then all I remember is seeing Kane and his men coming out of nowhere. It was like a miracle. They took me back to their place, a palace outside Falluja. Gold taps in the bathrooms. Everything covered in marble and shit. The Kingdom of Zach.' Cody grinned at the memory. 'Rock and roll, beer, Jack Daniel's on ice. It was a long way from Dreamland. There was this car pool of Ferraris, Porsches, a gold Ford Mustang, all just abandoned out there.'

'What about your unit, what about the army, the war?'

Cody screwed up his face. 'I knew you wouldn't understand.'

'I'm trying, son, but you had a duty to fulfil.'

'That's the whole point, Dad. I started out believing, I truly did. That's why I joined up. I believed in the mission, or at least, I thought so. We were there to help, right? I thought of us as like the Peace Corps but with guns. Before long I began to realise that the Iraqis hated us. Even little kids threw stones at us. And I'd heard all the stories about Haliburton and Brown and Root, how the politicians were making a ton of money out of this war. People were dying, getting maimed, all kinds of horrible shit. You think the people back home know about that? You think they care? You want me to come home a cripple, minus a leg and an arm, blind? And for what, so that some fat cat in Washington can make a fortune?' Cody shook his head slowly. 'Kane is right, you have to be a damn fool to fight their war for them.'

'So you decided to join him.'

'It made about as much sense as anything. This was a chance for us to clean up for once. The little guy. I figured I could disappear for a while. I was down as MIA. Kane could get me papers, get me back home. Shit, he could get anything he wanted. I wasn't asking for much, just enough to come home and set up a little business of my own, hiring out boats in Louisiana, or something.'

'Or something . . .' Cassidy rubbed a hand across his face. He was having trouble keeping his eyes open. His shirt was soaked in blood. Sindbad reappeared to report that everything appeared to be calm.

'You'd better check on Samari and the girl. They're in the kitchen.'

Sindbad sauntered off. He seemed to stand taller and straighter than he had before, as if the act of walking around with a gun had somehow revived some memory of his time in the army doing his national service. A moment later he was back, summoning Makana from the archway with a wave of his hand. The kitchen was deserted. Makana checked the storeroom. There was no one there.

'Afreets, *ya basha*?' asked Sindbad in a worried voice. 'Did they just turn into smoke?'

Makana had a feeling the explanation had to be a little more ordinary than fairy-tale spirits. He paced the room. There was no other exit. He walked back over to the door and surveyed the kitchen again. The light coming through the high windows opposite was stronger now. Sunlight illuminated one wall. Makana ran his eye carefully over every corner of the room, first the walls and cupboards and finally the floor, where he spotted a trail of blood spots. They led to an uneven patch in the floor tiles, where they disappeared. He felt with his hand until he found the hidden catch. Sindbad gave a gasp as Makana hauled up a trap-door. A set of steps led down into the gloom below.

'Stay here,' he said to Sindbad. 'Keep an eye on the others. Kane might come back.'

Then he pointed the Browning down below him and began to descend. He half expected a knife blade to come up at him out of the darkness. When he reached the bottom step he found himself in complete blackness. He closed his eyes for a moment and waited for them to adjust. When he opened them again he could detect a faint glow somewhere up ahead. He moved slowly towards it, feeling his way with each foot he put forward. He felt a cool gust of air against his face. The path descended and the light grew steadily stronger. A shimmer appeared in the distance. It took him a moment to realise that he was looking at the end of a tunnel. The path carried on, dropping at a shallow angle, and Makana began to move faster now, suddenly sure that he would arrive too late. The tunnel led down through the mountain behind the house, roughly towards the south. There was no sign of anyone ahead or behind him.

By now he was jogging along at a steady pace, cautious, not wanting to trip with a loaded gun in his hand. The tunnel widened as the angle eased off and then began to rise. The light grew like an eye opening in the darkness. He glimpsed them now, a scattering of shadows. Samari limping, the slighter figure of Bilquis alongside, holding the child in her arms.

'Wait!'

They came to a halt in the mouth of the tunnel, apparently exhausted. Bilquis let the child slip to the ground. Samari slumped against a stack of crates piled just inside the entrance. Beyond them was an open space, a circular arena hemmed in by rocky pinnacles. The man in the jumpsuit was coming towards them.

'Leave those,' Samari said, as the pilot went to lift up another flat crate. 'We don't have time. Prepare for immediate take-off.'

The pilot jogged back onto the open ground towards the helicopter. It was a military grey, an old British Sea King without markings. Who it belonged to was unclear – more of Samari's contacts, Makana guessed. Another figure was busy untying guy lines that secured the rotors, removing protective covers from the engines.

Clearly in pain, Samari straightened up. 'Well, this is it, Makana, you'll have to shoot us to stop me getting on that aircraft, but I sense that you are not the kind of person who takes the idea of shooting an unarmed man lightly.' He turned and began limping away.

'You don't have to do this,' Makana said. 'It's not too late.'

Bilquis hesitated. The boy clutched at her leg. She pressed him to her side.

'It's always been too late for us,' said Bilquis. 'In another life perhaps. I know too much about you and you about me.' She stared at him for a long moment. 'Goodbye Makana.'

Then she turned and hurried after Samari, stooping to put her arm under him to lend support, her son clutching her other hand. Makana let the gun drop to his side as the three of them walked out into the sunlight. Samari was right. Shooting a man in cold blood was not something he was capable of.

Makana watched as the helicopter rotors began to turn, beating themselves into a frenzy. Dust kicked up around the feet of the three passengers. Hands reached down to help them climb aboard. By now the whine of the engine had risen to a low scream. Makana watched Bilquis climb aboard last, the door sliding shut behind her. Then the rotors gathered force. They churned up the stinging sand, making Makana duck his head and cover his eyes. As he turned away he spotted the figure standing on a rocky ledge off to his left, on the periphery of the circle, a man whose head seemed to flutter in the wind. Kane. He was holding something to his shoulder. Makana knew what it was but there was barely time to register it before the cough of flame announced the launch of the rocket. The helicopter was about ten metres in the air, vertically above the wheel marks it had left in the sand. It had begun to turn, spinning slowly round. A few seconds more and it would have been clear, taking her into another life. Instead it exploded into an angry fist of flame and smoke. Makana ducked, hearing the whine of metal flying overhead, striking the rock with a resounding clang. For a moment the little arena was choked with dust and the smell of burning aviation fuel. The smoke cleared to reveal the helicopter had sunk back down into its tracks, a skeletal frame of its former self, flames and black smoke billowing from the fuselage.

Kane was striding towards him out of the blast, the rocket launcher cocked on one shoulder, the other hand thrown out wide.

'Now, that's entertainment!' he yelled, throwing his head back and laughing. He tossed aside the spent rocket launcher. Then a shot rang out from behind Makana. Kane jerked backwards, lifted off his feet and fell to the ground. Makana turned to see Cody, Kane's Desert Eagle held in both hands. He lowered the gun slowly.

'Your father?' Makana asked, although he knew the answer. Cody shook his head.

Makana turned back to the remains of the helicopter. Thick black smoke still billowed from the interior. It would have been instantaneous. She wouldn't have felt a thing he told himself. He stood and watched it burn, thinking about what might have been and the pointlessness of it all.

A few hours later found Makana steering the Thunderbird down the last stretch towards the coast. In the back seat Sindbad was sleeping, dreaming of the feast he imagined awaited him in Cairo. Next to him in the passenger seat Cody sat and stared sullenly out at the landscape.

Marwan had been happy: his task was taken care of and he was in on another high-profile incident. Makana could see him working out what this would mean to him personally, how it would improve his chances of promotion. And Okasha had Kasabian's killer. He had promised Cody that his father's body would be transported back to Cairo and then repatriated by the embassy. He would take care of all the details. Cody sat on the front steps of the villa as they carried Frank Cassidy out on a stretcher.

'He was a good man,' Makana heard him say, 'but sometimes being good just isn't enough.'

To Makana it seemed that whenever he tried to help someone he ended up hurting them. Every time he closed his eyes he saw the image of the exploding fireball in front of him. He knew now that he would never be free of that feeling of guilt that he had carried with him all these years. Nasra's and Muna's deaths had changed him for ever. They would always weigh heavily upon him. He understood that in some way he had hoped that Bilquis would take the guilt from him. She couldn't, of course. Nobody could. He realised that now, only now it was too late.

Below them, the sea appeared, a deep indigo blue that seemed full of promise. They dropped down towards the crossroads, where he stopped for a moment before swinging the wheel west and turning towards Cairo. Makana was in no mood for conversation. A part of him was curious to know what exactly the helicopter had been carrying. After all, it would be interesting to know how many of the old masterpieces had perished in the explosion. Was it a fascination with beauty or a desire for immortality that drove men to possess these objects? Perhaps it was just plain greed. Whatever it was, like moths drawn to a flame, it had cost Kasabian his life and now Samari and Kane theirs too, along with all the others they had taken with them. As for those items which had not been destroyed, he didn't want to think about what would happen to them; didn't want to know who would profit. He could imagine, and that was bad enough. Instead he lit another Cleopatra and focused his eyes on the road.

Ahead of them the sky grew ominously dark as thick ochre clouds gathered in the distance. A wall of dust rising up from the ground was sweeping towards them across the horizon. There was a *haboob* coming. He put his foot down and felt the big engine respond as they gathered speed and headed straight into the dust storm.

ALSO AVAILABLE BY PARKER BILAL

THE GOLDEN SCALES

A MAKANA INVESTIGATION

A stolen child. A missing hero. In this city forgiveness cannot always be bought . . .

Former police inspector Makana is a Sudanese refugee who lives on a rickety Nile houseboat in Cairo. Out of the blue he receives a call from the notorious and powerful Saad Hanafi, owner of a star-studded football team. Their most valuable player has vanished, and his disappearance threatens to bring down not only Hanafi's private empire but the entire country. Thrust into a dangerous and glittering world, Makana encounters Muslim extremists, Russian gangsters and a desperate mother hunting for her missing daughter. His search stirs up painful memories, leading him back into the sights of an old and dangerous enemy . . .

'*The Golden Scales* shows modern Cairo as a superbly exciting, edgy and dangerous setting for crime fiction . . . An absorbing, complex, lively novel *****'
THE TIMES

DOGSTAR RISING

A MAKANA INVESTIGATION

A city divided. A killer on the streets. A past that refuses to be forgotten

The unsolved murders of young homeless boys are fanning the embers of religious hatred. As tensions mount, Makana, who fled his native Sudan a decade ago, has been hired to investigate threats that have been made to a hapless travel agent. The case draws him close to Meera, a woman who knows what it is like to lose everything and who needs his help. But Makana's troubled past is trying to lay claim to him once again, this time in the form of a dubious businessman who possesses a powerful secret. When Makana witnesses a brutal killing he uncovers a web of intrigue, violence and old secrets, and attracts the attention of some very dangerous people.

'An excellent series'
NEW YORK TIMES BOOK REVIEW

THE GHOST RUNNER

A MAKANA INVESTIGATION

A question of honour. An eye for an eye. The truth cannot stay buried for ever

It is 2002 and as tanks roll into the West Bank and the reverberations of 9/11 echo across the globe, tensions are running high on Cairo's streets when a routine surveillance job leads Private Investigator Makana to the horrific murder of a teenage girl. Seeking answers, he travels to Siwa, an oasis town on the edge of the great Sahara desert, where the law seems disturbingly far away. As violence follows him through the twisting, sand-blown streets, Makana discovers that the truth can be as deadly and as changeable as the desert beneath his feet.

'Bilal whisks the reader straight to the dark heart of Cairo . . . His prose has a subtlety that is rarely found in crime novels'
ECONOMIST

CITY OF JACKALS

A MAKANA INVESTIGATION

When the remains of a body wash up on the riverbank alongside his houseboat, Makana is caught up in what looks like a series of ritual murders of young refugees. When the authorities show little interest in investigating the refugee killings, Makana once again feels the pull of his Sudanese past, and is impelled to seek justice for the victims himself. But when he enlists the help of the exacting – and beguiling – pathologist, Doctora Siham he soon discovers that his two cases may be connected in dangerous and unexpected ways . . .

'Like all the best crime fiction, Bilal's story has a depth and resonance which stretches far beyond its cast of characters into the wider world'
INDEPENDENT

Order your copy:

B L O O M S B U R Y